GRAY MOUNTAIN

ALSO BY JOHN GRISHAM

JOHN GRISHAM

GRAY MOUNTAIN

DOUBLEDAY

New York London Toronto Sydney Auckland

Copyright © 2014 by Belfry Holdings, Inc.

All rights reserved. Published in the United States by Doubleday, a division of Random House LLC, New York, and in Canada by Random House of Canada Limited, Toronto, Penguin Random House companies.

www.doubleday.com

DOUBLEDAY and the portrayal of an anchor with a dolphin are registered trademarks of Random House LLC.

Book design by Maria Carella
Jacket design by John Fontana
Jacket illustration © Henry Steadman
Jacket photographs: mountain and road © Doug Meikle Dreaming Track Images/Photolibrary/Getty Images; trees: © Denis Jr. Tangney/Vetta/ Getty Images; sky and mountains: © Ken Howard/ImageBrief.com; woman: © Henry Steadman

Library of Congress Cataloging-in-Publication Data is on file with the Library of Congress.

ISBN 978-0-385-53714-8 (hardcover)
ISBN 978-0-385-53916-6 (eBook)

MANUFACTURED IN THE UNITED STATES OF AMERICA

1   3   5   7   9   10   8   6   4   2

First Edition

To the memory of

Rick Hemba

1954–2013

So long, Ace

GRAY MOUNTAIN

1

The horror was in the waiting—the unknown, the insomnia, the ulcers. Co-workers ignored each other and hid behind locked doors. Secretaries and paralegals passed along the rumors and refused eye contact. Everyone was on edge, wondering, "Who might be next?" The partners, the big boys, appeared shell-shocked and wanted no contact with their underlings. They might soon be ordered to slaughter them.

The gossip was brutal. Ten associates in Litigation terminated; partially true—only seven. The entire Estate division closed, partners and all; true. Eight partners in Antitrust jumping to another firm; false, for now.

The atmosphere was so toxic that Samantha left the building whenever possible and worked with her laptop in coffee shops around lower Manhattan. She sat on a park bench one pleasant day—day ten after the fall of Lehman Brothers—and gazed at the tall building down the street. It was called 110 Broad, and the top half was leased by Scully & Pershing, the biggest law firm the world had ever seen. Her firm, for now, though the future was anything but certain. Two thousand lawyers in twenty countries, half of them in New York City alone, a thousand right up there packed together on floors 30 through 65. How many wanted to jump? She couldn't guess, but she wasn't the only one. The world's largest firm was shrinking in chaos, as were its competitors. Big Law, as it was known, was just as panicked as the hedge funds, investment banks, real banks, insurance conglomerates, Washington, and on down the food chain to the merchants on Main Street.

Day ten passed without bloodshed, as did the next. On day twelve there was a flash of optimism as Ben, one of Samantha's colleagues, shared a rumor that credit markets in London were loosening a bit. Borrowers might find some cash after all. But late that afternoon the rumor had run out of gas; nothing to it. And so they waited.

Two partners ran Commercial Real Estate at Scully & Pershing. One was nearing retirement age and had already been shoved out. The other was Andy Grubman, a forty-year-old pencil pusher who'd never seen a courtroom. As a partner, he had a nice office with a distant view of the Hudson, water he hadn't noticed in years. On a shelf behind his desk, and squarely in the center of his Ego Wall, there was a collection of miniature skyscrapers. "My buildings" he liked to call them. Upon completion of one of his buildings, he commissioned a sculptor to replicate it on a smaller scale, and he generously gave an even smaller trophy to each member of "my team." In her three years at S&P, Samantha's collection had six buildings, and that was as large as it would get.

"Have a seat," he ordered as he closed the door. Samantha sat in a chair next to Ben, who was next to Izabelle. The three associates studied their feet, waiting. Samantha felt the urge to grab Ben's hand, like a terrified prisoner facing a firing squad. Andy fell into his chair, and, avoiding eye contact but desperate to get things over with, he recapped the mess they were in.

"As you know, Lehman Brothers folded fourteen days ago."

No kidding, Andy! The financial crisis and credit meltdown had the world on the brink of a catastrophe and everyone knew it. But then, Andy rarely had an original thought.

"We have five projects in the works, all funded by Lehman. I've talked at length with the owners, and all five are pulling the plug. We had three more in the distance, two with Lehman, one with Lloyd's, and, well, all credit is frozen. The bankers are in their bunkers, afraid to loan a dime."

Yes, Andy, we know this too. It's front-page. Just get it over with before we jump.

"The exec committee met yesterday and made some cuts. Thirty first-year associates are being let go; some terminated outright, others laid off. All new hires are deferred indefinitely. Probate is gone. And, well, there is no easy way to say this, but our entire division is on the block. Cut. Eliminated. Who knows when owners will start building again, if ever. The firm is unwilling to keep you on the payroll while the world waits for loose credit. Hell, we could be headed for a major depression. This is probably just the first round of cuts. Sorry, guys. I'm really sorry."

Ben spoke first. "So we're being terminated outright?"

"No. I fought for you guys, okay? At first they planned to do the pink slip thing. I don't have to remind you that CRE is the smallest division in the firm and probably the hardest hit right now. I talked them into something we're calling a furlough. You'll leave now, come back later, maybe."

"Maybe?" Samantha asked. Izabelle wiped a tear but kept her composure.

"Yes, a big fat maybe. Nothing is definite right now, Samantha, okay? We're all chasing our tails. In six months we could all be at the soup kitchen. You've seen the old photos from 1929."

Come on, Andy, a soup kitchen? As a partner, your take-home last year was $2.8 million, average at S&P, which, by the way, came in fourth in net-per-partner. And fourth was not good enough, at least it wasn't until Lehman croaked and Bear Stearns imploded and the sub-prime mortgage bubble burst. Suddenly, fourth place was looking pretty good, for some anyway.

"What's a furlough?" Ben asked.

"Here's the deal. The firm keeps you under contract for the next twelve months, but you don't get a paycheck."

"Sweet," Izabelle mumbled.

Ignoring her, Andy plowed ahead: "You keep your health benefits, but only if you intern with a qualified nonprofit. HR is putting together a list of suitable outfits. You go away, do your little do-gooder bit, save the world, hope like hell the economy bounces back, then in a year or so you're back with the firm and you don't lose any seniority. You won't be in CRE but the firm will find a place for you."

"Are our jobs guaranteed when the furlough is over?" Samantha asked.

"No, nothing is guaranteed. Frankly, no one is smart enough to predict where we'll be next year. We're in the middle of an election, Europe is going to hell, the Chinese are freaking out, banks are folding, markets are crashing, nobody's building or buying. The world's coming to an end."

They sat for a moment in the gloomy silence of Andy's office, all four crushed with the reality of the end of the world. Finally, Ben asked, "You, too, Andy?"

"No, they're transferring me to Tax. Can you believe it? I hate Tax, but it was either Tax or driving a cab. I got a master's in taxation, though, so they figured they could spare me."

"Congratulations," Ben said.

"I'm sorry, guys."

"No, I mean it. I'm happy for you."

"I could be gone in a month. Who knows?"

"When do we leave?" Izabelle asked.

"Right now. The procedure is to sign a furlough agreement, pack up your stuff, clean off your desk, and hit the street. HR will e-mail you a list of nonprofits and all the paperwork. Sorry, guys."

"Please stop saying that," Samantha said. "There's nothing you can say that helps matters here."

"True, but it could be worse. The majority of those in your boat are not being offered a furlough. They're being fired on the spot."

"I'm sorry, Andy," Samantha said. "There are a lot of emotions right now."

"It's okay. I understand. You have the right to be angry and upset. Look at you—all three have Ivy League law degrees and you're being escorted out of the building like thieves. Laid off like factory workers. It's awful, just awful. Some of the partners offered to cut their salaries in half to prevent this."

"I'll bet that was a small group," Ben said.

"It was, yes. Very small, I'm afraid. But the decision has been made."

A woman in a black suit and a black necktie stood at the quad where Samantha shared a "space" with three others, including Izabelle. Ben was just down the hall. The woman tried to smile as she said, "I'm Carmen. Can I help you?" She was holding an empty cardboard box, blank on all sides so no one would know it was the official Scully & Pershing repository for the office junk of those furloughed or fired or whatever.

"No, thanks," Samantha said, and she managed to do so politely. She could have snapped and been rude, but Carmen was only doing her job. Samantha began opening drawers and removing all things personal. In one drawer she had some S&P files and asked, "What about these?"

"They stay here," Carmen said, watching every move, as if Samantha might attempt to pilfer some valuable asset. The truth was that everything of value was stored in the computers—a desktop she used in her space and a laptop she took almost everywhere. A Scully & Pershing laptop. It, too, would remain behind. She could access everything from her personal laptop, but she knew the codes had already been changed.

As if sleepwalking, she cleaned out the drawers and gently tucked away the six miniature skyscrapers from her collection, though she thought about tossing them into the trash can. Izabelle arrived and was given her own personal cardboard box. All others—associates, secretaries, paralegals—had suddenly found business elsewhere. Protocol had been quickly adopted—when someone cleans out a desk, let them do it in peace. No witnesses, no gawking, no hollow farewells.

Izabelle's eyes were puffy and red; she had obviously been in the restroom crying. She whispered, "Call me. Let's have a drink tonight."

"Sure," Samantha said. She finished stuffing it all into the box, her briefcase, and her bulky designer bag, and without looking over her shoulder she marched behind Carmen down the hallway and to the elevators on the forty-eighth floor. As they waited, she refused to look around and absorb it one last time. The door opened and thankfully the elevator was empty. "I'll carry that," Carmen said, pointing to the box, which was already increasing in bulk and weight. "No," Samantha said as she stepped inside. Carmen pushed the button for the lobby. Why, exactly, was she being escorted out of the building? The longer she pondered the question the angrier she became. She wanted to cry and she wanted to lash out, but what she really wanted was to call her mother. The elevator stopped on the forty-third floor and a well-dressed young man stepped in. He was holding an identical cardboard box, with a large bag strapped over his shoulder and a leather briefcase under an arm. He had the same stunned look of fear and confusion. Samantha had seen him in the elevator but never met him. What a firm. So mammoth the associates wore name badges at the dreadful Christmas party. Another security guard in a black suit stepped in behind him, and when everyone was in place Carmen again pressed the button for the lobby. Samantha studied the floor, determined not to speak even if spoken to. On the thirty-ninth floor, the elevator stopped again, and Mr. Kirk Knight got on board while studying his cell phone. Once the door closed, he glanced around, saw the two cardboard boxes, and seemed to gasp as his spine stiffened. Knight was senior partner in Mergers & Acquisitions and a member of the executive committee. Suddenly face-to-face with two of his victims, he swallowed hard and stared at the door. Then he suddenly punched the button for floor number 28.

Samantha was too numb to insult him. The other associate had his eyes closed. When the elevator stopped, Knight hustled off. After the door closed, Samantha remembered the firm leased floors 30 through 65. Why would Knight make a sudden exit onto 28? Who cared?

Carmen walked her through the lobby and out the door onto Broad Street. She offered a meek "I'm sorry," but Samantha did not respond. Laden like a pack mule, she drifted with the foot traffic, going nowhere in particular. Then she remembered the newspaper photos of the Lehman and Bear Stearns employees leaving their office buildings with boxes filled with their stuff, as if the buildings were on fire and they were fleeing for their lives. In one photo, a large color one on the front of the *Times*'s section B, a Lehman trader was caught with tears on her cheeks as she stood helplessly on the sidewalk.

But those photos were old news now and Samantha did not see any cameras. She set the box down at the corner of Broad and Wall and waited for a cab.

2

In a chic SoHo loft that cost her $2,000 a month, Samantha flung her office crap at the floor and fell onto the sofa. She clutched her cell phone, but waited. She breathed deeply, eyes closed, emotions somewhat in check. She needed her mother's voice and reassurance, but she did not want to sound weak, wounded, and vulnerable.

The relief came from the sudden realization that she had just been freed from a job she despised. Tonight at seven she might be watching a movie or having dinner with friends, not slaving away at the office with the meter running. This Sunday she could leave the city with no thoughts whatsoever about Andy Grubman and the pile of paperwork for his next crucial deal. The FirmFone, a monstrous little gadget that had been glued to her body for three years now, had been surrendered. She felt liberated and wonderfully unburdened.

The fear came from the loss of income and the sudden detour in her career. As a third-year associate, she was earning $180,000 a year in base salary, plus a nice bonus. A lot of money, but life in the city had a way of devouring it. Half evaporated in taxes. She had a savings account, one she halfheartedly acknowledged. When you're twenty-nine, single, and free in the city, in a profession where next year's package will exceed this year's salary plus bonus, why worry too much about saving money? She had a friend from Columbia Law who'd been at S&P for five years, had just made junior partner, and would earn about half a million this year. Samantha had been on that track.

She also had friends who jumped off the treadmill after twelve months and happily fled the awful world of Big Law. One was now a ski instructor in Vermont, a former editor of the *Columbia Law Review*, a refugee from the bowels of S&P who lived in a cabin by a stream and rarely answered his cell. In just thirteen months he had gone from an ambitious young associate to a mildly deranged idiot who slept at his desk. Just before HR intervened, he cracked up and left the city. Samantha thought of him often, usually with a twinge of jealousy.

Relief, fear, and humiliation. Her parents paid for a pricey prep school education in D.C. She graduated magna cum laude from Georgetown with a degree in political science. She breezed through law school and finished with honors. A dozen megafirms offered her jobs after a federal court clerkship. The first twenty-nine years of her life had seen overwhelming success and little failure. To be discharged in such a manner was crushing. To be escorted out of the building was degrading. This was not just a minor bump in a long, rewarding career.

There was some comfort in the numbers. Since Lehman collapsed, thousands of young professionals had been tossed into the streets. Misery loves company and all that, but at the moment she couldn't muster much sympathy for anyone else.

"Karen Kofer, please," she said to her phone. She was lying on the sofa, perfectly still, timing her breaths. Then, "Mom, it's me. They did it. I've been sacked." She bit her lip and fought back tears.

"I'm so sorry, Samantha. When did it happen?"

"About an hour ago. No real surprise, but it's still hard to believe."

"I know it, baby. I'm so sorry."

For the past week, they had talked of nothing but a likely termination. "Are you at home?" Karen asked.

"I am, and I'm okay. Blythe is at work. I haven't told her yet. I haven't told anyone."

"I'm so sorry."

Blythe was a friend and classmate from Columbia who worked at another megafirm. They shared an apartment but not much of their lives. When you work seventy-five to a hundred hours a week, there's so little to share. Things were not going well at Blythe's firm either and she was expecting the worst.

"I'm fine, Mom."

"No you're not. Why don't you come home for a few days?" Home was a moving target. Her mother rented a lovely apartment near Dupont Circle, and her father leased a small condo near the river in Alexandria. Samantha had never spent more than a month in either place and wasn't thinking about it now.

"I will," she said, "but not right now."

A long pause, then a soft "What are your plans, Samantha?"

"I have no plans, Mom. Right now I'm in shock and can't think past the next hour."

"I understand. I wish I could be there."

"I'm okay, Mom. I promise." The last thing Samantha needed at that moment was her mother's hovering presence and endless advice on what to do next.

"Is it a termination or some type of layoff?"

"The firm is calling it a furlough, a deal whereby we intern with a nonprofit for a year or two and keep our health benefits. Then, if things turn around, the firm will take us back without a loss of seniority."

"Sounds like a pathetic effort to keep you on a string."

Thanks, Mom, for your typical bluntness. Karen went on, "Why don't you tell those creeps to take a hike?"

"Because I'd like to keep my health insurance, and I'd like to know there might be the option of returning one day."

"You can find a job somewhere else."

Spoken like a career bureaucrat. Karen Kofer was a senior attorney with the Department of Justice in Washington, the only law job she'd ever had, and for almost thirty years now. Her position, like that of every person around her, was thoroughly protected. Regardless of depressions, wars, government shutdowns, national catastrophes, political upheavals, or any other possible calamity,

Karen Kofer's paycheck was inviolable. And with that came the casual arrogance of so many entrenched bureaucrats.

We are so valuable because we are so necessary.

Samantha said, "No, Mom, there are no jobs right now. In case you haven't heard, we are in a financial crisis with a depression right around the corner. Law firms are tossing out associates in droves, then locking the doors."

"I doubt if things are that bad."

"Oh really. Scully & Pershing has deferred all new hires, which means that a dozen or so of the brightest from the Harvard Law School have just been informed that the jobs they were promised next September won't be there. Same for Yale, Stanford, Columbia."

"But you are so talented, Samantha."

Never argue with a bureaucrat. Samantha took a deep breath and was about to sign off when an urgent call "from the White House" came through and Karen had to go. She promised to call right back, as soon as she saved the Republic. Fine, Mom, Samantha said. She received as much of her mother's attention as she could possibly want. She was an only child, which was a good thing in retrospect, in light of the wreckage strewn high and low by her parents' divorce.

It was a clear, beautiful day, weatherwise, and Samantha needed a walk. She zigzagged through SoHo, then through the West Village. In an empty coffee shop, she finally called her father. Marshall Kofer had once been a high-octane plaintiffs' lawyer whose expertise had been suing airlines after crashes. He built an aggressive and successful firm in D.C. and spent six nights a week in hotels around the world, either chasing cases or trying them. He made a fortune, spent lavishly, and as an adolescent Samantha was keenly aware that her family had more than many of the kids in her D.C. prep school. While her father was leaping from one high-profile case to the next, her mother quietly raised her while doggedly pursing her own career at Justice. If her parents fought, Samantha was not aware of it; her father was simply never at home. At some point, no one would ever know exactly when, a young and pretty para-

legal entered the picture and Marshall took the plunge. The fling
became an affair, then a romance, and after a couple of years Karen
Kofer was suspicious. She confronted her husband, who lied at first
but soon admitted the truth. He wanted a divorce; he'd found the
love of his life.

Coincidentally, at about the same time Marshall was compli-
cating his family life, he made a few other bad decisions. One
involved a scheme to take a large fee offshore. A United Asia Airlines jumbo jet had crashed on Sri Lanka, with forty Americans on
board. There were no survivors, and, true to form, Marshall Kofer
got there before anyone else. During the settlement negotiations,
he set up a series of shell companies throughout the Caribbean and
Asia to route, reroute, and outright hide his substantial fees.

Samantha had a thick file with newspaper accounts and investi-
gative reports of her father's rather clumsy attempt at corruption. It
would make a compelling book, but she had no interest in writing
it. He got caught, humiliated, embarrassed on the front page, convicted, disbarred, and sent to prison for three years. He was paroled
two weeks before she graduated from Georgetown. These days,
Marshall worked as a consultant of some variety in a small office in
the old section of Alexandria. According to him, he advised other
plaintiffs' lawyers on mass tort cases but was always vague with the
details. Samantha was convinced, as was her mother, that Marshall
had managed to bury a pile of loot somewhere in the Caribbean.
Karen had stopped looking.

Though Marshall would always suspect it and Karen would
always deny it, he had a hunch his ex-wife had a finger in his
criminal prosecution. She had rank at Justice, plenty of it, and lots
of friends.

"Dad, I got fired," she said softly into her cell. The coffee shop
was empty but the barista was close by.

"Oh, Sam, I'm so sorry," Marshall said. "Tell me what happened."

As far as she could tell, her father had learned only one thing
in prison. Not humility, nor patience, nor understanding, nor for-
giveness, nor any of the standard attributes one picks up after such

a humiliating fall. He was just as wired and ambitious as before, still eager to tackle each day and run over anyone stalling in front of him. For some reason, though, Marshall Kofer had learned to listen, at least to his daughter. She replayed the narrative slowly, and he hung on every word. She assured him she would be fine. At one point he sounded as if he might cry.

Normally, he would have made snide comments about the way she chose to pursue the law. He hated big firms because he had fought them for years. He viewed them as mere corporations, not partnerships with real lawyers fighting for their clients. He had a soapbox from which he could deliver a dozen sermons on the evils of Big Law. Samantha had heard every one of them and was in no mood to hear them again.

"Shall I come see you, Sam?" he asked. "I can be there in three hours."

"Thanks, but no. Not yet. Give me a day or so. I need a break and I'm thinking about getting out of the city for a few days."

"I'll come and get you."

"Maybe, but not now. I'm fine, Dad, I swear."

"No you're not. You need your father."

It was still odd to hear this from a man who had been absent for the first twenty years of her life. At least he was trying, though.

"Thanks, Dad. I'll call later."

"Let's take a trip, find a beach somewhere and drink rum."

She had to laugh because they had never taken a trip together, not just the two of them. There had been a few hurried vacations when she was a kid, typical trips to the cities of Europe, almost always cut short by pressing business back home. The idea of hanging out on a beach with her father was not immediately appealing, regardless of the circumstances.

"Thanks, Dad. Maybe later but not now. I need to take care of business here."

"I can get you a job," he said. "A real one."

Here we go again, she thought, but let it pass. Her father had been trying to entice her into a real law job for several years now, real in the sense that it would involve suing big corporations for all manner of malfeasance. In Marshall Kofer's world, every company of a certain size must have committed egregious sins to succeed in the cutthroat world of Western capitalism. It was the calling of lawyers (and maybe ex-lawyers) like him to uncover the wrongdoing and sue like crazy.

"Thanks, Dad. I'll call you later."

How ironic that her father would still be so eager for her to pursue the same brand of law that had landed him in prison. She had no interest in the courtroom, or in conflict. She wasn't sure what she wanted, probably a nice desk job with a handsome salary. Primarily because of her gender and brains, she once had a decent chance of making partner at Scully & Pershing. But at what cost?

Perhaps she wanted that career, perhaps not. Right now she just wanted to roam the streets of lower Manhattan and clear her head. She drifted through Tribeca as the hours passed. Her mother called twice and her father called once, but she declined to answer. Izabelle and Ben checked in too, but she didn't want to talk. She found herself at Moke's Pub near Chinatown, and for a moment stood outside looking in. Her first drink with Henry had been at Moke's, so many years ago. Friends introduced them. He was an aspiring actor, one of a million in the city, and she was a rookie associate at S&P. They dated for a year before the romance fizzled under the strain of her brutal work schedule and his unemployment. He fled to L.A. where, at last sighting, he was driving limos for unknown actors and doing bit parts in commercials, nonspeaking.

She could have loved Henry under different circumstances. He had the time, the interest, and the passion. She had been too exhausted. It was not unusual in Big Law for women to wake up at the age of forty and realize they were still single and a decade had just passed by.

She walked away from Moke's and headed north to SoHo.

Anna from Human Resources proved remarkably efficient. At 5:00 p.m., Samantha received a long e-mail that included the names of ten nonprofits someone had deemed suitable for non-paying internships by the battered and bruised souls suddenly furloughed by the world's largest law firm. Marshkeepers in Lafayette, Louisiana. The Pittsburgh Women's Shelter. Immigrant Initiative in Tampa. Mountain Legal Aid Clinic in Brady, Virginia. The Euthanasia Society of Greater Tucson. A homeless organization in Louisville. Lake Erie Defense Fund. And so on. None of the ten were anywhere near the New York metropolitan area.

She stared at the list for a long time and contemplated the reality of leaving the city. She had lived there for six of the past seven years—three at Columbia and three as an associate. After law school, she had clerked for a federal judge in D.C., then hurriedly returned to New York. Between there and Washington she had never lived beyond the bright lights.

Lafayette, Louisiana? Brady, Virginia?

In language that was far too chipper for the occasion, Anna advised those furloughed that space could possibly be limited at some of the above nonprofits. In other words, sign up in a hurry or you might not get the chance to move to the boondocks and work the next twelve months for free. But Samantha was too numb to do anything in a hurry.

Blythe popped in for a quick hello and microwave pasta. Samantha had delivered the big news via text and her roommate was near tears when she arrived. After a few minutes, though, Samantha managed to calm her and assure her that life would go on. Blythe's firm represented a pack of mortgage lenders, and the mood there was just as dark as at Scully & Pershing. For days now, the two had talked of almost nothing but being terminated. Halfway through the pasta, Blythe's cell began vibrating. It was her supervising partner, looking for her. So at 6:30 she dashed from the apartment, frantic to get back to the office and fearful that the slightest delay might get her sacked.

Samantha poured a glass of wine and filled the tub with warm water. She soaked and drank and decided that, in spite of the money, she hated Big Law and would never go back. She would never again allow herself to get yelled at because she was not at the office after dark or before sunrise. She would never again be seduced by the money. She would never again do a lot of things.

On the financial front, things were unsteady but not altogether bleak. She had $31,000 in savings and no debt, except for three more months on the loft rental. If she downsized considerably and pieced together income through part-time jobs, she could possibly hang on until the storm blew over. Assuming, of course, that the end of the world did not materialize. She couldn't see herself waiting tables or selling shoes, but then she had never dreamed her prestigious career would end so abruptly. The city would soon be crowded with even more waitresses and retail clerks holding graduate degrees.

Back to Big Law. Her goal had been to make partner by the age of thirty-five, one of few women at the top, and nail down a corner office from which she would play hardball with the boys. She would have a secretary, an assistant, some paralegals, and a driver on call, a golden expense account, and a designer wardrobe. The hundred-hour workweeks would shrink into something manageable. She would knock down two million plus a year for twenty years, then retire and travel the world. Along the way she would pick up a husband, a kid or two, and life would be grand.

It had all been planned and was seemingly within reach.

She met Izabelle for martinis in the lobby of the Mercer Hotel, four blocks from her loft. They had invited Ben but he had a new wife and was otherwise distracted. The furloughs were having opposite effects. Samantha was in the process of coping, even shrugging it off and thinking about ways to survive. She was lucky, though, because she had no student debt. Her parents had the money for a fine education. But Izabelle was choking under old loans and agonizing over the future. She slurped her martini and the gin went straight to her brain.

"I can't go a year with no income," she said. "Can you?"

"Possibly," Samantha said. "If I shrink everything and live off soup, I can scrimp along and stay in the city."

"Not me," Izabelle said sadly as she took another gulp. "I know this guy in Litigation. He got the furlough deal last Friday. He's already called five of the nonprofits, and all five said the internships had been grabbed by other associates. Can you believe it? So he called HR and raised hell and they said they're still working on the list, still getting inquiries from nonprofits looking for extremely cheap labor. So not only do we get sacked, but the little furlough scheme is not working too well. No one wants us even if we'll work for free. That's pretty sick."

Samantha took a tiny sip and savored the numbing liquid. "I'm not inclined to take the furlough deal."

"Then what do you do about health insurance? You can't go naked."

"Maybe I can."

"But if you get sick, you'll lose everything."

"I don't have much."

"That's foolish, Sam." Another pull on the martini, though a bit smaller. "So you're giving up on a bright future at dear old Scully & Pershing."

"The firm has given up on me, and you, and a lot of others. There has to be a better place to work, and a better way to make a living."

"I'll drink to that." A waitress appeared, and they ordered another round.

3

Samantha slept for twelve hours and woke up with an overwhelming urge to flee the city. Lying in bed and staring at the ancient wooden beams across her ceiling, she replayed the last month or so and realized she had not left Manhattan in seven weeks. A long August weekend in Southampton had been abruptly canceled by Andy Grubman, and instead of sleeping and partying she had spent Saturday and Sunday at the office proofreading contracts a foot thick.

Seven weeks. She showered quickly and stuffed a suitcase with some essentials. At ten, she boarded a train at Penn Station and left a voice message on Blythe's cell. She was headed to D.C. for a few days. Call me if you get the ax.

As the train rolled through New Jersey, curiosity got the best of her. She sent an e-mail to the Lake Erie Defense Fund, and one to the Pittsburgh Women's Shelter. Thirty minutes passed without replies as she read the *Times*. Not a word about the carnage at S&P as the economic meltdown continued unabated. Massive layoffs at financial firms. Banks refusing to lend while other banks were closing their doors. Congress chasing its tail. Obama blaming Bush. McCain/Palin blaming the Democrats. She checked her laptop and saw another e-mail from happy Anna in HR. Six new nonprofits had emerged and joined the party. Better get busy!

The Women's Shelter sent back a pleasant note, thanking Ms.

Kofer for her interest but the position had just been filled. Five minutes later, the good folks fighting to save Lake Erie said pretty much the same thing. Feeling the challenge now, Samantha sent a flurry of e-mails to five more nonprofits on Anna's list, then sent one to Anna politely asking her to become a bit more enthusiastic with her updates. Between Philadelphia and Wilmington, Marshkeepers down in Louisiana said no. The Georgia Innocence Project said no. The Immigrant Initiative in Tampa said no. The Death Penalty Clearinghouse said no, and Legal Aid of Greater St. Louis said no. No, but thanks for your interest. The intern positions have already been filled.

Zero for seven. She couldn't land a job as a volunteer!

She got a cab at Union Station near the Capitol and sank low in the rear seat as it inched through D.C. traffic. Block after block of government offices, headquarters for a thousand organizations and associations, hotels and gleaming new condos, sprawling offices packed with lawyers and lobbyists, the sidewalks crawling with busy people hurrying back and forth, urgently pursuing the nation's business as the world teetered on the brink. She had lived the first twenty-two years of her life in D.C., but now found it boring. It still attracted bright young people in droves, but all they talked about was politics and real estate. The lobbyists were the worst. They now outnumbered the lawyers and politicians combined, and they ran the city. They owned Congress and thus controlled the money, and over cocktails or dinner they would bore you to death with the details of their latest heroic efforts to secure a bit of pork or rewrite a loophole in the tax code. Every friend from childhood and Georgetown earned a paycheck that in some way had federal dollars attached to it. Her own mother earned $145,000 a year as a lawyer at Justice.

Samantha wasn't sure how her father earned his money. She decided to visit him first. Her mother worked long hours and wouldn't be home until after dark. Samantha let herself into her mother's apartment, left her suitcase, and took the same cab across the Potomac to Old Town in Alexandria. Her father was waiting with a hug and a smile and all the time in the world. He had moved into a much nicer building and renamed his firm the Kofer Group. "Sounds like a bunch of lobbyists," she said as she looked around his well-appointed reception area.

"Oh no," Marshall said. "We stay away from that circus over there," he said, pointing in the general direction of D.C. as if it were a ghetto. They were walking down a hallway, passing open doors to small offices.

Then what exactly do you do, Dad? But she decided to postpone that question. He led her into a large corner office with a distant view of the Potomac River, not unlike Andy Grubman's from another lifetime. They sat in leather chairs around a small table as a secretary fetched coffee.

"How are you doing?" he asked sincerely, a hand on her knee as if she'd fallen down the steps.

"I'm okay," Samantha said and immediately felt her throat tighten. Get a grip. She swallowed hard and said, "It's just been so sudden. A month ago things were fine, you know, on track, no problems. A lot of hours but that's life on the treadmill. Then we started hearing rumors, distant drumbeats of things going wrong. It seems so sudden now."

"Yes it does. This crash is more like a bomb."

The coffee arrived on a tray and the secretary closed the door as she left.

"Do you read Trottman?" he asked.

"Who?"

"Okay, he writes a weekly newsletter on the markets and politics. Based here in D.C. and been around for some time, and he's pretty good. Six months ago he predicted a meltdown in the sub-prime mortgage game, said it's been building for years and so on, said there would be a crash and a major recession. He advised everyone to get out of the markets, all markets."

"Did you?"

"Didn't have anything in the markets, really. And if I did I'm not sure I would have taken his advice. Six months ago we were living the dream and real estate values would never decline. Credit was dirt cheap and everybody was borrowing heavily. The sky was the limit."

"What does this Trottman say now?"

"Well, when he's not crowing, he's telling the Fed what to do. He's predicting a major recession, and worldwide, but nothing like 1929. He thinks the markets will sink by half, unemployment will jump to new levels, the Democrats will win in November, a couple of major banks will go under, a lot of fear and uncertainty but the world will survive somehow. What do you hear up there, on Wall Street? You're in the thick of things. Or you were, I suppose."

He was wearing the same style of black tasseled loafers he'd worn forever. The dark suit was probably handmade, just like in the glory days. Worsted wool and very expensive. Silk tie with perfect knot. Cuff links. The first time she visited him in prison he wore a khaki shirt and olive dungarees, his standard uniform, and he'd whined about how much he missed his wardrobe. Marshall Kofer had always loved fine clothes, and now that he was back he was clearly spending some money.

"Nothing but panic," she said. "Two suicides yesterday, according to the *Times*."

"Have you had lunch?"

"I had a sandwich on the train."

"Let's do dinner, just the two of us."

"I promised Mom, but I'm free for lunch tomorrow."

"Booked. How is Karen?" he asked. According to him, her parents had a friendly chat at least once a month by phone. According to her mother, the conversations happened about once a year. Marshall would like to be friends, but Karen carried too much baggage. Samantha had never tried to broker a truce.

"She's fine, I guess. Works hard and all that."

"Is she seeing anyone?"

"I don't ask. What about you?"

The young and pretty paralegal ditched him two months after he landed in prison, so Marshall had been single for many years. Single but seldom alone. He was almost sixty, still fit and thin with slicked-back gray hair and a killer smile. "Oh, I'm still in the game," he said with a laugh. "And you. Anybody significant?"

"No, Dad, afraid not. I've spent the last three years in a cave while the world went by. I'm twenty-nine and a virgin once again."

"No need to go there. How long are you in town?"

"I just got here. I don't know. I told you about the furlough scheme the firm is offering and I'm checking that out."

"You volunteer for a year, then get your old job back without losing rank?"

"Something like that."

"Smells bad. You don't really trust those guys, do you?"

She took a deep breath, then a sip of coffee. At this point, the conversation could spiral down into topics she couldn't stomach at the moment. "No, not really. I can honestly say that I do not trust the partners who run Scully & Pershing. No."

Marshall was already shaking his head, happily agreeing with her. "And you don't really want to go back there, not now, not twelve months from now. Right?"

"I'm not sure what I'll be thinking in twelve months, but I can't see much of a future at the firm."

"Right, right." He set his coffee cup on the table and leaned forward. "Look, Samantha, I can offer you a job right here, one that will pay well and keep you busy for a year or so while you sort things out. Maybe it can become permanent, maybe not, but you'll have plenty of time to make that decision. You will not be practicing law, real law as they say, but then I'm not sure you've been doing much of that for the past three years."

"Mom said you have two partners and that they've also been disbarred."

He faked a laugh, but the truth was uncomfortable. "Karen would say that, wouldn't she? But yes, Samantha, there are three of us here, all convicted, sentenced, disbarred, incarcerated, and, I'm happy to say, fully rehabilitated."

"I'm sorry, Dad, but I can't see myself working for a firm run by three disbarred lawyers."

Marshall's shoulders sagged a bit. The smile went away.

"It's not really a law firm, right?"

"Right. We can't practice because we have not been reinstated."

"Then what do you do?"

He bounced back quickly and said, "We make a lot of money, dear. We work as consultants."

"Everybody is a consultant, Dad. Who do you consult and what do you tell them?"

"Are you familiar with litigation funders?"

"For discussion purposes, let's say the answer is no."

"Okay, litigation funders are private companies that raise money from their investors to buy into big lawsuits. For example, let's say a small software company is convinced one of the big guys, say Microsoft, has stolen its software, but there's no way the small company can afford to sue Microsoft and go toe-to-toe in court. Impossible. So the small company goes to a litigation fund, and the fund reviews the case, and if it has merit, then the fund puts up some serious cash for legal fees and expenses. Ten million, twenty million, doesn't really matter. There's plenty of cash. The fund of course gets a piece of the action. The fight becomes a fair one, and there's usually a lucrative settlement. Our job here is to advise the litigation funds on whether or not they should get involved. Not all potential lawsuits should be pursued, not even in this country. My two partners, non-equity partners, I might add, were also experts in complex tort litigation until, shall we say, they were asked to leave the legal profession. Our business is booming, regardless of this little recession. In fact, we think this current mess will actually help our business. A lot of banks are about to get sued, and for huge sums."

Samantha listened, sipped her coffee, and reminded herself that she was listening to a man who once cajoled millions out of jurors on a regular basis.

"What do you think?" he asked.

Sounds dreadful, she thought, but kept frowning as if deep in thought. "Interesting," she managed to say.

"We see huge growth potential," he said.

Yes, and with three ex-cons running the show it's only a matter of time before there's trouble. "I don't know beans about litigation, Dad. I've always tried to stay away from it. I was in finance, remember?"

"Oh, you'll pick it up. I'll teach you, Samantha. We'll have a ball. Give it a shot. Try it for a few months while you sort things out."

"But I'm not disbarred yet," she said. They both laughed, but it really wasn't that funny. "I'll think about it, Dad. Thanks."

"You'll fit in, I promise. Forty hours a week, a nice office, nice people. It'll sure beat the rat race in New York."

"But New York is home, Dad. Not D.C."

"Okay, okay. I'm not going to push. The offer is on the table."

"And I appreciate it."

A secretary tapped on the door and stuck her head in. "Your four o'clock meeting, sir."

Marshall frowned as he glanced at his watch to confirm the time. "I'll be there in a moment," he said and she disappeared. Samantha grabbed her purse and said, "I need to be going."

"No rush, dear. It can wait."

"I know you're busy. I'll see you tomorrow for lunch."

"We'll have some fun. Say hello to Karen. I'd love to see her."

Not a chance. "Sure, Dad. See you tomorrow."

They hugged by the door and she hurried away.

The eighth rejection came from the Chesapeake Society in Baltimore, and the ninth came from an outfit fighting to save the redwoods in Northern California. Never, in her privileged life, had Samantha Kofer been rejected nine times in one day from any endeavor. Nor in a week, nor a month. She was not sure she could handle number ten.

She was sipping decaf in the café at Kramerbooks near Dupont Circle, waiting and swapping e-mails with friends. Blythe still had a job but things were changing by the hour. She passed along the gossip that her firm, the world's fourth largest, was also slaughtering associates right and left, and that it too had cooked up the same furlough scheme to dump its brightest on as many broke and struggling nonprofits as possible. She wrote: "Must be 1000s out there knocking doors begging for work."

Samantha didn't have the spine to admit she was zero for nine.

Then number ten chimed in. It was a terse message from a Mattie Wyatt at Mountain Legal Aid Clinic in Brady, Virginia: "If you can talk right now call my cell," and she gave her number. After nine straight stiff-arms, it felt like an invitation to the Inauguration.

Samantha took a deep breath and another sip, glanced around to make sure she could not be heard, as if the other customers were concerned with her business, then punched the numbers of her cell phone.

4

The Mountain Legal Aid Clinic ran its low-budget operations from an abandoned hardware store on Main Street in Brady, Virginia, population twenty-two hundred and declining with each census. Brady was in southwest Virginia, Appalachia, the coal country. From the affluent D.C. suburbs of northern Virginia, Brady was about three hundred miles away in distance and a century in time.

Mattie Wyatt had been the clinic's executive director from the day she founded the organization twenty-six years earlier. She picked up her cell phone and gave her usual greeting: "Mattie Wyatt."

A somewhat timid voice on the other end said, "Yes, this is Samantha Kofer. I just got your e-mail."

"Thank you, Ms. Kofer. I got your inquiry this afternoon, along with some others. Looks like things are pretty tough at some of these big law firms."

"You could say that, yes."

"Well, we've never had an intern from one of the big New York firms, but we could always use some help around here. There's no shortage of poor folk and their problems. You ever been to southwest Virginia?"

Samantha had not. She had seen the world but had never ventured into Appalachia. "I'm afraid not," she said as politely as possible. Mattie's voice was friendly, her accent slightly twangy, and Samantha decided that her best manners were needed.

"Well you're in for a jolt," Mattie said. "Look, Ms. Kofer, I've had three of you guys send e-mails today and we don't have room for three rookies who are clueless, know what I mean? So the only way I know to pick one is to do interviews. Can you come down here for a look around? The other two said they would try. I think one is from your law firm."

"Well, sure, I could drive down," Samantha said. What else could she say? Any hint of reluctance and she would indeed pick up the tenth rejection. "When did you have in mind?"

"Tomorrow, the next day, whenever. I didn't expect to get flooded with laid-off lawyers scrambling to find work, even if it doesn't pay. Suddenly there's competition for the job, so I guess the sooner the better. New York is a long way off."

"I'm actually in D.C. I can be there tomorrow afternoon, I suppose."

"Okay. I don't have much time to spend with interviews, so I'll likely just hire the first one to show up and cancel the rest. That is, if I like the first one."

Samantha closed her eyes for a few seconds and tried to put it all in perspective. Yesterday morning she had arrived at her desk in the world's largest law firm, one that paid her handsomely and had the promise of a long, profitable career. Now, about thirty hours later, she was unemployed, sitting in the café at Kramerbooks and trying to hustle her way into a temporary, unpaid gig about as deep in the boonies as one could possibly wander.

Mattie continued, "I drove to D.C. last year for a conference, took me six hours. You wanna say around four tomorrow afternoon?"

"Sure. I'll see you then. And thanks Ms. Wyatt."

"No, thank *you*, and it's Mattie."

Samantha searched the Web and found a site for the legal aid clinic. Its mission was simple: "Provide free legal services for low-income clients in southwest Virginia." Its areas of service included domestic relations, debt relief, housing, health care, education, and benefits due to black lung disease. Her legal education had touched briefly on some of these specialties; her career had not. The clinic did not deal with criminal matters. In addition to Mattie Wyatt, there was another attorney, a paralegal, a receptionist, all women.

Samantha decided she would discuss it with her mother, then sleep on it. She did not own a car and, frankly, could not see herself wasting the time to travel to Appalachia. Waiting tables in SoHo was looking better. As she stared at her laptop, the homeless shelter in Louisville checked in with a polite no. Ten rejections in one day. That was enough: she would end her quest to save the world.

Karen Kofer arrived at Firefly just after seven. Her eyes watered as she hugged her only child, and after a few words of sympathy Samantha asked her to please stop. They went to the bar and ordered wine while they waited for a table. Karen was fifty-five and aging beautifully. She spent most of her cash on clothes and was always trendy, even chic. As long as Samantha could remember, her mother had complained about the lack of style around her at Justice, as if it were her job to spice things up. She had been single for ten years and there had been no shortage of men, but never the right one. Out of habit, she sized up her daughter, from earrings down to shoes, and made her assessment in a matter of seconds. No comment. Samantha didn't really care. On this awful day, she had other things on her mind.

"Dad says hello," she said in an effort to steer the conversation away from the urgent matters at Justice.

"Oh, you've seen him?" Karen asked, eyebrows arched, radar suddenly on high alert.

"Yes. I stopped by his office. He seems to be doing well, looking good, expanding his business, he says."

"Did he offer you a job?"

"He did. Starting right away, forty hours a week in an office filled with wonderful people."

"They've all been disbarred, you know?"

"Yes, you told me that."

"It seems to be legitimate, for now anyway. Surely you're not thinking about working for Marshall. It's a gang of thieves and they'll probably be in trouble before long."

"So you're watching them?"

"Let's say I have friends, Samantha. Lots of friends in the right places."

"And you'd like to see him busted again?"

"No, dear, I'm over your father. We split years ago and it took a long time to recover. He hid assets and screwed me in the divorce, but I finally let it go. I have a good life and I'll not waste negative energy on Marshall Kofer."

In tandem, they sipped their wine and watched the bartender, a hunky boy in his mid-twenties in a tight black T-shirt.

"No, Mom, I'm not going to work for Dad. It would be a disaster."

The hostess led them to their table and a waiter poured ice water. When they were alone, Karen said, "I'm so sorry, Samantha. I can't believe this."

"Please, Mom, that's enough."

"I know, but I'm your mother and I can't help myself."

"Can I borrow your car for the next couple of days?"

"Well, sure. Why do you need my car?"

"There's a legal aid clinic in Brady, Virginia, one of the non-profits on my list, and I'm thinking of driving down for a look around. It's probably a waste of time, but I'm really not that busy these days. In fact, I have nothing to do tomorrow and a long drive might help to clear my head."

"But legal aid?"

"Why not? It's just an interview for an internship. If I don't get the job, then I'll remain unemployed. If I do get the job, I can always quit if I don't like it."

"And it pays nothing?"

"Nothing. That's part of the deal. I do the internship for twelve months and the firm keeps me in the system."

"But surely you can find a nice little firm in New York."

"We've already discussed this, Mom. Big law firms are laying off and small firms are folding. You don't understand the hysteria on the streets of New York these days. You're safe and secure and none of your friends will lose their jobs. Out in the real world it's nothing but fear and chaos."

"I'm not in the real world?"

Fortunately the waiter was back, and with a long narrative about the specials. When he left, they finished their wine and gazed at the tables around them. Finally, Karen said, "Samantha, I think you're making a mistake. You can't just go off and disappear for a year. What about your apartment? And your friends?"

"My friends are just as furloughed as I am, most of them anyway. And I don't have a lot of friends."

"I just don't like the sound of it."

"Great, Mom, and what are my options? Taking a job with the Kofer Group."

"Heaven forbid. You'd probably end up in jail."

"Would you visit me? You never visited him."

"Never thought about visiting him. I was delighted when they put him away. You'll understand one day, dear, but only if the man you love dumps you for someone else, and I pray that never happens."

"Okay, I think I understand that. But it was a long time ago."

"Some things you never forget."

"Are you trying to forget?"

"Look, Samantha, every child wants their parents to stay together. It's a basic survival instinct. And when they split, the child wants them to at least be friends. Some are able to do this, some are not. I do not want to be in the same room with Marshall Kofer, and I prefer not to talk about him. Let's just leave it at that."

"Fair enough." It was as close to a mediation as Samantha had ever been, and she quickly backed away. The waiter brought salads and they ordered a bottle of wine. "How is Blythe?" Karen asked, heading toward easier topics.

"Worried, but still employed." They talked about Blythe for a few minutes, then on to a man named Forest who'd been hanging around Karen's apartment for a month or so. He was a few years younger, her preference, but there was no romance. Forest was a lawyer advising the Obama campaign, and the conversation drifted in that direction. With fresh wine, they analyzed the first presidential debate. Samantha, though, was tired of the election, and Karen, because of her job, shied away from the politics. She said, "I forgot you don't own a car."

"I haven't needed one in years. I guess I could lease one for a few months if I need to."

"Come to think of it, I'll need mine tomorrow night. I'm playing bridge at a friend's house in McLean."

"No problem. I'll rent one for a couple of days. The more I think about it, the more I'm looking forward to a long drive, alone."

"How long?"

"Six hours."

"You can drive to New York in six hours."

"Well, tomorrow I'm going the other way."

The entrées arrived and they were both starving.

5

It took an hour to rent a red Toyota Prius, and as Samantha worked her way through D.C. traffic she gripped the wheel and constantly scanned the mirrors. She had not driven in months and was quite uncomfortable. The incoming lanes were packed with commuters hustling from the suburbs to the city, but the traffic headed west moved without too much congestion. Past Manassas, the interstate cleared considerably and she finally relaxed. Izabelle called and they gossiped for fifteen minutes. Scully & Pershing had furloughed more associates late the day before, including another friend from law school. Another batch of non-equity partners had hit the street. A dozen or so senior partners took early retirement, apparently at gunpoint. Support staff was cut by 15 percent. The place was paralyzed with fear, with lawyers locking their doors and hiding under their desks. Izabelle said she might go to Wilmington and live in her sister's basement, intern for a child advocacy program, and look for part-time work. She doubted she would return to New York, but it was too early to make predictions. Things were too unsettled, and changing rapidly, and, well, no one could say where they might be in a year. Samantha admitted she was thrilled to be out of the law firm and on the open road.

She called her father and canceled lunch. He seemed disappointed, but was quick to advise her against rushing into a meaningless internship deep in "the third world." He mentioned the job offer again and pressed a little too hard. So she said no. "No, Dad, I don't want the job, but thanks anyway."

"You're making a mistake, Sam," he said.

"I didn't ask for your advice, Dad."

"Perhaps you need my advice. Please listen to someone with some sense."

"Good-bye, Dad. I'll call later."

Near the small town of Strasburg, she turned south on Interstate 81 and fell in with a stampede of eighteen-wheelers, all seemingly oblivious to the speed limit. Looking at the map, she had envisioned a lovely drive through the Shenandoah Valley. Instead, she found herself dodging the big rigs on a crowded four-lane. Thousands of them. She managed to steal an occasional glance to the east and the foothills of the Blue Ridge, and to the west and the Appalachian Mountains. It was the first day of October and the leaves were beginning to turn, but sightseeing was not prudent in such traffic. Her phone kept buzzing with texts but she managed to ignore them. She stopped at a fast-food place near Staunton and had a stale salad. As she ate, she breathed deeply, listened to the locals, and tried to calm herself.

There was an e-mail from Henry, the old boyfriend, back in the city and looking for a drink. He had heard the bad news and wanted to commiserate. His acting career had fallen flatter in L.A. than it had in New York, and he was tired of driving limousines for D-list actors with inferior talent. He said he missed her, thought of her often, and now that she was unemployed perhaps they could spend some time together, polishing their résumés and watching the want ads. She decided not to respond, not then anyway. Perhaps when she was back in New York, and bored and really lonely.

In spite of the trucks and the traffic, she was beginning to enjoy the solitude of the drive. She tried NPR a few times, but always found the same story—the economic meltdown, the great recession. Plenty of smart people were predicting a depression. Others were thinking the panic would pass, the world would survive. In Washington, the brains appeared to be frozen as conflicting strategies were offered, debated, and discarded. She eventually ignored the radio, and the cell phone, and drove on in silence, lost in her thoughts. The GPS directed her to leave the interstate at Abingdon, Virginia, and she happily did so. For two hours she wound her way westward, into the mountains. As the roads became narrower, she asked herself more than once what, exactly, was she doing? Where was she going? What could she possibly find in Brady, Virginia, that would entice her to spend the next year there? Nothing—that was the answer. But she was determined to get there and to complete this little adventure. Maybe it would make for a bit of amusing chitchat over cocktails back in the city; perhaps not. At the moment, she was still relieved to be away from New York.

When she crossed into Noland County, she turned onto Route 36 and the road became even narrower, the mountains became steeper, the foliage brighter with yellow and burnt orange. She was alone on the highway, and the deeper she sank into the mountains the more she wondered if, in fact, there was another way out. Wherever Brady was, it seemed to be at the dead end of the road. Her ears popped and she realized she and her little red Prius were slowly climbing. A battered sign announced the approach to Dunne Spring, population 201, and she topped a hill and passed a gas station on the left and a country store on the right.

Seconds later, there was a car on her bumper, one with flashing blue lights. Then she heard the wail of a siren. She panicked, hit her brakes and almost caused the cop to ram her, then hurriedly stopped on some gravel next to a bridge. By the time the officer approached her door, she was fighting back tears. She grabbed her phone to text someone, but there was no service.

He said something that vaguely resembled "Driver's license please." She grabbed her bag and eventually found her license. Her hands were shaking as she gave him the card. He took it and pulled it almost to his nose, as if visually impaired. She finally looked at him; other impairments were obvious. His uniform was a mismatched ensemble of frayed and stained khaki pants, a faded brown shirt covered with all manner of insignia, unpolished black combat boots, and a Smokey the Bear trooper's hat at least two sizes too big and resting on his oversized ears. Unruly black hair crept from under the hat.

"New York?" he said. His diction was far from crisp but his belligerent tone was clear.

"Yes sir. I live in New York City."

"Then why are you driving a car from Vermont?"

"It's a rental car," she said, grabbing the Avis agreement on the console. She offered it to him but he was still staring at her license, as if he had trouble reading.

"What's a Prius?" he asked. Long *i*, like "Pryus."

"It's a hybrid, from Toyota."

"A what?"

She knew nothing about cars, but at that moment it did not matter. An abundance of knowledge would not help her explain the concept of a hybrid. "A hybrid, you know, it runs on both gas and electricity."

"You don't say."

She could not think of the proper response, and while he waited she just smiled at him. His left eye seemed to drift toward his nose.

He said, "Well, it must go pretty fast. I clocked you doing fifty-one back there in a twenty-mile-an-hour zone. That's thirty over. That's reckless driving down here in Virginia. Not sure about New York and Vermont, but it's reckless down here. Yes ma'am, it sure is."

"But I didn't see a speed limit sign."

"I can't help what you don't see, ma'am, now can I?"

An old pickup truck approached from ahead, slowed, and seemed ready to stop. The driver leaned out and yelled, "Come on, Romey, not again."

The cop turned around and yelled back, "Get outta here!"

The truck stopped on the center line, and the driver yelled, "You gotta stop that, man."

The cop unsnapped his holster, whipped out his black pistol, and said, "You heard me, get outta here."

The truck lurched forward, spun its rear tires, and sped away.

When it was twenty yards down the road, the cop aimed his pistol at the sky and fired a loud, thundering shot that cracked through the valley and echoed off the ridges. Samantha screamed and began crying. The cop watched the truck disappear, then said, "It's okay, it's okay. He's always butting in. Now, where were we?" He stuck the pistol back into the holster and fiddled with the snap as he talked.

"I don't know," she said, trying to wipe her eyes with trembling hands.

Frustrated, the cop said, "It's okay, ma'am. It's okay. Now, you got a New York driver's license and Vermont tags on this little weird car, and you were thirty miles over. What are you doing down here?"

Is it really any of your business? she almost blurted, but an attitude would only cause more trouble. She looked straight ahead, took deep breaths, and fought to compose herself. Finally she said, "I'm headed to Brady. I have a job interview." Her ears were ringing.

He laughed awkwardly and said, "Ain't no jobs in Brady, I can guarantee you that."

"I have an interview with the Mountain Legal Aid Clinic," she said, teeth clenched, her own words hollow and surreal.

This baffled him and he seemed uncertain as to his next move. "Well, I gotta take you in. Thirty over is extreme recklessness. Judge'll probably throw the book at you. Gotta take you in."

"In where?"

"To the county jail in Brady."

Her chin dropped to her chest and she massaged her temples. "I don't believe this," she said.

"Sorry ma'am. Get out of the car. I'll let you sit in my front seat." He was standing with his hands on his hips, his right one dangerously close to his holster.

"Are you serious?" she asked.

"As a heart attack."

"Can I make a phone call?"

"No way. Maybe at the jail. Besides, ain't no service out here."

"You're arresting me and taking me to jail?"

"Now you're catching on. I'm sure we do things different down here in Virginia. Let's go."

"What about my car?"

"Tow truck'll come get it. Cost you another forty bucks. Let's go."

She couldn't think clearly, but all other options seemed to end with more gunfire. Slowly, she grabbed her bag and got out of the car. At five foot seven and in flat shoes, she had at least two inches on Romey. She walked back to his car, its blue grille lights still flashing. She looked at the driver's door and saw nothing. He sensed what she was thinking and said, "It's an unmarked car. That's why you didn't see me back there. Works every time. Get in the front seat. I'll take you in with no handcuffs."

She managed to mumble a weak "Thanks."

It was a dark blue Ford of some variety, and it vaguely resembled an old patrol car, one retired a decade earlier. The front seat was of the bench style, vinyl with large cracks that revealed dirty foam padding. Two radios were stuck on the dashboard. Romey grabbed a mike and said, in rapid words barely decipherable, something like, "Unit ten, inbound to Brady with subject. ETA five minutes. Notify the judge. Need a wrecker at Thack's Bridge, some kinda little weird Japanese car."

There was no response, as if no one was listening. Samantha wondered if the radio really worked. On the bench between them was a police scanner, it too as quiet as the radio. Romey hit a switch and turned off his lights. "You wanna hear the siren?" he asked with a grin, a kid and his toys.

She shook her head. No.

And she thought yesterday had been the pits, with the ten rejections and all. And the day before she'd been laid off and escorted out of the building. But now this—arrested in Podunk and hauled away to jail. Her heart pounded and she had trouble swallowing.

There were no seat belts. Romey hit the gas and they were

soon flying down the center of the highway, the old Ford rattling from bumper to bumper. After a mile or two he said, "I'm really sorry about this. Just doing my job."

She asked, "Are you a policeman or a deputy sheriff or something like that?"

"I'm a constable. Do primarily traffic enforcement."

She nodded as if this cleared up everything. He drove with his left wrist limped over the steering wheel, which was vibrating. On a flat stretch of road, he gunned the engine and the turbulence increased. She glanced at the speedometer, which was not working. He barked into his mike again like a bad actor, and again no one answered. They slid into a steep curve, much too fast, but when the car fishtailed, Romey calmly turned in to the spin and tapped the brakes.

I'm going to die, she thought. Either at the hands of a deranged killer or in a fiery crash. Her stomach flipped and she felt faint. She clutched her bag, closed her eyes, and began to pray.

On the outskirts of Brady, she finally managed to breathe normally. If he planned to rape and murder her, and toss her body off a mountain, he wouldn't do it in town. They passed shops with gravel parking lots, and rows of neat little houses, all painted white. There were church steeples rising above the trees when she looked up. Before they got to Main Street, Romey turned abruptly and slid into the unpaved parking lot of the Noland County Jail. "Just follow me," he said. For a split second, she was actually relieved to be at the jail.

As she followed him toward the front door, she glanced around to make sure no one was watching. And who, exactly, was she worried about? Inside, they stopped in a cramped and dusty waiting area. To the left was a door with the word "Jail" stenciled on it. Romey pointed to the right and said, "You take a seat over there while I get the paperwork. And no funny stuff, okay?" No one else was present.

"Where would I go?" she asked. "I've lost my car."

"You just sit down and keep quiet." She sat in a plastic chair and he disappeared through the door. Evidently, the walls were quite thin because she heard him say, "Got a girl from New York out there, picked her up at Dunne Spring, doing fifty-one. Can you believe that?"

A male voice responded sharply, "Oh come on, Romey, not again."

"Yep. Nailed her."

"You gotta stop that crap, Romey."

"Don't start with me again, Doug."

There were heavy footsteps as the voices grew muted, then disappeared. Then, from deeper in the jail, loud angry voices erupted. Though she couldn't understand what was being said, it was obvious that at least two men were arguing with Romey. The voices went silent as the minutes passed. A chubby man in a blue uniform walked through the jail door and said, "Howdy. Are you Miss Kofer?"

"I am, yes," she answered, glancing around at the empty room.

He handed back her license and said, "Just wait a minute, okay?"

"Sure." What else could she say?

From the back, voices rose and fell and then stopped completely. She sent a text to her mother, one to her father, and one to Blythe. If her body was never found, they would at least know a few of the details.

The door opened again and a young man entered the waiting room. He wore faded jeans, hiking boots, a fashionable sports coat, no tie. He offered her an easy smile and said, "Are you Samantha Kofer?"

"I am."

He pulled over another plastic chair, sat with their knees almost touching, and said, "My name is Donovan Gray. I'm your attorney, and I've just gotten all charges dismissed. I suggest we get out of here as soon as possible." As he spoke, he gave her a business card, which she glanced at. It appeared to be legitimate. His office was on Main Street in Brady.

"Okay, and where will we be going?" she asked carefully.

"Back to get your car."

"What about that constable?"

"I'll explain as we go."

They hurried from the jail and got into a late-model Jeep Cherokee. When he started the engine, Springsteen roared from the stereo and he quickly turned it off. He was between thirty-five and forty, she guessed, with shaggy dark hair, at least three days' worth of stubble, and dark sad eyes. As they backed away, she said, "Wait, I need to text some people."

"Sure. You'll have good service for a few miles."

She texted her mother, father, and Blythe with the news that she was no longer at the jail and things seemed to be improving, under the circumstances. Don't worry, yet. She felt safer, for the moment. She would call and explain later.

When the town was behind them, he began: "Romey's not really a cop, or a constable, or anyone with any authority. The first thing you need to understand is that he's not all there, got a couple of screws loose. Maybe more. He's always wanted to be the sheriff, and so from time to time he feels compelled to go on patrol, always around Dunne Spring. If you're passing through, and you're from out of state, then Romey will take notice. If your license plates are from, say, Tennessee or North Carolina, then Romey won't bother you. But if you're from up north, then Romey gets excited and he might do what he did to you. He really thinks he's doing a good thing by hauling in reckless drivers, especially folks from New York and Vermont."

"Why doesn't someone stop him?"

"Oh we try. Everybody yells at him, but you can't watch him twenty-four hours a day. He's very sneaky and he knows these roads better than anyone. Usually, he'll just pull over the reckless driver, some poor guy from New Jersey, scare the hell out of him, and let him go. No one ever knows about it. But occasionally he'll show up at the jail with someone in custody and insist that they be locked up."

"I'm not believing this."

"He's never hurt anyone, but—"

"He fired a shot at another driver. My ears are still ringing."

"Okay, look he's crazy, like a lot of folks around here."

"Then lock him up. Surely there are laws against false arrest and kidnapping."

"His cousin is the sheriff."

She took a deep breath and shook her head.

"It's true. His cousin has been our sheriff for a long time. Romey is very envious of this; in fact, he once ran against the sheriff. Got about ten votes county-wide and that really upset him. He was stopping Yankees right and left until they sent him away for a few months."

"Send him away again."

"It's not that simple. You're actually lucky he didn't take you to his jail."

"*His* jail?"

Donovan was smiling and enjoying his narrative. "Oh yes. About five years ago, Romey's brother found a late-model sedan with Ohio tags parked behind a barn on their family's farm. He looked around, heard a noise, and found this guy from Ohio locked in a horse stall. It turns out Romey had fixed up the stall with chicken wire and barbed wire, and the poor guy had been there for three days. He had plenty of food and was quite comfortable. He said Romey checked on him several times a day and couldn't have been nicer."

"You're making this up."

"I am not. Romey was off his meds and going through a bad time. Things got ugly. The guy from Ohio raised hell and hired lawyers. They sued Romey for false imprisonment and a bunch of other stuff, but the case went nowhere. He has no assets, except for his patrol car, so a civil suit is worthless. They insisted he be prosecuted for kidnapping and so on, and Romey eventually pled guilty to a minor charge. He spent thirty days in jail, not his jail but the county jail, then got sent back to the state mental facility for a tune-up. He's not a bad guy, really."

"A charmer."

"Frankly, some of the other cops around here are more dangerous. I like Romey. I once handled a case for his uncle. Meth."

"Meth?"

"Crystal methamphetamine. After coal, it's probably the biggest cash crop in these parts."

"Can I ask you something that might seem a bit personal?"

"Sure. I'm your lawyer, you can ask me anything."

"Why do you have that gun in the console?" She nodded at the console just below her left elbow. In plain view was a rather large black pistol.

"It's legal. I make a lot of enemies."

"What kind of enemies?"

"I sue coal companies."

She assumed an explanation would take some time, so she took a deep breath and watched the road. After recounting Romey's adventures, Donovan seemed content to enjoy the silence. She realized he had not asked what she was doing in Noland County, the obvious question. At Thack's Bridge, he turned around in the middle of the road and parked behind the Prius.

She said, "So, do I owe you a fee?"

"Sure. A cup of coffee."

"Coffee, around here?"

"No, there's a nice café back in town. Mattie's in court and will likely be tied up until five, so you have some time to kill."

She wanted to say something but words failed her. He continued, "Mattie's my aunt. She's the reason I went to law school and she helped me through. I worked with her clinic while I was a student, then for three years after I passed the bar. Now I'm on my own."

"And Mattie told you I would show up for an interview?" For the first time she noticed a wedding ring on his finger.

"A coincidence. I often stop by her office early in the morning for coffee and gossip. She mentioned all these e-mails from New York lawyers suddenly looking for do-gooder work, said one might show up today for an interview. It's kind of amusing, really, for lawyers like us down here to see big-firm lawyers running for the hills, our hills. Then I happened to be at the jail seeing a client when your pal Romey showed up with a new trophy. And here we are."

"I wasn't planning to return to Brady. In fact, I was planning to turn that little red car around and get the hell out of here."

"Well, slow down when you go through Dunne Spring."

"Don't worry."

A pause as they stared at the Prius, then he said, "Okay, I'll buy the coffee. I think you'll enjoy meeting Mattie. I wouldn't blame you for leaving, but first impressions are often wrong. Brady is a nice town, and Mattie has a lot of clients who could use your help."

"I didn't bring my gun."

He smiled and said, "Mattie doesn't carry one either."

"Then what kind of lawyer is she?"

"She's a great lawyer who's totally committed to her clients, none of whom can pay her. Give it a shot. At least talk to her."

"My specialty is financing skyscrapers in Manhattan. I'm not sure I'm cut out for whatever work Mattie does."

"You'll catch on quick, and you'll love it because you'll be helping people who need you, people with real problems."

Samantha took a deep breath. Her instincts said, Run! To where, exactly? But her sense of adventure convinced her to at least see the town again. If her lawyer carried a gun, wasn't that some measure of protection?

"I'm buying," she said. "Consider it your fee."

"Okay, follow me."

"Should I worry about Romey?"

"No, I had a chat with him. As did his cousin. Just stay on my bumper."

A quick tour of Main Street revealed six blocks of turn-of-the-century buildings, a fourth of them empty with fading "For Sale" signs taped to the windows. Donovan's law office was a two-story with large windows and his name painted in small letters. Upstairs, a balcony hung over the sidewalk. Across the street and down three blocks was the old hardware store, now the home of the Mountain Legal Aid Clinic. At the far west end was a small, handsome courthouse, home to most of the folks who ran Noland County.

They stepped into the Brady Grill and took a booth near the back. As they walked by a table, three men glared at Donovan, who seemed not to notice. A waitress brought them coffee. Samantha leaned in low and said quietly, "Those three men up there, they seemed to dislike you. Do you know them?"

He glanced over his shoulder, then nodded and said, "I know everyone in Brady, and I'd guess that maybe half of them hate my guts. As I said, I sue coal companies, and coal is the biggest employer around here. It's the biggest employer throughout Appalachia."

"And why do you sue them?"

He smiled, took a sip of coffee, and glanced at his watch. "This might take some time."

"I'm really not that busy."

"Well, coal companies create a lot of problems, most of them anyway. There are a couple of decent ones, but most care nothing about the environment or their employees. Mining coal is dirty business, always has been. But it's far worse now. Have you heard of mountaintop removal?"

"No."

"Also known as strip-mining. They started mining coal in these parts back in the 1800s. Deep mining, where they bore tunnels into the mountains and extracted the coal. Mining has been a way of life here since then. My grandfather was a miner, so was his father. My dad was another story. Anyway, by 1920, there were 800,000 coal miners in the coalfields, from Pennsylvania down to Tennessee. Coal mining is dangerous work, and it has a rich history of labor troubles, union fights, violence, corruption, all manner of historical drama. All deep mining, which was the traditional way. Very labor-intensive. Around 1970, coal companies decided they could strip-mine and save millions on labor costs. Strip-mining is far cheaper than deep mining because it requires much fewer workers. Today there are only 80,000 coal miners left and half of them work above the ground, for the strip miners."

The waitress walked by and Donovan stopped for a second. He took a sip of coffee, glanced casually around, waited until she was gone, and continued. "Mountaintop removal is nothing but strip-mining on steroids. Appalachian coal is found in seams, sort of like layers of a cake. At the top of the mountain there is the forest, then a layer of topsoil, then a layer of rock, and finally a seam of coal. Could be four feet thick, could be twenty. When a coal company gets a permit to strip-mine, it literally attacks the mountain with all manner of heavy equipment. First it clear-cuts the trees, total deforestation with no effort at saving the hardwoods. They are bulldozed away as the earth is scalped. Same for the topsoil, which is not very thick. Next comes the layer of rock, which is blasted out of the ground. The trees, topsoil, and rock are often shoved into the valleys between the mountains, creating what's known as valley fills. These wipe out vegetation, wildlife, and natural streams. Just another environmental disaster. If you're downstream, you're just screwed. As you'll learn around here, we're all downstream."

"And this is legal?"

"Yes and no. Strip-mining is legal because of federal law, but the actual process is loaded with illegal activities. We have a long, ugly history of the regulators and watchdogs being too cozy with the coal companies. Reality is always the same: the coal companies run roughshod over the land and the people because they have the money and the power."

"Back to the cake. You were down to the seam of coal."

"Yeah, well, once they find the coal, they bring in more machines, extract it, haul it out, and continue blasting down to the next seam. It's not unusual to demolish the top five hundred feet of a mountain. This takes relatively few workers. In fact, a small crew can thoroughly destroy a mountain in a matter of months." The waitress refilled their cups and Donovan watched in silence, totally ignoring her. When she disappeared, he leaned in a bit lower and said, "Once the coal is hauled out by truck, it's washed, which is another disaster. Coal washing creates a black sludge that contains toxic chemicals and heavy metals. The sludge is also known as slurry, a term you'll hear often. Since it can't be disposed of, the coal companies store it behind earthen dams in sludge ponds, or slurry ponds. The engineering is slipshod and half-assed and these things break all the time with catastrophic results."

"They store it for how long?"

Donovan shrugged and glanced around. He wasn't nervous or frightened; he just didn't want to be heard. He was calm and articulate with a slight mountain twang, and Samantha was captivated, both by his narrative and his dark eyes.

"They store it forever; no one cares. They store it until the dam breaks and there's a tidal wave of toxic crud running down the mountain, into homes and schools and towns, destroying everything. You've heard of the famous *Exxon Valdez* tanker spill, where a tanker ran into the rocks in Alaska. Thirty million gallons of crude oil dumped into pristine waters. Front-page news for weeks and the entire country was pissed. Remember all those otters covered with black muck? But I'll bet you haven't heard of the Martin County spill, the largest environmental disaster east of the Mississippi. It happened eight years ago in Kentucky when a slurry impoundment broke and 300 million gallons of sludge rolled down the valley. Ten times more than the *Valdez*, and it was a nonevent around the country. You know why?"

"Okay, why?"

"Because it's Appalachia. The coal companies are destroying our mountains, towns, culture, and lives, and it's not a story."

"So why do these guys hate your guts?"

"Because they believe strip-mining is a good thing. It provides jobs, and there are few jobs around here. They're not bad people, they're just misinformed and misguided. Mountaintop removal is killing our communities. It has single-handedly wiped out tens of thousands of jobs. People are forced to leave their homes because of blasting, dust, sludge, and flooding. The roads aren't safe because of these massive trucks flying down the mountains. I filed five wrongful death cases in the past five years, folks crushed by trucks carrying ninety tons of coal. Many towns have simply vanished.

The coal companies often buy up surrounding homes and tear them down. Every county in coal country has lost population in the past twenty years. Yet a lot of people, including those three gentlemen over there, think that a few jobs are better than none."

"If they are gentlemen, then why do you carry a gun?"

"Because certain coal companies have been known to hire thugs. It's intimidation, or worse, and it's nothing new. Look, Samantha, I'm a son of the coal country, a hillbilly and a proud one, and I could tell you stories for hours about the bloody history of Big Coal."

"Do you really fear for your life?"

He paused and looked away for a second. "There were a thousand murders in New York City last year. Did you fear for your life?"

"Not really."

He smiled and nodded and said, "Same here. We had three murders last year, all related to meth. You just have to be careful." A phone vibrated in his pocket and he yanked it out. He read the text, then said, "It's Mattie. She's out of court, back at the office and ready to see you."

"Wait, how did she know I would be with you?"

"It's a small town, Samantha."

6

They walked along the sidewalk until they came to his office where they shook hands. She thanked him for his pro bono work as her attorney and complimented him on a job well done. And if she decided to hang around the town for a few months, they promised to do lunch at the Brady Grill someday.

It was almost 5:00 p.m. when she hustled across the street, jaywalking and half expecting to be arrested for it. She glanced to the west, where the mountains were already blocking the late afternoon sun. The shadows consumed the town and gave it the feel of early winter. A bell clinked on the door when she entered the cluttered front room of the legal aid clinic. A busy desk indicated that someone was usually there to answer the phone and greet the clients, but for the moment the reception area was empty. She looked around, waited, took in the surroundings. The office layout was simple—a narrow hall ran straight down the middle of what had been for decades the busy domain of the town's hardware store. Everything had the look and feel of being old and well used. The walls were whitewashed partitions that did not quite make it all the way to the copper-tiled ceiling. The floors were covered with thin, ragged carpet. The furniture, at least in the reception, was a mismatched collection of flea market leftovers. The walls, though, were exhibiting an interesting collection of oils and pastels by local artists, all for sale at very reasonable prices.

The artwork. The prior year the equity partners at Scully & Pershing had gone to war over a designer's proposal to spend $2 million on some baffling avant-garde paintings to be hung in the firm's main foyer. The designer was ultimately fired, the paintings forgotten, and the money split into bonuses.

Halfway down the hall a door opened, and a short, slightly stocky woman in bare feet stepped out. "I take it you're Samantha," she said, walking toward her. "I'm Mattie Wyatt. I understand you've had a rather rude welcome to Noland County. I'm so sorry."

"Nice to meet you," Samantha said as she stared at the bright pink and square reading glasses perched on the end of Mattie's nose. The pink of her glasses matched the pink tips of her hair, which was short, spiked, and dyed a severe white. It was a look Samantha had never seen before, but one that was working, here at least. Of course, she had seen looks far funkier in Manhattan, but never on a lawyer.

"In here," Mattie said as she waved at her office. Once inside, she closed the door and said, "I guess that nut Romey will have to hurt someone before the sheriff does anything. I'm very sorry. Have a seat."

"It's okay. I'm fine, and now I have a story that I'm sure I'll tell for many years."

"Indeed you will, and if you hang around here, you'll collect a lot of stories. Would you like some coffee?" She fell into a rocking chair behind a desk that seemed perfectly organized.

"No thanks. I just had coffee with your nephew."

"Yes, of course. I'm so glad you met Donovan. He's one of the bright spots around here. I practically raised him, you know. Tragic family and all. He's thoroughly committed to his work and rather pleasant to look at, don't you think?"

"He's nice," Samantha said cautiously, unwilling to comment on his looks and determined to stay away from his family's tragedy.

"Anyway, here's where we are. I'm supposed to meet another castaway from Wall Street tomorrow and that's it. I don't have a lot of time to spend interviewing, you know. I got four more e-mails today and I've stopped answering them. I'll check out this guy tomorrow and then our board will meet and pick the winner."

"Okay. Who's on the board?"

"It's basically just Donovan and me. Annette is another lawyer here and she would be invited to the interviews but she's out of town. We work pretty quick, not a lot of red tape. If we decide to go with you, when can you start?"

"I don't know. Things are happening pretty fast."

"I thought you weren't that busy these days."

"True. I guess I could start sooner rather than later, but I would like a day or two to think about it," Samantha said, trying to relax in a stiff wooden chair that tilted when she breathed. "I'm just not sure—"

"Okay, that's fine. It's not like a new intern will make a big difference around here. We've had them before, you know. In fact, we had a full-blown fellow for two years a while back, a kid from the coalfields who went to law school at Stanford then hired on with a big firm in Philadelphia."

"What did he do here?"

"She. Evelyn, and she worked with black lung and mine safety. A hard worker, and very bright, but then she was gone after two years and left us with a bunch of open files. Wonder if she's on the streets these days. Must be awful up there."

"It is. Pardon me for saying so, Ms. Wyatt, but—"

"It's Mattie."

"Okay, Mattie, but you don't seem too thrilled at the idea of an intern."

"Oh, forgive me. I'm sorry. No, actually we need all the help we can get. As I told you on the phone, there's no shortage of poor folks with legal problems around here. These people can't afford lawyers. Unemployment is high, meth use is even higher, and the coal companies are brilliant when it comes to finding new ways to screw people. Believe me, dear, we need all the help we can get."

"What will I be doing?"

"Everything from answering the phone to opening the mail

to filing federal lawsuits. Your résumé says you're licensed in both Virginia and New York."

"I clerked for a judge in D.C. after law school and passed the Virginia bar exam."

"Have you seen the inside of a courtroom in the past three years?"

"No."

Mattie hesitated for a second, as if this might be a deal breaker. "Well, I guess you're lucky in one sense. Don't suppose you've been to jail either?"

"Not since this afternoon."

"Oh, right. Again, sorry about that. You'll catch on quick. What type of work were you doing in New York?"

Samantha took a deep breath and thought of ways to truthfully duck the question. Invention failed her and she said, "I was in commercial real estate, pretty boring stuff actually. Incredibly boring. We represented a bunch of unpleasant rich guys who build tall buildings up and down the East Coast, primarily in New York. As a mid-level associate I normally spent my time reviewing financing agreements with banks, thick contracts that had to be prepared and proofread by someone."

Just above the pink and square frames, Mattie's eyes offered a look of pure pity. "Sounds awful."

"It was, still is, I guess."

"Are you relieved to be away from that?"

"I don't know how I feel, Mattie, to be honest. A month ago I was scrambling along in the rat race, elbowing others and getting elbowed myself, racing toward something, I can't even remember what it was. There were dark clouds out there but we were too busy to notice. Then Lehman went under, and for two weeks I was afraid of my shadow. We worked even harder, hoping that someone might notice, hoping that a hundred hours a week might save us where ninety hours would not. Suddenly it was over, and we were tossed into the street. No severance, nothing. Nothing but a few promises that I doubt anyone can keep."

Mattie looked as if she might cry. "Would you go back?"

"I don't know right now. I don't think so. I didn't like the work, didn't like most of the people in the firm, and certainly didn't like the clients. Sadly, most of the lawyers I know feel the same way."

"Well, dear, here at the Mountain Legal Aid Clinic, we love our clients and they love us."

"I'm sure they're much nicer than the ones I dealt with."

Mattie glanced at her watch, a bright yellow dial strapped to her wrist with green vinyl, and said, "What are your plans for the evening?"

Samantha shrugged and shook her head. "Haven't thought that far ahead."

"Well, you certainly can't drive back to Washington tonight."

"Does Romey work the night shift? Are the roads safe?"

Mattie chuckled and said, "The roads are treacherous. You can't go. Let's start with dinner and then we'll go from there."

"No, seriously, I can't—"

"Nonsense. Samantha, you're in Appalachia now, deep in the mountains, and we do not turn visitors away at dinnertime. My house is just around the corner and my husband is an excellent cook. Let's have a drink on the porch and talk about stuff. I'll tell you everything you need to know about Brady."

Mattie found her shoes and locked up the office. She said the Prius was safe where it was parked, on Main Street. "I walk to work," Mattie said. "About my only exercise." The shops and offices were closed. The two cafés were serving an early dinner to thin crowds. They trudged up the side of a hill, passing kids on the sidewalk and neighbors on porches. After two blocks they turned onto Third Street, a leafy row of turn-of-the-century, neat, redbrick homes, almost all identical with white porches and gabled roofs. Samantha wanted to hit the road, to hurry back toward Abingdon where she had noticed several chain motels at the interchange. But there was no way to gracefully say no to Mattie's hospitality.

Chester Wyatt was in a rocking chair reading a newspaper

when he was introduced to Samantha. "I told her you are an excellent cook," Mattie said.

"I guess that means I'm cooking dinner," he said with a grin. "Welcome."

"And she's starving," Mattie said.

"What would you like?" he asked.

"I'm fine," Samantha said.

Mattie said, "What about baked chicken with Spanish rice?"

"Just what I was thinking," Chester said. "A glass of wine first?"

They drank red wine for an hour as darkness settled around them. Samantha sipped slowly, careful not to have too much because she was worrying about her drive out of Noland County. There appeared to be no hotels or motels in Brady, and given the town's declining appearance she doubted there was a suitable room anywhere. As they talked, she politely probed here and there, and learned that the Wyatts had two adult children who had fled the area after college. There were three grandchildren they rarely saw. Donovan was like a son. Chester was a retired postal worker who had delivered rural mail for decades and knew everyone. Now he volunteered for an environmental group that monitored strip-mining and filed complaints with a dozen bureaucracies. His father and grandfather had been coal miners. Mattie's father had worked the deep mines for almost thirty years before dying of black lung at the age of sixty-one. "I'm sixty-one now," she said. "It was horrible."

While the women sat and talked, Chester eased back and forth to the kitchen, checking on the chicken and pouring wine. Once, when he was gone, Mattie said, "Don't worry, dear, we have an extra bedroom."

"No, really, I—"

"Please, I insist. There's not a decent room in town, believe me. A couple of hot-sheets joints that charge by the hour, but even they're about to close. A sad commentary, I suppose. Folks used to sneak off to the motel for illicit sex; now they just move in together and play house."

"So there is sex around here?" Samantha asked.

"I should hope so. My mother had seven kids, Chester's had six. There's not much else to do. And this time of the year, September and October, they're popping out like rabbits."

"Why?"

"Big storm just after Christmas."

Chester stepped through the screen door and asked, "What are we talking about?"

"Sex," Mattie said. "Samantha's surprised that folks have sex around here."

"Some of them do," he said.

"So I've heard," Mattie shot back with a grin.

"I didn't bring up sex," Samantha said defensively. "Mattie mentioned an extra bedroom for the night."

"Yes, and it's all yours. Just keep your door locked and we'll stay out of trouble," Chester said as he disappeared into the house.

"He's harmless, believe me," Mattie whispered.

Donovan arrived to say hello and thankfully missed that part of the conversation. He lived "on a mountain out in the country" and was on his way home from the office. He declined an offer of wine and left after fifteen minutes. He seemed distracted and said he was tired.

"Poor thing," Mattie said when he was gone. "He and his wife have separated. She moved back to Roanoke with their daughter, a five-year-old who's about the cutest thing you'll ever see. His wife, Judy, never adjusted to life here in the mountains and just got fed up. I don't feel good about them, do you Chester?"

Chester said, "Not really. Judy is a wonderful person but she was never happy here. Then, when the trouble started, she sort of cracked up. That's when she left."

The word "trouble" hung in the air for a few seconds, and when neither of the Wyatts chose to pursue it, Chester said, "Dinner's ready." Samantha followed them into the kitchen where the table was set for three. Chester served from the stove—steaming chicken with rice and homemade rolls. Mattie placed a salad bowl in the center of the table and poured water from a large plastic jug. Evidently, enough wine had already been served.

"Smells delicious," Samantha said as she pulled out a chair and sat down.

"Help yourself to the salad," Mattie said as she buttered a roll. They began eating and for a moment the conversation lagged. Samantha wanted to keep the conversation on their side of things, not hers, but before she could preempt them, Chester said, "Tell us about your family, Samantha."

She smiled and politely said, "Well, there's not much to talk about."

"Oh, we'll help you along," Mattie said with a laugh. "You grew up in D.C., right? That must have been interesting."

She hit the high points: the only child of two ambitious lawyers, a privileged upbringing, private schools, undergrad at Georgetown, her father's troubles, his indictment and imprisonment, the humiliation of his widely covered fall from power.

"I think I remember that," Chester said.

"It was all over the press." She described visiting him in prison, something he discouraged. The pain of the divorce, the desire to get out of D.C. and away from her parents, law school at Columbia, the federal clerkship, the seduction of Big Law, and the three less than pleasant years at Scully & Pershing. She loved Manhattan and could not imagine living anywhere else, but her world was upside down now, and, well, there was nothing certain in her future. As she talked, they watched her closely and absorbed every word. When she'd said enough, she took a mouthful of chicken and planned to chew it for a long time.

"That's certainly a harsh way to treat people," Chester said.

"Trusted employees just tossed into the street," Mattie said, shaking her head in disbelief and disapproval. Samantha nodded and kept chewing. She did not need to be reminded. As Chester poured more water, she asked, "Does all drinking water come from a bottle?"

For some reason this was amusing. "Oh yes," Mattie replied.

"No one drinks the water around here. Our fearless regulators promise us it's safe to drink, but no one believes them. We clean ourselves, our clothes, and our dishes with it, and some folks brush their teeth with it, but not me."

Chester said, "Many of our streams, rivers, and wells have been contaminated by strip-mining. The headwater streams have been choked off with valley fills. The slurry ponds leak into the deep wells. Burning coal creates tons of ash, and the companies dump this into our rivers. So please, Samantha, don't drink the tap water."

"Got it."

"That's one reason we drink so much wine," Mattie said. "I believe I'll have another glass, Chester, if you don't mind." Chester, who evidently was both chef and bartender, did not hesitate to grab a bottle off the counter. Since she would not be driving, Samantha agreed to another glass. Almost instantly, the wine seemed to hit Mattie and she began talking about her career and the legal clinic she founded twenty-six years earlier. As she prattled on, Samantha prodded her with enough questions to keep her going, though she needed no assistance.

The warmth of the cozy kitchen, the lingering aroma of the baked chicken, the taste of home-cooked food, the buzz from the wine, the openness of two extremely hospitable people, and the promise of a warm bed all came together halfway through the dinner and Samantha truly relaxed for the first time in months. She couldn't chill out in the city; every moment of downtime was monitored by the clock. She hadn't slept in the past three weeks. Both parents kept her on edge. The six-hour drive had been nerve-racking, for the most part. Then, the episode with Romey. Finally, Samantha felt her burdens floating away. Suddenly she had an appetite. She helped herself to more chicken, which pleased her hosts greatly.

She said, "On the porch, earlier, when we were talking about Donovan, you mentioned the 'trouble.' Is that off-limits?"

The Wyatts looked at each other; both shrugged. It was, after all, a small town and few things were off-limits. Chester quickly deferred and poured himself more wine. Mattie pushed her plate away and said, "He's had a tragic life, Donovan."

"If it's too personal, then we can skip it," Samantha said, but only out of courtesy. She wanted the scoop.

Mattie would not be denied. She ignored Samantha's offer and plowed ahead. "It's well-known around here; there's nothing secret about it," she said, sweeping away any obstacles to confidentiality. "Donovan is the son of my sister Rose, my late sister, I'm sorry to say. She died when he was sixteen."

"It's a long story," Chester added, as if there might be too much involved to properly tell it all.

Mattie ignored him. "Donovan's father is a man named Webster Gray, still alive, somewhere, and he inherited three hundred acres next door in Curry County. The land was in the Gray family forever, way back to the early 1800s. Beautiful land, hills and mountains, creeks and valleys, just gorgeous and pristine. That's where Donovan and his brother, Jeff, were born and raised. His father and grandfather, Curtis Gray, had the boys in the woods as soon as they could walk, hunting and fishing and exploring. Like so many kids in Appalachia, they grew up on the land. There's a lot of natural beauty here, what's left of it, but the Gray property was something special. After Rose married Webster, we would go there for family picnics and gatherings. I can remember Donovan and Jeff and my kids and all the cousins swimming in Crooked Creek, next to our favorite camping site." A pause, a careful sip of wine. "Curtis died in I think it was 1980, and Webster inherited the land. Curtis was a miner, a deep miner, a tough union man, and he was proud of it, like most of the older guys. But he never wanted Webster to work in the mines. Webster, as it turned out, didn't much care for work of any kind, and he bounced around from job to job, never amounting to much. The family struggled and his marriage with Rose became rather rocky. He took to the bottle and this caused more problems. He once spent six months in jail for stolen goods and the family almost starved. We were worried sick about them."

"Webster was not a good person," Chester added the obvious.

"The highest point on their property was called Gray Mountain, three thousand feet up and covered with hardwoods. The coal companies know where every pound of coal is buried throughout Appalachia; they did their geological surveys decades ago. And it was no secret that Gray Mountain had some of the thickest seams around here. Over the years, Webster had dropped hints about leasing some of his land for mining, but we just didn't believe him. Strip-mining had been around and was causing concern."

"Nothing like today, though," Chester added.

"Oh no, nothing like today. Anyway, without telling his family, Webster signed a lease with a company out of Richmond, Vayden Coal, to surface-mine Gray Mountain."

"I don't like the term 'surface-mine,'" Chester said. "It sounds too legitimate. It's nothing more than strip-mining."

"Webster was careful, I mean the man wasn't stupid. He saw it as his chance to make some real money, and he had a good lawyer prepare the lease. Webster would get two dollars for every ton, which back then was a lot more than other folks were getting. The day before the bulldozers showed up, Webster finally told Rose and the boys what he had done. He sugarcoated everything, said the coal company would be watched closely by the regulators and lawyers, that the land would be reclaimed after the coal was gone, and that the big money would more than offset the short-term headaches. Rose called me that night in tears. Around here, property owners who sell out to the coal companies are not held in high regard, and she was terrified of what her neighbors would think. She was also worried about their land. She said Webster and Donovan were in a big fight, said things were terrible. And that was only the beginning. The next morning a small army of bulldozers plowed its way up to the top of Gray Mountain and began—"

"The rape of the land," Chester added, shaking his head.

"Yes, that and more. They clear-cut the forest, shaved it clean, and shoved thousands of hardwoods into the valleys below. Next they scraped off the topsoil and pushed it down on top of the trees. When the blasting started all hell broke loose." Mattie took a sip of wine and Chester jumped into the narrative. "They had this wonderful old house down in a valley, next to Crooked Creek. It had been in the family for decades. I think Curtis's father built it around the turn of the century. The foundation was made of stone, and before long the stones began to crack. Webster started raising hell with the coal company, but it was a waste of time."

Mattie jumped back in. "The dust was awful, like a fog over the valleys around the mountain. Rose was beside herself and I often went over there to sit with her. The ground would shake several times a day when they were blasting. The house began to tilt and the doors wouldn't close. Needless to say, this was a nightmare for the family, and for the marriage. After Vayden knocked off the top of the mountain, about three hundred feet, they hit the first seam, and when they finally started hauling coal off the mountain, Webster began demanding his checks. The company stalled and stalled, then finally sent a payment or two. Not nearly what Webster was expecting. He got his lawyers involved and this really irritated the coal company. The war was on and everybody knew who would win."

Chester was shaking his head at the nightmare. He said, "The creek ran dry, choked off by the valley fill. That's what happens. In the last twenty years, we've lost over a thousand miles of headwaters in Appalachia. Just awful."

Mattie said, "Rose finally left. She and the boys came to live with us, but Webster refused to leave. He was drinking and acting crazy. He would sit on the porch with his shotgun and just dare anyone from the company to get close. Rose was worried about him, so she and the boys returned home. He promised to repair the house and fix everything as soon as the money came in. He filed complaints with the regulators, and even filed a lawsuit against Vayden, but they tied him up in court. It's hard to beat a coal company."

Chester said, "Their well water was contaminated with sulfur. The air was always thick with dust from the blasting and coal trucks. It just wasn't safe, and so Rose left again. She and the boys stayed in a motel for a few weeks, then they came here again, then off to somewhere else. This went on for about a year, wouldn't you say Mattie?"

"At least. The mountain continued to shrink as they went from seam to seam. It was sickening to watch it disappear. The price of coal was up, so Vayden mined like crazy, seven days a week with all the machinery and trucks they could throw at the site. Webster got a check one day for $30,000. His lawyer sent it back with an angry demand. That was the last of the checks."

Chester said, "Suddenly it was all over. The price of coal dropped dramatically and Vayden disappeared overnight. Webster's lawyer submitted a bill for $400,000, along with another lawsuit. About a month later Vayden filed for bankruptcy and walked away. It restructured itself into a new company, and it's still around. Owned by some billionaire in New York."

"So the family got nothing?" Samantha asked.

"Not much," Mattie replied. "A few small checks in the beginning, but only a fraction of what the lease called for."

Chester said, "It's a favorite trick in the coalfields. A company mines the coal, then goes bankrupt to avoid payments and the reclamation requirements. Sooner or later they usually pop up with another name. Same bad actors, just a new logo."

"That's disgusting," Samantha said.

"No, that's the law."

"What happened to the family?"

Chester and Mattie exchanged a long, sad look. "You tell the story, Chester," she said, and took a sip of wine.

"Not long after Vayden left, there was a big rain, and a flood. Because the creeks and rivers are choked off, the water is diverted to other runoffs. Flooding is a huge problem, to say the least. An avalanche of mud and trees and topsoil swept through the valley and took out the Gray home. Crushed it and scattered it for miles downstream. Fortunately, no one was in the house; by then it was uninhabitable, not even Webster could stay there. Another lawsuit, another waste of time and money. Bankruptcy laws are like Teflon. Rose drove out one sunny day and found a few of the stones from the foundation. She picked her spot, and she killed herself."

Samantha moaned and rubbed her forehead and mumbled, "Oh no."

"Webster disappeared for good. When we last heard from him he was living in Montana, doing who knows what. Jeff went to stay with another aunt and Donovan lived with us until he finished high school. He worked three jobs getting through college. By the time he graduated he knew exactly what he wanted to do: become a lawyer and spend the rest of his life fighting coal companies. We helped him through law school. Mattie gave him a job at the clinic, and he worked there a few years before opening his own shop. He's filed hundreds of lawsuits and taken on every coal company that ever thought about operating a strip mine. He's ruthless and fearless."

"And he's brilliant," Mattie said proudly.

"Indeed he is."

"Does he win?"

They paused and exchanged uncertain looks. Mattie said, "Yes and no. It's tough litigating against the coal companies. They play hardball. They lie and cheat and cover up, and they hire huge law firms like yours to stonewall anyone with a claim. He wins and he loses but he's always on the attack."

"And of course they hate him," Chester said.

"Oh yes, they certainly do. I said he was ruthless, right? Donovan does not always play by the book. He figures the coal companies bend the rules of legal procedure, so they force him to do the same."

"And this led to the 'trouble'?" Samantha asked.

Mattie replied, "It did. Five years ago, a dam broke in Madison County, West Virginia, about a hundred miles from here, and a wall of coal sludge slid down a valley and covered the small town of Prentiss. Four people were killed, virtually all the homes were destroyed, a real mess. Donovan got the case, teamed up with some other environmental lawyers in West Virginia, and filed a big federal lawsuit. He got his picture in the paper, lots of press, and he probably said too much. Among other things, he called the coal company 'the dirtiest corporation in America.' That's when the harassment started. Anonymous phone calls. Threatening letters. Goons back there in the shadows. They began following him, and still do."

"Donovan is followed?" Samantha asked.

"Oh yes," Mattie said.

"So that's why he carries a gun."

"Guns, plural. And he knows how to use them," Chester said.

"Do you worry about him?"

Chester and Mattie both managed a chuckle. Chester said, "Not really. He knows what he's doing and he can take care of himself."

"How about some coffee on the porch?" Mattie said.

"Sure, I'll brew a pot," Chester said as he rose from the table. Samantha followed Mattie back to the front porch and retook her position in a wicker rocker. The air was almost too cool to be outside. The street was silent; many of the homes were already dark.

Encouraged by the wine, Samantha asked, "What happened to the lawsuit?"

"It was settled last year. A confidential settlement that's still under wraps."

"If the lawsuit was settled, why are they still following him?"

"Because he's their number one enemy. He plays dirty when he has to, and the coal companies know it."

Chester arrived with a tray of coffee, decaf, and left to do the dishes. After a few sips, and a few minutes of gentle rocking, Samantha was about to nod off. She said, "I have a small overnight bag in my car. I need to get it."

"I'll walk with you," Mattie said.

"We won't be followed, will we?"

"No, dear, we're not a threat."

They disappeared into the darkness.

7

The two gentlemen to her right were slugging whiskeys and feverishly discussing ways to save Fannie Mae. The three to her left apparently worked at Treasury, which seemed to be the epicenter of the collapse. They were knocking back martinis, courtesy of the taxpayers. Up and down the bar of Bistro Venezia the talk was of nothing but the end of time. A windbag behind her was recounting at full volume his conversation that very afternoon with a senior advisor to the McCain/Palin campaign. He had unloaded a wave of solid advice, all of which was being ignored, he feared. Two bartenders were lamenting the crash of the stock market, as if they were losing millions. Someone argued that the Fed might do this, or it might do that. Bush was getting bad advice. Obama was surging in the polls. Goldman needed cash. Factory orders in China had dipped dramatically.

In the midst of the storm, Samantha sipped a diet soda and waited for her father, who was running late. It occurred to her that no one in Brady had seemed even remotely aware that the world was teetering on the brink of a catastrophic depression. Perhaps the mountains kept the place isolated and secure. Or perhaps life there had been depressed for so long another crash wouldn't matter. Her phone vibrated and she took it out of her pocket. It was Mattie Wyatt. "Samantha, how was your drive?" she asked.

"Fine, Mattie. I'm in D.C. now."

"Good. Look, the board just met and voted unanimously to offer you the internship. I interviewed the other applicant this afternoon, a rather nervous young fellow, actually from your law firm, and he doesn't interest us. I got the impression he was just passing through, probably got in his car and kept driving to some place far away from New York. Not sure how stable he is. Anyway, Donovan and I didn't see much potential there and we nixed him on the spot. When can you start?"

"Did he meet Romey?"

Mattie cackled on the other end and said, "I don't think so."

"I need to go to New York and get some things. I'll be there Monday."

"Excellent. Call me in a day or so."

"Thanks Mattie. I'm looking forward to it."

She saw her father across the way and left the bar. A hostess led them to a table in a corner and hurriedly whipped out menus. The restaurant was packed and a nervous chatter roared from all directions. A minute later, a manager in a tuxedo appeared and announced gravely, "I'm so sorry, but we need this table."

Marshall replied rudely, "I beg your pardon."

"Please sir, we have another table for you."

At that moment, a caravan of black SUVs wheeled to a stop on N Street outside the restaurant. Doors flew open and an army of agents spilled onto the sidewalk. Samantha and Marshall eased away from the table, watching, with everyone else, the circus outside. Such shows were commonplace in D.C., and at that moment everyone was guessing. Could it be the President? Dick Cheney? Which big shot can we say we had dinner with? The VIP eventually emerged and was escorted inside, where the crowd, suddenly frozen, gawked and waited.

"Who the hell is that?" someone asked.

"Never seen him before."

"Oh, I think he's that Israeli guy, the ambassador."

A noticeable rush of air left the restaurant as the diners realized that the fuss was over some lower-ranking celebrity. Though thoroughly unrecognizable, the VIP was evidently a marked man. His table—the Kofers' old table—was pushed into a corner and shielded by partitions that materialized from nowhere. Every serious D.C. restaurant keeps lead partitions at the ready, right? The VIP sat with his female partner and tried to look normal, like an average guy out for a quick bite. Meanwhile, his gun thugs patrolled the sidewalk and watched N Street for suicide bombers.

Marshall cursed the manager and said to Samantha, "Let's get out of here. Sometimes I hate this city." They walked three blocks along Wisconsin Avenue and found a pub that was being neglected by jihadists. Samantha ordered another diet soda as Marshall went for a double vodka. "What happened down there?" he asked. He had grilled her on the phone but she wanted to save the stories for a real conversation.

She smiled and started with Romey. Halfway through the tale she realized how much she was enjoying the adventure. Marshall was incredulous and wanted to sue someone, but settled down after a few pulls on the vodka. They ordered a pizza and she described the dinner with Mattie and Chester.

"You're not serious about working down there, are you?" he asked.

"I got the job. I'll try it for a few months. If I get bored I'll go back to New York and get a job at Barneys selling shoes."

"You don't have to sell shoes and you don't have to work in legal aid. How much money do you have in the bank?"

"Enough to survive. How much do you have in the bank?"

He frowned and took another drink. She continued, "A lot, right? Mom's convinced you buried a ton offshore and gave her the shaft in the divorce. Is that true?"

"No, it's not true, but if it was do you think I'd admit it to you?"

"No, never. Deny, deny, deny—isn't that the first rule for a criminal defense lawyer?"

"I wouldn't know. And by the way, I admitted to my crimes and pled guilty. What do you know about criminal law?"

"Nothing, but I'm learning. I have now been arrested, for starters."

"Well, so have I and I wouldn't recommend it. At least you avoided the handcuffs. What else does your mother say about me?"

"Nothing good. Somewhere in the back of my overworked brain I've had this fantasy of the three of us sitting down to a nice dinner in a lovely restaurant, not as a family, heaven forbid, but as three adults who might just have a few things in common."

"I'm in."

"Yeah, but she's not. Too many issues."

"How did we get off on this subject?"

"I don't know. Sorry. Did you ever sue a coal company?"

Marshall rattled his ice cubes and thought for a second. He had sued so many wayward corporations. Sadly, he said, "No, don't think so. My specialty was plane crashes, but Frank, one of my partners, was once involved in some type of coal case. An environmental mess involving this gunk they keep in lakes. He doesn't talk about it much, so that probably means he lost the case."

"It's called sludge, or slurry, take your pick. It's toxic waste that's a by-product of washing coal. The companies store it behind earthen dams where it rots for years as it seeps into the ground and contaminates the drinking water."

"My, my, aren't you the smart one now?"

"Oh, I've learned a lot in the past twenty-four hours. Did you know that some of the counties in the coalfields have the highest rates of cancer in the country?"

"Sounds like a lawsuit."

"Lawsuits are hard to win down there because coal is king and a lot of jurors are sympathetic to the companies."

"This is wonderful, Samantha. We're talking about real law now, not building skyscrapers. I'm proud of you. Let's sue somebody."

The pizza arrived and they ate it from the stone. A shapely brunette sauntered by in a short skirt and Marshall instinctively gawked and stopped chewing for a second, then caught himself and tried to act as though he hadn't seen the woman. "What kind of work will you be doing down there?" he asked awkwardly, one eye still on the skirt.

"You're sixty years old and she's about my age. When will you ever stop looking?"

"Never. What's wrong with looking?"

"I don't know. I guess it's the first step."

"You just don't understand men, Samantha. Looking is automatic and it's harmless. We all look. Come on."

"So you can't help it?"

"No. And why are we talking about this? I'd rather talk about suing coal companies."

"I got nothing else. I've told you everything I know."

"Will you be suing them?"

"I doubt it. But I met a guy who takes nothing but coal cases. His family was destroyed by a strip mine when he was a kid and he's on a vendetta. He carries a gun. I saw it."

"A guy? Did you like him?"

"He's married."

"Good. I'd rather you not fall in love with a hillbilly. Why does he carry a gun?"

"I think a lot of them do down there. He says the coal companies don't like him and there's a long history of violence in the business."

Marshall wiped his mouth with a paper napkin and took a sip of water. "Allow me to summarize what I've heard. This is a place where the mentally ill are allowed to wear uniforms, call themselves constables, drive cars with flashing lights, stop out-of-state drivers, and sometimes even haul them to jail. Others, who are evidently not mentally ill, go about the practice of law with guns in their briefcases. Still others offer temporary jobs to laid-off lawyers and don't pay them anything."

"That's a pretty fair analysis."

"And you're starting Monday morning?"

"You got it."

Marshall shook his head as he selected another slice of pizza. "I guess it beats Big Law on Wall Street."

"We'll see."

Blythe was able to escape her firm for a quick lunch. They met in a crowded deli not far from her office and over salads managed to reach an agreement. Samantha would pay her share of the rent for the three months left on the lease, but beyond that she could not commit. Blythe was clinging to her job and slightly optimistic about not losing it. She wanted to keep the apartment but could not handle the full rent. Samantha assured her there was an excellent chance she would be back in the city in short order, doing something.

Later in the afternoon, she met Izabelle for coffee and gossip. Izabelle's bags were packed and she was on her way home, to Wilmington, to live with a sister who had a spare room in the basement. She would intern with a child advocacy group and scramble for real work. She was depressed and bitter and uncertain about her survival. When they hugged good-bye, both knew it would be a long time before they met again.

Common sense told Samantha to lease a vehicle in the New York metropolitan area, load it up, and then head south. However, as she soon discovered while working the phone, any leased car would have New York license plates. She could probably find one in New Jersey, or maybe in Connecticut, but all three would be a red flag in Brady. She couldn't get Romey off her mind. He was, after all, still at large, making his mischief.

Instead, she loaded two suitcases and a large canvas bag with everything she deemed appropriate for where she was headed. A cab unloaded her at Penn Station. Five hours later, another cab collected her at Union Station in D.C. She and Karen ate carryout sushi in their pajamas and watched an old movie. Marshall was never mentioned.

The Web site for Gasko Leasing over in Falls Church promised a wide selection of great used vehicles, convenient terms, paperwork that was virtually hassle-free, easy-to-buy insurance, complete customer satisfaction. Her knowledge of automobiles was limited, but something told her a domestic model might have less potential for causing trouble than something from, say, Japan. Browsing online, she saw a midsized 2004 Ford hatchback that looked suitable. On the phone, the salesman said it was still available, and, more important, he guaranteed her it would have Virginia tags. "Yes ma'am, front and back." She took a cab to Falls Church, and met with Ernie, the salesman. Ernie was a flirt who talked far too much and observed very little. Had he been more astute, he would have realized how terrified Samantha was of the process of leasing a used car for twelve months.

In fact, she had thought about calling her father for help, but let it pass. She convinced herself she was tough enough for this relatively unimportant task. After two long hours with Ernie, she finally drove away in a thoroughly unnoticeable Ford, one obviously owned by someone living in the Commonwealth of Virginia.

8

Orientation consisted of an 8:00 a.m. meeting with a new client. Fortunately for Samantha, who had no idea how to conduct such a meeting, Mattie assumed control. She whispered, "Just take notes, frown a lot, and try to look intelligent." No problem—that was exactly how she had survived the first two years at Scully & Pershing.

The client was Lady Purvis, a fortyish mother of three teenagers whose husband, Stocky, was currently in jail next door in Hopper County. Mattie did not ask if Lady was her real name; if important, that detail would emerge later. But, given her rustic appearance and salty language, it was difficult to imagine her parents officially naming her Lady. She had the look of a hard life earned somewhere deep in the hollows, and she became irritated when Mattie said she could not smoke in the office. Samantha, frowning, scribbled furiously and didn't say a word. From the first sentence there was nothing but hard luck and misery. The family was living in a trailer, one with a mortgage, and they were behind on the payments; they were behind on everything. Her two oldest teenagers had dropped out of school to look for jobs that did not exist, not in Noland, Hopper, and Curry Counties. They were threatening to run away, somewhere out west where they could maybe find a paycheck picking oranges. Lady worked here and there, cleaning houses on the weekends, babysitting for five bucks an hour—anything, really, to make a dollar.

Stocky's crime: speeding. Which then led to an examination by the deputy of his driver's license, which had expired two days earlier. His total fines and court costs were $175, money he did not have. Hopper County had contracted with a private outfit to strong-arm the money out of Stocky and other poor people unlucky enough to commit petty crimes and traffic offenses. If Stocky could have written the check, he would have done so and gone home. But because he was poor and broke, his case was handled differently. The judge ordered it to be administered by the crooks at Judicial Response Associates. Lady and Stocky met with a JRA operative the day they went to court, and he explained how the payment plan would work. His company tacked on fees—one called the Primary Fee at $75, one called the Monthly Service Fee at $35 per, and one at the end, assuming they ever got there, called the Termination Fee, a bargain at only $25. Court costs and a few other vague add-ons brought their total to $400. They figured they might be able to pay $50 a month, the minimum allowed by JRA; however, they soon realized that $35 of the $50 was gobbled up with the Monthly Service Fee. They tried to renegotiate, but JRA wouldn't budge. After two payments, Stocky quit and that was when the serious trouble started. Two deputies came to their trailer after midnight and arrested Stocky. Lady protested, as did their oldest son, and the deputies threatened to zap them with their brand-new Tasers. When Stocky was dragged before the judge again, more fines and fees were added. The new total was $550. Stocky explained that he was broke and out of work, and the judge sent him back to jail. He'd been there for two months. Meanwhile, JRA was still tacking on its beloved monthly service charge, which for some mysterious reason had been increased to $45 per.

"The longer he stays there the deeper we get," Lady said, thoroughly defeated. In a small paper sack she had her paperwork, and Mattie began sorting through it. There were angry letters from the maker of the trailer who was also financing its purchase, and foreclosure notices, past-due utility bills, tax notices, court documents, and a stack of various papers from JRA. Mattie read them and handed them over to Samantha, who had no idea what to do except to make a list of all the misery.

Lady finally broke and said, "I gotta smoke. Gimme five minutes." Her hands were trembling.

"Sure," Mattie said. "Just step outside."

"Thanks."

"How many packs a day?"

"Just two."

"What's your brand?"

"Charlie's. I know I ought to quit, and I've tried, but it's the only thing that settles my nerves." She grabbed her purse and left the room. Mattie said, "Charlie's is a favorite in Appalachia, a cheaper brand, though it's still $4 a pack. That's eight bucks a day, two-fifty a month, and I'll bet Stocky smokes just as much. They're probably spending $500 a month on cigarettes and who knows how much on beer. If there's ever a spare dollar, they probably buy lottery tickets."

"That's ridiculous," Samantha said, relieved to finally say something. "Why? They could pay off his fines in one month and he's out of jail."

"They don't think that way. Smoking is an addiction, something they can't simply walk away from."

"Okay, can I ask a question?"

"Sure. I'll bet you want to know how a person like Stocky can be thrown into a debtors' prison, something this country outlawed about two hundred years ago. Right?"

Samantha slowly nodded. Mattie continued, "More than likely, you're also certain that throwing someone in jail because he cannot pay a fine or a fee violates the Equal Protection Clause of the Fourteenth Amendment. And, you are no doubt familiar with the 1983 Supreme Court decision, the name escapes me right now, in which the Court ruled that before a person can be thrown in jail for not paying a fine it must be proven that he or she was willfully not paying. In other words, he could pay but he refused. All this and more, right?"

"That's a nice summary."

"It's happening everywhere. JRA hustles the misdemeanor courts in a dozen southern states. On the average, local governments collect about 30 percent of their fine monies. JRA rolls in and promises 70 percent, at no taxpayer expense. They claim it's all funded by the folks like Stocky who get sucked into the scam. Every city and county needs money, so they sign up with JRA and the courts hand over the cases. The victims are placed on probation and when they can't pay, they get thrown in jail, where of course the taxpayers start picking up the expenses again. They're spending $30 a day to feed and house Stocky."

"This can't be legal."

"It's legal because it's not specifically illegal. They are poor people, Samantha, at the bottom of the pile, and down here the laws are different. That's why we're in business, so to speak."

"This is awful."

"It is, and it can get worse. As a delinquent probationer, Stocky might be excluded from food stamps, housing assistance, a driver's license, hell, in some states they might take away his right to vote, assuming he's ever bothered to register."

Lady was back, reeking of tobacco smoke and still just as jumpy. They plowed through the rest of her unpaid bills. "Is there any way you can help me?" she said, her eyes moist.

"Of course," Mattie said with far too much optimism. "I've had some success negotiating with JRA. They're not accustomed to lawyers getting involved, and for such tough guys, they're easy to bully. They know they're wrong and they're afraid someone might bust them. I know the judge over there and by now they're tired of feeding Stocky. We can get him out and get him back to work. Then we'll probably consider a bankruptcy to save the home and wipe out some of these bills. I'll haggle with the utility companies." She clicked off these bold moves as if they had already been accomplished, and Samantha suddenly felt better. Lady managed a smile, the first and only.

Mattie said, "Give us a couple of days and we'll put together a plan. Feel free to call Samantha here if you have any questions. She'll know everything about your case." The intern's heart skipped a beat as she heard her name mentioned. At the moment, she felt as though she knew nothing about anything.

"So we have two lawyers?" Lady asked.

"You certainly do."

"And you are, uh, free?"

"That's right, Lady. We are legal aid. We do not charge for our services."

Lady covered her eyes with both hands and began crying.

Samantha had not recovered from the first client meeting when she was called in to her second. Annette Brevard, the "junior partner" at Mountain Legal Aid Clinic, thought it would be educational for their new intern to get a real taste of domestic violence.

Annette was a divorced mother of two who had been in Brady for ten years. She had once lived in Richmond and practiced law in a midsized firm until a bad divorce sent her packing. She escaped to Brady with her children and took a job with Mattie because there was nothing else available in the Commonwealth. She certainly had no plans to stay in Brady, but then who's smart enough to plan the rest of their life? She lived in an old house downtown. Behind her house was a separate garage. Above the garage was a two-room apartment, Samantha's home for the next few months. Annette decided that if the internship was free, then so was the rent. They had haggled over this, but Annette was adamant. Samantha had no other viable option and moved in with promises of free babysitting. She was even allowed to park her hatchback in the garage.

The client was a thirty-six-year-old woman named Phoebe. She was married to Randy, and they had just gone through a bad weekend. Randy was in jail about six blocks away (the same jail Samantha had narrowly avoided) and Phoebe was sitting in a lawyer's office with a swollen left eye, a cut on her nose, and terror in her eyes. With compassion and feeling, Annette walked Phoebe through her story. Again, Samantha frowned intelligently without making a sound, took pages of notes, and wondered how many crazy people lived in those parts.

With a voice so calm it soothed even Samantha, Annette prodded Phoebe along. There were a lot of tears and emotion. Randy was a meth addict and dealer, also a drunk who'd been beating her for a year and a half. He never hit her as long as her father was alive—Randy was terrified of him—but after he died two years ago the physical abuse started. He threatened to kill her all the time. Yes, she used meth too, but she was careful and certainly not an addict. They had three kids, all under the age of ten. Her second marriage, his third. Randy was forty-two, older, and had a lot of rough friends in the meth business. She was afraid of these people. They had cash and they would arrange for his bail any moment now. Once free, Randy would almost certainly track her down. He was furious that she had finally called the police and had him arrested. But he knew the sheriff well and they wouldn't keep him in jail. He would beat her until she dropped the assault charges. She went through a pile of tissues as she sobbed her way through the story.

Occasionally, Samantha would scribble important questions such as "Where am I?" And "What am I doing here?"

Phoebe was afraid to go back to their rented home. Her three children were being hidden by an aunt in Kentucky. She was told by a deputy that Randy was scheduled to be in court sometime on Monday. He could even be there right now getting his bond set by the judge, and once it's set his buddies will plop down the cash and he'll walk. "You gotta help me," Phoebe said over and over. "He'll kill me."

"No he won't," Annette said with an odd sense of confidence. Judging from Phoebe's tears, looks of fear, and body language, Samantha agreed with her and suspected Randy might show up any moment and start trouble. Annette, though, seemed perfectly unbothered by that possibility.

She's been here before a hundred times, Samantha thought.

Annette said, "Samantha, go online and check the court docket."

She rattled off the Web site for Noland County's government list-
ings, and the intern was quick to open her laptop, start the search,
and for a moment ignore Phoebe and her emotions.

"I have to get a divorce," Phoebe was saying. "There's no way
I'll go back there."

"Okay, we'll file for divorce tomorrow and get an injunction to
keep him away from you."

"What's an injunction?"

"It's an order from the court, and if he violates it he'll really
anger the judge, who'll throw him back in jail."

This made her smile, but just for a second. She said, "I gotta
leave town. I can't stay here. He'll get stoned again and forget the
injunction and the judge and come after me. They gotta keep him
locked up for a while. Can they do that?"

"What's he charged with, Samantha?" Annette asked.

"Malicious wounding," she said just as she found the case
online. "Due in court this afternoon at 1:00. No bail has been set."

"Malicious wounding? What did he hit you with?"

The tears poured instantly and Phoebe wiped her cheeks with
the back of her hand. "He had a gun, a pistol we keep in a drawer
in the kitchen, unloaded because of the kids, but the bullets are on
top of the refrigerator, just in case, you know. We were fighting
and yelling and he pulled out the pistol like he was about to load it
and I suppose finish me off. I tried to grab it and he hit me on the
side of the head with the butt of it. Then it dropped to the floor
and he slapped me around with his hands. I got out of the house,
ran next door, and called the cops."

Annette calmly raised a hand to stop her. "That's the malicious
part—the use of a weapon." She looked at Phoebe and Samantha as
she said this, to enlighten both of them. "In Virginia, the sentence
can be from five to twenty years, depending on the circumstances—
weapon, injury, etc." Samantha was once again taking furious notes.
She had heard some of this in law school, so many years ago.

Annette continued, "Now, Phoebe, we can expect your husband to say that you went for the gun first, that you hit him and so

on, and he might even try to press charges against you. How would you respond to this?"

"This guy is eight inches taller and a hundred pounds heavier. No one in their right mind would believe I picked a fight with him. The cops, if they tell the truth, will say he was drunk and out of his mind. He even wrestled with them until they Tasered his big ass."

Annette smiled, satisfied. She glanced at her watch, opened a file, and removed some paperwork. "I have to make a phone call in five minutes. Samantha, this is our divorce questionnaire. It's pretty straightforward. Go through it with Phoebe and gather all the information you can. I'll be back in half an hour."

Samantha took the questionnaire as if she had handled dozens of them.

An hour later, alone and safe in her own makeshift office, Samantha closed her eyes and breathed deeply. The office appeared to be a former storage room, tiny and cramped with two unbalanced chairs and a round table with a vinyl covering. Mattie and Annette had apologized and promised an upgrade at some point in the future. One wall was dominated by a large window that looked out over the rear parking lot. Samantha was thankful for the light.

As small as it was, her space in New York had not been much larger. Against her wishes, her thoughts stayed on New York, the big firm and all its promises and horrors. She smiled when she realized she was not on the clock; gone was the unrelenting pressure to bill more hours, to make more money for the big boys at the top, to impress them with the goal of one day becoming just like them. She glanced at her watch. It was 11:00 and she had not billed a single minute, nor would she. The ancient phone rattled and she had no choice but to pick it up. "There's a call on line two," Barb said.

"Who is it?" Samantha asked nervously, her first phone call.

"Guy named Joe Duncan. Doesn't ring a bell."

"Why does he want to speak with me?"

"He didn't say that. Said he needs a lawyer and at the moment Mattie and Annette are tied up. He's yours by default."

"What kind of case?" Samantha asked, glancing at her six skyscrapers standing together on top of an army surplus file cabinet.

"Social Security. Be careful. Line two."

Barb worked part-time and ran the front. Samantha had spoken to her for only a few seconds early that morning as she was being introduced. The clinic also had a part-time paralegal named Claudelle. An all-girls show.

She punched line two and said, "Samantha Kofer."

Mr. Duncan said hello and quizzed her to make sure she was really a lawyer. She assured him she was but at that moment had doubts. Soon he was off and running. He was going through a rough spell and really wanted to chat about it. All manner of misfortune had hit him and his family, and based on the first ten minutes of his narrative he had enough problems to keep a small law firm busy for several months. He was unemployed—had been wrongfully terminated but that would be yet another story—but his real problem was his health. He had ruptured a lower disk and couldn't work. He had applied for disability status under Social Security, and had been denied. Now he was losing everything.

Because Samantha had so little to offer, she was content to let him ramble. After half an hour, though, she got bored. Ending the conversation was a challenge—he was desperate and clinging—but she finally convinced him she would immediately review his case with their Social Security specialist and get back to him.

By noon, Samantha was famished and exhausted. It was not the fatigue brought on by hours of reading and poring over thick documents, or the relentless pressure to impress people, or the fear of not measuring up and being shoved off the track to partnership. It was not the exhaustion she had lived with for the past three years. She was drained from the shock and fear of looking at the emotional wreckage of real humans, desperate people with little hope and looking to her for help.

For the rest of the firm, though, it was a typical Monday morning. They met for a brown-bag lunch in the main conference room, a weekly ritual, to eat quickly while discussing cases, clients, or any other business deemed necessary. But on this Monday the main topic was the new intern. They were keen to examine her. Finally, she was encouraged to speak.

"Well, I need some help," Samantha said. "I just got off the phone with a man whose claim for Social Security disability was denied. Whatever that means."

This was met with a mix of laughter and amusement. The word "disability" seemed to draw a reaction from the rest of the firm. "We no longer take Social Security cases," Barb said from the front line. She met the clients first, as they came through the front door.

"What was his name?" Claudelle asked.

Samantha hesitated and looked at the eager faces. "Okay, first things first. I'm not sure where we are with confidentiality. Do you—do we—discuss each other's cases openly, or are we each bound by rules of the attorney-client privilege?"

This drew even more laughter. All four talked at once, as they laughed and chuckled and nibbled on their sandwiches. It was immediately clear to Samantha that, within these walls, these four ladies talked about everyone and everything.

"Inside the firm, it's all fair game," Mattie said. "But outside, not a word."

"Good enough."

Barb said, "His name was Joe Duncan. Kinda rings a bell."

Claudelle said, "I had him a few years ago, filed a claim, got denied. I think it was a bad shoulder."

"Well, now it's spread to his lower lumbar," Samantha said. "Sounds like a mess."

"He's a serial claimant," Claudelle said. "And that's one reason we don't take Social Security cases anymore. There is so much fraud in the system. It's pretty rotten, especially around here."

"So what do I tell Mr. Duncan?"

"There's a law firm down in Abingdon that does nothing but disability cases."

Annette chimed in, "Cockrell and Rhodes, better known as

Cock and Roach, or Cockroach for short. Really bad boys who have a racket with some doctors and Social Security judges. All of their clients get checks. They're batting a thousand."

Mattie added, "A triathlete could file a claim and the Cockroaches could get him disability benefits."

"So we never—"

"Never."

Samantha took a bite of her highly processed turkey sandwich and looked directly at Barb. She almost asked the obvious: "If we don't take these cases, then why did you send the phone call back to me?" Instead, she made a mental note to keep the radar on high alert. Three years in Big Law had honed her survival skills razor sharp. Throat cutting and backstabbing were the norm, and she had learned to avoid both.

She would not discuss it now with Barb, but she would bring it up when the moment was right.

Claudelle seemed to be the clown of the group. She was only twenty-four, married for less than a year, pregnant, and having a rough time of it. She had spent the morning in the bathroom, fighting nausea and thinking vile thoughts about her unborn baby, a boy who had already been named after his father and was already causing as much trouble.

The tone was surprisingly raunchy. In forty-five minutes they not only covered the firm's pressing business but managed to explore morning sickness, menstrual cramps, labor and childbirth, men, and sex—no one seemed to be getting enough.

Annette broke up the meeting when she looked at Samantha and said, "We're in court in fifteen minutes."

9

Generally speaking, her experience with courtrooms had not been pleasant. Some visits had been required, others voluntary. When she was in the ninth grade, the great Marshall Kofer was trying an airline crash case in federal court in downtown D.C., and he convinced Samantha's civics teacher that her students' learning experience would be greatly enriched by watching him in action. For two full days, the kids sat in stultifying boredom as expert witnesses argued over the aerodynamics of severe icing. Far from being proud of her father, Samantha had been mortified at the unwanted attention. Fortunately for him, the students were back in class when the jury returned a verdict in favor of the manufacturer, handing him a rare loss. Seven years later she returned to the same building, but a different courtroom, to watch her father plead guilty to his crimes. It was a fine day for her mother, who never considered showing up, and so Samantha sat with an uncle, one of Marshall's brothers, and dabbed her eyes with tissues. A pre-law class at Georgetown had required her to watch a portion of a criminal trial, but a mild case of the flu kept her away. All law students do mock trials, and she had enjoyed them to a point, but wanted no part of the real thing. During her clerkship she seldom saw a courtroom. During her interviews, she had made it clear she wanted to stay far away from litigation.

And now she was walking into the Noland County Courthouse, headed for the main courtroom. The building itself was a handsome old redbrick structure with a sagging, bright tin roof over the third floor. Inside, a dusty foyer displayed fading portraits of bearded heroes, and one wall was covered with legal notices stapled slapdash to bulletin boards. She followed Annette to the second floor where they passed an ancient bailiff napping in his chair. They eased through thick double doors and stepped into the rear of the courtroom. Ahead, a judge was working at his bench as a few lawyers shuffled paperwork and bantered back and forth. To the right was the empty jury box. The high walls were covered with even more fading portraits, all men, all bearded and apparently serious about legal matters. A couple of clerks chatted and flirted with the lawyers. Several spectators watched and waited for justice to prevail.

Annette cornered a prosecutor, a man she hurriedly introduced to her intern as Richard, and said they represented Phoebe Fanning, who would be filing for a divorce as soon as possible. "How much do you know?" she asked Richard.

The three moved to a corner near the jury box so no one could hear. Richard said, "According to the cops, they were both stoned and decided they ought to settle their differences with a good fight. He won, she lost. Somehow a gun was involved, unloaded, and he whacked her in the head with it."

Annette recounted Phoebe's version as Richard listened carefully. He said, "Hump's his lawyer and all he wants now is a low bond. I'll argue for a higher one and maybe we can keep this old boy in jail a few more days, let him cool off while she clears out." Annette nodded, agreed, and said, "Thanks, Richard."

Hump was Cal Humphrey, a fixture from down the street; they had just walked past his storefront office. Annette said hello and introduced Samantha, who was appalled at the size of his stomach. A pair of gaudy suspenders strained under the load and seemed ready to pop, with consequences that would be too gross to consider. Hump whispered that "his man" Randy (for a second he could not remember his last name) needed to get out of jail because he was missing work. Hump didn't buy Phoebe's version of events, but instead suggested that the entire conflict had been started when she attacked his client with the unloaded pistol.

"That's why we have trials," Annette mumbled as they eased away from Hump. Randy Fanning and two other inmates were escorted into the courtroom and placed on the front row. Their handcuffs were removed and a deputy stood close. The three could have been members of the same gang—faded orange jail overalls, unshaven faces, messy hair, hard looks. Annette and Samantha sat in the audience, as far away as possible. Barb tiptoed into the courtroom, handed Annette a file, and said, "Here's the divorce."

When the judge called Randy Fanning to the bench, Annette sent a text message to Phoebe, who was sitting in her car outside the courthouse. Randy stood before the judge, with Hump to his right and Richard to his left, but farther away. Hump began a windy narrative about how much his client needed to be at work, how deep his roots were in Noland County, how he could be trusted to show up in court anytime he was needed, and so on. It was just a garden-variety marital dispute and things could be worked out without getting the judicial system further involved. As he rambled, Phoebe eased into the courtroom and sat beside Annette. Her hands were trembling, her eyes moist.

Richard, for the prosecution, dwelt on the gravity of the charges and the real possibility of a lengthy jail term for Fanning. Nonsense, said Hump. His man was innocent. His man had been attacked by his "unbalanced" wife. If she insisted on pushing matters, she just might be the one going to jail. Back and forth the lawyers argued.

The judge, a peaceful old gentleman with a slick head, asked calmly, "I understand the alleged victim is here in the courtroom. Is that correct, Ms. Brevard?" he asked, scanning the audience.

Annette jumped to her feet and said, "She's right here, Your Honor." She walked through the bar as if she owned the courtroom, Phoebe in tow. "We represent Phoebe Fanning, whose divorce we'll be filing within the next ten minutes."

Samantha, still safely in the audience, watched as Randy Fanning glared at his wife. Richard seized the moment and said, "Your

Honor, it might be helpful to notice the apparent wounds to the face of Ms. Fanning. This woman has had the hell beaten out of her."

"I'm not blind," replied the judge. "I don't see any damage to *your* face, Mr. Fanning. The court also takes note of the fact that you're over six feet tall and rather stout. Your wife is, let's say, quite a bit smaller. Did you slap her around?"

Randy shuffled his considerable weight from foot to foot, obviously guilty, and managed to say, "We had a fight, Judge. She started it."

"I'm sure she did. I think it's best if you continue to settle down for a day or two. I'm sending you back to jail and we'll meet again on Thursday. In the meantime, Ms. Brevard, you and your client tend to her pressing legal matters and keep me posted."

Hump said, "But, Your Honor, my client will lose his job."

Phoebe blurted, "He doesn't have a job. He cuts timber part-time and sells meth full-time."

Everyone seemed to swallow hard as her words rattled around the courtroom. Randy was ready to resume the fight and glared at his wife with murderous hatred. The judge finally said, "That's enough. Bring him back Thursday." A bailiff grabbed Randy and led him away and out of the courtroom.

Standing at the main door were two men, a couple of ruffians with matted hair and tattoos. They stared at Annette, Samantha, and Phoebe as they walked by. In the hallway, Phoebe whispered, "Those thugs are with Randy, all in the meth business. I gotta get out of this town."

Samantha thought: I might be right behind you.

They walked into the office of the Circuit Court and filed the divorce. Annette was asking for an immediate hearing for a restraining order to keep Randy away from the family. "The earliest slot is Wednesday afternoon," a clerk said.

"We'll take it," Annette said.

The two thugs were waiting just outside the front door of the courthouse, and they had been joined by a third angry young man.

He stepped in front of Phoebe and growled, "You better drop the charges, girl, or you'll be sorry."

Phoebe did not back away; instead, she looked at him in a way that conveyed years of familiarity and contempt. She said to Annette, "This is Randy's brother Tony, fresh from prison."

"Did you hear me? I said drop the charges," Tony said in a louder growl.

"I just filed for divorce, Tony. It's over. I'm leaving town as fast as I can, but I'll be sure and come back when he goes to court. I'm not dropping the charges, so please get out of the way."

One thug stared at Samantha, the other at Annette. The brief confrontation ended when Hump and Richard walked out of the courthouse and saw what was happening. "That's enough," Richard said, and Tony backed away.

Hump said, "Let's go gals. I'll walk you back to the office." As Hump lumbered down Main Street, talking nonstop about another case he and Annette were contesting, Samantha followed along, rattled by the incident and wondering if she needed a handgun in her purse. No wonder Donovan practiced law with a small arsenal.

The rest of her afternoon was client-free, thankfully. She had heard enough misery for one day, and she needed to study. Annette loaned her some well-used seminar materials designed for rookie lawyers, with sections on divorce and domestic relations, wills and estates, bankruptcy, landlord and tenant, employment, immigration, and government assistance. A section on black lung benefits had been added later. It was dry and dull, at least to read about, but she had already learned firsthand that the cases were anything but boring.

At five o'clock, she finally called Mr. Joe Duncan and informed him she could not handle his Social Security appeal. Her bosses prohibited such representation. She passed along the names of two private attorneys who took such cases and wished him well. He was not too happy with the call.

She stopped by Mattie's office and they recapped her first day on the job. So far so good, though she was still rattled by the brief confrontation on the courthouse steps. "They won't mess with a lawyer," Mattie assured her. "Especially a girl. I've been doing this for twenty-six years and I've never been assaulted."

"Congratulations. Have you been threatened?"

"Maybe a couple of times, but nothing that really scared me. You'll be fine."

She felt fine leaving the office and walking to her car, though she couldn't help but glance around. A light mist was falling and the town was growing darker. She parked in the garage under her apartment and climbed the steps.

Annette's daughter, Kim, was thirteen; her son, Adam, was ten. They were intrigued by their new "roommate" and insisted that she join them at mealtime, but Samantha had no plans to crash their dinner every night. With her crazy schedule, and Blythe's, she had grown accustomed to eating alone.

As a professional with a stressful job, Annette had little time to cook. Evidently, cleaning was not a priority either. Dinner was mac and cheese from the microwave with sliced tomatoes from a client's garden. They drank water from plastic bottles, never from the tap. As they ate, the kids peppered Samantha with questions about her life, growing up in D.C., living and working in New York, and why in the world she had chosen to come to Brady. They were bright, confident, easy to humor, and not afraid to ask personal questions. They were courteous too, never failing to say "Yes ma'am" and "No ma'am." They decided she was too young to be called Miss Kofer, and Adam felt as though Samantha was too much of a mouthful. They eventually agreed on Miss Sam, though Samantha was hopeful the "Miss" would soon disappear. She told them that she would be their babysitter, and this seemed to puzzle them.

"Why do we need one?" Kim asked.

"So your mother can go out and do whatever she wants to do," Samantha said.

They found this amusing. Adam said, "But she never goes out."

"True," Annette said. "There's not much to do in Brady. In

fact, there's nothing to do if you don't go to church three nights a week."

"And you don't go to church?" Samantha asked. So far, in her brief time in Appalachia, she had become convinced that every five families had their own tiny church with a leaning white steeple. There were churches everywhere, all believing in the inerrancy of the Holy Scripture but evidently agreeing on little else.

"Sometimes on Sunday," Kim said.

After supper, Kim and Adam dutifully cleared the table and stacked the dishes in the sink. There was no dishwasher. They wanted to watch television with Miss Sam and ignore their homework, but Annette eventually shooed them off to the small bedrooms. Sensing that her guest might be getting bored, Annette said, "Let's have some tea and talk."

With nothing else to do, Samantha said yes. Annette scooped up a pile of dirty clothes and tossed them into the clothes washer beside the refrigerator. She added soap and cranked a dial. "The noise will drown out anything we say," she said as she reached into a cabinet for tea bags. "Decaf okay?"

"Sure," Samantha said as she stepped into the den, a room overrun with sagging bookshelves, stacks of magazines, and soft furniture that had not been dusted in months. In one corner there was a flat-screen TV (the garage apartment did not have one), and in another corner Annette kept a small desk with a computer and a stack of files. She brought two cups of steaming tea, handed one to Samantha, and said, "Let's sit on the sofa and talk about girl stuff."

"Okay, what do you have in mind?"

As they settled in, Annette said, "Well, sex for one. How often do you get laid in New York?"

Samantha laughed at the frankness, then hesitated as if she couldn't remember the last time. "It's not that wild, really. I mean, it is if you're in the game, but in my crowd we work too much to have any fun. A night out for us is a nice dinner and drinks, after which I'm always too tired to do anything but go to sleep, alone."

"That's hard to believe, all those rich, young professionals on the prowl. I've watched *Sex and the City*, over and over. By myself, of course, after the kids go to bed."

"Well, I haven't. I've heard about it, but I'm usually at the office. I've had one boyfriend in the past three years. Henry, a starving actor, really cute and fun in the sack, but he got tired of my hours and my fatigue. Sure, you meet a lot of guys, but most of them are just as driven. Women are disposable. A lot of jerks too, a lot of arrogant brats who talk of nothing but money and brag about what they can buy."

"I'm crushed."

"Don't be. It's not as glamorous as you think."

"Never?"

"Oh sure, the occasional hookup, but nothing I care to remember." Samantha sipped her tea and wanted to shift the conversation. "What about you? You get much action in Brady?"

It was Annette's turn to laugh. She paused, took a sip, and became sad. "There's not much happening here. I made the choice, now I live it, and that's okay."

"The choice?"

"Yes, I came here ten years ago, in full retreat. My divorce was a nightmare and I had to get away from my ex. Get my kids away too. He has almost no contact. Now, I'm forty-five years old, somewhat attractive, in fairly good shape, unlike, well—"

"Got it."

"Let's just say there's not much competition in Noland County. There have been a couple of nice men along the way, but no one I wanted to live with. One guy was twenty years older, and I just couldn't do that to my kids. For the first few years, it seemed as though half the women in town were trying to fix me up with a cousin. Then I realized they really wanted me to get married so they wouldn't have to worry about their own husbands. Married men, though, do not tempt me. Far too much trouble, here or in the city."

"Why do you stay?"

"That's a great question, and I'm not sure I will. It's a safe place to raise kids, though we do worry about the environmental hazards. Brady's okay, but not far from here, back in the settlements and hollows, kids are constantly sick from contaminated water and coal dust. To answer your question, I've stayed because I love the work. I love the people who need my help. I can make a small difference in their lives. You met them today. You saw their fear and hopelessness. They need me. If I leave, there may be someone to take my place, and maybe not."

"How do you turn it off when you leave the office?"

"I can't always do that. Their problems are too personal, so I lose a lot of sleep."

"I'm glad to hear that because I keep thinking about Phoebe Fanning, with her busted face and kids hidden with a relative, and a goon for a husband who'll probably kill her when he gets out."

Annette offered a caring smile. "I've seen a lot of women in her situation, and they've all survived. Phoebe will be fine, eventually. She'll relocate somewhere—we'll help her—and she'll divorce him. Keep in mind, Samantha, he's in jail right now, getting a good taste of life behind bars. If he does something stupid, he could spend the rest of his days in prison."

"I didn't get the impression he's that much of a thinker."

"You're right. He's an idiot and an addict. I'm not making light of her situation, but she'll be okay."

Samantha exhaled and set her cup on the coffee table. "I'm sorry, this is just so new to me."

"Dealing with real people?"

"Yes, so caught up in their problems, and expected to fix them. The last file I worked on in New York involved a really shady guy, worth about a billion or so, our client, who wanted to build this very tall and sleek hotel in the middle of Greenwich Village. It was by far the ugliest model I ever saw, really gaudy. He fired three or four architects and his building just got taller and uglier. The city said hell no, so he sued and cozied up to the politicians and conducted himself like a lot of Manhattan developers. I met him once briefly when he came to the office to yell at my partner. A total sleazeball. And he was our client, my client. I detested the man. I wanted him to fail."

"And why not?"

"He did fail, and we were secretly thrilled. Imagine that, we put in tons of hours, charged the guy a fortune, and felt like celebrating when his project got rejected. How's that for client relations?"

"I'd celebrate too."

"Now I'm worried about Lady Purvis whose husband is serving time in a debtors' prison, and I'm fretting about Phoebe getting out of town before her husband is free on bond."

"Welcome to our world, Samantha. There'll be even more tomorrow."

"I'm not sure I'm cut out for this."

"Yes, you are. You gotta be tough in this business, and you're a lot tougher than you think."

Adam was back, homework suddenly finished, and he wanted to challenge Miss Sam to a game of gin rummy. "He thinks he's a card shark," Annette said. "And he cheats."

"I've never played gin rummy," Miss Sam said.

Adam was shuffling the deck like a Vegas dealer.

10

Most of Mattie's workdays began with coffee at eight o'clock sharp, office door closed, phone ignored, and Donovan sitting across from her sharing the latest gossip. There was really no need to close her door because no one else arrived for work until around 8:30, when Annette punched in after dropping her kids off at school. Nonetheless, Mattie treasured the privacy with her nephew and protected it.

Office rules and procedures appeared to be lax, and Samantha had been told to show up "around nine" and work until she found a good stopping place late in the afternoon. At first, she worried that the transition from a hundred hours a week to forty might be difficult, but not so. She had not slept until seven in years and was finding it quite agreeable. By eight, however, she was climbing the walls and eager to start the day. On Tuesday, she eased through the front door, passed Mattie's office, heard low voices, and checked the kitchen for the coffeepot. She had just settled behind her compact desk for an hour or two of studying, or until she was fetched to sit through another client interview, when Donovan suddenly appeared and said, "Welcome to town."

"Well, hello," she said.

He glanced around and said, "I'll bet your office in New York was a lot bigger."

"Not really. They stuffed us rookies into what they called

'quads,' these cramped little work spaces where you could reach over and touch your colleague, if you needed to. They saved on rent so the partners could protect their bottom line."

"Sounds like you really miss it."

"I think I'm still numb." She waved at the only other chair and said, "Have a seat."

Donovan casually folded himself into the small chair and said, "Mattie tells me you made it to court on your very first day."

"I did. What else did she tell you?" Samantha wondered if her daily movements would be recapped each morning over their coffee.

"Nothing, just the idle chatter of small-town lawyers. Randy Fanning was once an okay guy, then he got into meth. He'll wind up dead or in prison, like a lot of guys around here."

"Can I borrow one of your guns?"

A laugh, then, "You won't need one. The meth dealers are not nearly as nasty as the coal companies. Start suing them all the time and I'll get you a gun. I know it's early, but have you thought about lunch?"

"I haven't thought about breakfast yet."

"I'm offering lunch, a working lunch in my office. Chicken salad sandwich?"

"How can I refuse that?"

"Does noon work in your schedule?"

She pretended to consult her busy daily planner, and said, "Your lucky day. I happen to have an opening."

He jumped to his feet and said, "See ya."

She studied quietly for a while, hoping to be left undisturbed. Through the thin walls she heard Annette discussing a case with Mattie. The phone rang occasionally, and each time Samantha held her breath and hoped that Barb would send the caller to another office, to a lawyer who knew what to do. Her luck lasted until almost ten, when Barb stuck her head around the door and said, "I'll be out for an hour. You have the front." She disappeared before Samantha could inquire as to what, exactly, that meant.

It meant sitting at Barb's desk in the reception area, alone and vulnerable and likely to be approached by some poor soul with no money to hire a real lawyer. It meant answering the phone and routing the calls to either Mattie or Annette, or simply stalling. One person asked for Annette, who was with a client. Another asked for Mattie, who had gone to court. Another needed advice on a Social Security disability claim, and Samantha happily referred him to a private firm. Finally, the front door opened and Mrs. Francine Crump walked in with a legal matter that would haunt Samantha for months.

All she wanted was a will, one "that didn't cost anything." Simple wills are straightforward documents, the preparation of which can easily be undertaken by even the greenest of lawyers. Indeed, rookies jump at the chance to draft them because it's difficult to screw them up. Suddenly confident, Samantha led Mrs. Crump back to a small meeting room and left the door open so she could keep an eye on the front.

Mrs. Crump was eighty years old and looked all of it. Her husband died long ago, and her five children were scattered around the country, none close to home. She said she had been forgotten by them; they seldom came to visit, seldom called. She wanted to sign a simple will that gave them nothing. "Cut 'em all out," she said with astonishing bitterness. Judging from her appearance, and from the fact that she was looking for a free will, Samantha assumed there was little in the way of assets. Mrs. Crump lived in Eufaula, a small community "deep in Jacob's Holler." Samantha wrote this down as if she knew exactly where it was. There were no debts, nothing in the way of real assets except for an old house and eighty acres, land that had been in her family forever.

"Any idea what the land is worth?" Samantha asked.

Mrs. Crump crunched her dentures and said, "A lot more than anybody knows. You see, the coal company came out last year and tried to buy the land, been trying for some time, but I ran 'em off again. Ain't selling to no coal company, no ma'am. They're blasting away not far from my land, taking down Cat Mountain, and it's a real shame. Ain't got no use for no coal company."

"How much did they offer?"

"A lot, and I ain't told my kids either. Won't tell them. I'm in bad health, you see, and I'll be gone pretty soon. If my kids get the land, they'll sell to the coal company before I'm cold in the ground. That's exactly what they'll do. I know 'em." She reached into her purse and pulled out some folded papers. "Here's a will I signed five years ago. My kids took me down to a lawyer's office, just down the street, and they made me sign it."

Samantha slowly unfolded the papers and read the last will and testament of Francine Cooper Crump. The third paragraph left everything to her five children in equal shares. Samantha scribbled some useless notes and said, "Okay, Mrs. Crump, for estate tax purposes, I need to know the approximate value of this land."

"The what?"

"How much did the coal company offer you?"

She looked as if she'd been insulted, then leaned in low and whispered. "Two hundred thousand and change, but it's worth double that. Maybe triple. You can't trust a coal company. They lowball everybody, then figure out ways to steal from you at the end."

Suddenly the simple will was not so simple. Samantha proceeded cautiously, asking, "All right, so who gets the eighty acres under a new will?"

"I want to give it to my neighbor, Jolene. She lives across the creek on her own land and she ain't selling either. I trust her and she's already promised to take care of my land."

"You've discussed this with her?"

"Talk about it all the time. She and her husband, Hank, say they'll make new wills too, and leave their land to me in case they go first. But they're in better health, you know? I figure I'll pass first."

"But what if they pass first?"

"I doubt it. I got high blood pressure and a bad heart, plus bursitis."

"Sure, but what if they pass first, and you inherit their land to go along with your land, and then you die, who gets all this land?"

"Not my kids, and not their kids either. God help us. You think mine are bad."

"Got that, but someone has to inherit the land. Who do you have in mind?"

"That's what I came here for, to talk to a lawyer. I need some advice on what to do."

Suddenly, with assets on the line, there were different scenarios. The new will would certainly be contested by the five children, and other than what she had just skimmed in the seminar materials, Samantha knew nothing about will contests. She vaguely recalled a case or two from a class in law school, but that seemed like so long ago. She managed to stall, take notes, and ask semi-relevant questions for half an hour, and succeeded in convincing Mrs. Crump that she should return in a few days after the firm had reviewed her situation. Barb was back, and she proved skillful in helping to ease the new client out the front door.

"What was that all about?" Barb asked when Mrs. Crump was gone.

"I'm not sure. I'll be in my room."

Donovan's office was in much better shape than the legal aid clinic's. Leather chairs, thick rugs, hardwood floors with a nice finish. A funky chandelier hung in the center of the foyer. Samantha's first thought was that, finally, there was someone in Brady who might be making a buck or two. His receptionist, Dawn, greeted her politely and said the boss was waiting upstairs. She was off to lunch. As she climbed the circular staircase, Samantha heard the front door close and lock. There was no sign of anyone else.

Donovan was on the phone behind a large wooden desk that appeared to be very old. He waved her in, pointed to a bulky chair, and said, "Gotta go." He slammed the phone down and said, "Welcome to my domain. This is where all the long balls are hit."

"Nice," she said, looking around. The room was large and opened onto the balcony. The walls were covered with handsome bookcases, all packed with the usual assortment of treatises and thick tomes meant to impress. In one corner was a gun rack displaying at least eight deadly weapons. Samantha didn't know a shotgun from a deer rifle, but the collection appeared to be primed and ready.

"Guns everywhere," she observed.

"I hunt a lot, always have. When you grow up in these mountains, you grow up in the woods. I killed my first deer at the age of six, with a bow."

"Congratulations. And why do you want to have lunch?"

"You promised, remember? Last week, just after you were arrested and I rescued you from jail."

"But we agreed on lunch at the diner down the street."

"I thought we might have more privacy here. Plus, I try and avoid the local spots. As I told you, there are a lot of people around here who don't like me. Sometimes they say things and make a scene in public. It can really ruin a good lunch."

"I don't see any food."

"It's in the war room. Come with me." He jumped to his feet and she followed him down a short hallway to a long, windowless room. At one end of a cluttered table were two plastic carryout containers and two bottles of water. He pointed and said, "Lunch is served."

Samantha walked to a side wall and stared at an enlarged photo that was at least eight feet tall. It was in color, and it portrayed a scene that was shocking and tragic. A massive boulder, the size of a small car, had crashed through a mobile home, shearing it in half and causing serious damage. "What's this?" she asked.

Donovan stepped beside her and said, "Well, it's a lawsuit, to begin with. For about a million years, that boulder was part of Enid Mountain, about forty miles from here, over in Hopper County. A couple of years ago, they began strip-mining the mountain, blew its top off, and dug out the coal. On March 14 of last year, at four in the morning, a bulldozer owned and operated by a roguish outfit called Strayhorn Coal was clearing rock, without a permit, and this boulder was shoved into the fill area down the valley.

Because of its size, it picked up momentum as it descended along this steep creek bed." He was pointing to an enlarged map next to the photo. "Almost a mile from where it left the blade of the bulldozer, it crashed into this little trailer. In the back bedroom were two brothers, Eddie Tate, age eleven, and Brandon Tate, age eight. Sound asleep, as you might expect. Their father was in prison for cooking meth. Their mother was at work at a convenience store. The boys were killed instantly, crushed, flattened."

Samantha gawked at the photo in disbelief. "That's horrible."

"Indeed it was, and is. Life near a strip mine is never dull. The ground shakes and cracks foundations. Coal dust fills the air and blankets everything. The well water turns orange. Rocks fly all the time. I had a case two years ago in West Virginia where a Mr. and Mrs. Herzog were sitting by their small pool on a warm Saturday afternoon and a one-ton boulder came from nowhere and landed square in the middle of the pool. They got drenched. The pool cracked. We sued the company and got a few bucks, but not much."

"And you've sued Strayhorn Coal?"

"Oh, yes. We go to trial next Monday in Colton, Circuit Court."

"The company won't settle?"

"The company was fined by our fearless regulators. Hit 'em hard for twenty thousand bucks, which they have appealed. No, they won't settle. They, along with their insurance company, have offered a hundred thousand."

"A hundred thousand dollars for two dead kids?"

"Dead kids are not worth much, especially in Appalachia. They have no economic value because they, obviously, are not employed. It's a great case for punitive damages—Strayhorn Coal is capitalized at half a billion dollars—and I'll ask for a million or two. But the wise people who make the laws in Virginia decided years ago to cap punitive damages."

"I think I remember this from the bar exam."

"The cap is $350,000, regardless of how bad the defendant acted. It was a gift from our General Assembly to the insurance industry, like all caps."

"You sound like my father."

"You want to eat or stand here for the next hour."

"I'm not sure I'm hungry."

"Well, I am." They sat at the table and unwrapped their sandwiches. Samantha took a small bite but had no appetite. "Have you tried to settle the case?" she asked.

"I put a million on the table, they countered with a hundred thousand, so we're miles apart. They, the insurance lawyers along with the coal company, are banking on the fact that the family was screwed up and not that close. They're also banking on the fact that a lot of jurors in these parts are either afraid of Big Coal or quietly supportive of it. When you sue a coal company in Appalachia you can't always count on an unbiased jury. Even those who despise the companies tend to stay quiet about it. Everybody has a relative or a friend who's got a job. It makes for some interesting dynamics in the courtroom."

Samantha tried another small bite and looked around the room. The walls were covered with enlarged color photos and maps, some marked as trial exhibits, others apparently waiting for trial. She said, "This reminds me of my father's office, once upon a time."

"Marshall Kofer. I checked him out. He was quite the trial lawyer in his day."

"Yes, he was. When I was a kid, if I wanted to see him I usually had to go to his office, if he was in town. He worked nonstop. Ran a big firm. When he wasn't jetting around the world chasing the latest aviation disaster, he was in his office preparing for trial. They had this large, cluttered room—come to think of it, they called it the war room."

"I didn't invent the term. Most trial lawyers have one."

"And the walls were covered with large photos and diagrams and all sorts of exhibits. It was impressive, even to a kid. I can still feel the tension, the anxiety in the room as he and his staff got ready for the courtroom. These were big crashes, with lots of dead people, lots of lawyers and all. He explained later that most of his cases were settled right before trial. Liability was seldom an issue.

The plane went down, it wasn't the fault of the passengers. The airlines have plenty of money and insurance, and they worry about their image, so they settle. For huge sums."

"Did you ever consider working with him?"

"No, never. He's impossible, or at least he was back then. Massive ego, total workaholic, pretty much of an ass. I wanted no part of his world."

"Then he crashed himself."

"Indeed he did." She stood and walked to another photo, one of a mangled car. Rescue personnel were trying to remove someone trapped inside.

Donovan kept his seat and chewed on a chip. He said, "I tried that case in Martin County, West Virginia, three years ago. Lost."

"What happened?"

"A coal truck came down the mountain, overweight and speeding, and it veered across the center line and ran over that little Honda. The driver was Gretchen Bane, age sixteen, my client, and she died at the scene. If you look closely, you can see her left foot at the bottom there, sort of hanging out the door."

"I was afraid of that. Did the jury see this?"

"Oh yes. They saw everything. For five days I laid it all out for the jury, but it didn't matter."

"How'd you lose?"

"I lose about half of them. In that case, the truck driver took the stand, swore to tell the truth, then lied for three hours. He said Gretchen crossed the center line and caused the wreck, made it sound as though she was trying to kill herself. The coal companies are clever and they never send down one truck at a time. They travel in pairs, so there's always a witness ready to testify. Trucks hauling coal that weighs a hundred tons, racing across old, twenty-ton bridges still used by school buses, and absolutely ignoring every rule of the road. If there's an accident, it's usually bad. In West Virginia, they're killing one innocent driver per week. The trucker swears he was doing nothing wrong, his buddy backs him up, there are no other witnesses, so the jury falls in line with Big Coal."

"Can't you appeal?"

Donovan laughed as though she'd nailed her punch line. He took a swig of water and said, "Sure, we still have that right. But West Virginia elects its judges, which is an abomination. Virginia has some screwed-up laws, but at least we don't elect judges. Not so over there. There are five members of the West Virginia Supreme Court. They serve four-year terms and run for reelection. Guess who contributes the big money to the campaigns."

"The coal companies."

"Bingo. They influence the politicians, the regulators, the judges, and they often control the juries. So it's not exactly an ideal climate for us litigators."

"So much for a fair trial," she said, still looking at the photos.

"We win occasionally. In Gretchen's case, we got a break. A month after the trial, the same driver hit another car. Luckily, no one was killed, just a few broken bones. The deputy on the scene got curious and took the driver in for questioning. He was acting weird and finally admitted he'd been driving for fifteen hours straight. To help matters he was drinking Red Bull with vodka and snorting crystal meth. The deputy turned on a recorder and quizzed him about the Bane accident. He admitted he'd been threatened into lying by his employer. I got a copy of the transcript and filed a bunch of motions. The court finally granted a new trial, one we're still waiting for. Eventually, I'll nail them."

"What happened to the driver?"

"He became a whistle-blower and spilled the beans on East-point Mining, his employer. Someone slashed his tires and fired two shots through his kitchen window, so he's now in hiding, in another state. I give him cash to live on."

"Is that legal?"

"That's not a fair question in coal country. Nothing is black-and-white in my world. The enemy breaks every rule in the book, so the fight is never fair. If you play by the rules, you lose, even when you're on the right side."

She returned to the table and nibbled on a chip. She said, "I knew I was wise to avoid litigation."

"I hate to hear that," he said, smiling, his dark eyes absorbing every move she made. "I was thinking about offering you a job."

"I'm sorry."

"I'm serious. I could use some research, and I'll pay you. I know how much you're earning over at the legal clinic, so I figured you might want to moonlight as a research assistant."

"Here, in your office?"

"Where else? Nothing that would interfere with your internship, strictly after hours and on weekends. If you're not already bored here in Brady, it won't be long."

"Why me?"

"There's no one else. I have two paralegals and one is leaving tomorrow. I can't trust any other lawyer in town, nor anyone from any law office. I'm paranoid about secrecy, and you obviously haven't been here long enough to know anything or anybody. You're the perfect hire."

"I don't know what to say. Have you talked to Mattie?"

"Not about this, no. But if you're interested, I'll have a chat with her. She rarely says no to me. Think about it. If you don't want to, I'll understand completely."

"Okay, I'll think about it. But I've just started one job and wasn't planning on looking for another, not so soon anyway. Plus, I really don't like litigation."

"You won't have to go to court. Just hide in here, do the research, write the briefs, work the long hours you're accustomed to working."

"I was trying to get away from that."

"I understand. Mull it over and we'll chat later."

They worked on their sandwiches for a moment but the silence was too heavy. Samantha finally said, "Mattie told me about your past."

He smiled and shoved his food away. "What do you want to know? I'm an open book."

She doubted that. She could think of several questions: What happened to your father? How serious is the separation from your wife? How often do you see her?

Maybe later. She said, "Nothing really. It's an interesting background, that's all."

"Interesting, sad, tragic, filled with adventure. All of the above. I'm thirty-eight years old, and I'll die young."

She could think of no response.

11

The highway to Colton snaked through the mountains, rising and falling, offering breathtaking views of the dense ridges, then dipping into valleys filled with clusters of dilapidated shacks and mobile homes with junk cars scattered about. It clung to creeks with shallow rapids and water clear enough to drink, and just as the beauty sunk in it passed another settlement of tiny, forlorn houses stuck close together and shaded eternally by the mountains. The contrast was startling: the beauty of the ridges against the poverty of the people who lived between them. There were some pretty homes with neat lawns and white picket fences, but the neighbors were usually not as prosperous.

Mattie drove and talked while Samantha took in the scenery. As they climbed a stretch of road, a rare straightaway, a long truck approached from the other direction. It was dirty, covered with dust, with a canvas top over its bed. It was flying down the mountain, obviously speeding, but staying in the proper lane. After it passed, Samantha said, "I assume that was a coal truck."

Mattie checked a mirror as though she hadn't noticed. "Oh, yes. They haul it out after it's been washed and it's ready for the market. They're everywhere."

"Donovan talked about them yesterday. He doesn't think too highly of them."

"I'll bet good money that truck was overweight and probably couldn't pass inspection."

"And no one checks them?"

"It's spotty. And usually when the inspectors arrive the coal companies already know they're coming. My favorites are the mine safety inspectors who monitor the blasting. They have a schedule so when they show up at a strip mine, guess what? Everything is by the book. As soon as they leave, the company blasts away with little regard for the rules."

Samantha assumed Mattie knew everything about her lunch the day before with Donovan. She waited a moment to see if the job offer was mentioned. It was not. They topped a mountain and began another descent. Mattie said, "Let me show you something. Won't take but a minute." She hit the brakes and turned onto a smaller highway, one with more curves and steeper ridges. They were going up again. A sign said a picnic area with a scenic view was just ahead. They stopped at a small strip of land with two wooden tables and a garbage can. Before them lay miles of rolling mountains covered with dense hardwoods. They got out of the car and walked to a rickety fence built to keep people and vehicles from tumbling deep into a valley where they would never be found.

Mattie said, "This is a good spot to see mountaintop removal from a distance. Three sites—" She pointed to her left. "That's the Cat Mountain Mine not far from Brady. Straight ahead is the Loose Creek Mine in Kentucky. And to the right there is the Little Utah Mine, also in Kentucky. All active, all stripping coal as fast as humanly possible. Those mountains were once three thousand feet high, like their neighbors. Look at them now."

They were scalped of all greenery and reduced to rock and dirt. Their tops were gone and they stood like missing fingers, the nubs on a mangled hand. They were surrounded by unspoiled mountains, all ablaze with the orange and yellow of mid-autumn, and perfectly beautiful if not for the eyesores across the ridge.

Samantha stood motionless, staring in disbelief and trying to absorb the devastation. She finally said, "This can't be legal."

"Afraid so, according to federal law. Technically it's legal. But the way they go about it is quite illegal."

"There's no way to stop it."

"Litigation is still raging, has been for twenty years. We've had a few victories at the federal level, but all the good decisions have been overturned on appeal. The Fourth Circuit is loaded with Republican appointees. We're still fighting, though."

"We?"

"The good guys, the opponents of strip-mining. I'm not personally involved as a lawyer, but I'm on the right team. We're in a distinct minority around here, but we're fighting." Mattie glanced at her watch and said, "We'd better go."

Back in the car, Samantha said, "Kinda makes you sick, doesn't it?"

"Yes, they've destroyed so much of our way of life here in Appalachia, so, yes, it makes me sick."

As they entered the town of Colton, the highway became Center Street and after a few blocks the courthouse appeared on the right. Samantha said, "Donovan has a trial here next week."

"Oh yes, a big one. Those two little boys, so sad."

"You know the case?"

"Oh yes, it was quite the story when they were killed. I know more than I care to know. I just hope he wins. I advised him to settle, to take something for the family, but he wants to make a statement."

"So he doesn't take your advice."

"Donovan usually does what he wants to do, and he's usually right."

They parked behind the courthouse and walked inside. Unlike Noland County's, the Hopper County Courthouse was a baffling modern structure that had undoubtedly once looked thrilling on paper. All glass and rock, it jutted here and folded there, and wasted a lot of space in its daring design. Samantha figured the architect had eventually lost his license.

"The old one burned," Mattie said as they climbed the stairs. "But then they all burn."

Samantha wasn't sure what this meant. Lady Purvis was sitting nervously in the hallway outside the courtroom, and she smiled with great relief when she saw her lawyers. A few others loitered about, waiting for court to convene. After a few preliminaries, Lady pointed to a dough-faced young man in a polyester sports coat and shiny boots with pointed toes. "That's him, works for JRA, name's Snowden, Laney Snowden."

"Wait here," Mattie said. With Samantha following her, she made a beeline for Mr. Snowden, whose eyes got bigger the closer she got. "You're the representative for JRA?" Mattie demanded.

"I am," Snowden said proudly.

She thrust a card at him as if it were a switchblade and said, "I'm Mattie Wyatt, attorney for Stocky Purvis. This is my associate, Samantha Kofer. We've been hired to get our client out of jail."

Snowden took a step back as Mattie pressed ahead. Samantha, treading water, wasn't sure what to do, so she quickly adopted an aggressive posture and look. She scowled at Snowden as he looked blankly at her and tried to absorb the reality that a deadbeat like Stocky Purvis could hire not one but two lawyers.

"Fine," Snowden said. "Fork over the money and we'll get him out."

"He doesn't have any money, Mr. Snowden. That much should be clear by now. And he can't make any money as long as you've got him locked up in jail. Tack on all the illegal fees you want, but the truth is my client can't earn a dime sitting where he's sitting right now."

"I have a court order," Snowden said with bravado.

"Well, we're about to talk to the judge about his court order. It's going to be amended so Stocky walks. If you don't negotiate, you'll get left holding the bag."

"Okay, what do you gals have in mind?"

"Don't call me a gal!" Mattie barked at him. Snowden recoiled fearfully, as if he might get hit with one of those sexual harassment claims you read about. Mattie, inching closer to Snowden as her face changed colors, said, "Here's the deal. My client owes the county about $200 in fines and fees. You boys have tacked on four hundred more for your own fun and games. We'll pay a hundred of that, total of three hundred max, and we'll have six months to pay it. That's it, take it or leave it."

Snowden put on a phony smile, shook his head, and said, "Sorry, Ms. Wyatt, but we can't live with that."

Without taking her eyes off Snowden, Mattie reached into her briefcase and whipped out some papers. "Then try living with this," she said, waving the papers in his face. "It's a lawsuit to be filed in federal court against Judicial Response Associates—I'll add you later as a defendant—for wrongful arrest and wrongful imprisonment. You see, Mr. Snowden, the Constitution says, quite clearly, that you cannot imprison a poor person for failing to pay his debts. I don't expect you to know this because you work for a bunch of crooks. However, trust me on this, the federal judges understand it because they've read the Constitution, most of them anyway. Debtors' prisons are illegal. Ever heard of the Equal Protection Clause?"

Snowden's mouth was open but words failed him.

She pressed on. "Didn't think so. Maybe your lawyers can explain it, at three hundred bucks an hour. I'm telling you so you can tell your bosses that I'll keep you in court for the next two years. I'll drown you in paperwork. I'll drag your asses through hours of depositions and discover all your dirty little tricks. It'll all come out. I'll hound you into the ground and make your lives miserable. You'll have nightmares about me. And in the end I'll win the case, plus I'll collect attorneys' fees." She pushed the lawsuit into his chest and he reluctantly took it.

They wheeled about and marched away, leaving Snowden weak-kneed and shell-shocked and already having glimpses of the nightmares. Samantha, stunned in her own way, whispered, "Can't we bankrupt the $300?"

Suddenly composed, Mattie said with a grin, "Of course we can. And we will."

Thirty minutes later, Mattie stood before the judge and

announced they had reached a deal for the immediate release of her client, Mr. Stocky Purvis. Lady was in tears as she left the courthouse and headed for the jail.

Driving back to Brady, Mattie said, "A license to practice law is a powerful tool, Samantha, when it's used to help little people. Crooks like Snowden are accustomed to bullying folks who can't afford representation. But you get a good lawyer involved and the bullying stops immediately."

"You're a pretty good bully yourself."

"I've had practice."

"When did you prepare the lawsuit?"

"We keep them in inventory. The file is actually called 'Dummy Lawsuits.' Just plug in a different name, splash the words 'Federal Court' all over it, and they scatter like squirrels."

Dummy lawsuits. Scattering like squirrels. Samantha wondered how many of her classmates at Columbia had been exposed to such legal tactics.

At two that afternoon, Samantha was sitting in the main courtroom of the Noland County Courthouse patting the knee of a terrified Phoebe Fanning. Her facial wounds had now turned dark blue and looked even worse. She had arrived at court with a thick layer of makeup, which Annette didn't approve of. She instructed their client to go to the restroom and scrub it off.

Once again, Randy Fanning was driven over with his escort and entered the courtroom looking even rougher than he had two days earlier. He had been served a copy of the divorce and appeared perturbed by it. He glared at his wife, and at Samantha, as a deputy removed his handcuffs.

The Circuit Court judge was Jeb Battle, an eager youngster who looked no more than thirty. Since the legal aid clinic handled a lot of domestic work, Annette was a regular and claimed to get on well with His Honor. The judge called things to order and approved a few uncontested matters while they waited. When he called *Fanning versus Fanning*, Annette and Samantha moved with their client through the bar to a table near the bench. Randy Fanning walked to another table, with a deputy close by, and waited for Hump to waddle into place. Judge Battle looked closely at Phoebe, at her bruised face, and, without saying a word, made his decision.

He said, "This divorce was filed Monday. Have you been served a copy, Mr. Fanning? You may remain seated."

"Yes sir, I have a copy."

"Mr. Humphrey, I understand a bond will be set in the morning, is that right?"

"Yes sir."

"We are here on a motion for a temporary restraining order. Phoebe Fanning is asking the court to order Randall Fanning to stay away from the couple's residence, the couple's three children, Phoebe herself, and anyone in her immediate family. Do you object to this, Mr. Humphrey?"

"Of course we do, Your Honor. This matter is getting blown way out of proportion." Hump was on his feet, waving his hands dramatically, his voice getting twangier with each sentence. "The couple had a fight, and it's not the first one, and not all fights have been caused by my client, but, yes, he was in a fight with his wife. Obviously, they are having problems, but they're trying to work things out. If we could all just take a deep breath, get Randy out of jail and back to work, I feel sure these two can iron out some of their differences. My client misses his children and he really wants to go home."

"She's filed for divorce, Mr. Humphrey," the judge said sternly. "Looks like she's pretty serious about splitting up."

"And divorces can be dismissed as quickly as they are filed, see it all the time, Your Honor. My client is even willing to go to one of those marriage counselors if that'll make her happy."

Annette interrupted: "Judge, we're far beyond counseling. Mr. Humphrey's client is facing a malicious wounding charge, and possibly jail time. He's hoping all of this will simply go away and his client walks free. That will not happen. This divorce will not be dismissed."

Judge Battle asked, "Who owns the house?"

Annette replied, "A landlord. They're renting."

"And where are the children?"

"They're away, out of town, in a safe place."

Other than a few pieces of mismatched furniture, the house was already empty. Phoebe had moved most of their belongings to a storage unit. She was hiding in a motel in Grundy, Virginia, an hour away. Through an emergency fund, the legal clinic was paying for her room and meals. Her plans were to move to Kentucky and live near a relative, but nothing was certain.

Judge Battle looked directly at Randy Fanning and said, "Mr. Fanning, I'm granting the relief asked for in this motion, word for word. When you get out of jail, you are not to have any contact with your wife, your own children, or anyone in your wife's immediate family. Until further orders, you are not to go near the home you and your wife are renting. No contact. Just stay away, understood?"

Randy leaned over and whispered something to his lawyer. Hump said, "Judge, can he have an hour to get his clothes and things?"

"One hour. And I'll send a deputy with him. Let me know when he's released."

Annette stood and said, "Your Honor, my client feels threatened and frightened. When we left court on Monday, we were confronted on the front steps of the courthouse by Mr. Fanning's brother Tony and a couple of other tough guys. My client was told to dismiss the criminal charges, or else. It was a brief altercation, but unsettling nonetheless."

Judge Battle again glared at Randy Fanning, and asked, "This true?"

Randy said, "I don't know, Judge, I wasn't there."

"Was your brother?"

"Maybe. If she says so."

"I take a dim view of intimidation, Mr. Fanning. I suggest you have a chat with your brother and get him in line. Otherwise, I'll call in the sheriff."

"Thank you, Your Honor," Annette said.

Randy was handcuffed and led away, Hump following along whispering that things were going to be okay. Judge Battle tapped his gavel and called for a recess. Samantha, Annette, and Phoebe left the courtroom and stepped outside, half expecting more trouble.

Tony Fanning and a friend were waiting behind a pickup truck parked on Main Street. They saw the ladies and began walking toward them, both smoking and looking tough. "Oh boy," Annette said under her breath. "He doesn't scare me," Phoebe said. The two men blocked the sidewalk, but just as Tony was about to speak, Donovan Gray appeared from nowhere and said loudly, "Well, ladies, how did it go?"

Tony and his buddy lost every ounce of badness they'd had only seconds earlier. They backed away, avoiding eye contact, and wanting no part of Donovan. "Excuse us, fellas," Donovan said in an effort to provoke them. As he walked by, his eyes flashed at Tony, who held the glare for only a second before looking away.

After three straight dinners with Annette and her kids, Samantha begged off, saying she needed to study and retire early. She fixed a bowl of soup on a hot plate, spent another hour on the seminar materials, and put them aside. It was hard to imagine running a general practice on Main Street and trying to survive on no-fault divorces and real estate closings. Annette had said more than once that most of the lawyers in Brady were just scratching out livelihoods and trying to net $30,000 a year. Her salary was $40,000, same as Mattie's. Annette had laughed when she said, "It's probably the only place in the country where the legal aid lawyers make more than the average private practitioner." She said Donovan made far more than anyone else, but then he took greater risks.

He was also the biggest contributor to the clinic, where all funding was private. There was some foundation money, and a few big law firms from "up north" kicked in generously, but Mattie still struggled to raise the $200,000 annual goal. Annette said,

"We'd love to pay you something, but the money's just not here." Samantha assured her she was content with the arrangement.

Her Internet connection was through Annette's satellite system, perhaps the slowest in North America. "It takes patience," she had said. Luckily, patience was plentiful these days as Samantha found herself happily settling into a routine that included quiet nights and plenty of sleep. She went online to check the local newspapers, the *Times* out of Roanoke and the *Gazette* out of Charleston, West Virginia. In the *Gazette* she found an interesting story under the headline "Ecoterrorists Suspected in Latest Spree."

For the past two years, a gang had been attacking heavy equipment in several strip mines in southern West Virginia. A spokesman for a coal company referred to them as "ecoterrorists" and threatened all manner of reprisals if and when they were caught. Their favorite method of destruction was to wait until predawn hours and fire away from the safety of surrounding hills. They were excellent snipers, used the latest military rifles, and were proving quite efficient in disabling the hundred-ton off-road coal-mining trucks built by Caterpillar. Their rubber tires were fifteen feet in circumference, weighed a thousand pounds, and sold for $18,000 apiece. Each mining truck had six tires, and evidently these were easy targets for the snipers. There was a photo of a dozen yellow trucks, all idle and lined up neatly in an impressive show of muscle. A foreman was pointing to the flat tires—twenty-eight of them. He said a night watchman was startled at 3:40 a.m. when the assault began. In a perfectly coordinated attack, the bullets began hitting the tires, which exploded like small bombs. He wisely took cover in a ditch while calling the sheriff. By the time law enforcement arrived, the snipers had had their fun and were long gone. The sheriff said he was hard at work on the case but conceded it would be difficult to track down the "thugs." The site, known as the Bull Forge Mine, was next to Winnow Mountain and Helley's Bluff, both over three thousand feet in height and thick with untouched hardwoods. From deep in those forests, it was easy to hide and easy to fire at trucks, day or night. However, the sheriff said that in his opinion these were not just a bunch of guys with deer rifles having some fun. From wherever they were hiding, they were hitting targets a thousand yards away. The bullets found in some of the tires were 51-millimeter military-style slugs, obviously fired from sophisticated sniper rifles.

The story recapped recent attacks. The ecoterrorists picked their targets carefully, and since there was no shortage of strip mines on the map, they seemed to wait patiently until the mining trucks were parked in just the right places. It was noted that the snipers seemed to be concerned with avoiding injury to others. They had yet to fire upon a vehicle that wasn't parked, and many of the mines worked twenty-four hours a day. Six weeks earlier, at the Red Valley site in Martin County, twenty-two tires had been ruined in a barrage that seemed to last only seconds, according to another night watchman. As of now, four coal companies were offering rewards totaling $200,000.

There was no link to the Bullington Mine attack two years earlier, where, in the most brazen act of sabotage in decades, explosives from the company's own warehouse were used to damage six dump trucks, two draglines, two track loaders, a temporary office building, and the warehouse itself. Damages exceeded $5 million. No suspects had been arrested; none existed.

Samantha dug through the newspaper's archives, and found herself cheering for the ecoterrorists. Later, as she began to doze off, she reluctantly pulled up the *New York Times*. Except for a rare Sunday morning, back in her New York days, she seldom did more than scan it. Now, avoiding the Business section, she zipped through it but stopped cold in the Dining section. The food critic was trashing a new restaurant in Tribeca, a hot spot she had been to a month earlier. There was a photo of the bar scene, with young professionals stacked two deep, sipping and smiling and waiting for their tables. She remembered the food as excellent and soon lost interest in the reviewer's complaints. Instead, she stared at the photo. She could hear the din of the crowd; she could feel the frenetic energy. How good would a martini taste right now? And a two-hour dinner with friends, all the while keeping an eye out for cute guys?

For the first time she felt a bit homesick, but soon brushed it off. She could leave tomorrow if she wanted to. She could certainly earn more money back in the city than she was making in Brady. If she wanted to leave, there was nothing to hold her back.

12

The hike began at the end of a long-abandoned logging trail no one but Donovan could have possibly found. The drive getting there required the skill and nerve of a stunt driver, and at times Samantha was certain they were sliding into the valley. But he made it to a small opening heavily shaded with oak, gum, and chestnut, and said, "This is the end of the road."

"You call that a road?" she said as she slowly opened her door. He laughed and said, "It's a four-lane compared to some of these trails." She was thinking that life in the big city had done nothing to prepare her for this, but she was also thrilled at the thought of adventure. His only advice had been to "wear boots to hike in and neutral clothing." She understood the boots, but the clothing required an explanation.

"We have to blend in," he said. "They'll be watching for us and we'll be trespassing."

"Any chance of getting arrested again?" she had asked.

"Slim. They can't catch us."

The boots had been purchased the day before at the dollar store in Brady—$45 and a bit stiff and tight. She wore old khakis and a gray sweatshirt with "Columbia Law" across the front in small letters. He, on the other hand, wore green hunter's camouflage and state-of-the-art, mail-order hiking boots with a thousand miles on them. He opened the rear hatch of the Jeep and removed a backpack which he slung over his shoulders. When it was in place, he removed a rifle with a large scope. When she saw it she said, "Hunting, are we?"

"No, it's for protection. A lot of bears in these parts."

She doubted that, but was not sure what to believe. For a few minutes, they walked a trail that someone had used before, but not often. The incline was slight, the undergrowth thick with sassafras, redbud, foamflower, and red catchfly, plant life he casually pointed out as if fluent in another language. For her benefit, he moved at an easy pace, but she knew he could sprint up the mountain anytime he wanted. Soon she was panting and sweating, but she was determined to stay on his heels.

It was mandatory for all single professionals in the city to own a gym membership, and not just any gym. It had to be the right one—the right place and the right outfit, the right time of the day or night to be seen sweating and grunting and getting properly toned for $250 a month. Samantha's membership had collapsed under the ruthless demands of Scully & Pershing, had expired two years earlier, and had not been missed in the least. Her workouts had been reduced to long walks in the city. Those, along with light eating habits, had kept the weight off, but she was far from fit. The new boots grew heavier with each turn as they zigzagged upward.

They stopped at a small clearing and looked through the woods into a long, deep valley with mountain ridges in the distance. The view was spectacular, and she appreciated the break. He waved an arm and said, "These are the most biodiverse mountains in North America, much older than any other range. Home to thousands of species of plants and wildlife not found anywhere else. It took an eternity for them to become what they are." A pause as he soaked in the scenery. Like a tour guide who needed no prompting, he went on. "About a million years ago, coal began to form, seams of it. That was the curse. Now we're destroying the mountains as fast as possible to extract it so we can have all the cheap energy we can eat. Every person in this country uses twenty pounds of coal per day. I did some research into coal usage per region; there's a Web site. Did you know that the average person in Manhattan uses eight pounds of coal each day that comes from strip-mining here in Appalachia?"

"Sorry, I didn't know that. Where do the other twelve pounds come from?"

"Deep mines here in the East. Ohio, Pennsylvania, places where they mine coal the old-fashioned way and protect the mountains." He sat his backpack on the ground and pulled out binoculars. Through them he scanned the view and found what he wanted. He handed them to her and said, "Over there, at about two o'clock, you can barely see an area that's gray and brown." She looked through the binoculars, focused them, and said, "Okay, got it."

"That's the Bull Forge Mine in West Virginia, one of the largest stripping operations we've seen."

"I read about it last night. They had a little trouble a few months back. Some truck tires were used as target practice."

He turned and smiled at her. "Doing your homework, huh?"

"I have a laptop and it can find Google in Brady. The ecoterrorists struck again, right?"

"That's what they say."

"Who are these guys?"

"Hopefully, we'll never know." He was standing slightly ahead of her, still gazing in the distance, and as he spoke his left hand instinctively reached back an inch or two and touched the stock of his rifle. She barely caught it.

They left the clearing and began the real climb. The trail, when there was one, was barely discernible, and Donovan seemed not to notice it. He went from tree to tree, looking ahead for the next landmark, glancing down to check his footing. The hike became steeper and Samantha's thighs and calves began to ache. The cheap boots pinched the arches of her feet. Her breathing was labored, and after fifteen minutes of silent climbing she said, "Did you bring any water?"

A rotting log made a pleasant resting place as they shared a bottle. He didn't ask how she was doing and she didn't inquire as to how much longer they would hike. When they caught their breath, he said, "We're sitting on Dublin Mountain, about three hundred feet from the top. It's next door to Enid Mountain, which you'll see in a few minutes. If all goes as planned, in about six months Strayhorn Coal will bring in the dozers, thoroughly scalp this mountain, destroy all of these beautiful hardwoods, scatter all the animals, and start blasting away. Their application for a strip-mining permit is nearing approval. We've fought it for two years, but the fix is in." He waved an arm at the trees and said, "This will all be gone before we know it."

"Why not at least harvest the trees?"

"Because they're brutes. Once a coal company gets the green light, it goes crazy. They're after the coal, dammit, and nothing else matters. They destroy everything in their path—forests, timber, wildlife—and they run over anyone who gets in their way: landowners, local residents, regulators, politicians, and especially activists and environmentalists. It's a war, with no middle ground."

Samantha looked at the dense forest and shook her head in disbelief. She said, "It can't be legal."

"It's legal because it's not illegal. The legality of mountaintop removal has been litigated for years; it's still in the courts. But nothing has stopped it."

"Who owns this land?"

"Strayhorn does now, so we're trespassing, and, believe me, they would love to catch me up here, three days before the trial. Don't worry, though, we're safe. For about a hundred years this land was owned by the Herman family. They sold out two years ago and built a mansion on a beach somewhere." He pointed to his right and said, "There is an old family home just over that hill, about half a mile down the valley, been in the family for decades. It's abandoned now, empty. It'll take the bulldozers about two hours to level the house and outbuildings. There's a small family cemetery under an old oak not far from the house, a little white picket fence around the graves. Very quaint. It'll all be shoved down the valley—headstones, coffins, bones, whatever. Strayhorn doesn't give a damn and the Hermans are rich enough to forget where they came from."

She took another sip of water and tried to wiggle her toes. He reached into his backpack, removed two granola bars, and handed her one. "Thanks."

"Does Mattie know you're here?" he asked.

"I'm living under the assumption that Mattie, and Annette and Barb and probably even Claudelle, know just about every move I make. As you like to say, 'It's a small town.'"

"I've said nothing."

"It's Friday afternoon and things were slow around the office. I told Mattie you asked me if I wanted to go sightseeing. That's all."

"Good, then we went sightseeing. She doesn't need to know where."

"She thinks you should settle the lawsuit, to at least get something for the mother of the two boys."

He smiled and took a large bite. Seconds passed, then a full minute, and Samantha realized that long gaps in conversation did not make him uncomfortable. Finally, he said, "I love my aunt, but she knows nothing about litigation. I left her little legal clinic because I wanted to do big things, take on big lawsuits, get big verdicts, make big coal companies pay for their sins. I've had big wins and big losses, and like a lot of trial lawyers I live on the edge. Up and down. Flush one year and broke the next. I'm sure you got a taste of that as a kid."

"No, we were never broke, far from it. I was aware that my father sometimes lost, but there was always plenty of money. At least, until he lost it and went to prison."

"What was that like, from your standpoint? You were a teenager, right?"

"Look, Donovan, you're separated from your wife and you don't want to talk about it. Fine. My father went to prison and I don't want to talk about it. Let's make a deal."

"Fair enough. We should move on."

They trekked upward, slower and slower as the trail disappeared and the terrain became even steeper. Pebbles and stones trickled behind them as they grabbed saplings to pull themselves up. At one point, as they stopped to catch a breath, Donovan suggested that Samantha take the lead so that he could catch her if she stumbled and slid backward. She did so, and he stayed close, with one hand on her hip, sort of guiding, soft of shoving. Finally they reached the summit of Dublin Mountain, and as they emerged from the forest into a small, rocky clearing, he said, "We have to be careful here. This is our hiding place. Just over those rocks is Enid Mountain where Strayhorn is hard at work. They have some security guys who occasionally pay attention to this area. We've been in litigation for over a year, and we've had a couple of nasty altercations."

"Such as?"

He removed his backpack and leaned his rifle against a rock. "You've seen the photographs in my office. The first time we came here with a photographer they caught us and tried to press charges. I ran to the judge and got an order which allowed us access on a very limited basis. After that, the judge told us to stay off their property."

"I haven't seen any bears. Why the rifle?"

"Protection. Get down and come here." They crouched and walked a few steps to a gap between two boulders. Below them lay the remains of Enid Mountain, which in years past rose to thirty-two hundred feet, but was now reduced to a pockmarked landscape of dust and rock and crawling machinery. The operation was vast, stretching from the remains of the mountain and jutting over the ridges around it. Mining trucks hauling a hundred tons of fresh, unwashed coal bounced along a myriad of switchbacks, descending steadily like ants marching mindlessly in formation. A massive dragline the size of her apartment building swung back and forth, its bucket clawing into the earth and digging out two hundred cubic yards of overburden and dumping it into neat piles. Loaders with smaller buckets worked methodically to scoop it up and dump it into another fleet of trucks that hauled it to an area where bulldozers shoved it down the valley. Lower on the mountain, or the mine site, track shovels dug coal from the exposed seam and dumped it into the mining trucks that slowly inched away when loaded, straining under their cargo as they bounced along. Clouds of dust hung over every phase of the operation.

Donovan, in a low, somber voice as if he might be overheard, said, "Quite a shock, huh?"

" 'Shock' is the right word," she said. "Mattie showed me three strip mines on the way to Colton on Wednesday, but we were not this close. Kinda makes you sick."

"Yes, and you never get used to it. It's an ongoing rape of the land, a new assault every day."

The violence was slow, methodical, and efficient. After a few minutes, he said, "In two years, they've knocked off eight hundred feet of the mountain. They've gone through four or five seams, with about that many left to strip. When it's over, Enid Mountain will yield about three million tons of coal, at an average price of sixty bucks a ton. The math gets easy."

They huddled close together, careful not to actually touch, and watched the desolation. A bulldozer shoved a load perilously close to the edge, and the larger rocks tumbled down a wall of fill a thousand feet in height. The rocks bounced and fell until they were out of sight far below. He said, "And that's how it happened. Try and imagine the mountain about five hundred feet higher, where it was nineteen months ago. That's when one of those dozers pushed the boulder that traveled almost a mile before it hit the trailer where the Tate boys were asleep." He found his binoculars and began searching, then handed them to her. "Stay low, now," he said. "Far down in the valley there, beyond the fill, you can barely see a little white building. Used to be a church. Got it?"

After a few seconds she said, "Got it."

"Just beyond the church there was a tiny settlement of a few houses and trailers. You can't see it from here. As I said, it's about a mile away and the trees are blocking the view. At trial, we plan to show a video that reenacts the path of the boulder. It actually flew over the church, probably at about eighty miles an hour, based on its weight, and bounced once or twice, then banged into the Tate trailer."

"You have the boulder?"

"Yes and no. It weighs six tons, so we will not be hauling it into the courtroom. But it's still there and we have plenty of photographs. Four days after the accident, the coal company tried to remove it with explosives and machinery, but we were able to stop them. Thugs, nothing but thugs. They actually showed up with a full crew the day after the funeral, entered onto property they had no claim to, and were all set to dismantle the boulder, regardless of how much damage they did to everything else. I called the sheriff and there were some tense moments."

"You had the case four days after the accident?"

"No, I had the case the day after the accident. Less than twenty-four hours. I got to the mother's brother. You have to be quick out here."

"My father would be impressed."

Donovan glanced at his watch and looked at Enid Mountain. He said, "They're scheduled to blast at 4:00 p.m., so you're in for some excitement."

"Can't wait."

"You see that odd-looking truck with a tall boom attached to the rear, over there to the far left?"

"Are you kidding? There are a hundred trucks."

"It's not a haul truck; it's much smaller. All by itself."

"Okay, yes, I got it. What is it?"

"Don't know if it has an official name, but it's known as the blasting truck." With the binoculars, Samantha zeroed in on the truck and the busy crew around it. "What are they doing?"

"Right now, they're starting to drill. The regulations allow them to go down sixty feet with a blast hole that's seven inches in diameter. The holes are ten feet apart, sort of in a grid. The regulations limit them to forty holes per blast. Regs here and regs there, lots of rules on the books. Not surprisingly, they are routinely ignored and companies like Strayhorn are accustomed to doing whatever they want. No one is really watching, except for maybe an environmental group here and there. They'll take a video, file a complaint, the company gets a nuisance fine, a slap on the wrist, life goes on. The regulators are drawing their checks and sleeping peacefully."

A large bearded man crept silently behind them and slapped Donovan on the shoulders with a loud "Boom!" Donovan yelled, "Shit!" as Samantha yelped and dropped the binoculars. Stricken, they wheeled about and gasped at the grinning face of a burly man you wouldn't want to fistfight. "Sonofabitch," Donovan hissed without reaching for his rifle. Samantha desperately looked for an escape trail.

The man stayed low and laughed at the two. He stuck out a hand in Samantha's direction and said, "Vic Canzarro, friend of the mountains." She was trying to catch her breath and unable to extend a hand.

"Did you have to scare the hell out of us?" Donovan growled.

"No, but it sure is fun."

"You know him?" Samantha asked.

"Afraid so. He's a friend, or more of an acquaintance, actually. Vic, this is Samantha Kofer, an intern with Mattie's legal clinic." They finally shook hands. "A pleasure," Vic said. "What brings you to the coalfields?"

"It's a long story," she said, exhaling, heart and lungs now working. "A very long story."

Vic dropped a backpack and sat on a rock. He was sweating from the trek up and needed water. He offered a bottle to Samantha but she declined. "Columbia Law?" he asked, looking at her sweatshirt.

"Yes. I worked in New York until ten days ago when the world crashed and I got laid off or furloughed or something like that. Are you a lawyer?" She sat on another rock where Donovan joined her.

"Hell no. I used to be a mine safety inspector but managed to get myself fired. It's another long story."

"We all have long stories," Donovan said, taking a bottle of water. "Vic here is my expert witness. Typical expert—pay him enough and he'll tell the jury anything you want. Next week he'll spend a long day on the stand having a delightful time clicking off a never-ending list of Strayhorn Coal's safety violations. Then the defense lawyers will eat his lunch."

Vic laughed at this. "I'm looking forward to it," he said. "Going to trial with Donovan is always exciting, especially when he wins, which is not very often."

"I win as many as I lose."

Vic wore a flannel shirt, faded jeans, boots caked with old mud, and had the look of a veteran hiker who could whip out a tent from his backpack and spend the next week in the woods. "Are they drilling?" he asked Donovan.

"Just started, supposed to blast at four."

Vic checked his watch and asked, "Are we ready for trial?"

"Oh, yes. They doubled their offer this afternoon to two hundred thousand. I countered at nine-fifty."

"You're crazy, you know that? Take the money and get something for the family." He looked at Samantha and asked, "Do you know the facts?"

"Most of them," she said. "I've seen the photographs and maps."

"Never trust a jury around here. I keep telling Donovan this but he won't listen."

"Are you filming?" Donovan asked, changing the subject.

"Of course." They chatted for a few minutes as both men kept glancing at their watches. Vic removed a small camera from his backpack and took a position between two boulders. Donovan said to Samantha, "Since the inspectors are not watching, it's safe to assume Strayhorn will break a few rules when they start blasting. We'll catch it on video, and maybe show it to the jury next week. It's not that we really need it, because we have so much dirt on the company. They'll put their engineers on the stand and they'll lie about how closely they follow all regulations. We'll prove otherwise."

He and Samantha eased into positions next to Vic, who was filming and lost in his work. Donovan said, "They fill each hole with a concoction known as ANFO—an acronym for a combination of ammonium nitrate and fuel oil. It's too dangerous to transport so they mix it on the site. That's what they're doing now. That truck is funneling diesel fuel into the blast holes while that crew to the left there is rigging up the blasting caps and detonators. How many holes, Vic?"

"I count sixty."

"So they're clearly in violation, which is typical." Samantha watched through binoculars as men with shovels began backfilling the blast holes. A wire ran from the top of each one and two men were busy gathering them into a bundle. Sacks of ammonium nitrate were dropped into the blast holes, which were topped off with gallons of diesel fuel. The work was slow; 4:00 p.m. came and went. Finally, when the blasting truck backed away, Donovan said, "It won't be long now." The grid was cleared as the crews and trucks disappeared. A siren sounded and that area of the site became still.

The explosions were a distant rumble as plumes of dust and smoke shot into the air, each blast only a split second after the one before it. The plumes rose in perfect formation, like fountains in a Vegas water show, and the earth began to crumble. A wide swath of ancient rock fell in violent waves as the ground shook. Dust boiled from the blast site and formed a thick cloud above it. With no wind, the cloud hung over the rubble with nowhere to go. Much like a play-by-play announcer, Donovan said, "They're blasting three times a day. Their permit allows only twice. Multiply all of this by dozens of active surface mines, and they're using about a million pounds of explosives every day here in coal country."

"We got a problem," Vic said calmly. "We've been spotted."

"Where?" Donovan asked, taking the binoculars from Samantha.

"Up there, by the trailer."

Donovan focused on the trailer. On a platform next to it, two men with hard hats were apparently watching them through their own binoculars. Donovan waved; one of the men waved back. Donovan shot him the bird; the man returned the greeting.

"How long have they been there?" he asked.

"Don't know," Vic said. "But let's get outta here." They grabbed their backpacks and the rifle, and began a hurried descent down the mountain. Samantha slipped and almost fell. Vic caught her and kept her hand tight in his. They followed Donovan, ducking around trees, dodging boulders, clawing through underbrush, with no trail visible. After a few minutes, they stopped in a narrow open area. Vic pointed and said, "I came in this way. Call me when you get to your Jeep." He disappeared into the woods, and they continued downward. The trail was not as steep and they managed to carefully jog for a few hundred yards. "Are we okay?" Samantha finally asked.

"We're fine," he said calmly. "They don't know the trails like I do. And if they catch us they can't kill us."

She found little comfort in that. They picked up speed as the trail continued to flatten. The Jeep came into view a hundred yards away and Donovan paused for a second to search for other vehicles. "They haven't found us," he said. As they drove away, he sent a text to Vic. All was clear. They bounced down the mountain, dodging holes and ravines wide enough to swallow the Jeep, and after a few minutes he said, "We're no longer on Strayhorn's property." He turned onto a paved road just as a large, dust-covered pickup truck raced around a curve. "That's them," he said. The truck moved to the middle of the road to block the Jeep, but Donovan hit the gas and passed it on the shoulder. At least three rough-looking characters in hard hats were in the truck, scowling and looking for trouble. They stopped abruptly and began turning around to give chase, but the Jeep left them behind.

Racing through the back roads of Hopper County, Donovan kept one eye on his mirror and said nothing. "Do you think they got your license plate number?" she asked.

"Oh, they know it's me. They'll run to the judge Monday morning and cry like babies. I'll deny it all and tell them to stop whining. Let's pick a jury."

They passed the courthouse on Center Street in Colton. Donovan nodded in its direction and said, "There it is. Ground zero. The ugliest courthouse in Virginia."

"I was there Wednesday, with Mattie."

"Did you like the courtroom?"

"It's kind of weird, but I'm not much of an expert on court-rooms. I've always tried to avoid them."

"I love them. It's the only place where the little guy can go toe-to-toe on a level field with a big, crooked corporation. A person with nothing—no money, no power—nothing but a set of facts can file a lawsuit and force a billion-dollar company to show up for a fair fight."

"It's not always fair, is it?"

"Sure it is. If they cheat, then I cheat. They play dirty, I get even dirtier. You gotta love justice."

"You sound like my father. It's frightening."

"And you sound like my wife. She has no stomach for the work I do."

"Let's talk about something else."

"Okay, do you have plans for tomorrow?"

"Saturday in Brady. The clinic is closed, so what are my options?"

"How about another adventure?"

"Does it involve guns?"

"No, I promise I will not carry a gun."

"Will we trespass on someone's property? Is there a chance of getting arrested?"

"No, I promise."

"Sounds pretty dull. I'm in."

13

Blythe called bright and early on Saturday morning with the incredible news that she had the day off, a rarity in her world. Her employment situation had stabilized; her firm had apparently stopped its bloodletting. No one had been shown the door in the past five days and promises were finally trickling down from above. A gorgeous fall day in the city with nothing to do but shop and worry about lunch and enjoy being young and single. She missed her roommate, and at that moment Samantha was painfully homesick. She had been away now for only two weeks, but given the distance it seemed like a year. They talked for half an hour before both needed to get on with their day.

Samantha showered and dressed quickly, eager to ease out of the driveway before Kim and Adam came bouncing out of the house with a list of things to do. So far, it seemed as though Annette and her children allowed their guest to come and go without notice. She lived as quietly as possible, and had yet to see them peeking through screens and around curtains. But, she was also quite aware that most of Brady was curious about the alien from New York.

For that reason, and because his marital situation was unstable, Donovan had suggested that she meet him at the county airport, eleven miles east of town. They would rendezvous there and begin the next adventure, the details of which he kept to himself. She was surprised to learn there was an airport within a hundred miles of

Brady. Late Friday night, she searched it online and found nothing. How can an airport not have a Web site?

Not only was it missing a Web site, it also lacked aircraft, or at least none that she could see as the gravel road came to an end at the Noland County Airfield. Donovan's Jeep was parked next to a small, metal building, and was the only vehicle in sight. She walked through the only door she saw and crossed through what appeared to be the lobby, with folding chairs and metal tables strewn with flying magazines. The walls were covered with fading photos of planes and aerial shots. The other door opened onto the ramp, and there was Donovan puttering around a very small airplane. She walked outside and said, "What's that?"

"Good morning," he said with a big smile. "Did you sleep well?"

"Eight hours. Are you a pilot?"

"I am, and this is a Cessna 172, better known as a Skyhawk. I practice law in five states and this little dude helps me get around. Plus, it's a valuable tool when it comes to spying on coal companies."

"Of course. And we're going spying?"

"Something like that." He gently folded down and locked a cowling that covered the engine. "Preflight is finished and she's ready to go. Your door is on the other side."

She didn't move. "I'm not so sure about this. I've never flown in anything that small."

"It's the safest airplane ever built. I have three thousand hours and I'm highly skilled, especially on a perfect day like this. Not a cloud in the sky, ideal temperature, and the trees are alive with the colors of autumn. Today is a pilot's dream."

"I don't know."

"Come on, where's your sense of adventure?"

"But it only has one engine."

"That's all it needs. And if the engine quits it'll glide forever and we'll find a nice pasture somewhere."

"In these mountains?"

"Let's go Samantha." She slowly walked around the tail and to the right-side door under the wing. He helped her into the seat and gently secured the seat belt and shoulder harness. He closed the door, locked it, and went around to the left side. She looked behind her at the cramped rear seat, and she looked in front of her at the wall of instruments and gauges.

"Are you claustrophobic?" he asked as he snapped his seat belt and harness into place. Their shoulders were about an inch apart.

"I am now."

"You're gonna love it. You'll be flying it before the day is over." He handed her a headset and said, "Stick this on. It's pretty loud in here and we'll talk through these." They arranged their headsets. "Say something," he said.

"Something." Thumbs-up, the headsets were working. He grabbed a checklist and ran through the items, carefully touching each instrument and gauge as he went. He pulled the yoke back and forth. An identical one on her side moved in tandem. "Please don't touch that," he said.

She shook her head quickly; she wasn't touching anything. He said, "Clear," and turned the key. The engine jumped to life as the propeller began spinning. The airplane shook as he pushed the throttle. He announced his intentions over the radio, and they began taxiing down the runway, which seemed short and narrow, to her anyway. "Is anyone listening?" she asked.

"I doubt it. It's very quiet this morning."

"Do you have the only airplane in Noland County?"

He pointed to some small hangars ahead, along the runway. "There are a few more down there. Not many." At the end of the runway, he revved the engine again and rechecked the controls and instruments. "Hang on." He pushed the throttle forward, gently released the brakes, and they were rolling. As they picked up speed he calmly counted, "Eighty miles an hour, ninety, a hundred," then he pulled the yoke back and they left the asphalt. For a moment, she felt weightless and her stomach flipped. "You okay?" he asked without looking at her.

"Fine," she said with clenched jaws. As they were climbing, he began banking to the left and completed a 180-degree turn. They were low, not far above the trees, and he picked up the main highway. "See that green truck parked down there in front of that store?" he asked. She nodded. "That's the asshole who followed me this morning. Hang on." He jiggled the yoke and the wings dipped and rose, a salute to the asshole in the green truck. When it was out of sight, he began climbing again.

"Why would they follow you on a Saturday morning?" she asked, her white knuckles digging into her knees.

"You'll have to ask them. Maybe because of what happened yesterday. Maybe because we show up in court Monday for a big trial. Who knows. They follow me all the time." Suddenly she felt a bit safer in the air. By the time they reached Brady she was relaxed and taking in the scenery not far below. He buzzed the town at five hundred feet and gave her a bird's view of where she lived and worked. Except for a ride in a hot air balloon in the Catskills, she had never seen the earth from such a low altitude, and it was fascinating, even thrilling. He climbed to a thousand feet and leveled off as they skipped across the hills. The radio was as silent as the one in Romey's old fake patrol car, and she asked, "What about radar and air traffic controllers and stuff like that? Is anybody out there?"

"Probably not. We're flying VFR—visual flight rules—so we're not required to check in with air control. On a business trip, I would file a flight plan and get plugged into the air traffic system, but not today. We're just joyriding." He pointed to a screen and explained, "That's my radar. If we get close to another plane, it'll show up there. Relax, I've never had a crash."

"A close call?"

"None. I take it very seriously, like most pilots."

"That's nice. Where are we going?"

"I don't know. Where do you want to go?"

"You're the pilot, and you don't know where we're going?"

He smiled, banked to the left, and pointed to an instrument. "This is the altimeter; it monitors the altitude, which is pretty important when you're in the mountains." They were inching up to fifteen hundred feet, where they leveled off. He pointed outside and said, "That's Cat Mountain, or what's left of it. A big operation." Ahead and to her right was the strip mine, which looked like all the rest: a barren landscape of rock and dirt in the midst of beautiful mountains, with overfill shoved far below into the valleys. She thought of Francine Crump, the client in search of a free will, and the land she wanted to preserve. It was somewhere down there, somewhere close to Cat Mountain. There were small homes along the creeks, a settlement here and there. The Skyhawk banked steeply to the right, and as it did a perfect 360, Samantha looked straight down at the mining trucks and loaders and other machinery. A blasting truck, front-end loaders, a dragline, mining trucks and haul trucks, track shovels, track loaders. Her knowledge was expanding. She spotted a supervisor who was standing beside an office, straining to watch the airplane.

"They work on Saturday, huh?" she asked.

He nodded and said, "Seven days a week, sometimes. All the unions are gone."

They climbed to three thousand feet and leveled off. "We're over Kentucky now, heading west and north," he said. If not for the headsets, he would have been yelling into the roar of the engine. "Just look. Too many to count." The strip mines dotted the mountains like ugly scars, dozens of them as far as she could see. They flew directly over several. Between them she noticed vast open areas covered with patches of grass and a few small trees. "What's that?" she asked, pointing just ahead. "That flat spot with no woods?"

"A casualty, a reclaimed site that was once a strip mine. That one in particular used to be Persimmon Mountain, elevation twenty-five hundred feet. They took off the top, got the coal, then set about to reclaim it. The law requires it to have the 'approximate original contour'—that's the key language—but how do you replace a mountain once it's gone?"

"I've read about that. The land must be equal to or better than it was before the mining."

"What a joke. The coal companies will tell you that reclaimed land is great for development—shopping centers, condos, and the like. They built a prison on one in Virginia. And they built a golf course on another. Problem is, nobody plays golf around here. Reclamation is a joke."

They flew over another strip mine, then another. After a while they all looked the same. "How many are active, as of today?" she asked.

"Dozens. We've lost about six hundred mountains in the last thirty years to strip-mining, and at the rate we're going there won't be many left. Demand for coal is rising, the price is up, so the companies are aggressively seeking permits to start stripping." He banked to the right and said, "Now we're going north, into West Virginia."

"And you're licensed to practice there?" she asked.

"Yes, and in Virginia and Kentucky."

"You mentioned five states before we took off."

"Sometimes I go into Tennessee and North Carolina, but not that often. We're litigating a coal ash dump in North Carolina, a lot of lawyers involved. Big case."

He loved his big cases. The lost mountains in West Virginia looked the same as those in Kentucky. The Cessna zigzagged right and left, banking steeply so she could take another look at the devastation, then leveling off to check out another one. "That's the Bull Forge Mine, straight ahead," he said. "You saw it yesterday from the ground."

"Oh yes. The ecoterrorists. Those guys are really pissing off the coal companies."

"That seems to be their intention."

"Too bad you didn't bring a rifle. We could blow out a few tires from the air."

"I've thought about it."

After an hour in the air, Donovan began a slow descent. By then, she was familiar with the altimeter, the airspeed indicator, and the compass. At two thousand feet, she asked, "Do we have a destination?"

"Yes, but first I want to show you something else. Coming up on your side is an area known as Hammer Valley." He waited a minute for them to clear a ridge; a long, steep valley appeared.

"We're gonna start down here at the end of it, near the town of Rockville, population three hundred." Two church steeples rose through the trees, then the town came into view, a picturesque little village hugging a creek and surrounded by mountains. They flew over the town and followed the creek. Dozens of homes, mainly trailers, were scattered along narrow county roads.

"This is what's known as a cancer cluster. Hammer Valley has the highest rate of cancer in North America, almost twenty times the national average. Bad cancers—liver, kidney, stomach, uterine, and lots of leukemia." He gently pulled back on the yoke and the plane ascended as a large hump rose before them. They cleared it by two hundred feet and were suddenly over a reclaimed mine site. "And this is why," he said. "The Peck Mountain strip mine." The mountain was gone, replaced by small hills smoothed by bulldozers and covered in brown grass. Behind an earthen dam, a large body of black liquid sat ominously. "That's the slurry pond. A company called Starke Energy came in here about thirty years ago and stripped out all the coal, one of the first big removal sites in Appalachia. They washed it right here and dumped the waste into a small lake that was once pristine. Then they built that dam and made the lake a lot bigger."

They were circling the slurry pond at one thousand feet. "Starke eventually sold out to Krull Mining, another faceless ape of a company that's really owned by a Russian oligarch, a thug with his finger in a bunch of mines around the world."

"A Russian?"

"Oh yeah. We got Russians, Ukrainians, Chinese, Indians, Canadians, as well as the usual lineup of Wall Street cowboys and local turncoats. There are a lot of absentee owners here in the coalfields, and you can imagine how much they care about the land and the people."

He banked again and Samantha was staring straight down at the slurry, which, from a thousand feet, appeared to have the texture of crude oil. "That's pretty ugly," she said. "Another lawsuit?"

"The biggest ever."

They landed on a runway even smaller than Noland County's, with no hint that a town was anywhere close. As they taxied to the ramp, she saw Vic Canzarro leaning on a fence, waiting. They stopped near the terminal; there was not another aircraft in sight. Donovan killed the engine, ran through his postflight checklist, and they crawled out of the Skyhawk.

As expected, Vic drove an all-wheel-drive muscle truck, suitable for off-road encounters with security guards. Samantha sat in the rear seat with a cooler, some backpacks, and, of course, a couple of rifles.

Vic was a smoker, not of the chain variety, but an enthusiastic one nonetheless. He cracked the window on his driver's side about an inch, just enough for half of his exhaust to escape while the other half whirled around the club cab. After the second cigarette, Samantha was gagging and lowered the rear window behind Donovan. He asked her what she was doing. She told him in plain language, and this touched off a tense conversation between Donovan and Vic about his habits. He swore he was trying to quit, had in fact quit on numerous occasions, and freely admitted that he fretted over the likelihood of an awful death from lung cancer. Donovan hammered away, leaving Samantha with the clear impression that these two had been bickering over the same issue for some time. Nothing got resolved and Vic fired up another.

The hills and trails led them deep into Hammer Valley, and finally to the crumbling home of one Jesse McKeever. "Who is Mr. McKeever, and why are we visiting him?" she asked from the rear seat as they turned in to the driveway.

"A potential client," Donovan said. "He's lost his wife, one son, one daughter, one brother, and two cousins to cancer. Kidney, liver, lung, brain, pretty much entire body." The truck stopped, and they waited a second for the dog. An angry pit bull flew off the porch and raced at them, ready to eat the tires. Vic honked and Jesse finally emerged. He called the dog, struck him with his cane, cursed him, and ordered him into the backyard. The stricken dog obeyed and disappeared.

They sat on crates and battered lawn chairs under a tree in the front yard. Samantha was not introduced to Jesse, who completely ignored her. He was a rugged old cuss who looked much older than sixty, with few teeth and thick wrinkles made permanent by a hard life and a harsh scowl that never left his face. Vic had tested the water from the McKeever well, and the results, while predictable, were grim. The water was polluted with VOCs—volatile organic compounds—poisons such as vinyl chloride, trichloroethylene, mercury, lead, and a dozen others. With great patience, Vic explained what the big words meant. Jesse got the gist of the message. Not only was it unsafe to drink; it should not be used for anything, period. Not for cooking, bathing, brushing teeth, washing clothes or dishes. Nothing. Jesse explained that they had started hauling in their drinking water some fifteen years earlier, but had continued to use well water for bathing and household cleaning. His boy died first, cancer in his digestive tract.

Donovan turned on a tape recorder and placed it on a rubber milk crate. Casually, and with complete empathy, he elicited an hour's worth of background on Jesse's family and the cancers that had ravaged it. Vic listened and smoked and occasionally asked a question himself. The stories were gut-wrenching, but Jesse went through them with little emotion. He had seen so much misery and he had been hardened by it.

"I want you to join our lawsuit, Mr. McKeever," Donovan said after he turned off the recorder. "We're planning to sue Krull Mining in federal court. We think we can prove that they dumped a lot of waste in their pond up there, and that they've known for years that it was leaking into the groundwater down here."

Jesse rested his chin on his cane and seemed to doze. "No lawsuit'll bring 'em back. They're gone forever."

"True, but they didn't have to die. That slurry pond killed them, and the men who own it should have to pay."

"How much?"

"I can't promise you a dime, but we'll sue Krull for millions.

You'll have plenty of company, Mr. McKeever. As of now I have about thirty other families here in Hammer Valley signed up and ready to go. All lost someone to cancer, all within the past ten years."

Jesse spat to his side, wiped his mouth on a sleeve, and said, "I heard about you. Plenty of talk up and down the valley. Some folks want to sue; others are still scared of the coal company, even though it's finished up there. I don't know what to do, really. I'll just tell you that. Don't know which way to go."

"Okay, think about it. But promise me one thing; when you get ready to fight, call me, not some other lawyer. I've been working on this case for three years, and we haven't even filed suit yet. I need you on my side, Mr. McKeever."

He agreed to think it over, and Donovan promised to come back in a couple weeks. They left Jesse in the shade, the dog once again by his side, and drove away. Nothing was said until Samantha asked, "Okay, how do you prove the company knew its sludge pond was contaminating Mr. McKeever's water?"

The two in the front seat exchanged a look, and for a few seconds there was no response. Vic reached for a cigarette and Donovan finally said, "The company has internal documents that clearly prove it knew of the contamination and did nothing; in fact it has covered up everything for the past ten years."

She opened her window again, took a long breath, and asked, "How did you get the documents if you haven't filed suit yet?"

"I didn't say we have the documents," Donovan said a bit defensively.

Vic added, "There have been a few investigations, by the EPA and other regulatory agencies. There's a lot of paperwork."

"Did the EPA find these bad documents?" she asked. Both men seemed tentative.

"Not all of them," Vic replied.

There was a gap in the conversation as she backed off. They turned onto a gravel road and bounced along for a mile or so. "When will you file the lawsuit?" she asked.

"Soon," Donovan said.

"Well, if I'm going to work in your office, I need to know these things, right?"

Donovan did not respond. They turned in to the front yard of an old trailer and parked behind a dirty car with no hubcaps and a bumper hanging by a wire. "And who is this?" she asked.

"Dolly Swaney," Donovan said. "Her husband died of liver cancer two years ago, at the age of forty-one."

"Is she a client?"

"Not yet," Donovan said as he opened the door. Dolly Swaney appeared on the front porch, a crumbling addition with broken steps. She was huge and wore a large, stained gown that fell almost to her bare feet.

"I think I'll wait in the truck," Samantha said.

They had an early lunch at the only diner in downtown Rockville, a hot, stuffy café with the smell of grease heavy in the air. The waitress placed three glasses of ice water on the table; all three glasses went untouched. Instead, they ordered diet sodas to go with their sandwiches. With no one sitting close, Samantha decided to continue the questioning.

"So, if you already have thirty clients, and you've been working on the case for three years, why haven't you filed suit by now?"

Both men glanced around as if someone might be listening. Satisfied, Donovan answered in a low voice, "This is a huge case, Samantha. Dozens of deaths, a defendant with enormously deep pockets, and liability that I think we can make clear at trial. I've already spent a hundred thousand bucks on the case, and it'll take much more than that to get it before a jury. It takes time: time to sign up the clients, time to do the research, time to put together a legal team that can fight the army of lawyers and experts Krull Mining will throw at its defense."

"It's also dangerous," Vic added. "There are a lot of bad actors in the coalfields, and Krull Mining is one of the worst. Not only is it a ruthless strip miner, it's also a vicious litigator. It's a beautiful lawsuit, but dealing with Krull Mining has scared away a lot of lawyers, guys who are usually on board in the big environmental cases."

Donovan said, "That's why I need some help. If you're bored and looking for some excitement, then let's go to work. I have a ton of documents that need to be reviewed."

She suppressed a laugh and said, "Great, more document review. I spent the first year with the firm buried in a vault doing nothing but document review. In Big Law, it's the curse of every rookie associate."

"This will be different, I assure you."

"Are these the incriminating documents, the good stuff?"

Both men glanced around again. The waitress arrived with the diet sodas and left them. It was doubtful she cared anything about litigation. Samantha leaned in low and hit them hard with "You already have these documents, don't you?"

Donovan replied, "Let's just say we have access to them. They went missing. Krull Mining knows they're missing, but they don't know who has them. After I file the lawsuit, the company will learn that I have access to them. That's all I can say."

As he spoke, Vic stared at her intently, watching for her reaction. His look said, "Can she be trusted?" His look was also skeptical. He wanted to talk about something else.

She asked, "What will Krull Mining do when it knows you have access?"

"Go berserk, but what the hell. We'll be in federal court, hopefully with a good judge, one who'll hold their feet to the fire."

Their platters arrived, scrawny sandwiches beside piles of fries, and they began eating. Vic asked her about New York and her life there. They were intrigued by her work in a firm with a thousand lawyers in the same building, and by her specialty in building sky-scrapers. She was tempted to make it sound slightly glamorous, but couldn't muster the necessary deceit. As she ignored the sand-wich and played with the fries, she couldn't help but wonder where Blythe and her friends were lunching; no doubt some chic restau-rant in the Village with cloth napkins, a wine list, and designer cuisine. Another world.

14

The Skyhawk climbed to five thousand feet, leveled off, and Donovan asked, "Are you ready?" By then she was enjoying flying at lower altitudes and absorbing the views, but she had no desire to take the controls. "Gently grab the yoke," he said, and she did.

"I've got it too, so don't worry," he said calmly. "The yoke controls the pitch of the nose, up and down, and it also turns the airplane. All movements are small and slow. Turn it slightly to the right." She did and they began a gradual bank to her side. She turned back to the left and they leveled off. She pushed the yoke forward, the nose dipped, and they began losing altitude. She glanced at the altimeter. "Level off at forty-five hundred," he said. "Keep the wings level." From forty-five hundred feet, they ascended back to five thousand, and Donovan put his hands in his lap. "How does it feel?"

"Awesome," she said. "I can't believe I'm doing this. It's so easy." The Skyhawk responded to the slightest movement of the yoke. Once she realized she was not going to crash it, she managed to relax a little and enjoy the thrill of her first flight.

"It's a great airplane, simple and safe, and you're flying it. You could go solo in a month."

"Let's not rush things."

They flew straight and level for a few minutes without talking. Samantha watched the instruments closely, glancing only briefly at the mountains below. He asked, "So, Captain, where are we going?"

"I have no idea. Not sure where we are and not sure where we're going."

"What would you like to see?"

She thought for a moment. "Mattie told me about your family's place and what happened there. I'd like to see Gray Mountain."

He hesitated for a second and said, "Then look at the heading indicator and turn left to a heading of 190 degrees. Do it slow and stay level." She executed the turn perfectly and kept the Skyhawk at five thousand feet. After a few minutes, she asked, "Okay, what would happen right now if the engine quit?"

He sort of shrugged as if this never crossed his mind. "First, I would try and restart it. If that didn't work, I'd start looking for a flat surface, a pasture or pipeline, maybe even a highway. At five thousand feet, a Skyhawk will glide for about seven miles so there's a lot of time. When I found my spot, I would circle around it, try and gauge the wind on the descent, and pull off a perfect emergency landing."

"I don't see any open areas down there."

"Then just pick your mountain and hope for the best."

"Sorry I asked."

"Relax. Fatalities in these planes are rare, and they're always caused by pilot error." He yawned and went quiet for a while. Samantha found it impossible to relax entirely, but was growing more confident by the minute. After a long break in conversation, she glanced at her co-pilot, who appeared to be dozing. Was he joking with her, or was he really asleep? Her first impulse was to yell into her mike and startle him; instead, she checked the instruments, made sure the airplane was flying straight and the wings were perfectly level, and fought the urge to panic. She caught herself gripping the yoke and let go for a second. The fuel gauge showed half a tank. If he wanted to sleep, go ahead. She would give him a few minutes to nap, then panic. She released the yoke again and realized the plane would fly by itself, with only a light touch here and there for corrections. She glanced at her watch. Five minutes, ten, fifteen. The mountains were slowly passing under them. There was nothing on the radar to indicate traffic. She kept her cool, but there was a growing sense that she needed to scream.

He awoke with a cough and quickly scanned the instruments. "Nice job, Samantha."

"How was your nap?"

"Fine. Sometimes I get sleepy up here. The drone of the engine gets monotonous and I have trouble staying awake. On long trips, I'll turn on the autopilot and doze off for a few minutes."

She wasn't sure how to respond to this and let it pass. "Do you know where we are?" she asked. He looked ahead and without hesitation said, "Sure, we're approaching Noland County. At eleven o'clock is Cat Mountain. You'll fly just to the left of it, and I'll take over from there. Descend to four thousand feet."

They flew over the edge of Brady at three thousand feet, and Donovan took the controls. "You want to fly it again sometime?" he asked.

"Maybe, I don't know. How long does it take to learn everything?"

"About thirty hours of ground school, or self-study, and another thirty in the air. The problem is there's no instructor around here. Had one, but he died. In a plane crash."

"I think I'll just stick to cars. I grew up in a world of plane crashes so I've always been wary of aviation. I'll let you do the flying."

"Anytime," he said, smiling. He kept the nose pitched downward until they were a thousand feet above the terrain. They flew beside a strip mine where blasting was under way; a thick cloud of black smoke hung close to the ground. On the horizon, steeples were peeking above the trees. "Have you been to Knox?" he asked.

"No, not yet."

"It's the seat of Curry County, where I was born. Nice town, about the same size and sophistication as Brady, so you haven't missed much." They flew over the town, but there wasn't much to see, at least not from one thousand feet. They began climbing again, weaving around the taller peaks until they were deep in the mountains. They topped one and Donovan said, "There it is, what's left of Gray Mountain. The company abandoned it twenty years ago, but by the time they left most of the coal was gone. Lawsuits tied up everything for years. Obviously, the site did not get reclaimed. Probably the ugliest spot in all of Appalachia."

It was a desolate landscape, with open gashes where coal was being extracted when the crews suddenly stopped, and mounds of overfill left to sit forever, and all over the site scrawny trees trying desperately to survive. Most of the mine was rock and soil, but patches of brown grass had grown up. The valley fill dropping from the site was partially covered with vines and shrubbery. As Donovan began to circle, he said, "The only thing worse than a reclaimed strip mine is one that's been abandoned. That's what happened here. It still makes me sick."

"Who owns it now?"

"My father, it's still in the family, but it's not worth much. The land is ruined. The streams disappeared under the valley fill, all the fish are gone. The water is poison. The wildlife ran off to a safer place. Did Mattie tell you what happened to my mother?"

"She did, but not in detail."

He descended and banked steeply to the right so she looked straight down. "Do you see that white cross down there, with rocks around it?"

"Yes, I see it."

"That's where she died. Our home was over there, an old family place built by my grandfather, who was a deep miner. After the flood destroyed the home, my mother found a spot there, near the rocks, and that's where it happened. My brother, Jeff, and I found some old timbers from the house and built that cross."

"Who found her?"

He took a deep breath, and said, "So Mattie didn't tell you everything?"

"I guess not."

"I found her."

Nothing was said for a few minutes as Donovan buzzed the valley on the east side of Gray Mountain. There were no roads, homes, or signs of people. He banked again and said, "Just over this ridge here is the only part of the property that wasn't ruined. The water flows in another direction and the valley was safe from the strip mine. You see that creek down there?" He banked steeper so she could.

"Yes, I got it."

"Yellow Creek. I have a little cabin on that creek, a hiding place few people know about. I'll show it to you sometime."

I'm not so sure about that, Samantha thought. We are now close enough, and pending some change in your marital status, I have no plans to get closer. But she nodded and said, "I'd like to see it."

"There's the chimney," he said. "It's barely visible, both from here and on the ground. No plumbing, no electricity, you sleep in hammocks. I built it myself, with help from my brother, Jeff."

"Where's your father?"

"Last I heard he was in Montana, but I haven't spoken to him in many years. Have you seen enough?"

"I believe so."

At the Noland County Airfield, Donovan taxied close to the terminal but did not kill the engine. Instead, he said, "Okay, I want you to get out here, carefully, and walk behind the airplane. The prop is still spinning."

"You're not getting out?" she asked, pulling the latch on her shoulder harness.

"No, I'm going to Roanoke to see my wife and daughter. Be back tomorrow, and at the office." Samantha got out under the wing, felt the rush of air from the propeller, walked behind the tail, and waited at the door. She waved at Donovan, who gave her the thumbs-up and began taxiing away. She watched him take off and drove back to Brady.

Saturday dinner was a pot of Chester's legendary Texas chili. He'd never been to Texas, as best he could remember, but found a great recipe (only two years ago) on a Web site. The legend part seemed more or less a creation of his own imagination, but his enthusiasm for cooking and entertaining was infectious. Mattie baked corn bread and Annette brought a chocolate pie for dessert. Samantha had never learned to cook and was now living in a tiny apartment with only a hot plate and a toaster, so she got a pass. While Chester stirred the pot and added spices and talked nonstop, Kim and Adam made a pizza in Aunt Mattie's kitchen. Saturday was always pizza night for them, and Samantha was delighted to be at the Wyatts' and not stuck again with Annette and the kids. In their eyes she was no longer a roommate/babysitter, but in one week had risen to the hallowed status of big sister. They loved her and she loved them, but the walls were closing in. Annette seemed content to allow the kids to smother her.

They ate in the backyard, at a picnic table under a maple tree ablaze with bright yellow leaves. The ground was covered with them too, a beautiful carpet that would soon be gone. Candles were lit as the sun disappeared behind the mountains. Claudelle, their paralegal, joined them late. Mattie had a rule that over dinner there would be no shop talk—nothing about the clinic, their work, their clients, and, especially, nothing even remotely related to coal. So they dwelt on politics—Obama versus McCain, Biden versus Palin. Politics naturally led to discussions about the economic disaster unfolding around the world. All news was bad, and while the experts disagreed on whether it would be a minor depression or just a deep recession, it still seemed far away, like another genocide in Africa. Awful, but not really touching Brady, yet. They were curious about Samantha's friends in New York.

For the third or fourth time that afternoon and evening,

Samantha noticed a detached coolness in Annette's words and attitude toward her. She seemed fine when talking to everyone else, but slightly abrupt when she said anything to Samantha. At first, she thought nothing of it. But by the time dinner was over, she was certain something was gnawing at Annette. It was puzzling because nothing had happened between them.

Finally, she suspected it had something to do with Donovan.

15

Samantha awoke to the pleasant sounds of distant church bells. There seemed to be several melodies in the air, some closer, or louder, others farther away, but all busy rousing the town folk with not so gentle reminders that the Sabbath had arrived and the doors were open. It was two minutes past nine, according to her digital clock, and she once again marveled at her ability to sleep. She thought about rolling over and going for more, but after ten hours enough was enough. The coffee was ready, the aroma drifting from the other room. She poured a cup and sat on the sofa and thought about her day. With little to do, her first goal was to avoid Annette and the kids.

She called her mother and gabbed for thirty minutes about this and that. Karen, typically, was absorbed in the latest crisis at Justice and rattled on about it. Her boss was having urgent, preliminary meetings to organize plans to investigate big banks and purveyors of sub-prime mortgages and all manner of Wall Street crooks, and this would begin as soon as the dust settled and they figured out exactly who was responsible for the mess. Such talk bored Samantha, but she gamely held on, sipping coffee in her pajamas and listening to the nonstop church bells. Karen mentioned driving down to Brady in the near future for her first real look at life in the mountains, but Samantha knew it was all talk. Her mother rarely left D.C.; her work was too important. She finally asked about the internship and the legal clinic. How long will you stay? she asked. Samantha said she had no plans to leave anytime soon.

When the bells stopped, she put on jeans and left her apartment. Annette's car was still parked in front of the house, an indication that she and the kids were skipping church on this beautiful Sunday. From a rack near Donovan's office on Main Street, Samantha bought a copy of the *Roanoke Times* and read it in an empty café while she ate a waffle with bacon. After breakfast, she walked the streets of Brady for a while; it didn't take long to see all of it. She passed a dozen churches, which all seemed to be packed, judging by the crowded parking lots, and tried to remember the last time she had seen the inside of one. Her father was a lapsed Catholic, her mother an indifferent Protestant, and Samantha had not been raised in any faith.

She found the schools, all as old as the courthouse, all with rusting air conditioners sagging from the windows. She said hello to a porch full of ancient people rocking their time away at the nursing home, evidently too old even for church. She walked past the tiny hospital and vowed to never get sick in Brady. She walked along Main Street and wondered how in the world the small merchants stayed in business. When the tour was over she got in her car and left.

On the map, Highway 119 wiggled through the coal country of far eastern Kentucky and into West Virginia. The day before, she had seen Appalachia from the air; now she would try it from the road. With Charleston a vague destination, she took off with nothing but a road map and a bottle of water. Soon she was in Kentucky, though the state line made little difference. Appalachia was Appalachia, regardless of boundaries someone had set an eternity ago. A land of breathtaking beauty, of steep hills and rolling mountains covered in dense hardwood forests, of rushing streams and rapids cutting through deep valleys, of depressing poverty, of tidy little towns with redbrick buildings and whitewashed houses, of church after church. Most of them seemed to be of the Baptist variety, though the brands were hopelessly confusing. Southern Baptist; General Baptist; Primitive Baptist; Missionary Baptist.

Regardless, they were all bustling with activity. She stopped in Pikeville, Kentucky, population seven thousand, found the center of town, and treated herself to coffee amongst the locals in a stuffy café. She got some looks but everyone was friendly. She listened hard to the chatter, at times uncertain if it was the same language, and even chuckled at the banter. Near the West Virginia line, she couldn't resist stopping at a country store that advertised "World Famous Beef Jerky, Homemade." She bought a package, took one bite, tossed the rest in a trash can, and sipped water for fifteen miles to get rid of the taste.

She was determined not to think about coal; she was tired of the subject. But it was everywhere: in the haul trucks that owned the roads, in the fading billboards urging union strength, in the occasional glimpse of a strip mine and a mountaintop being removed, in the battle of bumper stickers, with "Like Electricity? Love Coal" on one side and "Save the Mountains" on the other, and in the tiny museums honoring the heritage of mining. She stopped at a historical marker and read the account of the Bark Valley Disaster, a deep mine explosion that killed thirty men in 1961. Friends of Coal had an aggressive campaign under way, and she drove past many of their billboards declaring "Coal Equals Jobs." Coal was the fabric of life in these parts, but the strip-mining had divided the people. According to her Internet research, its opponents argued that it destroyed jobs, and they had the numbers to support them. Eighty thousand miners now, almost all non-union and half working in surface mines. Decades earlier, long before they began blasting tops off mountains, there were almost a million miners.

She eventually made it to Charleston, the capital. She still wasn't comfortable in traffic and found more than she expected. She had no idea where she was going and was suddenly afraid of getting lost. It was almost 2:00 p.m., past lunch and time to turn around. The first leg of her trip ended when she randomly pulled in to a strip mall surrounded by fast-food restaurants. She was craving a burger and fries.

———

All the lights were on in Donovan's office long after sunset. She walked by it once around 8:00, started to knock, but decided not to disturb him. At 9:00 she was at her desk, primarily because she wanted to avoid her apartment, and not really working. She called his cell and he answered it. "Are you busy?" she asked.

"Of course I'm busy. I start a trial tomorrow. What are you doing?"

"I'm at the office, puttering, bored."

"Come on over. I want you to meet someone."

They were in his war room, upstairs, the tables covered with open books and files and legal pads. Donovan introduced her to one Lenny Charlton, a jury consultant from Knoxville. He described the man as an overpaid but frequently effective analyst, and he described Samantha simply as a lawyer/friend who was on his side. Samantha wondered if Donovan insulted all the experts he hired.

He asked Lenny, "Ever hear of Marshall Kofer out of D.C.? Once a high-flying aviation trial lawyer?"

"Of course," Lenny said.

"Her dad. But there's nothing in the DNA. She avoids courtrooms."

"Smart lady."

They were ending a long session in which they had gone through the list of sixty prospective jurors. Lenny explained, for her benefit, that his firm was paid trifling wages to conduct background searches of every person on the list, and that the chore was difficult given the tight and incestuous nature of coalfield communities. "Excuses, excuses," Donovan mumbled, almost under his breath. Lenny explained further that picking juries in coal country was dicey because everyone had a friend or a relative who worked either for a company that mined coal or for one that provided services to the industry.

Samantha listened with fascination as they discussed the last few names on the list. One woman's brother worked at a strip mine. One woman's father had been a deep miner. One man lost his adult son in a construction accident, but it wasn't related to coal. And so on. There seemed to be something wrong with this spying game, of allowing litigants to peek into the private lives of unsuspecting people. She would ask Donovan about it later if she had the chance. He looked tired and seemed a bit edgy.

Lenny left a few minutes before ten. When they were alone, she asked, "Why don't you have co-counsel for this trial?"

"I often do, but not this case. I prefer to do it myself. Strayhorn and its insurance company will have a dozen dark suits swarming around their table. I like the contrast, just Lisa Tate and me."

"David and Goliath, huh?"

"Something like that."

"How late will you work?"

"I don't know. I won't sleep much tonight, or this week for that matter. Comes with the territory."

"Look, I know it's late and you have better things to worry about, but I have to ask you something. You've offered me a part-time job as a research assistant, a paid position, so I would become an employee of your firm, right?"

"Right. Where is this going?"

"Hang on. I'm not sure I want to work for you."

He shrugged. Whatever. "I'm not begging."

"Here's the question: Do you have in your possession documents—the bad documents as you and Vic call them—owned by Krull Mining pertaining to the contamination of the groundwater in Hammer Valley, documents that you're not supposed to have?"

His dark and tired eyes flashed with anger but he bit his tongue, hesitated, then smiled.

"It's a direct question, Counselor," she said.

"I get that. So, if the answer is yes, then I suppose you'll decline the job and we'll still be friends, right?"

"You answer my question first."

"And if the answer is no, then you might consider working for me, right?"

"I'm still waiting, Counselor."

"I plead the Fifth Amendment."

"Fair enough. Thank you for the offer but I'll say no."

"As you wish. I have lots of work to do."

Black lung is a legal term for a preventable, occupational lung disease. It is more formally known as coal workers' pneumoconiosis (CWP), and is caused by prolonged exposure to coal dust. Once coal dust is inhaled into the body it cannot be removed or discharged. It progressively builds up in the lungs and can lead to inflammation, fibrosis, even necrosis. There are two forms of the disease: "simple CWP" and "complicated CWP" (or progressive massive fibrosis).

Black lung is a common affliction among coal miners, both in deep mines and surface mines. It is estimated that 10% of all miners with 25 years experience develop the disease. It is debilitating and usually fatal. Approximately 1500 miners die each year from black lung, and because of the insidious nature of the disease, their deaths are almost always slow and agonizing. There is no cure and no effective medical treatment.

The symptoms are shortness of breath and a constant cough that often yields a black mucus. As these grow worse, the miner faces the dilemma of whether or not to pursue benefits. Diagnosis is fairly straightforward: (1) an exposure history to coal dust; (2) a chest X-ray; and (3) the exclusion of other causes.

In 1969, Congress passed the Federal Coal Mine Health and Safety Act which established a compensation system for victims of black lung. The law also set up standards to reduce coal dust. Two years later, Congress created the Black Lung Disability Trust Fund and funded it with a federal tax on coal production. In this law, the coal industry agreed to a system designed to ease the identification of the disease and to guarantee compensation. If a miner had worked ten years and had medical proof— either an X-ray or autopsy evidence of severe black lung—then in theory he was to be awarded benefits. Also, a miner still working with black lung was to be transferred to a job with less exposure to dust without the loss of pay, benefits, or seniority. As of July 1, 2008, a miner with black lung receives $900 a month from the Trust.

The intent of the new federal law was to sharply reduce exposure to coal dust. Tough standards were soon in place and miners were offered free chest X-rays every five years. The X-rays showed 4 in 10 miners tested had some level of black lung. But in the years after the law took effect, new cases of black lung plunged by 90 percent. Doctors and experts predicted the disease would be eradicated. However, by 1995 government studies began to indicate an increase in the rate of the disease; then an even bigger increase. Just as troublesome, the disease appeared to progress more rapidly and it was showing up in the lungs of younger miners. Experts share two theories for this: (1) miners are working longer shifts, and thus are exposed to more dust; and (2) coal operators are exposing miners to illegal concentrations of coal dust.

Black lung is now epidemic in the coalfields, and the only possible reason is a prolonged exposure to more dust than the law allows. For decades the coal companies have resisted efforts to strengthen the standards, and they have been successful.

The law does not allow a miner to pay a lawyer; therefore, a typical miner with a claim must try to navigate the federal black lung system by himself. The coal industry is harshly resistant to claims, regardless of the proof offered by the miner. The companies fight the claims with experienced attorneys who skillfully manipulate the system. For a miner who prevails, his process usually takes about five years.

For Thomas Wilcox, the ordeal lasted twelve years. He was born near Brady, Virginia, in 1925, fought in the war, was wounded twice, decorated, and upon his return home he got married and went to work in the mines. He was a proud miner, a staunch union man, a loyal Democrat, and a fine husband and father. In 1974, he was diagnosed with black lung disease and filed a claim. He had been sick for several years and was almost too weak to work. His chest X-ray clearly showed complicated CWP. He had worked underground for 28 years and had never smoked. His claim was initially approved, but the award was appealed by the coal company. In 1976, at the age of 51, Thomas had no choice but to retire. He continued to deteriorate and he was soon on oxygen around the clock. With no income, his family scrambled to support themselves and cover his medical expenses. He and his wife were forced to sell the family home and live with an older daughter. His black lung *claim was thoroughly choked up deep within the federal system by crafty attorneys working for the coal company. At the time, he was due about $300 a month, plus medical care.*

By the end, Thomas was a shriveled skeleton, stuck in a wheelchair and gasping for breath as the final days passed and his family prayed for a merciful end. He could not speak and was fed baby food by his wife and daughters. Through the generosity of friends and neighbors, and the tireless efforts of his family, the supply of oxygen was never depleted. He weighed 104 pounds when he died in 1986, at the age of 61. An autopsy yielded incontrovertible proof of black lung.

Four months later the coal company dropped its appeal. Twelve years after he filed his claim, his widow received a lump sum settlement for back benefits.

Note: Thomas Wilcox was my father. He was a proud war hero, though he never talked about his battles. He was a son of the mountains and loved their beauty, history, and way of life. He taught us all how to fish the clear streams, camp in the caves, and even hunt deer for food. He was an active man who slept little and preferred to read late into the night. We watched him gradually slow down as the disease took its grip. Every miner fears black lung, but he never thinks it will happen to him. As reality set in, Thomas lost his energy and began to brood. The simple tasks around the farm became more difficult. When he was forced to quit the mines, he went into a prolonged period of deep depression. As his body grew weaker and smaller, talking became too strenuous. He needed all of his energy just for breathing. In his final days, we took turns sitting with him and reading his favorite books. Often, he had tears in his eyes.

MATTIE WYATT, JULY 1, 2008

It was in the last section of the thick binder of seminar materials, and had obviously been added later. Samantha had not noticed it before. She put away the binder, found her running shoes, and went for a long walk around Brady. It was after eleven on Sunday night, and she did not see another person outdoors.

16

Mattie was in court in Curry County, Annette was running late, part-time Barb had yet to show, and part-time Claudelle didn't arrive until noon on Mondays, so Samantha was all alone when Pamela Booker made a noisy entrance with two dirty kids behind her. She was crying by the time she gave her name and started begging for help. Samantha herded them into a conference room and spent the first five minutes trying to assure Pamela things would be okay, though she had no idea what "things" were in play. The kids were mute, with wide eyes and the startled looks of those traumatized. And they were hungry, Pamela said when she settled down. "Do you have anything to eat?"

Samantha raced to the kitchen, found some stale cookies, a pack of saltines, a bag of chips, and two diet sodas from Barb's stash, and placed it all on the table in front of the two children who grabbed the cookies and bit off huge chunks. Through more tears, Pamela said thanks, and began talking. The narrative spilled out so fast Samantha had no time to take notes. She watched the kids devour the food while their mother told their story.

They were living in a car. They were from a small town just over the line in Hopper County, and since they lost their home a month earlier Pamela had been looking for a lawyer to rescue them. No one would help, but one eventually mentioned the Mountain Legal Aid Clinic over in Brady. Here they were. She had a job in a factory making lamps for a motel chain. It wasn't a great job but one that paid the rent and bought groceries. There was no husband in the picture. Four months ago, a company she'd never heard of began garnishing her paycheck, took a third of it, and she couldn't stop it. She complained to her boss, but he just waved a court order at her. Then he threatened to fire her, said he hated garnishment orders because of the hassle. When she argued with him, he followed through with his threat and she was now unemployed. She went to see the judge and explained everything, told him she couldn't pay her rent and buy food at the same time, but he was not sympathetic. Said the law was the law. The problem was an old credit card judgment she hadn't thought about in ten years. Evidently, the credit card company sold her judgment to some bottom-feeding collection agency, and, without her knowledge, an order of garnishment was issued. When she couldn't pay the rent on her trailer, her landlord, a real asshole, called the sheriff and kicked her out. She piled in with a cousin for a few days, but that blew up and she left to live with a friend. That didn't work either, and for the past two weeks she and the kids had been living in their car, which was low on everything—oil, air, gas, and brake fluid, the dashboard lit up like a Christmas tree. Yesterday, she shoplifted some chocolate bars and gave them to the kids. She herself had not eaten in two days.

Samantha absorbed it all and managed to hide her shock. How, exactly, do you live in a car? She began taking notes without the slightest idea of what to do on the legal front.

Pamela pulled out paperwork from her fake designer bag and slid the pile across the table. Samantha scanned a court order while her new client explained she was down to her last two dollars, and she didn't know whether to spend them on gas or food. She finally took a cookie and held it with shaking hands. Two things dawned on Samantha. The first was that she was the last line of defense for this little family. The second was that they were not leaving anytime soon. There was nowhere to go.

When Barb finally arrived, Samantha gave her $20 and asked

her to hurry and buy as many sausage biscuits as possible. Barb said, "We keep a few bucks around the office."

Samantha replied, "We'll need it."

Phoebe Fanning was still hiding from her husband in a motel, courtesy of the clinic, and Samantha was aware that Mattie kept a few bucks on reserve for emergencies like this. After Barb left, Samantha looked through a back window at the parking lot. Pamela's car, even filled with gas and all other necessary fluids, looked as though it wouldn't make it back to Hopper County. It was a small import with a million miles on it, and now it was being used as a home.

The cookies and saltines were gone when she returned to the conference room. She told Pamela she had sent out for some food, and this made her cry. The boy, Trevor, age seven, said, "Thank you, Miss Kofer." The girl, Mandy, age eleven, asked, "Could I please use the bathroom?"

"Certainly," Samantha said. She showed her the way down the hall and sat down at the table to take more notes. They started at the beginning and went slowly through the story. The credit card judgment was dated July 1999 and had a balance of $3,398, which included all manner of court costs, obscure fees, even some interest thrown in for good measure. Pamela explained that her ex-husband had been ordered to satisfy the judgment in their divorce decree, a copy of which was in the paperwork. Nine years had passed without a word, at least nothing she was aware of. She had moved several times and perhaps the mail had not kept up. Who knew? At any rate, the collection agency had found her and started all this trouble.

Samantha noted that Trevor, at seven, had been born after the divorce, but this was not worth mentioning. There were several court orders holding the ex-husband in contempt for failure to pay child support for Mandy. "Where is he?" she asked.

"I have no idea," Pamela said. "I haven't heard from him in years."

Barb returned with a sack of sausage biscuits and spread the feast on the table. She rubbed Trevor's head and told Mandy how happy she was they had come to visit. All three Bookers offered polite thanks, then ate like refugees. Samantha closed the door and huddled with Barb in the reception area. "What's the deal?" Barb asked, and Samantha gave her the basics.

Barb, who thought she'd seen it all, was puzzled, but never timid. "I'd start with the boss. Give him a load of hell, threaten to sue for triple damages, then go after the collection company." The phone was ringing and she reached to answer it, leaving Samantha, the lawyer, alone in her confusion.

A load of hell? Triple damages? For what, exactly? And this advice was from a nonlawyer. Samantha thought about stalling until either Mattie or Annette returned, but she had been there for a week and orientation was over. She went to her office, closed the door, and nervously punched the number at the lamp factory. A Mr. Simmons was pleasantly surprised to learn that Pamela Booker had herself a lawyer. He said she was a good worker, he hated to lose her and all that, but damned those garnishment orders. It just made his bookkeeping a nightmare. He had already filled her spot, and he'd made sure the new employee had no legal problems.

Well, you might have some more legal problems, Samantha explained coolly. Bluffing, and not sure of the law, she explained that a company cannot fire an employee simply because his or her wages are being garnished. This irritated Mr. Simmons and he mumbled something about his lawyer. Great, Samantha said, give me her number and I'll pursue the matter with her. Wasn't a woman, he said, and the guy charged two hundred bucks an hour anyway. Give him some time to think about it. Samantha promised to call back that afternoon, and they eventually agreed that 3:00 p.m. would be convenient.

When she returned to the conference room, Barb had found a box of crayons and some coloring books and was busy organizing fun and games for Trevor and Mandy. Pamela was still holding half a sausage biscuit and staring at the floor, as if in a trance. When Annette finally arrived, Samantha met her in the hallway and, whispering, unloaded the details. Annette was still a bit aloof and bothered by something, but business was business. "The judgment expired years ago," was her first reaction. "Check the law on this. I'll bet the credit card company sold the judgment to the collection company for pennies on the dollar, and now it's enforcing an outdated court order."

"You've seen this before?"

"Something similar, a long time ago. Can't remember the case name. Do the research, then contact the collection agency. These are generally some nasty characters and they don't scare easily."

"Can we sue them?"

"We can certainly threaten. They are not accustomed to people like this suddenly showing up with a lawyer. Call the boss and burn his ass too."

"I've already done that."

Annette actually smiled. "What did he say?"

"I explained that he cannot fire an employee simply because of a garnishment order. I have no idea if this is accurate, but I made it sound authentic. It worried him and we're supposed to chat again this afternoon."

"It's not accurate but it's a nice bluff, which is often more important than whatever the law says. The lawsuit will be against the collection company, if in fact they are pinching her paychecks from an expired judgment."

"Thanks," Samantha said, taking a deep breath. "But we have more pressing matters. They are in there and they have no place to go."

"I suggest you spend the next few hours taking care of the basics—food, laundry, a place to sleep. The kids are obviously not in school; worry about that tomorrow. We have a slush fund to cover some expenses."

"Did you say laundry?"

"I did. Who said legal aid work was all glamour?"

The morning's second crisis erupted minutes later when Phoebe Fanning arrived unannounced with her husband, Randy, and informed Annette she was dropping her divorce. They had reconciled, so to speak, and she and the kids were back home, where things had settled down. Annette was furious and called Samantha into her office to witness the meeting.

Randy Fanning had been out of jail for three days and was only slightly more presentable absent the orange county jumpsuit. He sat with a smirk and kept one hand on Phoebe's arm as she tried her best to explain her change of plans. She loved him, plain and simple, couldn't survive without him, and their three children were much happier with their parents together. She was tired of hiding in a motel and the kids were tired of hiding with relatives, and everyone had made peace.

Annette reminded Phoebe that she had been beaten by her husband, who glared across the table as if he might erupt any moment. Annette seemed fearless while Samantha tried to hide in a corner. It had been a fight, Phoebe explained, not exactly a fair one but a fight nonetheless. They had been arguing too much, things got carried away; it'll never happen again. Randy, who preferred to say nothing, chimed in and confirmed that, yes, they had promised to stop the fighting.

Annette listened to him without believing a word. She reminded him that he was violating the terms of the temporary restraining order as he sat there. If the judge found out he'd go back to jail. He said, Hump, his lawyer, had promised to get the order dismissed without a hassle.

There were traces of dark bluish color still visible on the side of Phoebe's face from the last fight. Divorce was one matter; the criminal charges were another. Annette got to the serious part when she asked if they had spoken to the prosecutor about dropping the malicious wounding. Not yet, but they planned to do that as soon as the divorce was dismissed. Annette explained that it wouldn't be automatic. The police had a statement from the victim; they had photographs, other witnesses. This seemed a bit confusing, and even Samantha wasn't so sure. If the victim and star witness folds, how do you pursue the case?

The two lawyers had the same thought: Did he beat her again to coerce her to drop everything?

Annette was irritated and hammered away with tough questions, but neither backed down. They were determined to forget their troubles and move on to a happier life. When it was time for the meeting to end, Annette flipped through the file and estimated that she had spent twenty hours on the divorce. At no charge, of course.

Next time, find another lawyer.

After they left, Annette described them as a couple of meth addicts who were obviously unstable and probably needed each other. "Let's just hope he doesn't kill her," she said.

As the morning dragged on, it became clear that the Booker family had no plans to leave. Nor were they asked to; just the opposite. The staff embraced them and checked on them every few minutes. At one point Barb whispered to Samantha, "We've actually had clients sleep here for a couple of nights. Not ideal, but sometimes there's no choice."

With a roll of quarters, Pamela left to find the Laundromat. Mandy and Trevor stayed in the conference room, coloring with crayons and reading, occasionally giggling at something between them. Samantha worked at the other end of the table, digging through statutes and cases.

At 11:00 a.m. sharp, Mrs. Francine Crump arrived for what was scheduled to be a brief will signing. Samantha had prepared the document. Mattie had reviewed it. The little ceremony should take less than ten minutes, and Francine would leave with a proper last will and testament for which she would pay nothing. Instead, it became the third crisis of the morning.

As instructed, Samantha had drafted a will that left Francine's eighty acres to her neighbors, Hank and Jolene Mott. Francine's five adult children would get nothing, and this would inevitably lead to trouble down the road. Doesn't matter, Mattie had said. It's her land, clear and unencumbered, and she can dispose of it any way she wants. We'll deal with the trouble later. No, we are not required to notify the five children that they are being cut out. They'll learn of this after the funeral.

Or would they? As Samantha closed the door to her office and pulled out the file, Francine began crying. Dabbing her cheeks with a tissue, she unloaded her story. Three in a row, all crying, Samantha thought.

Over the weekend, Hank and Jolene Mott had finally told her a horrible secret: they had decided to sell their hundred acres to a coal company and move to Florida where they had grandkids. They didn't want to sell, of course, but they were getting old—hell, they were already old and being old was no excuse to sell and run, lots of old people hang on to their land around here—but anyway they needed the money for retirement and medical bills. Francine was furious with her longtime neighbors and still couldn't believe it. Not only had she lost her friends, she'd also lost the two people she trusted to protect her own land. And the worst was yet to come: a strip mine was being planned for next door! Folks all up and down Jacob's Holler were angry, but that's what the coal companies do to you. They turn neighbor against neighbor, brother against sister.

Rumor was the Motts were leaving as soon as possible. Running like chickens, according to Francine. Good riddance.

Samantha was patient, in fact she had been patient all morning as the office tissue supply dwindled, but she slowly realized that her first last will and testament was headed for the wastebasket. She managed to bring Francine around to the obvious question: If not the Motts, then who gets the land? Francine didn't know what to do. That's why she was talking to a lawyer.

The Monday brown-bag lunch in the main conference room was modified somewhat to include Mandy and Trevor Booker. Though the two children had been eating all morning, they were still hungry enough to split a sandwich with the staff. Their mother was doing laundry and they had no place to go. The conversation was light, church gossip and the weather, suitable topics for young ears and far from the raunchy topics Samantha had heard the week before. It was quite dull and the lunch was over in twenty minutes.

Samantha needed some advice and didn't want to bother with Annette. She asked Mattie for a moment or two, and closed the door to her office. She handed over some paperwork and said proudly, "This is my first lawsuit."

Mattie smiled and took it gingerly. "Well, well, congratulations. It's about time. Sit down and I'll read it."

The defendant was Top Market Solutions, a dodgy outfit out of Norfolk, Virginia, with offices in several southern states. Numerous phone calls had yielded little information about the company, but Samantha had all she needed to fire the first shot. The more she researched the clearer the issues became. Annette was right—the judgment expired seven years after it was entered, and had not been reenrolled. The credit card company sold the invalid judgment to Top Market at a deep discount. Top Market in turn took the judgment, reenrolled it in Hopper County, and began using the legal system to collect the money. One available tool was the garnishing of paychecks.

"Short and sweet," Mattie said when she finished. "And you're sure of the facts?"

"Yes, it's not that complicated, really."

"You can always amend it later. I like it. You feel like a real lawyer now?"

"I do. I've never thought about it before. I type up a lawsuit, alleging anything I choose, file it, serve notice on the defendant, who has no choice but to answer in court, and we either settle the dispute or go to trial."

"Welcome to America. You'll get used to it."

"I'm thinking about filing it this afternoon. They are homeless, you know. The sooner the better."

"Fire away," Mattie said, handing the lawsuit over. "I would also e-mail a copy to the defendant and put them on notice."

"Thanks. I'll polish it up and head for the courthouse."

At 3:00 p.m., Mr. Simmons at the lamp factory was much less

pleasant than he'd been during their first chat. He said he'd checked with his lawyer, who assured him that terminating an employee over a garnishment order was not illegal within the Common-wealth of Virginia, contrary to what Ms. Kofer had said that morning. "Don't you know the law?" he asked.

"I understand it very well," she said, eager to get off the phone. "I guess we'll just see you in court." With one lawsuit prepped and ready to go, she couldn't help but feel a bit trigger-happy.

"I've been sued by better lawyers," Mr. Simmons said and hung up.

The Bookers finally left. They followed Samantha to a motel on the east side of town, one of two in Brady. The entire staff had weighed in on which was less offensive, and the Starlight won by a narrow margin. It was a throwback to the 1950s with tiny rooms and doors that opened onto the parking lot. Samantha had spoken with the owner twice, had been promised two adjoining rooms that were clean, with televisions, and had negotiated a reduced rate of $25 a night per room. Mattie liked to describe it as a hot-sheets joint, but there was no evidence of illicit behavior, at least not at 3:30 on a Monday afternoon. The other eighteen rooms appeared to be empty. Pamela's clean laundry was folded neatly into grocery bags. As they unloaded the car, Samantha realized that the little family was taking a big step back up the ladder. Mandy and Trevor were excited about staying in a motel, even had their own room. Pamela had a spring in her step and a big smile. She hugged Saman-tha fiercely and said thanks for the umpteenth time. As she drove away, all three were standing beside the car, waving.

After an hour of twisting through the mountains and dodging a few coal trucks, Samantha arrived on Center Street in Colton a quarter before five. She filed the Booker lawsuit against Top Mar-ket Solutions, paid the filing fee with a check drawn on the clinic, and filled out the paperwork to execute service of process on the defendant, and when everything was tidied up she left the clerk's office quite proud that her first lawsuit was now on the books.

She hurried down to the courtroom, hoping the trial had not been recessed for the day. Far from it; the courtroom was half-filled and stuffy, with a layer of tension you could feel as scowling men in dark suits gazed upon the seven people sitting in the jury box. Jury selection was winding down; Donovan had hoped to complete it the first day.

He sat next to Lisa Tate, mother of the two boys. They were alone at the plaintiff's table, which was next to the jury box. On the other side of the courtroom, at the defense table, a small army of black suits swarmed around, all with hard, unpleasant looks, as if they had been outflanked in the initial phase of the trial.

The judge was talking to his new jury, giving them instructions on what and what not to do throughout the trial. He almost scolded them into promising to immediately report any contact with persons trying to discuss the trial. Samantha looked at the jurors and tried to determine which ones Donovan had wanted and which ones were considered favorable to coal. It was impossible. All white, four women, three men, youngest around twenty-five and oldest at least seventy. How could anyone predict the group dynamics of the jury as it weighed the evidence?

Perhaps Lenny Charlton, the consultant. Samantha saw him three rows up, watching the jurors as they listened to the judge's instructions. Others were watching too, no doubt consultants hired by Strayhorn Coal and its insurance company. All eyes were on the jurors. Big money was on the line, and it was their task to award it, or not.

Samantha smiled at the contrast. Here, in a tense courtroom, Donovan had dragged in another rich corporation to answer for its bad deeds. He would demand millions in damages. In the coming weeks, he would file a billion-dollar case against Krull Mining, a case that would devour several years and a small fortune in expenses. She, on the other hand, now had in her briefcase her first lawsuit, one seeking $5,000 in damages from a shady outfit that was probably one step away from bankruptcy.

Donovan stood to address the court. He was wearing his lawyer's finest, a handsome navy suit that hung fashionably on his lean frame. His long hair had been slightly trimmed for the occasion. He was clean shaven for a change. He moved around the courtroom as if he owned it. The jurors watched every move and absorbed every word as he announced that the plaintiff was satisfied with the jury and had no more challenges.

At 5:45 p.m., the judge adjourned for the day. Samantha hurried out and beat the rush. She drove four blocks to the lower school Mandy and Trevor attended. She had talked to the principal twice during the day. Their assignments had been put together by their teachers. The principal had heard the family was living in a car and was very concerned. Samantha assured her they were in a better place and things were looking up. She hoped they would be back in school in a matter of days. In the meantime, she would make sure they kept up their studies and finished their homework.

Driving away, Samantha admitted she felt more like a social worker than a lawyer, and there was nothing wrong with that. At Scully & Pershing, her work was more suitable for accountants or financial analysts, or at times minimum-wage clerks or simple pencil pushers. She reminded herself that she was a real lawyer, though she often had doubts.

As she was leaving Colton, a white pickup truck ran up behind her, then backed away. It followed her all the way to Brady, keeping the same distance, not too close but never out of sight.

17

Pizzerias in big cities benefit from Italian natives or descendants thereof, people who understand that real pizza comes from Naples where the crusts are thin and the toppings simple. Samantha's favorite was Lazio's, a hole-in-the-wall in Tribeca where the cooks yelled in Italian as they baked the crusts in brick ovens. Like most things in her life these days, Lazio's was far away. So was the pizza. The only place in Brady to get one to go was a sub shop in a cheap strip mall. Pizza Hut, along with most other national chains, had not penetrated deep into the small towns of Appalachia.

The pizza was an inch thick. She watched the guy slice it and slide it into the box. Eight bucks for a pepperoni and cheese, which seemed to weigh five pounds. She drove it to the motel where the Bookers were watching television and waiting. They had been scrubbed and looked much better in clean clothing, and they were embarrassingly grateful for the changes. Samantha also brought along the bad news that she now had the kids' homework for the next week, but this did nothing to dampen their moods.

They had dinner in Pamela's room, pizza and soft drinks, with *Wheel of Fortune* in the background on low volume. The kids talked about school, their teachers, and the friends they were missing in Colton. Their transformation from early that morning was startling. Frightened and hungry, they had hesitated to say a word. Now they wouldn't shut up.

When the pizza was gone, Pamela cracked the whip and made them buckle down and study. She was afraid they were falling behind. After a few timid objections, they went to their room and got to work. In low voices, Samantha and Pamela talked about the lawsuit and what it might mean. With a little luck, the company might realize its mistake and talk settlement. Otherwise, Samantha would have them in court as soon as possible. She managed to convey the confidence of a seasoned litigator and never hinted that this was her first real lawsuit. She also planned to meet with Mr. Simmons at the lamp factory and explain the mistakes that led to the garnishment. Pamela was not a deadbeat; rather, she was being mistreated by bad people abusing the legal system.

As she drove away from the Starlight Motel, Samantha realized she had spent the better part of the past twelve hours aggressively representing Pamela Booker and her children. Had they not stumbled into the clinic early that morning, they would be hiding somewhere in the backseat of their car, hungry, cold, hopeless, frightened, and vulnerable.

Her cell phone buzzed as she was changing into jeans. It was Annette, a hundred feet across the backyard. "The kids are in their rooms. Got time for some tea?" she asked.

The two needed to talk, to air things out and get to the bottom of whatever was bugging Annette. Kim and Adam managed to interrupt their homework long enough to say hello to Samantha. They preferred to have her there for dinner every night, with television afterward and maybe a video game or two. Samantha, though, needed some space. Annette was certainly helping matters.

When the kids were back in their rooms and the tea was poured, they sat in the semi-dark den and talked about their Monday. According to Annette, there were a lot of homeless people in the mountains. You don't see them panhandling on the streets, like in the cities, because they usually know someone who'll share a room or a garage for a week or so. Almost everybody has kinfolk not far away. There are no homeless shelters, no nonprofits dedicated to the homeless. She had a client once, a mother whose teenage son was mentally ill and violent, and she was forced to make him leave. He lived in a pup tent in the woods, surviving off stolen goods and an occasional handout. He almost froze in the winter and almost drowned in a flood. It took four years to get him committed to a facility. He escaped and had never been seen since. The mother still blamed herself. Very sad.

They talked about the Bookers, Phoebe Fanning, and poor Mrs. Crump, who didn't know whom to give her land to. This reminded Annette of a client once who needed a free will. He had plenty of money because he'd never spent any—"tight as a tick"—and he handed over a prior will, one drafted by a lawyer down the street. The old man had no family to speak of, didn't like his distant relatives, and wasn't sure whom to leave his money to. So the prior lawyer inserted several paragraphs of indecipherable drivel that, in effect, left everything to the lawyer. After a few months, the old man got suspicious and showed up in Annette's office. She prepared a much simpler will, one that gave it all to a church. When he died, the lawyer down the street cried at his wake, his funeral, and his burial, then blew up when he learned of the later will. Annette threatened to report him to the state bar association and he settled down.

Kim and Adam reappeared, now in pajamas, to say good night. Annette left to tuck them in. When their doors were closed, she poured more tea and sat on one end of the sofa. She took a sip and got down to business. "I know you're spending time with Donovan," she said, as if this were a violation of something.

Samantha couldn't deny it; why should she? And did she owe anyone an explanation? "We went flying last Saturday, and the day before we hiked up Dublin Mountain. Why?"

"You need to be careful, Samantha. Donovan is a complicated soul, plus he's still married, you know?"

"I've never slept with a married man. You?"

She ignored the question with "I'm not sure if being married means much to Donovan. He likes the ladies, always has, and now that he's living alone, I'm not sure anyone is safe. He has a reputation."

"Tell me about his wife."

A deep breath, another sip. "Judy is a beautiful girl, but it was a bad match. She's from Roanoke, kind of a city girl, certainly a stranger to the mountains. They met in college and really struggled with their future together. They say a woman marries a man with the belief she can change him, and she can't. A man marries a woman with the belief that she won't change, and she does. We do. Judy couldn't change Donovan; the more she tried the more he resisted. And she certainly changed. When she came to Brady she tried hard to fit in. She planted a garden and volunteered here and there. They joined a church and she sang in the choir. Donovan became more obsessed with his work and there were repercussions. Judy tried to get him to back off, to pass on some of the cases against the coal companies, but he just couldn't do it. I think the final straw was their daughter. Judy didn't want her educated in the schools around here, which is kind of a shame. My kids are doing just fine."

"Is the marriage over?"

"Who knows? They've been separated for a couple of years. Donovan's crazy about his daughter and sees her whenever he can. They say they're trying to find a solution, but I don't see one. He's not leaving the mountains. She's not leaving the city. I have a sister who lives in Atlanta, no children. Her husband lives in Chicago, a good job. He thinks the South is inbred and backward. She thinks Chicago is cold and harsh. Neither will budge, but they claim to be happy with their lives and have no plans to split. I guess it works for some folks. Seems odd, though."

"She doesn't know he fools around?"

"I don't know what she knows. It wouldn't surprise me, though, if they have an agreement, some type of open arrangement." She looked away as she said this, as if she knew more than she was saying. What should have been obvious suddenly became so, to

Samantha anyway. She asked, "Has he told you this?" It seemed a stretch for Annette to merely speculate on such a salacious matter.

A pause. "No, of course not," she said, without conviction.

Was Donovan using the married man's favorite line: Let's have a go, honey, because my wife is doing it too? Perhaps Annette was not as starved for companionship as she pretended to be. Another piece of the puzzle fell into place. Say she was having an affair with Donovan, for either lust or romance or both. Now the new girl in town had his eye. The tension between them was nothing but old-fashioned jealousy, something Annette could never admit, but couldn't hide either.

Samantha said, "Mattie and Chester talked about Donovan. They seem to think Judy got scared when the harassment started, said there were anonymous phone calls, threats, strange cars."

"True, and Donovan is not the most popular person in town. His work irritates a lot of people. Judy felt the sting a few times. And as he's gotten older, he's become even more reckless. He fights dirty, and so he wins a lot of cases. He's made a bunch of money and, typical of trial lawyers, his ego has expanded with his bank accounts."

"Sounds like there are a lot of reasons for the split."

"Afraid so," she said wistfully, but with little feeling.

They sipped and thought and said nothing for a moment. Samantha decided to go for it all, to get to the bottom of things. Annette was always so open when discussing sex, so give it a try. "Has he ever come on to you?"

"No. I'm forty-five years old with two kids. He sees me as too old. Donovan likes 'em younger." She did a passable job of selling this.

"Anybody in particular?"

"Not really. Have you met his brother, Jeff?"

"No, he's mentioned him a few times. Younger, right?"

"Seven years younger. After their mother killed herself, the boys lived here and there, with Mattie stepping in to raise Donovan while Jeff went to another relative. They are very close. Jeff's had a rougher time of it, dropping out of college, drifting here and there. Donovan has always looked out for him, and now Jeff works for him. Investigator, runner, bodyguard, errand boy, you name it and Jeff does it. He's also at least as cute as Donovan, and single."

"I'm not really in the market, if that's what you mean."

"We're always in the market, Samantha. Don't kid yourself. Maybe not for a permanent fix, but we're all looking for love, even the quick variety."

"I doubt my life would get less complicated if I return to New York with a mountain boy in tow. Talk about a bad match."

Annette laughed at this. The tension seemed to be easing, and now that Samantha understood it, she could deal with it. She had already decided that Donovan was close enough. He was charming, exciting, certainly sexy, but he was also nothing but trouble. With the exception of the first time they had met, Samantha had always felt as though they were just a step or two away from getting undressed. If she had taken his job offer, it would have been difficult, if not impossible, to avoid a fling, if for no other reason than boredom.

They said good night and Samantha walked back to her apartment. As she climbed the dark stairs above the garage, the question hit her: How many times has Annette put the kids to bed, then sneaked over here to her little love nest for a quick romp with Donovan?

Plenty, something told her. Plenty.

18

Samantha found the lamp factory in a badly neglected industrial park outside the town of Brushy in Hopper County. Most of the metal buildings had been abandoned. Those still in business had a few cars and pickups in their parking lots. It was a sad barometer of an economy long in decline, and far from the pretty poster envisioned by the Chamber of Commerce.

At first, over the phone, Mr. Simmons said he had no time for a meeting, but Samantha pressed and charmed her way into the promise of thirty minutes. The front reception area reeked of cigarette smoke and the linoleum floors had not been swept in weeks. A grouchy clerk led Samantha to a room down the hall. Voices penetrated the thin walls. Machinery roared from somewhere in the rear. The operation had the feel of a business trying gamely to avoid the fate of its industrial park neighbors as it churned out cheap lamps for cheap motels at the lowest wages possible, with absolutely no thought of additional benefits. Pamela Booker said the perks included one week of unpaid vacation and three sick days, also without pay. Don't even think about health insurance.

Samantha calmed herself by thinking of all the meetings she had suffered through before, meetings with some of the most incredible jerks the world had ever seen, really rich men who gobbled up Manhattan and ran roughshod over anyone in their way. She had seen these men devour and annihilate her partners, including Andy Grubman, a guy she actually missed occasionally. She had heard them yell and threaten and curse, and on several occasions their diatribes had been aimed at her. But she had survived. Regardless of what a prick Mr. Simmons was, he was a kitten compared to those monsters.

He was surprisingly cordial. He welcomed her, showed her a seat in his cheap office, and closed the door. "Thanks for seeing me," she said. "I'll be brief."

"Would you like some coffee?" he asked politely.

She thought of the dust and clouds of cigarette smoke and could almost visualize the brown stains caked along the insides of the communal coffeepot. "No thanks."

He glanced at her legs as he settled in behind his desk and relaxed as though he had all day. She silently tagged him as a flirt. She began by recapping the latest adventures of the Booker family. He was touched, didn't know they were homeless. She handed him an edited, bound copy of the documents involved, and walked him step-by-step through the legal mess. The last exhibit was a copy of the lawsuit she filed the day before, and she assured him there was no way out for Top Market Solutions. "I got 'em by the balls," she said, a deliberate effort at crudeness to judge his reaction. He smiled again.

In summary, the old credit card judgment had expired and Top Market knew it. The garnishment should never have been ordered, and Pamela Booker's paycheck should have been left alone. She should still have her job.

"And you want me to give her her job back?" he asked, the obvious.

"Yes sir. If she has her job she can survive. Her kids need to be in school. We can help her find a place to live. I'll drag Top Market into court, make them cough up what they clipped her for, and she'll get a nice check. But that will take some time. What she needs right now is her old job back. And you know that's only fair."

He stopped smiling and glanced at his watch. "Here's what I'll do. You get that damned garnishment order revoked so I don't have to fool with it, and I'll put her back on the payroll. How long will that take?"

Samantha had no idea but instinctively said, "Maybe a week."

"We got a deal?"

"A deal."

"Can I ask you a question?"

"Anything."

"How much is your hourly rate? I mean, I got a guy over in Grundy, not that sharp, really, and slow to return calls, slow with everything, and he charges me two hundred bucks an hour. That might not be much in the big leagues, but you see where we are. I'd send him more work, but, hell, it's not worth it. I've been looking around but there aren't many reasonable lawyers in these parts. I figure you gotta be real reasonable if Pamela Booker can hire you. So, what's your rate?"

"Nothing. Zero."

He stared at her, mouth open. "I work for legal aid," she said.

"What's legal aid?"

"It's free legal services for low-income people."

It was a foreign concept. He smiled and asked, "Do you take on lamp factories?"

"Sorry. Just poor folks."

"We're losing money, I swear. I'll show you the books."

"Thank you, Mr. Simmons."

As she raced back to Brady with the good news, she thought of the possible ways to quash the garnishment order. And the more she thought, the more she realized how little she knew about the basics of practicing everyday law.

In New York, she had seldom left the office late in the afternoon and gone straight home. There were too many bars for that, too many single professionals on the prowl, too much networking and socializing and hooking up and, well, drinking to be done. Every week someone discovered a new bar or a new club that had to be visited before it got discovered and the throngs ruined it.

The after hours were different in Brady. She had yet to see the inside of a bar; from the street they looked sketchy, both of them. She had yet to meet another young, unmarried professional. So, her choice boiled down to (1) hanging around the office so she wouldn't have to (2) go to her apartment and stare at the walls. Mattie preferred to hang around too, and each afternoon by 5:30 she was roaming around, shoeless, looking for Samantha. Their ritual was evolving, but for now it included sipping a diet soda in the conference room and gossiping while watching the street. Samantha was eager to pry about the possible hanky-panky between Annette and Donovan, but she did not. Maybe later, maybe one day when she had more proof, or probably never. She was still too new to town to involve herself in such sensitive matters. Plus, she knew Mattie was rabidly protective of her nephew.

They had just settled into their chairs and were ready for half an hour or so of debriefing when the bells clanged on the front door. Mattie frowned and said, "Guess I forgot to lock it."

"I'll see," Samantha said, as Mattie went to find her shoes.

It was the Ryzers, Buddy and Mavis, from deep in the woods, Samantha surmised after a quick introduction and once-over. Their paperwork filled two canvas shopping bags, with matching stains. Mavis said, "We got to have a lawyer."

Buddy said, "Nobody'll take my case."

"What is it?" Samantha asked.

"Black lung," he replied.

In the conference room, Samantha ignored the shopping bags as she took down the basics. Buddy was forty-one, and for the past twenty years had worked as a surface miner (not a strip miner) for Lonerock Coal, the third-largest producer in the U.S. He was currently earning $22 an hour operating a track shovel at the Murray Gap Mine in Mingo County, West Virginia. His breathing was labored as he spoke, and at times Mavis took over. Three children, all teenagers "still in school." A house and a mortgage. He was suffering from black lung caused by the coal dust he inhaled during his twelve-hour shifts.

Mattie finally found her shoes and entered the room. She introduced herself to the Ryzers, took a hard look at the shopping bags, sat down next to Samantha, and began taking her own notes. At one point she said, "We're seeing more and more surface miners with black lung, not sure why but one theory is that you guys are working longer shifts, thus you inhale more of the dust."

"He's had it for a long time," Mavis said. "Just gets worse every month."

"But I gotta keep working," Buddy said. About twelve years earlier, somewhere around 1996, they weren't sure, he began noticing a shortness of breath and a nagging cough. He'd never smoked and had always been healthy and active. He was playing T-ball with the kids one Sunday when his breathing became so labored he thought he was having a heart attack. That was the first time he mentioned anything to Mavis. The coughing continued and during one fit of wheezing he noticed black mucus on the tissues he was using. He was reluctant to seek benefits for his condition because he feared retaliation from Lonerock, so he kept working and said nothing. Finally, in 1999, he filed a claim under the federal black lung law. He was examined by a doctor certified by the Department of Labor. His condition was the most severe form of black lung disease, more formally known as "complicated coal workers' pneumoconiosis." The government ordered Lonerock to begin paying him monthly benefits of $939. He continued working and his condition continued to deteriorate.

As always, Lonerock Coal appealed the order and refused to begin payments.

Mattie, who'd dealt with black lung for fifty years, scribbled away and shook her head. She could write this story in her sleep.

Samantha said, "They appealed?" The case seemed clear-cut.

"They always appeal," Mattie said. "And about that time you folks met the nice boys at Casper Slate, right?"

Both heads dropped at the very sound of the name. Mattie looked at Samantha and said, "Casper Slate is a gang of thugs who wear expensive suits and hide behind the facade of a law firm, headquarters in Lexington and offices throughout Appalachia. Wherever you find a coal company, you'll find Casper Slate doing its dirty work. They defend companies who dump chemicals in rivers, pollute the oceans, hide toxic waste, violate clean air standards, discriminate against employees, rig government bids, you name the sleazy or illegal behavior and Casper Slate is there to defend it. Their specialty, though, is mining law. The firm was built here in the coalfields a hundred years ago, and almost every major operator has it on retainer. Their methods are ruthless and unethical. Their nickname is Castrate, and it's fitting."

Buddy couldn't help but mumble, "Sons of bitches." He didn't have a lawyer; thus, he and Mavis were forced to battle it out with a horde from Casper Slate, lawyers who had mastered the procedures and knew precisely how to manipulate the federal black lung system. Buddy was examined by their doctors—the same doctors whose research was being funded by the coal industry—and their report found no evidence of black lung. His medical condition was blamed on some benign spot on his left lung. Two years after he applied for benefits, his award was reversed by an administrative law judge who relied on the reams of medical evidence submitted by Lonerock's doctors.

Mattie said, "Their lawyers exploit the weaknesses in the system, and their doctors search for ways to blame the condition on anything but black lung. It's no surprise that only about 5 percent of the miners who have black lung get any benefits. So many legitimate claims are denied, and many miners are too discouraged to pursue their claims."

It was after 6:00 p.m. and the meeting could last for hours. Mattie took charge by saying, "Look folks, we'll read through your materials here and review your case. Give us a couple of days and we'll call you. Please don't call us. We will not forget about you, but it'll just take some time to plow through all this. Deal?"

Buddy and Mavis smiled and offered polite thanks. She said, "We've tried lawyers everywhere, but nobody'll help us."

Buddy said, "We're just glad you let us in the door."

Mattie followed them to the front, with Buddy gasping for air and tottering like a ninety-year-old. When they were gone, she returned to the conference room and sat across from Samantha. After a few seconds she said, "What do you think?"

"A lot. He's forty-one and looks sixty. It's hard to believe he's still working."

"They'll fire him soon, claim he's a danger, which is probably true. Lonerock Coal busted its unions twenty years ago, so there's no protection. He'll be out of work and out of luck. And he'll die a horrible death. I watched my father shrink and shrivel and gasp until the end."

"And that's why you do this."

"Yes. Donovan went to law school for one reason—to fight coal companies on a bigger stage. I went to law school for one reason—to help miners and their families. We're not winning our little wars, Samantha, the enemy is too big and powerful. The best we can hope for is to chip away, one case at a time, trying to make a difference in the lives of our clients."

"Will you take this case?"

Mattie took a sip through a straw, shrugged, and said, "How do you say no?"

"Exactly."

"It's not that easy, Samantha. We can't say yes to every black lung case. There are too many. Private lawyers won't touch them because they don't get paid until the very end, assuming they win. And the end is never in sight. It's not unusual for a black lung case to drag on for ten, fifteen, even twenty years. You can't blame a lawyer in private practice for saying no, so we get a lot of referrals. Half of my work is black lung, and if I didn't say no occasionally, I couldn't represent my other clients." Another sip as Mattie eyed her closely. "Do you have any interest?"

"I don't know. I'd like to help, but I don't know where to start."

"Same as your other cases, right?"

They smiled and enjoyed the moment. Mattie said, "Here's a problem. These cases take time, years and years because the coal companies fight hard and have all the resources. Time is on their side. The miner will die eventually, and prematurely, because there's no cure for it. Once coal dust gets in your body, there's no way to remove or destroy it. Once black lung sets in, it gets worse and worse. The coal companies pay the actuaries and they play the odds, so the cases drag on. They make it so difficult and cumbersome it discourages not only the miner who's sick but his friends as well. That's one reason they fight so hard. Another reason is to frighten away the attorneys. You'll be gone in a few months, back to New York, and when you leave you'll leave behind some files, work that will be dumped on our desks. Think about that, Samantha. You have compassion and you show great promise for this work, but you're only passing through. You're a city girl, and proud of it. Nothing wrong with that. But think about your office and the day you leave it, and how much work will be left undone."

"Good point."

"I'm going home. I'm tired and I think Chester said we're having leftovers. See you in the morning."

"Good night, Mattie."

Long after she left, Samantha sat in the dimly lit conference room and thought about the Ryzers. Occasionally, she looked at the shopping bags filled with the sad history of their fight to collect what was due. And there she sat, a perfectly capable and licensed attorney with the brains and resources to render real assistance, to come to the aid of someone in need of representation.

What was there to fear? Why was she feeling timid?

The Brady Grill closed at eight. She was hungry and went out for a walk. She passed Donovan's office and noticed every light was on. She wondered how the Tate trial was going but knew he was too busy to chat with her. At the café she bought a sandwich, took it back to the conference room, and carefully unloaded the Ryzers' shopping bags.

She hadn't pulled an all-nighter in several weeks.

19

Samantha skipped the office on Wednesday morning and left town as the school buses were making their rounds, which was not a good idea. Traffic on the twisting highway crept along, stopping and waiting while oblivious and sleep-deprived ten-year-olds, sagging under bulky backpacks, took their sweet time boarding. Across the mountain and into Kentucky, the buses disappeared and the coal trucks clogged the roads. After an hour and a half, she approached the small town of Madison, West Virginia, and stopped, as directed, at a country store under a faded Conoco sign. Buddy Ryzer was at a table in the rear, sipping coffee and reading a newspaper. He was thrilled to see Samantha and introduced her to one of his buddies as "my new lawyer." She accepted this without comment and produced a file with authorizations allowing her to obtain all of his medical records.

In 1997, before he filed his claim against Lonerock Coal, Buddy went through a routine physical exam. An X-ray revealed a small mass on his right lung. His doctor was certain it was benign, and he was right. In a two-hour operation, he removed the mass and sent Buddy and Mavis home with the good news. Since the operation had nothing to do with his subsequent claim for black lung benefits, it was not mentioned again. Mattie felt it was imperative to gather all medical records, thus Samantha's trip to Madison. Her destination was the hospital in Beckley, West Virginia, a town of twenty thousand.

Buddy followed her to her car, and when they were finally alone she politely informed him that they were still just investigating. No decision had been made about accepting him as a client. They would review the file, and so forth. Buddy said he certainly understood, but he was clearly on board. Telling him no would be painful.

She headed to Beckley, an hour's drive through the heart of coal country and ground zero for mountaintop removal. There was so much dust in the air she wondered if a motorist passing through might contract black lung. Without too much trouble, she found the hospital in Beckley, and worked her way through its layers until she found the right clerk in Records. She filled out request forms, handed over authorizations signed by Mr. Ryzer, and waited. An hour passed as she e-mailed everyone she could think of. She was in a cramped, windowless room with no ventilation. Another half hour passed. A door opened, and the clerk pushed a cart through it. A small box was on the cart, and this was a relief. Maybe it wouldn't take forever to review the records.

The clerk said, "Mr. Aaron F. Ryzer, admitted on August 15, 1997."

"That's it. Thank you." The clerk left without another word. Samantha removed the first file and was soon lost in an incredibly mundane hospital stay and surgery. It appeared that the pathologist who wrote the reports was not aware the patient was a miner, nor did he look for signs of black lung. In its early stages, the disease is not readily apparent, and at that point, in August 1997, Buddy was showing symptoms but had not filed his claim. The doctor's job had been straightforward—remove the mass, make sure it was benign, sew him up, and send him home. There was nothing remarkable about the surgery or Buddy's stay in the hospital.

Two years later, after Buddy had filed his black lung claim, the attorneys for Casper Slate entered the picture as they were combing through his medical history. She read their initial letters to the pathologist in Beckley. They had stumbled across the 1997 surgery, where they found a collection of slides of the lung tissue. They asked the doctor to send the slides to two of the firm's favorite experts, a Dr. Foy in Baltimore and a Dr. Aberdeen in Chicago. For some reason, Dr. Foy copied the pathologist in Beckley with a finding that the tissue revealed pneumoconiosis, or complicated black lung disease. Since the pathologist was no longer involved in Buddy's treatment, he did nothing with this information. And because Buddy did not have a lawyer at the time, no one working on his behalf had ever reviewed the records that Samantha was now holding.

Samantha took a deep breath. She sat down with the report, and slowly walked through it again. At that moment, it looked as though Casper Slate lawyers, in early 2000, learned from at least one of their own experts that Buddy had had black lung disease since 1997, yet they fought his claim and eventually prevailed.

He did not receive benefits, but went back to the mines while Casper Slate lawyers buried their crucial evidence.

She roused the clerk, who reluctantly agreed to make a few copies, at half a dollar a page. After three hours in the bowels of the hospital, Samantha saw sunlight and made her escape. She drove around town for fifteen minutes before spotting the federal building, where, seven years earlier, Buddy Ryzer had presented his case to an administrative law judge. His only advocate had been Mavis. Across the room, they had faced a phalanx of expensive Castrate lawyers who toiled daily in the murky world of the federal black lung system.

As Samantha entered the empty lobby of the building, she was practically strip-searched by a couple of bored guards of some nameless variety. A directory by the elevators led her to a file room on the second floor. A clerk, obviously federally tenured and pro-tected, eventually asked what she wanted. She was looking for a black lung file, she explained as politely as possible. Of course her paperwork was not in order. The clerk frowned and acted as though a crime had been committed. He produced some blank forms and rattled off instructions about how one must properly access such a file; it required two signatures from the claimant. She left with nothing but frustration.

At nine the following morning, Samantha again met Buddy at the Conoco station in Madison. He was excited to see his lawyer for the third day in a row, and introduced her to Weasel, the guy who owned the store. "All the way from New York," Buddy said proudly, as if his case was so important heavyweight legal talent had to be imported. When the paperwork was complete and perfect, she said good-bye and drove back to the courthouse in Beckley. The armed warriors who had so bravely guarded the front lobby on Wednesday were evidently off fishing on Thursday. There was no one to fondle and grope her. The metal detector was unplugged. Clever terrorists monitoring Beckley had only to wait until Thursdays to thwart Homeland Security and blow up the building.

The same clerk examined her forms and searched vainly for a reason to reject them, but he found nothing to nitpick. She followed him to a massive room lined with metal file cabinets filled with thousands of old cases. He punched buttons on a screen; machines hummed as shelves moved. He opened the drawer and extracted four large expandable files. "You can use one of those tables," he said, pointing, as if he owned them. Samantha thanked him, unloaded her briefcase, made her nest, and kicked off her shoes.

Mattie, too, was shoeless late Thursday afternoon when Samantha returned to the office. Everyone else was gone and the front door was locked. They went to the conference room so they could watch the traffic on Main Street as they talked. Throughout her thirty-year career as a lawyer, and especially the last twenty-six years at the clinic, Mattie had repeatedly butted heads with the boys (always men—never women) at Casper Slate. Their brand of aggressive advocacy often went even further, into the realm of unethical conduct, perhaps even criminal behavior. About a decade earlier, she had taken the extreme measure of filing an ethics complaint against the firm with the Virginia bar association. Two Castrate lawyers were reprimanded, nothing serious, and when it was all over it had not been worth the trouble. In retaliation, the firm targeted her whenever possible and backstabbed even more fiercely when defending one of her black lung cases. Her clients suffered, and she regretted challenging the firm head-on. She was quite aware of Dr. Foy and Dr. Aberdeen, two renowned and eminently qualified researchers who'd been purchased by the coal companies years ago. The hospitals where they worked received millions in research grants from the coal industry.

As jaded as Mattie was toward the law firm, she was still surprised at Samantha's discovery. She read the copy of Dr. Foy's report to the pathologist in Beckley. Oddly enough, neither Foy nor Aberdeen was mentioned in the Ryzer hearing. Foy's medical report was not submitted; rather, the lawyers at Casper Slate used another slew of doctors, none of whom mentioned the findings of Dr. Foy. Had they been told of these findings? "Highly unlikely," was Mattie's prediction. "These lawyers are known for concealing evidence that's not helpful to the coal company. It's safe to assume that both doctors saw the lung tissue and arrived at the same conclusion: that Buddy had complicated black lung disease. So the lawyers buried it and found more experts."

"How can you just bury evidence?" Samantha asked, a question she'd been repeating to herself for many hours.

"It's easy for these guys. Keep in mind this happens before an administrative law judge, not a real federal judge. It's a hearing, not a trial. In a real trial there are strict rules regarding discovery and full disclosure; not so in a black lung hearing. The rules are far more relaxed, and these guys have spent decades tweaking and manipulating the rules. In about half the cases, the miner, like Buddy, has no lawyer, so it's really not a fair fight."

"I get that, but tell me how the lawyers for Lonerock Coal could know for a fact that Buddy had the disease as early as 1997, then cover it up by finding the other doctors who testified, under oath, that he was not suffering from black lung."

"Because they're crooks."

"And we can't do anything about it? Sounds like fraud and conspiracy to me. Why can't they be sued? If they did it to Buddy Ryzer, you can bet they've done it to a thousand others."

"I thought you didn't like litigation."

"I'm coming around. This is not right, Mattie."

Mattie smiled and enjoyed her indignation. We've all been there, she thought. "It would be a massive effort to take on a law firm as powerful as Casper Slate."

"Yes, I know that, and I know nothing about litigation. But fraud is fraud, and in this case it would be easy to prove. Doesn't proving fraud pave the way to punitive damages?"

"Perhaps, but no law firm around here will sue Casper Slate directly. It would cost a fortune, take years, and if you got a big verdict you couldn't keep it. Remember, Samantha, they elect their Supreme Court over in West Virginia, and you know who makes the biggest campaign contributions."

"Sue them in federal court."

Mattie pondered this for a moment and finally said, "I don't know. I'm no expert on that type of litigation. You'll have to ask Donovan."

There was a knock on the door but neither made a move. It was after six, almost dark, and they were simply not up to another drop-in. Someone knocked again, then went away. Samantha asked, "So how do we proceed with his claim for benefits?"

"Are you taking his case?"

"Yes. I can't walk away from it knowing what I do now. If you'll help me, I'll file it and go to war."

"Okay, the first few steps are easy. File the claim and wait for a medical exam. After you receive it, and assuming it says what we expect, you'll wait about six months for the district director to award benefits, which are about $1,200 a month now. Lonerock will appeal the award, and the real war begins. That's the usual routine. However, in this case we'll ask the court to reconsider in light of new evidence and seek benefits dating back to his first claim. We'll probably win that too, and Lonerock will no doubt appeal."

"Can we threaten the company and its lawyers with exposure?"

Mattie smiled and seemed amused by her response. "Some people we can threaten, Samantha, because we're lawyers and our clients are right. Others we leave alone. Our goal is to get as much money as possible for Buddy Ryzer, not to crusade against crooked lawyers."

"It seems like a perfect case for Donovan."

"Then ask him. By the way, he wants us to stop by for a drink. All the testimony is in and the jury should get the case by noon tomorrow. According to him, things have gone his way and he's feeling very confident."

"No surprise there."

They were sipping whiskey around a cluttered table upstairs in the war room, with coats off, ties undone, the looks of weary warriors, but smug ones nonetheless. Donovan introduced Samantha to his younger brother, Jeff, while Vic Canzarro fetched two more crystal tumblers from a shelf. To her recollection, Samantha had never tasted a brown liquor, straight up. There could have been a few, heavily mixed into a concoction at a frat party, but she had not been aware of it. She preferred wine and beer and martinis, but had always shied away from the brown stuff. At that moment, though, there were no options. These boys were enjoying their George Dickel straight, no ice.

It burned her lips and scalded her tongue and set fire to her esophagus, but when Donovan asked, "How is it?" she managed a smile and said, "Fine." She smacked her lips as if she'd never tasted anything so delicious while vowing to pour it down the drain as soon as she could find a restroom.

Annette was right. Jeff was at least as cute as his older brother, had the same dark eyes and long unruly hair, though Donovan had tidied up a bit for his jury. Jeff wore a coat and tie, but also jeans and boots. He was not a lawyer, indeed according to Annette he had flunked out of college, but according to Mattie he worked closely with Donovan and did a lot of his dirty work.

Vic had spent four hours on the witness stand the day before, and he was still amused by his arguments with Strayhorn Coal's lawyers. One story led to another. Mattie asked Jeff, "What's your take on the jury?"

"They're all in," he said without hesitation. "Maybe with one exception, but we're in good shape."

Donovan said, "They offered half a million bucks to settle this afternoon, after the last witness. We got 'em on the run."

Vic said, "Take the money, you idiot."

Donovan asked, "Mattie, what would you do?"

"Well, a half a million is not much for two dead boys, but it's a lot for Hopper County. No one on that jury has ever seen such a sum, and they'll have a hard time handing it over to one of their own."

"Take it or roll the dice?" Donovan asked.

"Take it."

"Jeff?"

"Take the money."

"Samantha?"

Samantha was breathing through her mouth, trying to extinguish the flames. She licked her lips and said, "Well, two weeks ago I couldn't spell 'lawsuit,' now you want my advice on whether or not to settle one?"

"Yes, you have to vote, or we'll cut off the booze."

"Please do. I'm just a lowly legal aid lawyer, so I'd take the money and run."

Donovan took a small sip, smiled, and said, "Four against one. I love it." Only one vote counted, and it was clear the case would not be settled. Mattie asked, "What about your closing argument? Can we hear it?"

"Of course," he said, jumping to his feet, straightening his tie, and placing his tumbler on a shelf. Along one side of the long table, he began to pace, staring at his audience like a veteran stage actor. Mattie whispered to Samantha, "He likes to practice on us when we have the time."

He stopped, looked directly at Samantha, and began, "Ladies

and gentlemen of the jury, a pile of money will not bring back
Eddie and Brandon Tate. They've been dead now for nineteen
months, their lives crushed out of them by the men who work for
Strayhorn Coal. But money is all we have to measure damages in
cases like this. Cold hard cash, that's what the law says. It's now
up to you to decide how much. So let's start with Brandon, the
younger of the two, a frail little boy, only eight years old and born
two months premature. He could read by the time he was four and
loved his computer, which by the way was under his bed when the
six-ton boulder arrived. The computer, too, was found mangled
and without power, as dead as Brandon."

He was smooth without being showy. Sincere, without a hint
of anything but sincerity. He had no notes and didn't need them.
Samantha was immediately captivated and would have given him
any sum of money he asked for. He was pacing back and forth, very
much onstage and fully in command of his script. At one point,
though, Mattie startled them with "Objection, you can't say that."

Donovan laughed and said, "My apologies, Your Honor. I'll ask
the jurors to disregard what I just said, which of course is impossible and that's why I said it in the first place."

"Objection," Mattie said again.

There were no wasted words, no hyperbole, no flowery quo-
tations from the Bible or Shakespeare, no false emotions, nothing but a carefully nuanced argument in favor of his client, and
against an awful company, all delivered effortlessly, spontaneously.
He suggested the amount of $1 million per child, and $1 million
in punitive damages. Three million total, a large sum to him, and
certainly to the jurors, but a drop in the bucket for Strayhorn Coal.
Last year, the company's gross income was $14 million a week.

When he finished, that particular jury was already in his pocket.
The real one would not be as easy. As Vic poured more whiskey,
Donovan challenged them to pick apart his closing argument. He
said he would be up all night revising it. He claimed the whiskey
loosened his creative thoughts, and some of his best final summa-
tions were the result of a few hours of thoughtful sipping. Mattie
argued that $3 million was too much. It might work in larger cities

but not in Hopper County, or Noland County for that matter. She reminded him that neither county had ever seen a million-dollar verdict, and he reminded her that there was a first time for everything. And, no one could create a better set of facts, facts he had just clearly and masterfully laid out before the jury.

Back and forth, back and forth. Samantha excused herself and went to the restroom. She poured the whiskey down the drain and hoped she never encountered it again. She said good night, wished Donovan all the luck in the world, and drove to the Starlight Motel, where the Booker family was enjoying an extended stay. She had cookies for the kids and two romance novels for Pamela. While Mandy and Trevor toyed with their homework, the women eased outside, where they leaned on the hood of Samantha's Ford and talked business. Pamela was excited because a friend had found a small apartment in Colton, just $400 a month. The kids were falling behind in school, and after three nights at the motel she was ready to move on. They decided to leave early on the next morning, take the kids to school, and look at the apartment. Samantha would do the driving.

20

After two weeks in Brady, or more accurately three weeks away from Scully & Pershing, Samantha's sleep deprivation had been thoroughly exorcised and she was back to her old habits. At 5:00 on Friday morning, she was sipping coffee in bed and hammering out a three-page memo on the subject of Buddy Ryzer's black lungs and Casper Slate's fraudulent behavior in screwing him out of benefits. At 6:00, she e-mailed it to Mattie, Donovan, and her father. Marshall Kofer's reaction was something she was eager to hear.

Another big lawsuit was the last thing on Donovan's mind, and her intent was not to pester him on this momentous day. She was simply hoping he might find the time over the weekend to read about Mr. Ryzer and pass along his thoughts. Ten minutes later, she received his thoughts. His e-mail read: "I have battled with these slimeballs tooth and nail for the past 12 years, and I hate them with a passion. My fantasy trial is a huge courtroom showdown against Castrate, a grand exposé of all their sins. I love this case! Let's talk later. Off to war in Colton. Should be fun!!"

She replied: "Will do. Best of luck."

At 7:00, she drove to the Starlight Motel and gathered up the Bookers. Mandy and Trevor were dressed in their best and eager to get back to school. As Samantha drove, they ate her doughnuts and chattered nonstop. Again, the line between lawyering and social work was getting blurred, but it didn't matter. According to Mattie, in addition to providing legal advice, the job often included marriage counseling, carpooling, cooking, job searching, tutoring, financial advising, apartment hunting, and babysitting. She was fond of saying, "We don't work by the hour, but by the client."

Outside the school in Colton, Samantha stayed in the car while Pamela went inside with her children. She wanted to say hello to the teachers and explain things. Samantha had sent daily e-mails to the school, and the teachers and principal had been supportive.

With the kids securely in place back where they belonged, Samantha and Pamela spent the next two hours looking into the rather sparse selection of rental housing in and around Colton. The apartment Pamela's friend had gushed on about was only a few blocks from the school and one of four units in a run-down commercial building that had been partially converted. The place was clean enough, with a few sticks of furniture, which was important because Pamela had none. It was priced at $400 a month, which seemed reasonable given its condition. As they left, Pamela said, with no enthusiasm at all, "I guess we could live there."

Mattie's slush fund was good for a couple of months only, though Samantha did not divulge this. She gave the accurate impression that money was tight and that Pamela needed to find work as soon as possible. No hearing on the garnishment order had been set; in fact, Samantha had not heard a word from the defendant, Top Market Solutions. She had called the lamp factory twice to make sure Mr. Simmons was in a semi-pleasant mood and that Pamela could still get her job back as soon as the garnishment went away. Prospects for other employment in Hopper County were dim.

Samantha had never seen the inside of a mobile home, had never really thought about doing so, but two miles east of the city limits, at the end of a gravel road, she had her first experience. It was a nice trailer, furnished and clean and only $550 a month. Pamela confessed that she had grown up in a trailer, like so many of her friends, and was fond of the privacy. To Samantha, the place at first seemed incredibly cramped, but as she walked around it she had to confess she'd seen much tighter quarters in Manhattan.

There was a duplex on a hill above the town, nice views and all, but the folks next door gave all appearances of being insufferable. There was a vacant house in a shady part of town. They looked at it from the street and did not get out of the car. From there the search fizzled, and they decided to have coffee downtown, not far from the courthouse. Samantha resisted the temptation to walk over, sneak into the back row, and watch Donovan perform for the jury. A couple of locals in a booth nearby talked of nothing but the trial. One said he had gone by at 8:30 and the courtroom was already packed. In his windy opinion, it was the "biggest trial ever in Colton."

"What's it about?" Samantha asked pleasantly.

"You don't know about the Tate trial?" the man asked incredulously.

"Sorry, not from around here."

"Oh boy." He shook his head and sort of waved her off. His pancakes arrived and he lost interest in holding court. He knew far too much to share in such a short time.

Pamela had a friend in Colton she needed to check on. Samantha left her at the café and drove back to Brady. As soon as she walked into her office, Mattie was right behind her with "Just got a text from Jeff. Donovan wouldn't settle and the jury has the case. Let's grab a sandwich, eat in the car, and drive over."

"I just left there," Samantha said. "Besides, you can't get a seat."

"And how do you know this?"

"I have sources." Instead, they ate sandwiches in the conference room with Claudelle and waited nervously for the next text. When it did not arrive, they drifted back to their offices, puttering, still waiting.

At 1:00 p.m., Mrs. Francine Crump arrived on schedule for the formal signing of her free will. It seemed odd that a woman who owned land worth at least $200,000 would pinch pennies so tightly, but the truth was that she had nothing but the land (and the coal beneath it). Samantha had corresponded with the Mountain Trust, a well-established conservation group that specialized in taking title to land and preserving it. In Francine's simple will, she bequeathed her eighty acres to the Mountain Trust, and to the exclusion of her five adult children. As Samantha read the will to her and explained everything carefully, Francine began crying. It was one thing to get mad and "cut out the kids," but it was quite another when she saw the words on paper. Samantha began to worry about the signing. For the will to be valid, Francine had to be "legally competent" and certain of what she was doing. Instead, for the moment anyway, she was emotional and uncertain. At eighty, and in declining health, she would not be around much longer. Her children would certainly contest the will. Since they would not be able to argue that the Mountain Trust unduly influenced their mother, they would be forced to attack the will on the grounds that she was mentally unfit when she signed it. Samantha would be smack in the middle of an ugly family brawl.

For reinforcements, she summoned both Annette and Mattie. The two veterans had seen it before and spent a few minutes with Francine, chatting about this and that until the tears stopped. Annette asked about her children and grandchildren, but this did not brighten her mood. She said she rarely saw them. They had forgotten about her. The grandkids were growing up so fast, and she was missing it all. Mattie explained that once she died, and once the family learned about the gift of the land to the Mountain Trust, there would be trouble. They would likely hire a lawyer and contest the will. Was that what she wanted?

Francine held her ground. She was bitter at her neighbors for selling out to a coal company, and she was determined to protect her land. She didn't trust her children and knew they would grab the cash as quickly as possible. With her emotions in check, she signed the will, and the three lawyers witnessed it. They also signed affidavits attesting to their client's mental stability. After she left, Mattie said, "We'll see that one again."

At 2:00 p.m., and with no word from the courtroom, Samantha informed Mattie that she needed to return to Colton to pick up the Bookers. Mattie jumped to her feet and they left in a hurry.

———

Donovan was killing time in a gazebo behind the hideous courthouse. He was sitting on a bench and chatting with Lisa Tate, the boys' mother and his plaintiff. Jeff was nearby, on the phone, smoking a cigar and looking nervous.

Donovan introduced Mattie and Samantha to Lisa, and said nice things about the way she had held up during the five-day trial. The jury was still deliberating, he said as he pointed to a second-floor window in the courthouse. "That's their room," he said. "They've had the case about three hours."

Mattie said, "I'm so sorry about your boys, Lisa. Such a senseless tragedy."

"Thank you," she replied softly but had no interest in pursuing the conversation.

"So how was your closing argument?" Samantha asked after an awkward pause.

Donovan smiled the victor's smile and said, "Probably top three of all time. Had 'em in tears, didn't I, Lisa?"

She nodded and said, "It was very emotional."

Jeff finished his call and joined them. "What's taking so long?" he asked Donovan.

"Relax. They had a nice lunch, courtesy of the county. Now they're walking through the evidence. I'd give them another hour."

"Then what?" Mattie asked.

"A big verdict," he said with another smile. "A record for Hopper County."

Jeff said, "Strayhorn offered $900,000 when the jury retired. Perry Mason here said no." Donovan looked at his brother with a sneer, as if to say, "What do you know? Just hang on, I'll show you."

Samantha was struck by the sheer recklessness of Donovan's decisions. His client was a poor woman with little education and dim prospects for a better life. Her husband was in prison for selling drugs. She and her two sons had been living in a small trailer deep in the hills when the tragedy happened. Now she was alone with nothing but a lawsuit. She could walk away right now with at least half a million dollars in cash, more than she had ever dreamed of. Yet her lawyer had said no and rolled the dice. Blinded by the dream of striking gold, he had laughed at the chance of getting a decent sum. What if the jury marched off in the wrong direction and said no? What if the coal company managed to silently exert pressure in places never to be known?

Samantha could not imagine the horror of Lisa Tate walking out of the courtroom empty-handed, with nothing to show for the deaths of her little boys. Donovan, though, seemed unconcerned, even cocky. He certainly appeared calmer than anyone else in their little group. Her father had always said trial lawyers were a strange breed. They walked a fine line between big verdicts and catastrophic failures, and the great ones were not afraid of the risks.

Mattie and Samantha couldn't hang around. The Bookers were waiting. They said good-bye and Donovan invited them to stop by his office later to celebrate.

Pamela Booker preferred the trailer. She had spoken to the owner and negotiated the rent down to $500 a month for six months. Mattie said the clinic could swing the first three, but after that the rent was all hers. When they picked the kids up from school, Pamela told them about their new home, and they drove straight over to see it.

The call came at 5:20, and the news was great. Donovan had his million-dollar verdict; three million to be exact, the amount he asked from the jury. A million for each child, a million in punitive damages. An unheard-of verdict for that part of the world. Jeff told Mattie the courtroom was still packed when the verdict was read, and the crowd applauded wildly before the judge calmed things down.

Samantha was in the conference room with Mattie and Annette, and all three reveled in the verdict. They high-fived, fist-pumped, and chatted excitedly as if their own little firm had done something great. It wasn't Donovan's first million-dollar verdict—he'd had one in West Virginia and one in Kentucky, both coal truck collisions—but it was his largest. They were happy, even giddy, and no one was really sure if they were more excited over winning or relieved at not losing. It didn't matter.

So this is what litigation is all about, Samantha thought. Maybe she was beginning to understand. This was the rush, the high, the narcotic that pushed trial lawyers to the brink. This was the thrill that Donovan sought when he refused to settle for cash on the table. This was the overdose of testosterone that inspired men like her father to dash around the world chasing cases.

Mattie declared that they would throw a party. She called Chester and snapped him into high gear. Burgers on the grill in their backyard, with champagne to start and beer to finish. Two hours later, the party materialized perfectly in the cool evening. Donovan proved to be a graceful winner, deflecting congratulations and giving his client all the credit. Lisa was there, alone. In addition to the hosts and Samantha, the crowd included Annette with Kim and Adam; Barb and her husband, Wilt; Claudelle and her husband; Vic Canzarro and his girlfriend; and Jeff.

In a toast, Mattie said, "Victories are rare in our business, so let's savor this moment of triumph, good over evil and all that jazz, and wipe out these three bottles of champagne. Cheers!"

Samantha was sitting in a wicker patio swing chatting with Kim when Jeff asked if she needed a top-off. She did, and he took her empty glass. When he returned, he looked at the narrow empty spot beside her, and she invited him to have a seat. It was very cozy. Kim got bored and left them. The air was cool, but the champagne kept them warm.

21

Her second adventure in the Cessna Skyhawk was not quite as thrilling as the first. They waited at the Noland County Airfield an hour for some weather to move on. Perhaps they should have waited longer. Donovan at one point mumbled something about postponing the trip. Jeff, also a pilot, seemed to agree, but then saw a break in the front and thought they could make it. After watching them study a weather screen at the terminal and fret over "turbulence," Samantha was secretly hoping they would cancel. But they did not. They took off into the clouds, and for the first ten minutes she thought she might be sick. From the front, Donovan said, "Hang on," as the small plane was tossed about. Hang on to what, exactly? She was in the rear seat, which was cramped even for her. She had been relegated to second class and was already promising herself she would never do this again. Bullets of rain pecked vigorously at the windshield.

At six thousand feet the clouds thinned considerably and the ride became smooth. Up front both pilots seemed to relax. All three on board had headsets, and Samantha, breathing normally, was fascinated by the radio. The Skyhawk was being handled by Washington air traffic control, and there were at least four other aircraft on the same frequency. Everyone was terribly excited about the weather, with pilots calling in the latest updates based on what they had encountered. Her fascination, though, soon led to boredom as they hummed along, bouncing slightly on top of the clouds. She could see nothing below, and nothing on either side. An hour in and she almost nodded off.

Two hours and fifteen minutes after they left Brady, they landed at a small airport in Manassas, Virginia. They rented a car, found a drive-thru for carryout lunch tacos, and arrived at the Kofer Group's new digs in Alexandria at 1:00 p.m. Marshall greeted them warmly and apologized for the emptiness of the place. It was, after all, Saturday.

Marshall was delighted to see his daughter, especially under the circumstances. She was hanging around with a real trial lawyer and seemed keenly interested in pursuing a promising lawsuit against corporate bad guys. After just two weeks in the coalfields she was well on her way to a real conversion. He had been trying in vain for years to show her the light.

After some small talk, Marshall said to Donovan, "Congrats on the verdict down there. Tough place to get one."

Samantha had not mentioned the Tate verdict to her father. She had e-mailed him twice with details about the meeting, but nothing about the trial. Donovan said, "Thanks. There was a line or two in the Roanoke paper. I guess you saw it."

"Missed that," he said. "We monitor a lot of trials through a national network. Your story popped up late last night and I read the summary. A great set of facts."

They were seated around a square table with real flowers in the center, next to coffee in a silver pot. Marshall had dressed down and was slumming in a cashmere sweater and slacks. The Gray boys were in jeans and old sports coats. Samantha wore jeans and a sweater.

Donovan said thanks again and answered Marshall's questions about the trial. Jeff said nothing and missed nothing. He and Samantha exchanged looks occasionally. She poured more coffee and finally said, "Perhaps we should move along."

"Right," Marshall said as he took a sip. "How much do I know?"

"There's nothing new," Samantha said. "I've just started digging and I'm sure we'll learn a lot more after I file the claim for black lung benefits."

"Casper Slate has a nasty reputation," Marshall said.

"They've earned it," Donovan replied. "I've fought them for a long time."

"Give me your lawsuit. Give me your theory."

Donovan took a deep breath and glanced at Samantha. He said, "Federal court, probably in Kentucky. Maybe West Virginia. Certainly not Virginia because of the caps on damages. We file the lawsuit with one plaintiff, Buddy Ryzer, and we sue Casper Slate and Lonerock Coal. We allege fraud and conspiracy, perhaps racketeering, and we ask for the moon in punitive damages. It's a punitive case, plain and simple. Lonerock Coal is currently capitalized at six billion and insured to the hilt. Casper Slate is private and we don't know what it's worth, but we'll find out. As we dig, we hope we find other fraud cases. The more the better. But if we don't, we'll always be ready to take the Ryzer case to the jury and ask for a fortune in punitives."

Marshall nodded as if he agreed, as if he'd done this a hundred times.

Donovan paused and asked, "What's your take on it?"

"Agreed, so far. It sounds good, especially if the fraud really exists and there's no way to explain it away. It certainly looks legitimate, and the jury appeal is fantastic. Actually, I think it's brilliant. A corrupt law firm full of high-priced lawyers hiding medical evidence to beat some poor, sick miner out of his meager benefits. Wow! It's a trial lawyer's dream. It's a clear punitive case with tremendous upside potential." He paused, took a calculated sip, and continued. "But, first, of course, there is the little matter of the actual lawsuit. You practice alone, Donovan, with almost no staff and, shall we say, limited resources. A lawsuit like this will take five years and cost $2 million, minimum."

"One million," Donovan said.

"Split the difference. One and a half. I'm assuming that's still out of your reach."

"It is, but I have friends, Mr. Kofer."

"Let's go with Marshall, shall we?"

"Sure, Marshall. There are two law firms in West Virginia and two in Kentucky that I conspire with. We often pool our money and resources and divide the work. Still, I'm not sure we can risk that much. I suppose that's why we're here."

Marshall shrugged and laughed and said, "That's my business. The litigation wars. I consult with lawyers and with litigation funders. I play matchmaker between the guys with the cash and the guys with the cases."

"So you can arrange one or two million for the litigation expenses?"

"Sure, that's no problem, not in this line. Most of our work involves between ten and fifty million. Two mill is easy."

"And how much does it cost us, the lawyers?"

"That depends on the fund. The great thing about this case is that it'll cost two million, let's say, and not thirty million. The less you take for expenses, the more you keep in fees. I'm assuming you'll get 50 percent of the recovery."

"I've never asked for 50 percent."

"Well, welcome to the big leagues, Donovan. In all major cases the trial lawyers get 50 percent these days. And why not? You take all the risks, do all the work, and put up all the money. A big verdict is a windfall for a client like Buddy Ryzer. Poor guy's trying to get a thousand dollars a month. Get him a few million and he's a happy dude, right?"

"I'll think about it. I've never taken more than 40."

"Well, it may be difficult to arrange funding if we're not at 50. That's just the way it is. So we line up the money, now what about the manpower? Casper Slate will throw an army of lawyers at you, their best and brightest, meanest and slickest, and if you think they cheat now, just wait until their own necks are on the line and they're trying to hide their dirty underwear. It'll be a war, Donovan, one like we seldom see."

"You ever sue a law firm?"

"No. I was too busy suing airlines. Believe me, they were tough enough."

"What was your biggest verdict?"

Samantha almost said, "Please, come on." The last thing they needed was Marshall Kofer onstage telling his war stories. Without the slightest hesitation, he gave that smug smile and said, "I popped Braniff for forty million in San Juan, Puerto Rico, in 1982. Took seven weeks."

She wanted to ask, Great, Dad, and was that the fee you kept offshore and tried to bury until Mom got wind of it?

Marshall continued, "I was the lead lawyer, but there were four of us, and we worked our tails off. My point, Donovan, is that you will need some high-powered help. The fund will scrutinize you and your team before it commits the money."

Donovan said, "I'm not worried about the team, or the preparation, or the trial. I've spent my career looking for a case like this. The lawyers I bring in are all veteran trial lawyers and they know the terrain. This is our backyard. The jurors will be our people. The judge, we can only hope, will be beyond the reach of the defendants. And on appeal, the verdict will be in the hands of federal judges, not state judges elected by the coal companies."

"I realize this," Marshall said.

"You didn't answer the question," Jeff said, almost rudely. "How much do we give up in exchange for the funding?"

Marshall shot him a hard look, then instinctively smiled and said, "Depends. It's negotiable. That's my job to arrange the deal, but, just guessing, I'd say the fund I have in mind would ask for a fourth of the attorneys' fees. As you know, it's impossible to predict what a jury might do; therefore it's impossible to project what the fees might be. If the jury gives you, say, ten million, and the expenses are two, then the expenses come off the top and you split eight with your client. He gets four million, you get the same. The fund gets a quarter of that. You get the rest. Not a great deal for the fund, but not a loser either. A 50 percent return. Needless to say here, fellas, but the bigger the verdict the better. Personally, I think ten million is low. I can see a jury getting highly agitated with Casper Slate and Lonerock Coal and going for blood."

He was quite convincing, and Samantha had to remind herself that he once extracted huge sums from juries.

"Who are these guys?" Donovan asked.

"Investors, other funds, hedge funds, private equity guys, you name it. There is a surprising number of Asians who have discovered the game. They're petrified by our tort system but also captivated by it. They think they're missing something. I have several retired lawyers who struck gold in their day. They know litigation and are not afraid of the risks. They've done quite well in this business."

Donovan seemed unsure. "I'm sorry," he said. "This is all new to me. I've heard of litigation funds but I've never been near one."

Marshall said, "It's just old-fashioned capitalism, but from our side of the street. Now a plaintiffs' lawyer with a great case but no money can take on corporate thugs anywhere and level the field."

"And they review the case and predict the outcome?"

"That's my job, really. I consult with both sides—the trial lawyer and the fund. Based on what Samantha has told me, and a review of the pertinent documents, and especially because of your growing reputation in the courtroom, I have no hesitation in recommending this case to one of my funds. It will approve one to two million bucks in short order, and you're in business."

Donovan looked at Jeff, who looked at Marshall and asked, "Back in your prime, Mr. Kofer, would you take this case?"

"In a heartbeat. Big law firms make lousy defendants, especially when you catch 'em red-handed."

Donovan asked Samantha, "Do you think Buddy Ryzer is up to the challenge?"

She replied, "I have no idea. All he wants are his benefits, present and past. We haven't discussed a lawsuit like this. In fact, he doesn't even know all the stuff I found in his medical records. I was planning on meeting with him next week."

"What's your gut feeling?"

"You want my gut feeling about something I know nothing about?"

"Yes or no?"

"Yes. He's a fighter."

They walked down the street to a sports bar with five screens all showing college football. Donovan was a Hokie from Virginia Tech, rabid as all of them, and was keen to find scores. They ordered beers and gathered around a table. After the waiter placed four tall mugs in front of them, Marshall said to Donovan, "Your name popped up online last night. I was looking at contamination cases in the coalfields—sorry but that's how I spend my reading time—and I came across the Peck Mountain sludge pond and the Hammer Valley cancer cluster. According to a story in the Charleston paper, you've been investigating the case for some time. Anything in the works?"

Donovan made eye contact with Samantha, who quickly shook her head. No, I haven't said a word. He said, "We're still investigating, and signing up clients."

"Clients mean a lawsuit, right? Not prying here, just a bit curious. It sounds like a massive case, and a very expensive one. Krull Mining is a monster."

"I know Krull very well," Donovan said, with caution. Not for a split second would he trust Marshall Kofer with any information he might swap or barter in another deal. When it was obvious he preferred not to talk about the case, Marshall said, "Oh well, I know two funds that specialize in toxic waste cases. It's an extremely lucrative area, I might add."

Is everything lucrative, Dad? Samantha wanted to ask. Then she thought, What a perfect match! Donovan Gray and his gang who either have possession of, or access to, a treasure trove of ill-gotten documents once owned by Krull Mining, and the Kofer Group, a gang of disbarred lawyers who no doubt would bend the law again if put in a bind. That was just in one corner. In the other corner was Krull Mining, a company with the worst safety record in the history of U.S. coal production and an owner who was reputed to be one of the deadliest Russian gangsters in Putin's frat pack. And in the center of the ring, and dodging bullets, were the poor and suffering souls of Hammer Valley who'd been cajoled out of their trailers and sweet-talked into signing up for this thrilling adventure into American tort law. They would be named as plaintiffs and sue for a billion dollars. If they got a thousand they'd spend it on cigarettes and lottery tickets. Wow! Samantha chugged her beer and once again vowed to avoid serious litigation. She watched football on two screens but had no idea who was playing.

Marshall was telling a story about two jets—one from Korea and one from India—that collided over the Hanoi airport in 1992. Everybody was dead and nobody was from America; however, Marshall filed suit in Houston where the juries understand big verdicts. This fascinated Donovan, and Jeff seemed mildly interested. That was enough of an audience for Marshall. Samantha kept watching the game.

After one beer—Donovan was piloting—they walked back to the office and said good-bye. Samantha noticed that the sun was out and the sky was clear. Perhaps the ride home would be nice and smooth, with great visibility.

She pecked her father on the cheek and promised to call later.

22

The Tate verdict brought excitement to the area and was a source of endless gossip and speculation. According to a story in the Roanoke paper, Strayhorn Coal was promising a vigorous appeal. Its lawyers had little to say, but others were not so timid. A vice president of the company called the verdict "shocking." A mouthpiece for some economic development group worried that "such a huge verdict" might harm the state's reputation as a place favorable to business. One of the jurors (unnamed) was quoted and said there had been a lot of tears in the jury room. Lisa Tate was unavailable for comment, but her lawyer was not.

Samantha watched and listened and had late-night drinks with Donovan and Jeff. Diet soda for her, Dickel for them. Strayhorn might have been posturing when it promised an appeal, but Donovan said the company really wanted to settle. With two dead kids at issue, the company knew it would be difficult to ever win. The punitive damages would be automatically reduced from a million to $350,000, so roughly a quarter of the verdict was already gone. The company offered $1.5 million to settle on the Tuesday after the verdict, and Lisa Tate wanted to take it. Donovan let it slip that he was getting 40 percent, so he could smell a nice payday.

On Wednesday, he, Jeff, and Samantha met with Buddy and Mavis Ryzer to discuss the potential lawsuit against Lonerock Coal and Casper Slate. The Ryzers were devastated to learn that the law firm had known for years that Buddy was suffering from black lung, yet hid the evidence. Buddy angrily said, "Sue the bastards for everything," and never, during the two-hour meeting, backed down. The couple left Donovan's office mad and determined to fight until it was over. That night, again over drinks, Donovan confided to Samantha and Jeff that he had mentioned the lawsuit to two of his closest trial lawyer buddies, two guys in different firms in West Virginia. Neither had an interest in spending the next five years brawling with Casper Slate, regardless of how egregious its behavior.

A week later, Donovan flew to Charleston, West Virginia, to file the Hammer Valley contamination case. Outside the federal courthouse, facing a gang of reporters and with four other lawyers beside him, he laid out their case against Krull Mining. "Russian owned," of course. He claimed the company had been polluting the groundwater for fifteen years; that it knew what was happening and covered it up; and that Krull Mining had known for at least the last ten years that its chemicals were causing one of the highest rates of cancer in America. Donovan confidently said, "We'll prove it all, and we have the documents to back it up." He was lead counsel and his group represented over forty families in Hammer Valley.

Like most trial lawyers, Donovan loved the attention. Samantha suspected he rushed the Hammer Valley filing because he was still in the spotlight from the Tate verdict. She tried to back away and ignore the Gray brothers for a few days, but they were persistent. Jeff wanted to have dinner. Donovan needed her advice, he said, because both of them represented Buddy Ryzer. She was aware of his growing frustration with his trial lawyer friends, none of whom were showing any enthusiasm for tackling Casper Slate. Donovan said more than once he would go solo, if necessary. "More of the fee for me," he said. He became obsessed with the case and talked to Marshall Kofer every day. To their surprise, Marshall came through with the money. A litigation fund was offering a line of cash of up to $2 million for 30 percent of the recovery.

Donovan was again pressing Samantha to work in his office. The Hammer Valley case and the Ryzer case would soon be all-consuming, and he needed help. She felt strongly that he needed an entire staff of associates, not just a part-time intern. When he verbally settled the Tate case for $1.7 million, he offered her a full-time position with a generous salary. She declined, again. She reminded him that (a) she was still wary of litigation and not looking for a job; (b) she was just passing through, sort of on loan until the dust settled up in New York and she could figure out the next phase of her life, a phase that would have nothing to do with Brady, Virginia; and (c) she had made a commitment to the legal clinic and actually had real clients who needed her. What she didn't explain was that she was afraid of him and his cowboy style of lawyering. She was convinced that he, or someone working on his behalf, had stolen valuable documents from Krull Mining and that this would inevitably be exposed. He was not afraid to break rules and laws and wouldn't hesitate to violate court orders. He was driven by hatred and a burning desire for revenge, and, at least in her opinion, was headed for serious trouble. She could hardly admit to herself that she felt vulnerable around him. An affair could flare without much effort, and that would be a dreadful mistake. What she needed was less time with Donovan Gray, not more.

She wasn't sure how to handle Jeff. He was young, single, sexy; thus a rarity in those parts. He was also hot on her trail, and she knew that dinner, wherever one might find a nice dinner, would lead to something else. After three weeks in Brady, she rather liked that idea.

On November 12, Donovan, with no co-counsel in sight, marched into the federal courthouse in Lexington, Kentucky, home to an eight-hundred-member law firm officially known as Casper, Slate & Hughes, and sued the bastards. He also sued Lone-rock Coal, a Nevada corporation. Buddy and Mavis were with him, and, of course, he had alerted the press. They chatted with some reporters. One asked why the lawsuit had been filed in Lexington, and Donovan explained that he wanted to expose Casper Slate to its hometown folks. He was aiming for the scene of the crime, and so on. The press had a grand time with the story, and Donovan collected press clippings.

Two weeks earlier, he had filed the Hammer Valley lawsuit against Krull Mining in Charleston and received regional coverage.

Two weeks before that, he had won the Tate case with a spectacular verdict and got his name in a few newspapers.

On November 24, three days before Thanksgiving, they found him dead.

23

The nightmare began in the middle of Monday morning, as all the lawyers were working quietly at their desks, not a client in sight. The silence was shattered when Mattie screamed, a painful, piercing cry that Samantha was certain she would remember forever. They raced to her office. "He's dead!" she wailed. "He's dead! Donovan's dead!" She was standing with one hand on her forehead; the other hand held the phone in midair. Her mouth was open, her eyes filled with terror. "What!" Annette shrieked.

"They just found him. His plane crashed. He's dead."

Annette fell into a chair and began sobbing. Samantha stared into Mattie's eyes, both unable to speak for a second. Barb was in the door, both hands over her mouth. Samantha finally walked over and took the phone. "Who is it?" she asked.

"Jeff," Mattie said as she slowly sat down and buried her face in her hands. Samantha spoke into the receiver but the line was dead. Her knees were weak and she backed into a chair. Barb collapsed into another one. A moment passed, a moment laden with fear, shock, and uncertainty. Could there be a mistake? No, not if Donovan's only sibling called his beloved aunt to deliver the worst possible news. No, it was not a mistake or a joke or prank; it was the unbelievable truth. The phone was ringing again, all three incoming lines blinking as the word was spreading rapidly through the town.

Mattie swallowed hard and managed to say, "Jeff said Donovan flew to Charleston yesterday to meet with some lawyers. Jeff was out of town over the weekend and Donovan was by himself. Air traffic control lost contact with him around eleven last night. Somebody on the ground heard a noise, and they found his plane this morning in some woods a few miles south of Pikeville, Kentucky." Her quivering voice finally gave out and she lowered her head.

Annette was mumbling, "I can't believe this. I can't believe this." Samantha was speechless. Barb was a blubbering mess. More time passed as they cried and tried to come to grips with what was happening. They calmed a bit as the first hint of reality settled in. After a while, Samantha left the room and locked the front door. She moved quietly around the offices, closing curtains and blinds. Darkness engulfed the clinic.

They sat with Mattie as the phones rang and rang in the distance and all the clocks seemed to stop. Chester, with his own key, entered through the rear door and joined the mourning. He sat on the edge of the desk with one hand on his wife's shoulder and patted gently as she sobbed and whispered to herself.

Softly, Chester asked, "Have you talked to Judy?"

Mattie shook her head and said, "No. Jeff said he would call her."

"Poor Jeff. Where is he?"

"He was in Pikeville, taking care of things, whatever that means. He was not doing too well."

A few minutes later, Chester said, "Let's go home, Mattie. You need to lie down, and no one's working around here today."

Samantha closed her office door and fell into her chair. She was too stunned to think of anything else, so she stared at the window for a long time and tried to organize her thoughts. Organization failed her, and she was consumed with the sudden desire to flee Brady and Noland County and all of Appalachia and perhaps never come back. It was Thanksgiving week and she was planning to leave anyway, to head for D.C. and spend time with her parents and maybe some friends. Mattie had invited her to Thanksgiving lunch, but she had already declined.

Some Thanksgiving. They were now staring at a funeral.

Her cell phone vibrated. It was Jeff.

At four thirty that afternoon, he was sitting on a picnic table at a remote scenic overlook near Knox in Curry County. His truck was parked nearby and he was alone, as expected. He did not turn to see if it was her, did not move as she walked across the gravel toward him. He was gazing into the distance, lost in a world of jumbled thoughts.

She kissed him on the cheek and said, "I'm so sorry."

"Me too," Jeff said, and managed a quick smile, a forced one that lasted only a second. He took her hand as she sat beside him. Knee to knee, they silently watched the ancient hills below them. There were no tears and few words, at first. Jeff was a tough guy, far too macho to be anything but stoic. She suspected he would do his crying alone. Deserted by his father, orphaned by his mother, and now left abandoned by the death of the only person he ever truly loved. Samantha could not imagine his anguish at this awful moment. She herself felt as though there was a gaping hole in her stomach, and she had known Donovan for less than two months.

"You know they killed him," he said, finally putting into words what they had been wondering throughout the day.

"And who are they?" she asked.

"Who are they? They are the bad guys, and there are so many of them. They are ruthless and calculating and for them killing is no big deal. They kill miners with unsafe mines. They kill hillbillies with contaminated water. They kill little boys who are sound asleep in their trailer. They kill entire communities when their dams break and their slurry ponds flood the valleys. They killed my mother. Years ago they killed union men who were striking for better wages. I doubt if my brother is the first lawyer they've killed."

"Can you prove it?"

"I don't know, but we'll try. I was in Pikeville this morning—I had to identify the body—and I stopped by to see the sheriff. I told him I suspected foul play and I wanted the airplane treated like a crime scene. I've already notified the Feds. The plane did not burn up, just crashed. I don't think he suffered. Can you imagine having to identify the body of your brother?"

Her shoulders slumped at the thought. She shook her head.

He grunted and said, "They had him at the morgue, just like you see on television. Open the vault, slide him out, slowly pull back the white sheet. I almost threw up. His skull was cracked."

"That's enough," she said.

"Yes, that's enough. I suppose there are certain things in life you're never prepared to do, and after you do them you swear you'll never do them again. Do most people go through life without ever having to identify a body?"

"Let's talk about something else."

"Okay. Good idea. What do you want to talk about?"

"How do you prove it was a criminal act?"

"We'll hire experts to examine the plane from prop to tail. The NTSB will review the radio transmissions to see what was going on right before the crash. We'll piece this thing together and figure it out. A clear night, perfect weather, an experienced pilot with three thousand hours in his logbook, one of the safest airplanes in history; it just doesn't make sense otherwise. He finally pissed off the wrong people, I guess."

A breeze blew in from the east, scattering leaves and bringing a chill. They huddled closer together like old lovers, which they were not. Not old, not new, not current. They'd had dinner twice, nothing more. The last thing Samantha needed was a complicated romance with a definite expiration date. She wasn't sure what he wanted. He spent a lot of time away from Brady, and she suspected there was a girl involved. They had absolutely no future together. The present might be fun, a romp here, a frolic there, a little companionship on cold nights, but she wasn't about to rush in.

He said, "You know, I've always thought the worst day of my

life was the day Aunt Mattie came to my classroom at school and told me my mother was dead. I was nine years old. But this is worse, much worse. I'm numb, so numb you could stick knives in me and I wouldn't feel anything. I wish I'd been with him."

"No you don't. One loss is enough."

"I cannot imagine life without Donovan. We were basically orphans, you know, raised by relatives in different towns. He was always looking out for me, always had my back. I got into a lot of trouble, and I wasn't afraid of my relatives or schoolteachers or the cops or even the judges. I was afraid of Donovan, and not in a physical sense. I was afraid of letting him down. The last time I went to court I was nineteen years old. He had just finished law school. They'd caught me with some pot, a small amount that I was actually trying to sell but they didn't know it. The judge gave me a break—a few months in the county jail but nothing serious. When I was about to walk up to the bench and face the judge, I turned around and looked at the courtroom. There was my brother, standing next to Aunt Mattie, and he had tears in his eyes. I'd never seen him cry. So I cried too, and I told the judge he would never see my face again. And he didn't. I've had one speeding ticket since then." His voice cracked slightly as he pinched his nose. Still no tears, though. "He was my brother, my best friend, my hero, boss, confidant. Donovan was my world. I don't know what I'll do now."

Samantha felt like crying. Just listen, she said to herself. He needs to talk.

"I'm going to find these guys, Samantha, do you hear me? If it takes every dime I have and every dime I have to steal, I'll track them down and get revenge. Donovan wasn't afraid to die, neither am I. I hope they're not."

"Who's your number one suspect?"

"Krull Mining, I guess."

"And that's because of the documents?"

He turned and gave her a look. "How do you know about the documents?"

"I flew with Donovan to Hammer Valley one Saturday. We

had lunch with Vic in Rockville. They were talking about Krull Mining and let something slip."

"That's surprising. Donovan was more careful than that."

"Does Krull Mining know he has the documents?"

"They know the documents are missing and they strongly suspect we've got them. The documents are deadly, poisonous, and beautiful."

"You've seen them?"

He hesitated for a long time, then said, "Yes, I've seen them and I know where they are. You wouldn't believe what's in them. No one will." He paused for a moment as if he needed to shut up, but he also wanted to talk. If Donovan trusted her so much, then perhaps he could too. He went on, "There's one memo from the CEO in Pittsburgh to their headquarters in London in which the CEO estimates the cost of cleaning up the Peck Mountain mess at $80 million. The cost of paying a few tort claims to families hit by cancer was estimated at only ten million max, and that was on the high side. The tort claims at that time had not been filed and there was no certainty that they would ever be filed. Thus, it was far cheaper to let the people drink the water, die of cancer, and maybe spend a few bucks in a settlement than it was to stop the leaks in the slurry pond."

"And where is this memo?"

"With all the rest. Twenty thousand documents in four boxes, all tucked away."

"Somewhere close by?"

"Not far from here. I can't tell you because it's too dangerous."

"Don't tell me. I suddenly know more than I want to."

He released her hand and slipped off the picnic table. He bent down and picked up a handful of pebbles and began tossing them into the ravine below. He was mumbling something she could not understand. He went through another handful, then a third, tossing them at nothing in particular. Shadows were forming and clouds were moving in.

He walked back to the table, stood beside her and said, "There's something you should know. They're probably listening to you. Your phone at the office, maybe even a bug or two in your apartment. Last week we had a guy comb the office again, and, sure enough, there are bugs everywhere. Just be careful what you say because someone is listening."

"You're kidding, right?"

"For some strange reason, Samantha, today I'm not in the mood to bullshit."

"All right, all right, but why me?"

"They watch us closely, especially Donovan. He's been living for years with the assumption somebody was listening. That's probably why he flew to Charleston yesterday to meet with the lawyers face-to-face. They've been meeting in various hotel rooms, staying away from surveillance. The thugs have seen you hanging around with us. They have all the money in the world so they watch anybody who comes and goes, especially a new lawyer in town."

"I don't know what to say. I've talked to my father all afternoon about airplane crashes."

"Which phone?"

"Both, office and cell."

"Be careful with the office. Stick to the cell. We may even start using prepaid cell phones."

"I'm not believing this."

He sat next to her, took her hand, and flipped up the collar of his jacket. The sun was dipping behind the mountains and the breeze was stronger. With his left hand, he slowly wiped a tear from his cheek. When he spoke his voice was scratchy and hoarse. "I remember when my mother died I couldn't stop crying."

"It's okay to cry, Jeff."

"Well, if I can't cry for my brother I guess I'll never cry for anyone."

"Have a go. It might make you feel better."

He was quiet for a few minutes, silent but not tearful. They squeezed closer together as darkness settled in and the breeze came and went. After a long gap, she said, "I talked to my father this afternoon. Needless to say he's devastated. He and Donovan became real pals in the past month or so and Dad admired him a lot. He also knows everyone in this particular field and can find the right experts to analyze the crash. He said that over the years he's handled many small aircraft fatalities."

"Any that were deliberately caused?"

"Yes, as a matter of fact. Two of them. One in Idaho and one down in Colombia. If I know my dad, he's on the phone and computer right now looking, checking out experts for small Cessna crashes. He said the main thing is to make sure the airplane is secure at this point."

"It's secure."

"Anyway, Marshall Kofer is on board if we need him."

"Thanks. I like your father."

"So do I, most of the time."

"I'm cold, are you cold?"

"Yes."

"And we're supposed to go to Mattie's, right?"

"I think so."

Because there was so little left of the Gray family, and their home had been destroyed years earlier, the cakes and casseroles had to be delivered somewhere else, and Mattie's was the logical choice. The food began arriving late in the afternoon, and along with each dish came a lengthy visit by whoever prepared it. Tears were shed, condolences passed along, promises made to help in any way, and, most important, details were pursued. The men loitered on the front porch and by the driveway, smoking and gossiping and wondering what really caused the crash. Engine failure? Was he off course? Someone said he had not radioed Mayday—the universal distress call for pilots. What could this possibly mean? Most of the men had flown only once or twice in their lives, some never, but such inexperience did not diminish the speculation. Inside, the women organized the tide of food, often dipping in for quick taste tests, while fussing over Mattie and pondering aloud the current state of Donovan's marriage to Judy, a pretty young thing who'd never found her place in town but was now remembered with unrestrained affection.

Judy and Mattie had eventually worked out the arrangements. Judy at first preferred to wait until Saturday for a memorial service, but Mattie felt it was wrong to force folks to suffer through Thanksgiving with such unpleasant business still hanging. Samantha was learning, as she watched it all from as much distance as possible, that traditions were important in Appalachia, and there was no hurry in burying the dead. After six years in New York, she was accustomed to quick send-offs so the living could get on with life and work. Mattie, too, seemed eager to speed things along, and she finally convinced Judy to hold the service on Wednesday afternoon. Donovan would be in the ground when they awoke on Thursday and got on with the holiday.

The United Methodist Church, 4:00 p.m. Wednesday, November 26, with the burial to follow in the cemetery behind the church. Donovan and Judy were members there, though they had not attended in years.

Jeff wanted to bury his brother on Gray Mountain, but Judy didn't like the idea. Judy didn't like Jeff and the feelings were mutual. As Donovan's legally married wife, Judy had full authority over all arrangements. It was a tradition, not a law, and everyone understood it, including Jeff.

Samantha hung around Mattie's for an hour Monday night, but was soon tired of the ritual of sitting with other mourners, then grazing through the food covering the kitchen table, then stepping outside for fresh air. She was tired of the mindless chatter of people who knew Mattie and Chester well, but not their nephew. She was tired of the gossip and speculation. She was amused by the speed with which the small town embraced the tragedy and seemed determined to make the most of it, but the amusement soon became frustration.

Jeff, too, seemed bored and frustrated. After being hugged and fawned over by the large women he hardly knew, he quietly vanished. He pecked Samantha on the cheek and said he needed some time alone. She left soon thereafter and walked through the quiet town to her apartment. Annette called her over and they drank tea in the dark den until midnight, and talked of nothing but Donovan Gray.

Before sunrise, Samantha was wide awake, sipping coffee and online. The Roanoke paper ran a brief story about the accident, but there was nothing new. Donovan was described as a devoted advocate for the rights of coal miners and landowners. The Tate verdict was mentioned, along with the Hammer Valley lawsuit against Krull Mining and the Ryzer lawsuit against Lonerock Coal and its lawyers. A lawyer pal in West Virginia described him as "a fearless protector of the native beauty of Appalachia" and "a staunch enemy of wayward coal companies." There was no mention of possible foul play. All applicable agencies were investigating. He had just turned thirty-nine and left a wife and one child.

Her father called early and was curious about the funeral arrangements. He offered to drive down and sit with her during the service, but Samantha said no thanks. Marshall had spent most of Monday working the phone, digging for as much inside info as possible. He promised to have "something" by the time they got together in a few days. They would discuss the Ryzer case, which was now in limbo for obvious reasons.

The office was like a funeral home, dark and gloomy with no prospects of a pleasant day. Barb hung a wreath on the door and locked it. Mattie stayed home and the rest of them should have. Appointments were canceled and phone calls were ignored. The Mountain Legal Aid Clinic was not really open for business.

Nor was the law office of Donovan M. Gray, three blocks down Main Street. An identical wreath hung on its locked door, and inside Jeff huddled with the secretary and the paralegal and tried to put together a plan. The three were the only remaining employees of the firm, a firm that was now dead.

24

A tragic death, a well-known lawyer, free admission, a nosy little town, another boring Wednesday afternoon—mix all of these ingredients and the church was filled long before 4:00 p.m., when the Reverend Condry rose to begin the memorial service. He offered a windy prayer and sat down as the choir sang the first of several mournful dirges. He rose again for some Holy Scripture and a rambling, somber thought or two. The first eulogy was given by Mattie, who struggled to contain her emotions as she talked about her nephew. She proved quite capable of talking while crying, and at times had everyone else crying with her. When she told the story of Donovan finding the body of his mother, her dear sister Rose, her voice cracked and she stopped for a moment. She swallowed hard and forged ahead.

Samantha was five rows back, between Barb and Annette, all three clutching tissues and dabbing their cheeks. All three were thinking the same thought: Come on, Mattie, you can do it. Let's get to the end now. Mattie, though, was in no hurry. This was Donovan's only farewell service and no one would be rushed.

The closed casket was parked at the foot of the pulpit and covered with flowers. Annette had whispered that in these parts many funeral services took place with the casket open, so that the mourners were required to view the deceased while great things were said about him. It was an odd custom, one aimed at making the moment far more dramatic than necessary. Annette said she planned to be cremated. Samantha confessed she had not considered any of her options.

Fortunately, Judy had better sense than to allow such a spectacle. She and her daughter were seated in the front row, just a few feet from the casket. As advertised, she was gorgeous, a slender brunette with eyes as dark as Donovan's. Their daughter, Haley, was six years old and had been struggling with her parents' separation. Now she was thoroughly overwhelmed by her father's death. She clutched her mother and never stopped crying.

Samantha's car was packed and pointed north. She wanted desperately to leave Brady and race home to D.C., where her mother promised to be waiting with take-out sushi and a fine bottle of Chablis. Tomorrow, Thanksgiving, they would sleep late and have a long lunch at an Afghan kabob dive that was always packed on the holiday with Americans who either disliked turkey or wanted to avoid family.

Mattie finally succumbed to a wave of emotion. She apologized and sat down. Another hymn. A few more observations from the Reverend Condry, borrowing from the wisdom of the apostle Paul. And another lengthy eulogy, this from a close friend from their law school days at William & Mary. After an hour, a lot of the crying was over and folks were ready to go. When the reverend closed with the benediction, the crowd left. Most reassembled behind the church and huddled around a purple burial tent next to the grave. The reverend was brief. His remarks seemed off the cuff but on point. He prayed eloquently, and as he wound down Samantha began inching away. It was customary for each person to file past the grieving family and offer a few words of comfort, but Samantha had had enough.

Enough of the local customs. Enough of Brady. Enough of the Gray brothers and all their drama and baggage. With a full tank and an empty bladder, she drove with a purpose for five hours nonstop to her mother's apartment in central D.C. For a few moments, she stood on the sidewalk beside her car and took in the sights and sounds, the traffic and congestion and closeness of so many people

living so near to each other. This was her world. She longed for
SoHo and the frenetic energy of the big city.

Karen was already in her pajamas. Samantha quickly unpacked
and changed. For two hours they sat on cushions in the den, eating
and sipping wine, laughing and talking at the same time.

The litigation fund that promised to bankroll the fraud and
conspiracy case against Lonerock Coal and Casper Slate had already
yanked the money. The deal was off. Donovan had filed the lawsuit
as a lone gunman with the promise that other plaintiffs' lawyers
would soon hop on board to form a first-rate litigation team. Now,
though, with him dead and his pals ducking for cover, the case was
going nowhere. Marshall Kofer was greatly frustrated by this. It
was a "gorgeous lawsuit," one that he would tee up in an instant if
only he could.

He wasn't giving up. He explained to Samantha that he was
running the case through his vast network of trial lawyer contacts
from coast to coast, and was confident he could put together the
right team, one that would attract sufficient funding from another
investment group. He was willing to put up some of his own money
and to take an active role in the litigation. He envisioned himself as
the coach on the sideline, sending in plays to his quarterback.

They were at lunch the day after Thanksgiving. Samantha preferred to avoid the topics of lawsuits, Donovan, the Ryzer case,
Lonerock Coal, and so forth, anything, really, to do with Brady,
Virginia, and Appalachia. But as she toyed with her salad, she realized that she should be thankful for litigation. Without it, she and
her father would have so little to discuss. With it, they could talk
for hours.

He spoke quietly, his eyes flitting here and there as if the restaurant might be filled with spies. "I have a source at NTSB," he
said, as smug as always when he had some inside dirt. "Donovan
did not make a distress call. He was flying at seven thousand feet in
clear weather, no sign of trouble, then he vanished from the radar.

If there was an engine problem, he had ample time to report it and give his exact location. But, nothing."

"Maybe he just panicked," Samantha said.

"I'm sure he panicked. The plane starts going down; hell, they all panic."

"Can they determine if he was using the autopilot?"

"No. A small plane like that doesn't have a black box, so there's no data on what was happening. Why do you ask about the autopilot?"

"Because he told me once, when we were flying, that he sometimes takes a nap. The hum of the engine makes him sleepy, and so he simply flips on the autopilot and dozes off. I'm not sure how you engage it, but what if he fell asleep and somehow hit the wrong button? Is that possible?"

"A lot of things are possible, Samantha, and I like that theory better than the foul play scenario. I find it hard to believe that his airplane was sabotaged. That's murder, and it's far too risky for any of the bad guys he was dealing with. Lonerock Coal, Krull Mining, Casper Slate—all bad actors, sure, but would they run the risk of committing murder and getting caught? I don't think so. And a high-profile murder at that? One that is certain to be fully investigated? I don't buy it."

"Well Jeff certainly does."

"He has a different perspective and I appreciate that. I sympathize with him. But what do they gain by knocking off Donovan? In the Krull Mining case, there are three other law firms at the plaintiff's table, all, I might add, with far more experience with toxic torts than Donovan."

"But he has the documents."

Marshall pondered this for a moment. "Do the other three firms have the documents?"

"I don't think so. I get the impression they're buried somewhere."

"Well, anyway, Krull doesn't know that, not yet anyway. In fact, if I were counsel for Krull, I would assume all the lawyers on the plaintiff's team have access to the documents. So, again, what do they gain by knocking off only one of the four lawyers?"

"So, if we follow your line of reasoning, then Lonerock Coal and Casper Slate would have enormous incentive to take him out. He's the lone gunman, as you say. There's no other name on the lawsuit. He dies one day and within forty-eight hours the litigation funds are gone. Lawsuit's over. They win."

Marshall was shaking his head. He glanced around again; no one had noticed they were there. "Look, Samantha, I loathe companies like Lonerock and law firms like Casper Slate. I made a career fighting goons like them. Hate them, okay? But they are reputable—hell, Lonerock is publicly traded. You'll never convince me they're capable of murdering a lawyer who's sued them. Krull is another matter; it's a rogue outfit owned by a rich thug who roams the world causing trouble. Krull is capable of anything, but, again, why? Knocking off Donovan will not help its case in the long run."

"Let's talk about something else."

"I'm sorry. He was your friend and I liked him a lot. He reminded me of my younger days."

"It's pretty devastating, really. I have to go back, but I'm not sure I want to."

"You have clients now. Real people with real problems."

"I know, Dad. I'm a real lawyer, not some pencil pusher in a corporate firm. You win."

"I didn't say that, and this is not a contest."

"You've said it for three years, and everything is a contest with you."

"A bit edgy, are we?" Marshall said as he reached across the small table and touched her hand. "I'm sorry. I know it's been an emotional week."

Her eyes suddenly watered as her throat tightened. She said, "I'd like to go now."

25

There were four of them, all large, angry, rough-looking people, two men and two women, ages forty-five to sixty, she guessed, with gray hair and rolls of fat and cheap clothes. They were in town for a rare Thanksgiving visit with their momma but were now forced to stay over, to miss work, to deal with a legal mess that was not of their making. As Samantha approached on foot, she saw them loitering around the front door, waiting impatiently for the legal clinic to open, and she instinctively knew who they were and what they wanted. She thought about ducking into Betty's Quilts and hiding for an hour or so, but then what would she and Betty talk about? Instead, she walked around the block and entered the offices from the rear. She turned on lights, made coffee, and eventually drifted to the front, where she opened the door. They were still waiting, still angry; things had been simmering for some time.

"Good morning," she said as happily as possible. A blind person could see that the next hour would be most unpleasant.

The leader, the oldest, growled, "We're looking for Samantha Kofer." He took a step forward, as did the other three.

Still smiling, she said, "That's me. What can I do for you?"

A sister whipped out a folded document and asked, "Did you write this for Francine Crump?"

The other brother added, "It's our mother's will." He seemed ready to spit in her face.

They followed her into the conference room and gathered around the table. Samantha politely offered them coffee, and when all four refused she went to the kitchen and slowly poured herself a cup. She was stalling, waiting for someone else to arrive. It was 8:30, and normally Mattie would be holed up in her office chatting with Donovan. Today, though, she doubted Mattie would arrive before noon. With a fresh cup, she sat at the end of the table. Jonah, age sixty-one, lived in Bristol. Irma, age sixty, lived in Louisville. Euna Faye, age fifty-seven, lived in Rome, Georgia. Lonnie, age fifty-one, lived in Knoxville. DeLoss, the "baby" at forty-five, was living in Durham, and at the moment he was home with Momma, who was very upset. It had been a rough Thanksgiving. Samantha took notes and tried to burn some clock so they might take a breath and settle down. After ten minutes of one-way chitchat, though, it was obvious they were itching for a fight.

"What the hell is the Mountain Trust?" Jonah asked.

Samantha described the trust in great detail.

Euna Faye said, "Momma said she ain't never heard of no Mountain Trust. Said you're the one who come up with it. That so?"

Samantha patiently explained that Mrs. Crump sought her advice on how to bequeath her property. She wanted to leave it to someone or some organization that would protect it and keep it from being strip-mined. Samantha did her research and found two nonprofits in Appalachia that were appropriate.

They listened carefully but did not hear a word.

"Why didn't you notify us?" Lonnie demanded rudely. Fifteen minutes into the meeting it was apparent that there was no real pecking order in this family. Each of them wanted to be in charge. Each was trying to be the chief hard-ass. Though she was on her heels, Samantha stayed calm and tried to understand. These were not wealthy people; in fact they were struggling to stay in the middle class. Any inheritance would be a windfall, one that was certainly needed. The family plot was eighty acres, far more than any of them would ever own.

Samantha explained that her client was Francine Crump, not the family of Francine Crump. Her client did not want her children to know what she was doing.

"You think she don't trust us, her own flesh and blood?" demanded Irma.

Based on her conversations with Francine, it was abundantly clear she did not trust her own children, flesh and blood be damned. But Samantha calmly replied, "I only know what my client told me. She was very clear with what she wanted and didn't want."

"You've split our family, you know that?" Jonah said. "Driven a wedge between a mother and her five children. I don't know how you could do something so underhanded."

"It's our land," Irma mumbled. "It's our land."

Lonnie tapped the side of his head and said, "Momma ain't right, you know what I mean. She's been slipping for some time, probably Alzheimer's or something like that. We were afraid she might do something crazy with the land, you know, but nothing like this."

Samantha explained that she and two other lawyers in the clinic had spent time with Mrs. Crump on the day she signed her will, and that all three were convinced she knew precisely what she was doing. She was "legally competent," and that's what the law requires. The will would stand up in court.

"The hell it will," Jonah shot back. "It ain't going to court because it's gonna be changed."

"That's up to your mother," Samantha said.

Euna Faye looked at her phone and said, "They're here, DeLoss and Momma. Parked outside."

"Can they come in?" Lonnie asked.

"Of course," Samantha said, because there was nothing else to say.

Francine looked even weaker and feebler than she had a month earlier. All five siblings stood and tried to help their beloved mother as she shuffled through the front door, down the hallway, and into the conference room. They placed her in a chair and gathered around her. Then they all looked at Samantha. Francine adored the attention and smiled at her lawyer.

Lonnie said, "Go ahead, Momma, and tell her what you told us about signing the will, about how you don't remember it, and—"

Euna Faye interrupted, "And about how you never heard of no Mountain Trust and you don't want them to get our land. Go ahead."

"It's our land," Irma said for the tenth time.

Francine hesitated as if she needed even more prodding, and said, finally, "I really don't like this will anymore."

And what have they done, old woman, tied you to a tree and flogged you with a broom handle? Samantha wanted to ask. And how was Thanksgiving dinner, with the entire family passing around the new will and frothing in apoplectic fury? Before she could respond, though, Annette walked into the room and said good morning. Samantha quickly introduced her to the Crump brood, and just as quickly Annette read the situation perfectly and pulled up a chair. She never backed down from a confrontation, and at that moment Samantha could have hugged her.

She said, "The Crumps are unhappy with the will we did last month."

Jonah said, "And we're unhappy with you lawyers, too. Just don't understand how you can go behind our backs and try to cut us out like this. No wonder lawyers got such a bad reputation everywhere. Hell, you earn it every day."

Coolly, Annette asked, "And who found the new will?"

Euna Faye replied, "Nobody. Momma was talking about it the other day, one thing led to another, and she got out the will. We near 'bout died when we read what you folks had put in it. Going back to when we was kids Momma and Daddy have always said the land would stay in the family. And now you guys try and cut us out, give it to some bunch of tree huggers over in Lexington. You ought to be ashamed."

Annette asked, "Did your mother explain that she came to us

and asked us to prepare, at no charge, a will leaving the land to someone else? Was she clear about this?"

DeLoss said, "She's not always too sharp these days."

Francine glared at him and snapped, "I'm sharper than you think I am."

"Now Momma," Euna Faye said as Irma touched Francine to calm her.

Samantha looked at Francine and asked, "So, do you want me to prepare a new will?"

All six nodded their heads in unison, though Francine's nodded at a noticeably slower pace.

"Okay, and I assume that the new will leaves the land to your five children in equal shares, right?"

All six agreed. Annette said, "That's fine. We'll be happy to do just that. However, my colleague here spent several hours meeting with Mrs. Crump, consulting and preparing the current will. As you know, we don't charge for our services, but that doesn't mean we don't have limits. We have a lot of clients and we're always behind with our work. We will prepare one more will, and that's it. If you change your mind again, Mrs. Crump, then you'll have to go hire another lawyer. Do you understand?"

Francine looked blankly at the table while her five children nodded yes.

"How long will it take you?" Lonnie asked. "I'm missing work right now."

"So are we," Annette said sternly. "We have other clients, other business. In fact, both Ms. Kofer and I are due in court in thirty minutes. This is not a pressing matter."

"Oh come on," Jonah barked. "It's just a simple will, barely two pages long, won't take you fifteen minutes to fix up. We'll take Momma down to the café for breakfast while y'all do it, then we'll get her to sign it and be on our way."

"We ain't leaving till she signs the new one," Irma said boldly, as if they might set up camp right there in the conference room.

"Oh yes you are," Annette said. "Or else I'll call the sheriff. Samantha, when do you think you can have the will prepared?"

"Wednesday afternoon."

"Great. Mrs. Crump, we'll see you then."

"Come on!" DeLoss said, standing and red-faced. "You got the damned thing in your computer. Just spit it out. Won't take five minutes and Momma'll sign it. We can't wait around here all week. Should've left yesterday."

"I'm asking you to leave now, sir," Annette said. "And if you want faster service, there are plenty of lawyers up and down Main Street."

"And real lawyers at that," Euna Faye said, pushing back from the table. The rest of them slowly got to their feet and helped Francine to the door. As they were leaving the room, Samantha said, "And you do want the new will, Mrs. Crump?"

"Damned right she does," Jonah said, ready to throw a punch, but Francine did not respond. They left without another word and slammed the door behind them. When it stopped rattling, Annette said, "Don't prepare the will. Give them time to get out of town, then call Francine and tell her that we will not be a part of this. They have a gun to her head. The whole thing stinks. If she wants a new will, let her pay for one. They can scrape together $200. We've wasted enough time."

"Agreed. We're going to court?"

"Yes. I got a call last night. Phoebe and Randy Fanning are in jail, got busted Saturday with a truckload of meth. They're looking at years in the pen."

"Wow. So much for a quiet Monday. Where are their kids?"

"I don't know but we need to find out."

The roundup ensnared seven gang members, though the state police said more arrests were coming. Phoebe sat next to Randy on the front row, along with Tony, who'd been out of prison for only four months and was now headed back for a decade. Next to Tony was one of the thugs who had threatened Samantha weeks earlier during her first trip to court. The other three were from central casting—long, dirty hair, tattoos crawling up their necks, unshaven faces, the red puffy eyes of addicts who've been stoned for a long time. One by one they walked to the bench, told His Honor they were not guilty, and sat back down. Annette convinced Richard, the prosecutor, to allow her a private moment with Phoebe. They huddled in a corner with a deputy close by.

She had lost weight since they had last seen her, and her face showed the ravages of meth addiction. Her eyes watered immediately and her first words were "I'm so sorry. I can't believe this."

Annette showed no sympathy. "Don't apologize to me. I'm not your mother. I'm here because I'm worried about your kids. Where are they?" She was whispering, but forcefully.

"With a friend. Can you get me out of jail?"

"We don't do criminal law, Phoebe, only civil. The court will appoint another lawyer for you in a few minutes."

The tears vanished as quickly as they materialized. "What happens to my kids?" she asked.

"Well, if the charges are anywhere near the truth, you and Randy are about to spend several years in prison, separate facilities of course. Do you have a family member who can raise the kids?"

"I don't think so. No. My family turned their backs. His family is all locked up, except his mother and she's crazy. I can't go to prison, you understand. I gotta take care of my kids." The tears returned and were instantly dripping off her cheeks. She doubled over as if punched in the gut and began shaking. "They can't take my kids," she said too loudly, and the judge glanced at them.

Samantha could not help but think, Were you thinking about your kids when you were peddling meth? She handed her a tissue and patted her shoulder.

"I'll see what I can do," Annette said. Phoebe returned to the group in orange jumpsuits. Samantha and Annette took a seat across the aisle. Annette whispered, "She's not technically our client anymore. Our representation ended when we dismissed the divorce."

"Then why are we here?"

"The Commonwealth will try and terminate parental rights. That's something we need to monitor, but there's not much we can do." They watched and waited for a few minutes as the prosecutor and the judge discussed the matter of bail hearings. Annette read a text message and said, "Oh boy. The FBI is raiding Donovan's office, and Mattie needs help. Let's go."

"The FBI?"

"So you've heard of them?" Annette mumbled as she stood and hustled down the aisle.

A wreath was still on the front door of Donovan's office. The door was wedged open, and just inside Dawn, the secretary, was sitting at her desk, wiping tears. She pointed and said, "In there." Loud voices were coming from the conference room behind her. Mattie was yelling at someone, and when Annette and Samantha entered they were greeted with "Who the hell are you?"

There were at least four young men in dark suits, all tense and ready to go for their guns. Boxes of files were stacked on the floor; drawers were open; the table was covered in debris. The leader, one Agent Frohmeyer, was doing the barking. Before Annette could respond, he growled again, "Who the hell are you?"

"They're lawyers and they work with me," Mattie said. She was in jeans and a sweatshirt, and she was obviously agitated. "As I said, I am his aunt and I am the attorney for his estate."

"And I'll ask you again: Have you been appointed by the court?" Frohmeyer demanded.

"Not yet. My nephew was buried just last Wednesday. Don't you have any decency?"

"I have a search warrant, lady, that's all I care about."

"I get that. Can you at least allow us to read the search warrant before you start hauling stuff out of here?"

Frohmeyer grabbed the search warrant off the table and thrust it at Mattie. "You got five minutes, lady, that's all." The agents left the room. Mattie closed the door and pressed an index finger against her lips. Her message was clear: "Don't say anything important."

"What's going on here?" Annette asked.

"Who knows? Dawn called me in a panic after those goons barged in. Here we are." She was flipping through the search warrant. She began mumbling, "Any and all records, files, notes, exhibits, reports, summaries, whether on paper, video, audio, electronic, digital, or in any other form, relevant to, pertaining to, or in any way connected to Krull Mining or any of its subsidiaries, and—it goes on to list all forty-one plaintiffs in the Hammer Valley lawsuit." She flipped a page, skimmed it, flipped another.

Annette said, "Well, if they take the computers, they'll have access to everything, whether it's covered in the warrant or not."

Mattie said, "Yes, everything that's here." She winked at Annette and Samantha, then flipped another page. She read some more, mumbled some more, then tossed it on the table and said, "It's a blank check. They can take everything in the office, whether it's related to the Hammer Valley litigation or not."

Frohmeyer rapped on the door as he opened it. "Time's up, ladies," he said like a bad actor as the agents reappeared en masse. There were five of them now, all itching for trouble. Frohmeyer said, "Now, if you'll please get out of the way."

"Sure," Mattie said. "But as his executor, I'll need an inventory of all the stuff you haul out of here."

"Of course, once you're appointed." Two agents were already opening more file cabinets.

"Everything," Mattie almost yelled.

"Yeah, yeah," Frohmeyer said, waving her off. "Good day, ladies."

As the three lawyers walked out of the room, Frohmeyer added, "By the way, we have another unit searching his home right now, just so you know."

"Great, and what might you be looking for there?"

"You'll have to read the search warrant."

They were rattled and suspected someone was watching, so they decided to stay away from the office. They found a back booth at the coffee shop and felt somewhat secure. Mattie, who had not smiled in a week, almost laughed when she said, "They'll get nothing off the computers. Jeff took out the hard drives last Wednesday, before the funeral."

Samantha said, "So they'll be back, looking for the hard drives."

Mattie shrugged and said, "Who cares? We can't control what the FBI does."

Annette said, "So, let me get this straight. Krull Mining believes Donovan somehow got his hands on documents he shouldn't have, which is probably true. Now that he's filed the lawsuit, Krull is terrified the documents are about to be exposed. They go to the U.S. Attorney, who opens a case, for theft, I assume, and sends in the goons to find the documents. Now that Donovan is dead, they figure he can't hide the documents anymore."

Mattie added, "That's pretty close. Krull Mining is using the U.S. Attorney to bully the plaintiffs and their lawyers. Threaten a criminal action, and prison, and your opponents quickly throw in the towel. It's an old trick, and one that works."

"Another reason to avoid litigation," Samantha said.

"Are you really the executor of his estate?" Annette asked.

"No, Jeff is. I'm the attorney for the executor and the estate. Donovan updated his will two months ago. He kept his will current. The original has always been in my lockbox at the bank. He left half of his estate to Judy and his daughter, part of it in trust, and the other half he split three ways. One third to Jeff; one third to me; and one third to a group of nonprofits at work here in Appalachia, including the clinic. Jeff and I are going to court Wednesday morning to open probate. Looks like our first job will be to get an inventory from the FBI."

"Does Judy know she's not the executor?" Annette asked.

"Yes, we've talked several times since the funeral. She's okay with it. She and I have a good relationship. She and Jeff—that's another story."

"Any idea of the size of the estate?"

"Not really. Jeff has the hard drives and is putting together a list of open cases, some of which are years away from disposition. Hammer Valley was just filed and I assume the other plaintiffs' lawyers will pick up the ball and run with it. The Ryzer case appears to be dead now. There's a verbal agreement with Strayhorn Coal to settle the Tate case for $1.7 million."

Annette said, "I suspect there's some money in the bank."

"I'm sure of it. Plus, he had dozens of smaller cases. Not sure where they'll go. We might be able to handle a few of them, but not many. I often suggested to Donovan that he find a partner or at least a good associate, but he loved having the place to himself. He rarely took my advice."

"He adored you, Mattie, you know that," Annette said. There was a moment of silence for the dead. The waitress topped off their cups, and as she walked away Samantha realized it was the same gal who'd served her the first time she had entered the Brady Grill. Donovan had just rescued her from Romey and jail. Mattie was waiting at the clinic for an interview. It was hardly two months ago, yet it seemed like years. Now he was dead and they were talking about his estate.

Mattie swallowed hard and said, "We need to meet with Jeff late this afternoon and talk about some issues. Just the three of us, away from our offices."

"Why am I included?" Samantha asked. "I'm just an intern, just passing through, as you like to say."

"Good point," Annette said.

"Jeff wants you there," Mattie said.

26

Jeff rented a room at the Starlight Motel, twenty bucks an hour, and tried to convince the manager that nothing immoral was in the works. The manager feigned surprise and ignorance, even seemed a bit insulted that anyone would suggest bad behavior at a hot-sheets joint like his. Jeff explained that he was meeting three women, all lawyers, one of whom was his sixty-year-old aunt, and that they just needed a quiet place to discuss some sensitive issues. Whatever, said the manager. Would you like a receipt? No.

On another day, Mattie might have been nervous about her car being seen at the motel, but a week after Donovan's death she could not have cared less. She was too numb to worry about such trivial matters. It was a small town—let 'em talk. Her mind was focused on far more important matters. Annette rode in the front seat, Samantha the rear, and as they parked next to Jeff's truck she realized he was standing in the door of the room once occupied by Pamela Booker. Next door had been Trevor and Mandy. For four nights, long ago it seemed, they had taken shelter at the motel after living in their car for a month. With Samantha's fearless lawyering and the clinic's generosity, the Booker family had been rescued from the wilds and was now living peacefully in a rented trailer a few miles outside of Colton. Pamela was working at the lamp factory. The lawsuit against Top Market Solutions—Samantha's first—was still unresolved, but the family was safe and happy.

"He's probably been here before," Annette said as they looked at Jeff.

"Enough of that," Mattie said. The three lawyers got out of the car and walked into the tiny room.

"You're serious about this spying stuff, right?" Annette asked, obviously not serious about it.

Jeff leaned against the pillows on the rickety bed and waved at three cheap chairs. "Welcome to the Starlight."

"I've been here before," Samantha said.

"Who was the lucky guy?"

"None of your business." The three lawyers settled into the chairs. There were files and notepads on the bed.

Jeff said, "Yes, I'm dead serious about this spying stuff. Donovan's office was bugged. So was his house. He suspected they, whoever they are, were watching and listening, and it's best if we don't take chances."

"What did the FBI take from the house?" Mattie asked.

"They were there for two hours and found nothing. They took the computers, but by now they know the hard drives were replaced. All they'll find is a bunch of obscene greetings to anyone who might be snooping. So, they'll be back, I suppose. Doesn't matter. They'll never find anything."

"You know you're skirting around the edges of the law," Annette said.

Jeff smiled and shrugged. "Big deal. You think Krull Mining is sitting around right now worrying about who's playing by the rules? No, they are not. Right now they're on the phone with the U.S. Attorney desperate to find out what the Fibbies scooped up in their raids today."

"It's a criminal investigation, Jeff," Annette said with an edge. "One that is aimed at Donovan and those working with him, primarily you, if you in fact have possession of ill-gotten documents, or access to them. These guys are not going to disappear just because you outfoxed them with the hard drives."

"I don't have the documents," he said, a throwaway that no one in the room believed.

Mattie waved her hand and said, "All right, all right, enough of this. We're going to court Wednesday to probate his estate and I thought we were going to talk about that."

"Yes, but there are more pressing matters. I'm convinced my brother was murdered. The crash was not an accident. The airplane has been secured and I've hired two experts to work with the state police in Kentucky. So far there's nothing but they're running tests. Donovan made a lot of enemies, but none bigger than Krull Mining. Some documents disappeared and they suspect he got his hands on them. The documents are deadly and Krull Mining was sweating blood, just waiting to see if Donovan would file the lawsuit. He did, scared the hell out of them, but did not reveal anything from the documents. Now he's dead, and they figure it'll be difficult to produce the documents. The next target could be me. I know they are following me, and probably listening. They're using the FBI to do their dirty work. They're tightening the noose, so I'll be disappearing from time to time. If someone gets hurt it'll probably be the guy on my tail. I'm royally pissed off about my brother and my trigger finger is itchy."

"Come on, Jeff," Mattie said.

"I'm serious, Mattie. If they'll rub out someone as important as Donovan, they won't hesitate to take out a non-player like me, especially if they think I have the documents."

Samantha had cracked a window in a fruitless search for fresh air. The white plaster ceiling was stained with nicotine. The green shag carpet had old stains. She didn't remember the room as being so depressing when the Bookers lived in it. Now, though, she wanted to bolt. Finally, she blurted, "Time out. Excuse me. I'm not sure what I'm doing here. I am just an intern, just passing through as we all know, and I really don't want to hear what I'm hearing, okay? Could someone please tell me why I'm here?"

Annette rolled her eyes in frustration. Mattie sat with her arms folded across her chest. Jeff said, "Because I invited you. Donovan admired you and told you things in confidence."

"He did? Sorry, I just wasn't aware of that."

"You're part of the team, Samantha," Jeff said.

"What team? I didn't ask for this." She massaged her temples as if suffering a migraine. A quiet moment passed. Mattie finally said, "We need to talk about his estate."

Jeff reached for a pile of papers, took some, and passed them around. "This is a rough list of his ongoing cases." Samantha felt like a Peeping Tom as she looked at information that no law firm, large or small, would ever voluntarily divulge. At the top of page 1, under the heading "Major," were four cases—the Hammer Valley litigation, the Ryzer case against Lonerock Coal and its lawyers, and the Tate verdict. Number four was the Gretchen Bane wrongful death case versus Eastpoint Mining, the retrial of which was now scheduled for the following May.

"There is a handshake deal to settle Tate, but I can't find anything in writing," Jeff said as he flipped a page. "The other three are years away from being resolved."

Samantha said, "You can forget Ryzer, unless other lawyers get involved. The litigation fund has pulled the money. We'll pursue the black lung benefits, but Donovan's fraud and conspiracy lawsuit is going nowhere."

"Why don't you take it?" Jeff asked. "You know the facts."

Samantha was shocked at the suggestion and even faked a laugh. "Are you kidding? This is a complicated multistate federal tort case based on a theory that has yet to be proven. I have yet to win my first lawsuit and I'm still terrified of litigation."

Mattie was flipping pages and said, "We can handle some of these, Jeff, but not all of them. I'm counting fourteen black lung cases. Three wrongful deaths. About a dozen environmental claims. I don't know how he kept up with it all."

Jeff asked, "Okay, here's a question from a non-lawyer. Is it possible to hire someone to come in and run the firm, to handle the smaller claims and maybe help out with the bigger ones? I don't know. I'm just asking."

Annette was shaking her head. "The clients won't stick because the new lawyer would be a stranger. And you can be certain that the other lawyers in town are circling like vultures. The good cases on this list will be gone in a month."

Mattie said, "And we'll get stuck with the bad ones."

Annette said, "There's no way to keep the office open, Jeff, because there's no one to run it. We'll absorb what we can. The Hammer Valley litigation has plenty of legal talent behind it. Forget Ryzer. In the Bane case, Donovan has co-counsel in West Virginia, so his estate will be entitled to a fee there if it's ever resolved, but it won't be much. I'm not familiar with these other wrongful death cases, but it looks like liability is not too solid."

"I agree," Mattie said. "We'll look at them closer over the next few days. The most significant case is the Tate verdict, but that money is not in the bank."

"I'll be happy to step outside," Samantha said.

"Nonsense," Mattie said. "Probating a will for estate purposes is not a confidential matter, Samantha. The court file will be a public record, and anyone can walk into the clerk's office and take a look. Plus, there are no real secrets here in Brady. You should know that by now."

Jeff was handing over more papers and saying, "His secretary and I went over these accounts this weekend. The Tate fee is almost 700,000—"

"Less income taxes of course," Mattie said.

"Of course. And, as I said, it's just a verbal deal. I guess the lawyers for Strayhorn can back out, right Mattie?"

"Oh yes, and don't be surprised if they do. With Donovan out of the picture, they could easily change their strategy and flip us the bird."

Samantha was shaking her head. "Wait a minute. If they agreed to settle the case, how can they change their minds?"

"There's nothing in writing," Mattie explained. "Or at least nothing we've found so far. Typically, in a case like this, the two sides sign a brief settlement agreement and get it approved by the court."

Jeff said, "According to the secretary, there is a rough draft of one in the computer, but it was never signed."

"So we're screwed," Samantha said, allowing the word "we" to slip out unintentionally.

"Not necessarily," Mattie replied. "If they renege on the settlement, the case moves forward on appeal, something Donovan was not worried about. It was a clean trial with no reversible error, at least in his opinion. In about eighteen months the verdict should be affirmed on appeal. If the Supreme Court reverses, it comes back for another trial."

"Who'll try it?" Samantha asked.

"Let's worry about that when it happens."

"What else is in the estate?" Annette asked.

Jeff was looking at his handwritten notes. "Well, first of all, Donovan had a life insurance policy to the tune of half a million bucks. Judy is the beneficiary, and, according to the accountant, that money will pass outside his estate. So she's in pretty good shape. He had 40,000 in a personal bank account, 100,000 in his law firm checking account, 300,000 in a mutual fund, and he had a litigation expense fund with 200,000 in it. His other assets are the Cessna, which of course is now worth nothing but insured at 60,000. His house and acreage are appraised by the county at one-forty and he wants that to be sold. His office building is appraised by the city of Brady at one-ninety, and I get that, according to his will. The house has a small mortgage; the office does not. Beyond that it's all personal assets—his Jeep, his truck, his office furniture, etc."

"What about the family farm?" Annette asked.

"No, Gray Mountain is still owned by our father and we have not spoken in years. I don't have to remind you that he didn't make it to his son's funeral last week. Besides, the land is not worth much. I suppose I'll inherit it one day, but I'm not counting my money."

Samantha said, "I really don't think I should be included in this conversation. It's personal and private and right now I know more than his wife does."

Jeff shrugged and said, "Come on, Samantha."

She grabbed the doorknob and said, "You guys talk all the business you want. I've had enough. I'll walk home." Before they could respond, she was gone, outside the room and hustling across the gravel parking lot. The motel was on the edge of town, not far from the jail where Romey had taken her barely two months earlier. She needed the cool air and the walk, and she needed to get away from the Gray boys and their troubles. She had great sympathy for Jeff and the loss of his brother, she felt an emptiness herself, but she was also appalled at his recklessness. Tampering with the computers would guarantee more trouble from the FBI. Jeff was cocky enough to think he could outfox the Feds and disappear whenever he wanted, but she doubted it.

She passed some houses on Main Street and smiled at the scenes inside. Most families were either having dinner or clearing the table. Televisions were on; kids were at the tables. She passed Donovan's office and felt her throat tighten. He'd been dead for a week and she missed him greatly. Had he been single, there was no doubt some manner of romantic and physical relationship would have sprung to life not long after she arrived in Brady. Two young single lawyers in a small town, enjoying each other's company, both flirting and maneuvering; it would have been inevitable. She remembered Annette's warnings about Donovan and his fondness for the ladies, and wondered again if she had been truthful. Or was she simply protecting her own interests? Was she getting Donovan all to herself and didn't want to share? Jeff was convinced he was murdered; her father was not. How much did it really matter when Samantha considered what was obvious—he was gone forever?

She turned around and walked back to the Brady Grill, where she ordered a salad and coffee and tried to kill time. She did not want to return to the office, nor did she want to go sit in her apartment. After two months in Brady, she was feeling the boredom. She enjoyed the work and the daily drama around the clinic, but the lack of anything to do at night was getting monotonous. She ate quickly and paid her check to Sarge, the grumpy old man who owned the café, wished him a good night and pleasant dreams, and left. It was 7:30, still too early to turn in, so she marched on, taking in the brisk air and stretching her legs. She had walked every street in Brady and knew they were all safe. A dog might growl and a teenager might whistle, but she was a tough city girl who had endured far worse.

On a dark street behind the high school, she heard footsteps behind her, heavy sounds of someone who was not trying to follow in silence. She turned at a corner, and the footsteps did the same. She picked a street lined with homes, almost all with porch lights on, and turned onto it. The same footsteps followed. At an intersection, and at a place where she could scream and people would hear her, she stopped and turned around. The man kept walking until he was only five feet away.

"You want something?" she asked, ready to kick and scratch and yell if necessary.

"No, just out for a stroll, same as you." White male, age forty, heavy beard, six feet two, bushy hair boiling out from under an unmarked cap, and a thick barn coat with both hands stuffed into large pockets.

"Bullshit, you're following me. Say something quick before I start screaming."

"You're in way over your head, Ms. Kofer," he said. Slight mountain twang, definitely a local. But he knew her name!

"You know my name. What's yours?"

"Pick one. Call me Fred if you like."

"Oh, I like Bozo better. Fred sucks. Let's go with Bozo."

"Whatever. I'm so glad you think this is funny."

"What's on your mind, Bozo?"

Unfazed, unflinching, he said, "You're running with the wrong crowd, and you're playing a game in which you don't know the rules. You need to keep your cute little ass over in the legal clinic, where you can take care of the poor folks and stay out of trouble. Better yet, for you and for everyone else, pack your shit and go back to New York."

"Are you threatening me, Bozo?" Damned right he was. The threat was being delivered in a dramatic and unmistakable fashion.

"Take it any way you like, Ms. Kofer."

"So, I wonder who you work for. Krull Mining, Lonerock Coal, Strayhorn Coal, Eastpoint Mining—there are just so many thugs to choose from. And let's not forget those crooks in nice suits over at Casper Slate. Who signs your paycheck, Bozo?"

"They pay me in cash," he said as he took a step closer. She threw up both hands and said, "One more step, Bozo, and I'll scream so loud half of Brady will come running." A group of teenagers made a loud approach from behind him, and Bozo lost interest quickly. Almost under his breath he said, "We'll be watching."

"So will I," she retorted, but had no idea what she meant. She exhaled mightily and realized how dry her mouth was. Her heart pounded and she needed to sit down. Bozo disappeared as the teenagers passed without a word or a glance. Samantha began a rapid zigzag back to her apartment.

One block from it, another man materialized from the darkness and stopped her on the sidewalk. "We need to talk," Jeff said.

"This must be my night," she said, as they began walking away from her apartment. She replayed the encounter with Bozo, and kept her eyes moving for more signs of him. There was nothing, though, from the shadows. Jeff listened and nodded as if he knew Bozo personally.

He said, "Here's what's going down. The FBI paid a visit here today, but they also raided the offices of the other three law firms that signed on to sue Krull Mining in the Hammer Valley case. These guys are friends of Donovan's—they were all at his funeral last week. Two firms in Charleston, one in Louisville. Lawyers who specialize in toxic torts and pool their resources and manpower to fight the bad guys. Well, they got raided today, which means, among other things, that the FBI, and we assume Krull Mining too, now know the truth, and the truth is that Donovan did not turn over the stolen documents to the other lawyers. Not yet. That was not the plan. Donovan was very careful with the documents and he did not want to incriminate the other lawyers, so he simply described what's in the documents. The strategy among the lawyers was to file suit, drag Krull Mining into court, goad the company and its lawyers into telling a bunch of lies under oath, then produce the documents for the judge and jury to enjoy. In the general opinions of the lawyers, the documents are worth at least half a billion dollars in punitive damages. In all likelihood they will also lead to criminal investigations, indictments, and so on."

"So the FBI will be back shortly, this time looking for you."

"I think so, yes. They believe Donovan had the documents, now they know the other lawyers do not, so where are they?"

"Where are they?"

"Close by."

"And you have them?"

"Yes."

They walked a block in silence. Jeff called out to an old man sitting under a blanket on a porch. A few steps later, she asked, "How did he get the documents?"

"Do you really want to know?"

"I'm not sure. But knowledge is not a crime, is it?"

"You're the lawyer."

They turned a corner onto a darker street. Jeff coughed, cleared his throat, and began, "At first, Donovan hired a hacker, this Israeli guy who travels the world selling his talents for nice sums of money. Krull had digitized some of its internal stuff, and the hacker got inside without too much of a hassle. He found some pretty interesting material about the Peck Mountain mine site and slurry pond, enough to get Donovan excited. It was obvious, though, that Krull had kept a lot of records out of its digital storage system. The hacker went as far as he could, then bailed out, covered his tracks, and disappeared. Fifteen thousand bucks for a week's work. Not bad, I guess. Risky, though, because he got caught on another job three months ago and is now sitting in jail in Vancouver. Anyway, Donovan made the decision to scope out Krull's headquarters near Harlan, Kentucky. It's a small town and it's kinda strange having such a big operation based in such a rural area, but that's not unusual in the coalfields. Donovan visited a few times, always changing disguises; he loved the cloak-and-dagger stuff and thought he was a real genius at espionage. And he was very good. He picked a holiday weekend, Memorial Day of last year, and went in on a Friday afternoon, dressed like a phone repairman. He rented a white, unmarked cargo van and parked it with some other cars in a lot. He even put fake license plates on the van. Once inside, he vanished into an attic and waited until closing time. There were armed security guards and surveillance cameras outside, but not much inside. I was watching from nearby, so was Vic, both of us armed and ready with an emergency plan in case something went wrong. For three days, Donovan was on the inside and we were on the outside, hiding in the woods, watching, waiting, fighting off ticks and mosquitoes. It was miserable. We were using high-frequency radios to keep in touch and to keep each other awake. Donovan found the kitchen, ate all the food, and slept on a sofa in the lobby. Vic and I were sleeping in our trucks. Donovan also found the records, a treasure trove of incriminating documents that detailed Krull's cover-up of the Peck Mountain site and all its problems. He copied thousands of documents and put the originals back in the files as if nothing happened. On that Monday, Memorial Day, a cleaning crew showed up, and they almost caught him. I saw them first, called Donovan, and he barely made it back into the attic before the janitors entered the building. He stayed there for three hours, smothering in the heat."

"How did he get the documents out?"

"Trash bags, just another load of garbage. He put seven bags in a Dumpster behind the office building. We knew the garbage truck would run Tuesday morning. Vic and I followed it to the landfill. Donovan walked out of the office, changed costumes and became an FBI agent, and showed up at the landfill with a badge. The people who work at landfills really don't care where the stuff comes from, or what happens to it, and after a few harsh words from Agent Donovan they threw up their hands. We loaded the trash bags into the rental van and sprinted back to Brady. We worked around the clock for three days sorting, arranging, and indexing, then we hid the documents in a mini-storage not far from Vic's home near Beckley. Later, we moved them again, and again."

"And the good folks at Krull Mining had no clue that someone had vandalized their offices?"

"It wasn't that clean. Donovan had to jimmy some locks and break into some file cabinets, and he kept some of the original documents. He left a trail. There were surveillance cameras all over the exterior, and we're sure they recorded images of him. But you would never know it was him because of the disguises. Plus, Donovan and Vic thought it was important for Krull to know that someone had been there. We went back later that afternoon, that Tuesday, and watched from a distance. Police cars were coming and going. Folks were obviously agitated."

"It's a great story, but it strikes me as being incredibly reckless."

"Of course it was. But that was my brother. His philosophy was that since the bad guys are always cheating—"

"I know, I know. He told me more than once. What's on his computer hard drives?"

"Nothing sensitive. He wasn't stupid."

"Then why did you take them?"

"He told me to. I had strict instructions in the event something happened to him. There was a case in Mississippi a few years back where the FBI raided a law office and grabbed all the computers. Donovan lived in fear of that, so I had my orders."

"And what are you supposed to do with the Krull documents?"

"Deliver them to the other lawyers before the FBI finds them."

"Can the FBI find them?"

"Highly unlikely." They were approaching the courthouse from a narrow side street. Jeff pulled something out of his pocket and handed it to her. "It's a prepaid cell phone," he said. "Your very own."

She stared at it and said, "I have a phone. Thanks."

"But your phone is not secure. This one is."

She looked at him and did not reach for the phone. "And why might I need this?"

"To talk to me and Vic, no one else."

She took a step back and shook her head. "I don't believe this, Jeff. If I take that phone, then I join your little conspiracy. Why me?"

"Because we trust you."

"You don't even know me. I've only been here for two months."

"Exactly. You don't know anyone, or anything. You've yet to be corrupted. You don't talk because you have no one to talk to. You're smart as hell, fun to be around, and very cute."

"Oh great. Just what I need to hear. I'll look spectacular in an orange jumpsuit with chains around my ankles."

"You would, yes. You'd look great in anything, or nothing."

"Was that a pickup line?"

"Maybe."

"Okay, the answer is not now. Jeff, I'm seriously considering packing my bags, hopping in my rented car, slinging gravel out of here, as you locals like to say, and not stopping until I get to New York City, where I belong. I don't like what's happening around me and I did not ask for all this trouble."

"You can't leave. You know too much."

"After twenty-four hours in Manhattan I'll forget it all, believe me."

Down the street, Sarge slammed the door to the café and lumbered away. Nothing else moved on Main Street. Jeff gently took her arm and led her off the sidewalk to a dark spot beneath some trees near a memorial to Noland County's war dead. He pointed to something in the distance, far behind the courthouse, two blocks away. Almost whispering he said, "See that black Ford pickup truck parked next to the old Volkswagen?"

"I don't know a Ford from a Dodge. Who is it?"

"There are two of them, probably your new pal Bozo and a jackass I refer to as Jimmy."

"Jimmy?"

"Jimmy Carter. Big teeth, big smile, sandy hair."

"Got it. How clever. What are Bozo and Jimmy doing sitting in a parked truck at eight thirty tonight?"

"Talking about us."

"I want to go to New York, where it's safe."

"Can't really blame you. Look, I'm disappearing for a couple of days. Please take this phone so I'll have someone to talk to." He slid the prepaid cell phone into her hand, and after a second or two, she took it.

27

Early Tuesday morning, Samantha left Brady and headed for Madison, West Virginia, an hour-and-a-half drive that could take twice that long if the roads were choked with coal trucks and school buses. A strong breeze scattered the few leaves still on the trees. The color was gone, and the ridges and valleys were a dull, depressing shade of brown that wouldn't change until spring. There was a chance of light snow tomorrow, the first of the season. She caught herself glancing into the rearview mirror, and at times managed to smile at her paranoia. Why would anyone waste time following her through the mountains of Appalachia? She was just a temp, an unpaid intern who was growing more homesick by the day. She planned to spend Christmas in New York, to catch up with friends and places, and she was already wondering if she would have the guts to return to Appalachia.

Her new cell phone was on the passenger seat, and she glanced at it and wondered what Jeff was doing. For an hour she thought about calling him just to see if it worked, but she knew it did. And when, exactly, was she supposed to use the damned thing? And for what purpose?

On the main highway south of town she found the meeting place—the Cedar Grove Missionary Baptist Church. She had explained to her clients that they needed to talk, in private, and not at the gas station where Buddy drank his morning coffee and everyone felt free to participate in every conversation. The Ryzers suggested their church, and Samantha speculated it was because they did not want her to see their home. They were sitting in Buddy's truck in the parking lot, watching the occasional car go by, seemingly without a care in the world. Mavis hugged Samantha as if she were family, and they walked to the fellowship hall behind the small chapel. The door was unlocked; the large room was empty. They pulled folding chairs around a card table and talked about the weather and Christmas plans.

Finally, Samantha got around to business. "I assume you received the letter from Donovan's office with the tragic news."

Both nodded sadly. Buddy mumbled, "Such a good man." Mavis asked, "What does it mean, you know, for us and the case?"

"That's why I'm here. To explain and answer questions. The black lung claim will continue at full speed. It was filed last month and, as you know, we're waiting for the medical exam. But I'm afraid the big lawsuit is dead, for now anyway. When Donovan filed the case over in Lexington, he was acting alone. Usually, in these big cases, especially ones that take years and eat up a lot of cash, Donovan would put together a litigation team of several other lawyers and firms. They would split the labor and expenses. But in your case, he was still trying to convince some of his lawyer buddies to hop on board. Frankly, they were reluctant. Taking on Lonerock Coal and its law firm and trying to prove behavior that's criminal is a huge job."

"Y'all explained all this before," Buddy said bluntly.

"Donovan explained it. I was in the room, but, as I made clear, I was not joining the big case as a lawyer."

"So we have no one?" Mavis asked.

"That's correct. As of now, there's no one to handle the case, and it has to be dismissed. I'm sorry."

Buddy's breathing was labored enough when he was perfectly content, but the slightest bit of stress or unpleasantness made him gasp. "This ain't right," he said, his mouth wide open as he sucked in air. Mavis stared at her in disbelief, then wiped a tear from her cheek.

"No, it's not right," Samantha said. "But what happened to Donovan was not right either. He was only thirty-nine years old and was doing great work as a lawyer. His death was a senseless tragedy that has left all of his clients out in the cold. You're not the only ones who are looking for answers."

"Y'all suspect foul play?" Buddy asked.

"It's still under investigation and so far there's no evidence of wrongdoing. A lot of unanswered questions, but no real proof."

"Looks kinda fishy to me," he said. "We catch them sumbitches red-handed hiding documents and screwing people, then Donovan files a billion-dollar lawsuit, and then his airplane crashes under mysterious circumstances."

"Buddy, your language," Mavis scolded. "You are in church."

"I'm in the fellowship hall. The church is right over there."

"It's still the church. Watch your language."

Chastised, Buddy shrugged and said, "I'll bet they find something."

Mavis said, "They're harassing him at work. It started right after we filed the big lawsuit over in Lexington. Tell her about it, Buddy. Don't you think it's important, Samantha? Don't you need to know?"

"It ain't nothing I can't handle," Buddy said. "Just a little nuisance treatment. They put me back driving a haul truck, which is a little rougher than the track loader, but it ain't no big deal. And they put me to working nights three times last week. My schedule was set for months, and now they're jacking me around with different shifts. I can take it. I still got a job at a good wage. Hell, the way it is now with no union protection, they could walk in tomorrow and fire me on the spot. I couldn't do nothing about it. They busted our union twenty years ago and we've been fair game ever since. I'm lucky to have a job."

Mavis said, "True, but you can't work much longer. He has to climb up these steps to get in the haul truck, and he can barely make it. They watch him too, just waiting for him to collapse or something so they can say he's disabled and therefore a danger, then they can fire him."

"They can fire me anyway. I just said that."

Mavis bit her tongue as Buddy inhaled noisily. Samantha removed some papers from her briefcase and placed them on the table. She said, "This is a motion to dismiss, and I need you to sign it."

"Dismiss what?" Buddy asked, though he knew the answer. He refused to look at the papers.

"The federal lawsuit against Lonerock Coal and Casper Slate."

"Who files it?"

"You met Mattie, my boss at the clinic. She is Donovan's aunt and she's also the attorney for his estate. The court will give her the authority to wind up his business."

"And what if I don't sign it?"

Samantha had not anticipated this, and, knowing so little about federal procedure, she wasn't sure of her answer, but a quick response was needed nonetheless. "If the case is not pushed by you, the plaintiff, then it will eventually be dismissed by the court."

"So either way, it's dead?" Buddy asked.

"Yes."

"Okay, I'm not quitting. I'll not sign it."

Mavis blurted, "Why don't you take the case? You're a lawyer." Both eyed her intently, and it was obvious the question had been kicked around at length.

This, Samantha had anticipated. She replied, "Yes, but I am not experienced in federal court and I'm not licensed in Kentucky." They absorbed this without comment, and without really understanding it. A lawyer is a lawyer, right?

Mavis shifted gears with "Now, on this black lung claim, you said you were gonna calculate all the back benefits we're entitled to. And you said that if we win the case, we get to go back to the day we first filed the claim, some nine years ago. Is that right?"

"That's correct," Samantha said, shuffling for some notes. "And according to our numbers, it's about $85,000."

"That's not much money," Buddy said in disgust, as if the paltry sum could be blamed on Samantha. He drew in mightily and continued, "They ought to pay more, a helluva lot more after what they done. I should've quit working in the mines ten years ago when I got sick, and I would have if I'd had the benefits. But no, hell no, I had to keep working and keep breathing the dust."

"Just got sicker and sicker," Mavis added gravely.

"Now I won't be able to work another year, two at max. And if we ever get 'em in court they'll be liable for almost nothing. It ain't right."

"I agree," Samantha said. "But we've had this conversation, Buddy, and more than once."

"That's why I want to sue them bastards in federal court."

"Your language, Buddy,"

"I'll cuss if I want to, dammit Mavis."

"Look, I need to be going," Samantha said, reaching for her briefcase. "I wish you would reconsider your decision not to sign this dismissal."

"I'm not quitting," Buddy said, gasping.

"Fine, but I'm not driving over here again for this. Understood?"

He just nodded. Mavis walked out with her, leaving Buddy behind for a few moments. At the car, Mavis said, "Thank you so much, Samantha. We are grateful. We went years without a lawyer, and now it's comforting to know we have one. He's dying and he knows it, so he has some bad days when he's not too pleasant."

"I understand."

At the ancient Conoco station, Samantha stopped for gas and, hopefully, a drinkable cup of coffee. A few vehicles were parked to the side of the building, all with West Virginia license plates, and none of which she recognized. Jeff had told her to be more aware, to watch every car and truck, notice every license plate, look at faces without staring, and listen to voices while appearing uninterested. Assume someone is always watching, he had warned, but she found it difficult to accept.

"They believe we have something they desperately want," he had said. The "we" part still troubled her. She didn't recall joining anyone's team. As she stared at the pump, she saw a man enter the store, though she had not noticed another vehicle arrive in the past few minutes.

Bozo was back. She paid with a credit card at the pump and could have sped away, but she needed confirmation. She entered through the front door and said good morning to the clerk at the register. Several old men were sitting in rockers around a potbellied stove and none seemed to notice her. A few more steps and she was in the tiny café, which was nothing but a cheap add-on with a dozen tables adorned with checkered cloth. Five people were eating, sipping coffee, and talking.

He was seated at the counter, staring at the grill, where a cook was frying bacon. She couldn't see his face and didn't want a scene, and for a second she stood awkwardly in the middle of the café, uncertain. She caught a glance or two and decided to leave. She drove back into Madison and stopped at a convenience store where she bought a road map. Her leased Ford had a GPS but she had not bothered to program it. She needed directions fast.

Half an hour later, as she drifted along a county road somewhere in Lawrence County, Kentucky, her new cell phone finally found enough service for a call. Jeff answered after four rings. She calmly explained what was happening, and he made her repeat everything in slow motion.

"He wanted you to see him," Jeff said. "Why else would he risk being seen? It's not an unusual tactic. He knows you're not going to punch him or anything, so he just delivers a not so subtle message."

"Which is?"

"We're watching. We can always find you. You're hanging around with the wrong people and you might get hurt."

"Okay, I got the message. Now what?"

"Nothing. Just keep your eyes open and see if he's waiting when you get back to Brady."

"I don't want to go back to Brady."

"Sorry."

"Where are you?"

"I'm on the road for a few days."

"Vague enough."

She drove into Brady just before noon and saw no one suspicious. She parked on the street near the office, and from behind her sunglasses managed to scan the area before going inside. On the one hand, she felt like an idiot; on the other, she half expected to see Bozo lurking behind a tree. And what the hell was he going to do? Stalking her would bore any private eye to death.

The Crump brood was calling. Evidently, Francine had told one of them that she had changed her mind again and planned to meet with Ms. Kofer and make no changes to her existing will. This, of course, fired up the Crumps, and they were burning up the phone lines in an effort to find Ms. Kofer and set her straight, again. No one at the clinic had heard from Francine. Samantha reluctantly took the stack of phone messages from Barb, who offered the unsolicited suggestion that she should call only one, perhaps Jonah, the oldest, and explain that their dear mother had not called the clinic, and insist that they stop harassing the front desk.

She closed her door and called Jonah. He said hello pleasantly enough, then immediately threatened to sue her and get her disbarred if she again messed with "Momma's will." She said she hadn't seen nor heard from Francine in the past twenty-four hours. She had no appointment scheduled with her. Nothing. This calmed him a little, though he was ready to erupt any second.

She said, "Could it be possible that your mother is playing games with you?"

"Momma don't think like that," he said.

She politely asked him to call off the dogs, to ask his siblings to stop calling the clinic. He refused, and they finally brokered a deal: if Francine came to the office seeking legal advice, Samantha would ask her to call Jonah and inform him of what she was doing.

She quickly hung up, and two seconds later Barb buzzed her. "It's the FBI," she said.

The caller identified himself as Agent Banahan, from the Roanoke office, and said he was looking for a man named Jeff Gray. Samantha admitted to knowing Jeff Gray, and asked the agent how she might go about confirming his identity. Banahan said he would be happy to stop by her office in half an hour or so; he was in the area. She said she would not discuss anything over the phone and agreed to the meeting. Twenty minutes later, he was in the reception area being examined by Barb, who thought he was quite cute and thought of herself as quite the flirt. Banahan was not impressed and took a seat in the small conference room where Samantha and Mattie were waiting with a recorder on the table.

After terse introductions, and a close examination of his credentials by both lawyers, Mattie began by saying, "Jeff Gray is my nephew."

"We know that," Banahan said with a smirk, and the women instantly disliked him. "Do you know where he is?"

Mattie looked at Samantha and said, "I don't. Do you?"

"No." She wasn't lying; at that moment she had no idea where Jeff was hiding.

"When did you last speak to him?" he asked, in Samantha's direction.

Mattie interrupted by saying, "Look, his brother was killed Monday of last week; we buried him on Wednesday, five days before you boys raided his office. Under the terms of his will, Jeff is the executor and I'm the attorney for the executor. So, yes, I'll be talking a lot to my nephew. What is it you want?"

"We have a lot of questions."

"Do you have a warrant for his arrest?"

"No."

"Good, so he is not evading an arrest."

"That's right. We just want to talk."

"Any and all conversations with Jeff Gray will take place right here, at this table. Understood? I will advise him to say nothing outside the presence of Ms. Kofer and me, okay?"

"That's fine, Ms. Wyatt, so when can we chat with him?"

Mattie relaxed and said, "Well, I'm not sure where he is today. I just tried his cell and it went straight to voice mail." Samantha shook her head as if she hadn't spoken to Jeff in weeks. Mattie continued, "We were scheduled to go to court tomorrow to open the estate and start the process of probate, but the judge rescheduled it until next week. So, I don't know where he is at this moment."

Samantha asked, "Is this related to the actions the FBI took yesterday when it confiscated files from the office of Donovan Gray?"

Banahan showed her both palms and said, "Isn't that pretty obvious?"

"Seems like it is. Who are you investigating, now that Donovan Gray is dead?"

"I'm not at liberty to say."

Mattie asked, "Is Jeff a subject of your investigation?"

"No, not at this time."

"He's done nothing wrong," Mattie said.

28

The damage was inflicted at the Millard Break Mine near Wittsburg, Kentucky, in an attack similar to the others. Firing from a position on the east face of Trace Mountain, a densely wooded ridge five hundred feet above the strip mine, the snipers found their range from about seven hundred yards and had a grand time taking out forty-seven tires, each weighing nine hundred pounds and costing $18,000. The two night watchmen, both heavily armed themselves, told authorities the attack lasted about ten minutes and at times sounded like a war as sniper rifles snapped and echoed across the valley and tires exploded nearby. The first volley hit at 3:05 a.m. All mining machinery was idle; all operators safely at home. One security guard jumped into a truck for some idea of pursuit—he wasn't sure exactly where he might be headed—but was soon dissuaded when the pickup took fire and had two of its tires blown off. The other security guard ducked into an office trailer to call the law, but was forced to take cover when a burst of gunfire blew out all the windows. These were significant events because they directly endangered human life. In the other attacks, the snipers had been careful not to hurt anyone. They went after machinery, not people. Now, though, they were breaking serious laws. The guards thought there were at least three rifles in play, though, admittedly, it was difficult to tell in the chaos.

The owner, Krull Mining, made the usual harsh and threatening statements to the press. It offered an impressive reward. The county sheriff promised a thorough investigation and swift arrests, some rather blustery and shortsighted comments in light of the fact that "these ecoterrorists" had been marauding through southern Appalachia with impunity for the better part of two years now.

The news story went on to recap recent attacks and speculated that the snipers had used the same weaponry as before—the 51-millimeter cartridge that's normally fired from the M24E long-range rifle, the same one army snipers were using in Iraq and routinely scoring kills at over one thousand yards. An expert was quoted as saying that using such a rifle from such a distance, and in the dead of night with easily available optic technology, would make it virtually impossible to track down the snipers.

Krull Mining said there was a tight market for tires, a shortage in some places, and the mine could be closed for several days.

Samantha read the story on her laptop as she sipped coffee Friday morning at the office. She had a sick feeling that Jeff was involved with the gang, if not its leader. Almost two weeks after the death of his brother, he needed to make a statement, to lash out in his own brand of retribution, and strike a blow at Krull Mining. If her hunch was accurate, it was just another reason to pack her bags. She e-mailed the story to Mattie down the hall, then walked into her office and said, "To be perfectly honest, I think Jeff is involved in this."

Mattie responded with a fake laugh at such foolishness. She said, "Samantha, this is the first Friday in December, the day we decorate the office, along with everybody else in Brady. It's the first day I've managed to feel good and actually smile since Donovan died. I don't want to ruin the day by worrying about what Jeff is up to. Have you talked to him?"

"No, why should I? We're not involved, as you like to say. He doesn't check in with me."

"Good, let's forget about Jeff for a little while and try to muster up some Christmas cheer."

Barb cranked up the radio and soon carols were ringing throughout the offices. She was in charge of the tree, a sad little plastic reproduction they kept in a broom closet the rest of the year, but by the time they strung up lights and hung ornaments it was showing signs of life. Annette placed ivy and mistletoe all over the front porch and tacked a wreath to the door. They hauled in food, and lunch was a leisurely affair in the conference room, with Chester supplying a beef stew from a Crock-Pot. All work was forgotten; all clients ignored. The phone seldom rang, as if the rest of the county was also busy getting in the spirit. After lunch, Samantha went to the courthouse, and along the way noticed that every shop and office was being decorated. A city crew was busy hanging silver bells on light posts above the streets. Another was anchoring a large, freshly cut fir in the park next to the courthouse. Christmas was suddenly in the air and the entire town was catching the spirit.

At dark, all of Brady arrived and throngs of people clogged the sidewalks along Main Street, drifting from store to store, picking up hot cider and gingerbread cookies as they went. Traffic was blocked from the street and children waited excitedly for the parade. It materialized around seven, when sirens could be heard in the distance. The crowd pressed closer and lined Main. Samantha watched with Kim, Adam, and Annette. The sheriff led the procession, his brown-and-white patrol car gleaming with fresh polish. His entire fleet followed. Samantha wondered if ole Romey might sneak into the action, but there was no sign of him. The high school band marched by with a rather weak rendition of "O Come, All Ye Faithful." It was a small band from a small high school.

"They're not very good are they?" Adam whispered to Samantha. "I think they're great," she replied.

The Girl Scouts marched by, followed by the Boy Scouts. A float carried some disabled vets in wheelchairs, all happy to be alive and enjoying another Christmas. The star was Mr. Arnold Potter, age ninety-one, a survivor of D-day, sixty-four years ago. He was the county's greatest living hero. The Shriners zipped about on their mini-motorcycles, stealing the show as always. The Rotary Club's float was a Nativity scene with real sheep and goats, all behaving for the moment. A large float pulled by a late-model Ford pickup was packed with the children's choir from the First Baptist Church. The kids were dressed in white robes and their angelic voices sang "O Little Town of Bethlehem" in near-perfect pitch. The mayor rode in a 1958 convertible Thunderbird. He waved and smiled a lot but no one seemed to care. There were some more police cars, a fire truck from a volunteer brigade, and another float with a bluegrass band picking and strumming a rowdy interpretation of "Jingle Bells." A riding club trotted by on a herd of quarterhorses, all garbed up in rodeo splendor, humans and animals. Roy Rogers and Trigger would have been proud. The local gas jobber had a shiny new truck with a ten-thousand-gallon tank, and someone thought it would be a nice addition to the parade. For fun, the driver, a black guy, was blasting non-holiday rap with the windows down.

Finally, the reason for the season appeared in his sleigh. Old Saint Nick waved to the boys and girls and tossed candy at their feet. Through a loudspeaker he chanted, "Ho, Ho, Ho," but nothing else.

When the parade was out of sight, most of the spectators moved toward the courthouse and gathered in the park beside it. The mayor welcomed everyone and prattled on too long. Another children's choir sang "O Holy Night." Miss Noland County, a beautiful redhead, was singing "Sweet Little Jesus Boy" when Samantha felt someone touch her right elbow. It was Jeff, with a cap and eyeglasses she had never seen before. She backed away from Kim and Adam, eased through the crowd and away from it to a dark place near the war memorial. They had stood there last Monday night, looking at Bozo and Jimmy in the distance.

"Are you free tomorrow?" he asked, almost in a whisper.

"It's Saturday; of course I have nothing to do."

"Let's go hiking."

She hesitated and watched as the mayor flipped a switch and the official Christmas tree lit up. "Where?"

He slipped a piece of folded paper into her hand and said, "Directions. See you in the morning." He pecked her on the cheek and disappeared.

———

She drove to the town of Knox in Curry County and parked in the library lot a block off Main Street. If she had been followed, she was not aware of it. She walked nonchalantly to Main, west for three blocks, and into the Knox Market, a café and coffee shop. She asked about a restroom and was pointed toward the rear. She found a door that led to an alley that led to Fifth Street. As directed, she walked two blocks away from downtown and saw the river. As she approached Larry's Trout Dock under the bridge, Jeff appeared from the bait shop and pointed to a twenty-foot johnboat.

Without a word, both got in the boat; Samantha in the front bundled against the cold, and Jeff in the back where he started the outboard. He guided the boat away from the dock and eased down on the throttle. They were in the center of the Curry River, and the town was quickly disappearing. They passed under another bridge and civilization seemed to end. For miles, or however one measures distance on a crooked river—Samantha had no idea— they glided over the dark, still water. The Curry was a narrow, deep river with no rocks or rapids. It wiggled through the mountains, hidden from the sun by soaring cliffs that almost touched one another above the water. They passed a boat, a lone fisherman staring forlornly at his line, oblivious to them. They passed a small settlement near a sandbar, a collection of floating shacks and boats. "River rats," Jeff would later call them. They went deeper and deeper into the canyon, and around each bend the Curry grew narrower and darker.

The loud hum of the outboard prevented conversation, not that either had much to say. It was obvious he was taking her to a place she had never been, but she was not afraid, not hesitant in the least. In spite of his complications, his anger, his current emotional instability, and his recklessness, she trusted him. Or at least she trusted him enough to go hiking, or whatever he had in mind for the day.

Jeff eased off the throttle and the boat drifted toward the right. An old sign said, "Curry Cut-Off," and a concrete ramp came into view. Jeff swung the boat around and it skidded onto a sandbar. "Hop out here," he said, and she stepped out of the boat. He chained it to a metal rack near the ramp and stopped for a moment to stretch his legs. They had been in the boat for almost an hour.

"Well, good morning to you, sir," she said.

He smiled and said, "And to you. Thanks for coming."

"As if I had a choice. Where, exactly, are we?"

"We're lost in Curry County. Follow me."

"Whatever you say."

They left the sandbar, stepped into thick woods, and began climbing an unmarked trail that only someone like Jeff could follow. Or Donovan. As it grew steeper he seemed to pick up the pace. Just as her thighs and calves were beginning to scream, he stopped suddenly in a small clearing and grabbed some cedar branches. He shoved them out of the way, and, of course, there was a Honda four-wheeler just waiting for a ride.

"Boys and their toys," she said.

"Ever been on one?" he asked.

"I live in Manhattan."

"Hop on." She did. There was a sliver of a seat behind him. She locked her arms around his waist as he cranked the engine and let it roar. "Hold on," he said, and they were off, tearing along the same trail that, seconds earlier, had been barely wide enough for humans. It led to a gravel road, which Jeff attacked like a stunt driver. "Hold on!" he yelled again as he popped a wheelie and they were practically airborne. Samantha wanted to ask if he could slow down, but instead just squeezed harder and closed her eyes. The ride was thrilling and terrifying, but she knew he would not endanger her. From the gravel road, they turned onto another dirt trail, one that rose at a steep angle. The trees were too thick for stunt work, so Jeff became more cautious. Still, the ride was harrowing and dangerous. After half an hour on the four-wheeler, Samantha was having fond memories of the johnboat.

"May I ask where we're going?" she said into his ear.

"Hiking, right?" The trail peaked and they raced along a ridge. He turned onto another trail and they began a descent, a treacherous journey that involved sliding from one side to the other and dodging trees and boulders. They slowed for a second in a clearing and took in a view to their right. "Gray Mountain," he said, nodding at the shaved and barren hill in the distance. "We'll be on our land in just a moment."

She hung on for the last leg, and when they splashed across Yellow Creek she saw the cabin. It was tucked into the side of a hill, a rustic square made of old timbers, with a front porch and a chimney on one end. Jeff parked beside it and said, "Welcome to our little hiding place."

"I'm sure there's an easier way to get here."

"Oh, sure. There's a county road not far away. I'll show you later. Cool cabin, huh?"

"I guess. I'm not much on cabins. Donovan showed it to me one day, but we were a thousand feet in the air. If I remember correctly, he said there's no plumbing, heating, or electricity."

"You got it. If we stay tonight, we'll sleep by the fire."

Such a sleepover had not been discussed, but by then Samantha was not surprised. She followed him up the steps, across the porch, and into the main room of the cabin. A log was smoldering in the fireplace. "How long have you been here?" she asked.

"Got here late last night, slept by the fire. It's really nice and cozy. You want a beer?"

She glanced at her watch: 11:45. "It's a little early." There was a cooler next to a small dining table. "Do you have water?"

He handed her a bottle of water and opened a beer. They sat in two wooden chairs near the fireplace. He took a swig and said, "They were here this week. Someone, not sure who, but I doubt it was the FBI because they would need to produce a search warrant. It was probably operatives working for Krull or some other outfit."

"How do you know they were here?"

"Got 'em on video. Two months ago, Donovan and I rigged up two surveillance cameras. One is in a tree across the creek, the other is in a tree about fifty feet from the front porch. They're activated here, at the front door. If someone opens the door, the cameras come on and run for thirty minutes. The trespassers have no clue. Last Wednesday, at 3:21 to be exact, four goons showed up here and went through the cabin. I'm sure they were looking for the documents, hard drives, laptops, or anything else that might be of use. Interesting, though, that they did not leave a trace. Nothing. Not even the dust was disturbed, so you gotta figure these guys are pretty good. They also think I'm stupid, but now I know what they look like. I have the four faces, and when I see them I'll be ready."

"Are they watching now?"

"I doubt it. My truck is hidden in a place they'll never see. This is our land, Samantha, and we know it better than anyone. You want to take a look?"

"Let's go."

He grabbed a backpack and she followed him out of the cabin. They trekked along Yellow Creek for half a mile and stopped in a clearing to enjoy some rare sunshine. Jeff said, "I don't know how much Donovan told you, but this is the only part of our property that was not destroyed by the strip miners. We have about twenty acres here that was untouched. Beyond that ridge is Gray Mountain and the rest of our land, and it was all ruined."

They hiked on, climbing the ridge until the woods opened up and they stopped to take in the devastation. It was desolate enough from a thousand feet in the air, but from ground level it was truly depressing. The mountain itself had been reduced to an ugly, pockmarked hump of rock and weeds. With great effort, they climbed to the top of it and gazed through the choked-off valleys below. For lunch, they ate sandwiches in the shade of a dilapidated trailer once used as mining headquarters. Jeff told stories about watching the destruction as a kid. He'd been nine years old when the mining began.

Samantha was curious as to why he had chosen Gray Mountain as their Saturday hiking destination. Like Donovan, he preferred not to talk about what happened there. The hiking was far from pleasant. The landscapes and views were ruined, for the most part. They were smack in the middle of the Appalachian Mountains with thousands of miles of unspoiled trails at their disposal. The situation with Krull Mining was extremely dangerous; they could've been followed.

So why Gray Mountain? But she did not ask. She might later, but not right then.

As they were descending, they walked past a vine-covered waste yard of rusting machinery, obviously abandoned when Vayden Coal fled the site. Lying on its side and partially covered with weeds was a massive tire. Samantha walked closer and said, "What is this used for?"

"The haul trucks. That's a small one, actually, only about ten feet in diameter. Nowadays they're almost twice as big."

"I was reading the news yesterday. Did you see the story about the Millard Break shoot-out the other night? These ecoterrorists—"

"Sure, everybody knows about them."

She turned and stared at him with unblinking eyes. He took a step back and said, "What?"

She kept staring, and said, "Oh, nothing. It just seems to me that ecoterrorism would appeal to you and Donovan, and perhaps Vic Canzarro as well."

"I love those guys, whoever they are. But I really don't want to go to prison." He was walking away as he said this. At the foot of Gray Mountain, they walked along the edge of a creek bed. There was no water; there had been none in a long time. Jeff said he and Donovan used to fish at that spot with their father, long before the valley fill destroyed the creek. He took her to their old home site and described the house where they lived, the house built by his grandfather. They stopped at the cross where Donovan found their mother, Rose, and he knelt beside it for a long time.

The sun was disappearing over the mountains; the afternoon had slipped away. The wind was sharper, a cold front was moving through and bringing a chance of flurries by morning. When they were back by Yellow Creek, he asked, "Do you want to stay here tonight or go back to Brady?"

"Let's stay," she said.

———

They grilled two steaks over charcoal on the porch and ate them by the fire with red wine in paper cups. When the first bottle was empty, Jeff opened a second, and they stretched out on a pile of quilts in front of the fire. They began kissing, cautiously at first; there was no hurry because there was a long night ahead of them. Their lips and tongues were stained with cheap merlot and they laughed about it. They talked about her past, and his. He did not mention Donovan and she was careful to avoid him also. The past was easy compared to the future. Jeff was out of a job and had no idea what he might do. It had taken him five years to finish two years of college; he wasn't much of a student. He had spent four months in the county jail on a drug charge, a felony that was still on his record and would haunt him for a long time. He avoided drugs now; too many friends ruined by meth. Maybe some pot occasionally, but he wasn't much of a smoker, or a drinker. They slowly got around to the topic of their love lives. Samantha talked about Henry as if the romance had been more involved than it was. Frankly, though, she'd been too busy and too exhausted to begin and maintain a serious relationship. Jeff had once been engaged to his childhood sweetheart, but his jail time disrupted their plans. While he was locked up she ran away with another boy and broke his heart. For a long time he took a dim view of women and treated them as if they were good for only one thing. He was mellowing now, and for the past year had been seeing a young divorcée over in Wise. She worked at the college, had a nice job and two brats. Problem was, he couldn't stand her kids. Their father was schizophrenic and they were showing signs. The relationship had cooled considerably.

"You have your hand under my shirt," she said.

"Yes, it feels good under there."

"Actually, it does. It's been a long time."

They finally kissed as if they meant it, a long, probing kiss with hands groping wildly and buttons flying open. They took a break to undo belts and kick off shoes. The next kiss was more tender, but all four hands were still working, removing. When they were nice and perfectly naked, they made love by the glow of the fire. At first, their rhythms were awkward. He was a little rough and she was a little rusty, but they soon got the hang of each other's body. Round one was quick as both needed a release. Round two was far more satisfying as they explored and changed positions. When it was over, they lay sprawled on the quilts, gently touching each other, exhausted.

It was almost 9:00 p.m.

The dusting of snow was gone by mid-morning. The sun was bright, the air clear. They hiked for an hour around Gray Mountain, hopping across dried creeks that once brimmed with rainbow and brown trout, ducking into shallow caves the boys had used as forts in another lifetime, crawling over boulders blown from the earth two decades ago, and meandering through trails that no one else could possibly find.

Samantha wasn't sore from last night's marathon, but certain muscles seemed a bit tender. Jeff, though, seemed unfazed. Whether climbing mountains or having sex by the fire, his stamina was endless.

She followed him through a gorge at the base of the mountain, then to another trail that disappeared into thick woods. They climbed rocks, part of a natural formation, and entered a cave, one that was impossible to notice from twenty feet away. Jeff turned on a flashlight and looked over his shoulder. "Are you okay?"

"I'm right behind you," she said, practically clinging. "Where are we going?"

"I want to show you something." They crouched low to clear a wall of rock and climbed deeper into the cave, which, but for the flashlight, was pitch-black. They moved slowly, as if sneaking up on something. If he had yelled "Snake!" she would have either fainted or died instantly from a heart attack.

They entered a room, a semi-round cavern with a ray of sunlight somehow penetrating the rock. It was a storage room, one that had been in use for some time. Two rows of army surplus lockers stood against one wall, a stack of cardboard containers against another. A table made of a sheet of thick plywood sitting on cinder blocks held a collection of identical storage boxes. The boxes were plastic and sealed tightly. Jeff said, "We played here as kids. It's about two hundred feet into the base of Gray Mountain, too deep and low to have been ruined by the mining. This room was one of our favorites because there's light, and it's dry, no moisture whatsoever, and it's the same temperature year-round."

Samantha pointed to the table and said, "And those would be the records you stole from Krull Mining, right?"

He nodded with a smile and said, "Correct."

"I'm now an accessory to a crime. Why did you bring me here, Jeff?"

"You're not an accessory because you had nothing to do with the crime and you've never seen these boxes. You've never been here, right?"

"I don't know. This doesn't feel right. Why did you bring me here?"

"It's simple, Samantha, and it's not so simple. These documents have to be delivered to the other attorneys, Donovan's co-counsel. And soon. I'll figure out a way to do it, but it won't be easy. The FBI is looking. Krull is watching. Everybody would love to catch me with the documents. Hell, I helped steal them and now they're hidden on my family's property, so I wouldn't have much of a defense, would I?"

"You're toast."

"Exactly, and if something happens to me before I can deliver them, someone needs to know where they are."

"And that someone is me, I suppose?"

"You're smart enough to figure it out."

"I doubt that. And who else knows about this?"

"Vic Canzarro, and that's it. No one else."

She took a deep breath and walked closer to the table. She said, "There's nothing simple about it, Jeff. On the one hand, these are stolen documents that could cost Krull Mining a fortune and force the company to clean up its mess. On the other hand, they could mean a criminal prosecution for you or whoever happens to have possession of them. Have you talked to the other lawyers, to Donovan's co-counsel?"

"Not since he died. I want you to do that, Samantha. I'm not a lawyer. You are, and it needs to be done immediately. Some secret meeting where no one is watching or listening."

She shook her head as she felt herself fall deeper into the spiderweb. Had she finally reached the point of no return? "I'll have to think about that. Why can't you and Vic meet with the lawyers?"

"Vic won't do it. He's running scared. Plus, he has a lot of baggage here in the coalfields. It's a long story."

"Are there any short ones around here?"

She walked to the lockers and asked, "What's in here?"

"Our gun collection."

She thought about opening one of the doors for a peek inside, but she knew nothing about guns and didn't want to learn. Without looking at him, she asked, "What are the odds of finding a military sniper rifle, with night vision optics, and a stash of 51-millimeter cartridges?" She turned and stared at him, but he looked away and said, "I wouldn't open that if I were you."

She headed for the entrance, brushed beside him, and said, "Let's get out of here."

They left the cave and were soon zigzagging along the trails. It occurred to Samantha that if something did happen to Jeff she could never find her way back to the cave. And, furthermore, if something happened to Jeff she would be back in Manhattan before Mattie could organize another funeral.

Nothing was said for a long time. They shared a can of bad chili on the porch for lunch, washed it down with the last of the wine, and took a nap by the fire. When the naps were over, they found themselves kissing and groping again. The same clothes eventually came off again, tossed haphazardly around the room, and they spent a delightful Sunday afternoon together.

29

Phoebe Fanning's bail was reduced from $100,000 to a mere $1,000, and at 9:00 a.m. Monday morning she posted it through a bondsman. The deal came about after Samantha successfully badgered the judge into releasing the mother while the father remained in jail. The well-being of three innocent children was on the line, and after two days of harassment the judge had come around. Phoebe's court-appointed defense attorney claimed to be overworked and had little time for the preliminary matters; thus, Samantha had stepped in to secure the release. She walked out of the courthouse with Phoebe and drove her home. She waited with her there for an hour while a distant cousin brought the kids over. They had not seen their mother in over a week, and had obviously been warned that she would likely serve time. There were a lot of tears and hugging and so on, and Samantha was quickly bored with it. She had carefully explained to Phoebe that she was facing a minimum of five years in prison, much more for Randy if he took the fall, and that she needed to prepare her children for the inevitable catastrophe.

As she was leaving the Fannings, her cell phone buzzed. It was Mattie at the office. She had just received the news that Francine Crump had been stricken with a severe stroke and was in the hospital. The saga of the free last will and testament continued.

At the hospital, a frightening and antiquated facility that should have inspired healthy habits in every citizen in Noland County, Samantha found a nurse in the ICU who could spare a word or two. The patient had been brought in just after midnight, unresponsive and with almost no blood pressure. A CT scan revealed a massive hemorrhagic stroke, or severe bleeding into the brain. She had been intubated and was comatose. "Things are not good," the nurse said with a deep frown. "Looks like she went hours before they found her. Plus she's eighty years old." Because she was not a member of the family, Samantha was not allowed to peek into the ICU and see who might be sitting with Francine.

When she returned to the office, there were phone messages from Jonah and DeLoss Crump. As their mother lay dying, they were desperate to chat about her estate. If Francine had a new will, it had not been prepared by the attorneys at the Mountain Legal Aid Clinic. If there was no new will, and if Francine remained comatose until she died, then it was abundantly clear that Samantha would be dealing with these unpleasant people for many months to come. A hot will contest was taking shape.

She decided to ignore the calls for the moment. All five siblings were probably racing to Brady, and she would hear from them soon enough.

The firm's brown-bag lunch that Monday was spent digesting some ominous news. As Mattie had warned, the attorneys for Strayhorn Coal were reneging on their agreement to settle the Tate wrongful death case. They had sent her a letter, as the presumed attorney for Donovan's estate, and said that they would not settle; instead, they were aggressively appealing the verdict. She had fired back an e-mail with the flippant suggestion that they should try and control their aggression. Her theory was that they were willing to push the appeal, hope for a reversal, and roll the dice in a retrial with Donovan out of the way. Such a retrial would be three years down the road, at the earliest, and while they waited and got paid to stall, their client's money would be hard at work elsewhere. Annette was incensed and pushed Mattie to bring the matter to the attention of the judge. Strayhorn and Donovan had an agreement to settle for $1.7 million. It was unfair, even unconscionable, for the defendant to back out simply because the plaintiff's attorney was now dead. Mattie agreed; however, so far no one in Donovan's office could find anything in writing. It looked as though they reached a deal on the phone, but no settlement memo was prepared before he died. Without written guidelines, she doubted the court would force the settlement. She had consulted with a trial lawyer friend and a retired judge; both thought they were out of luck. She planned to have a chat with the trial judge, off the record, and get some idea of what he was thinking. The bottom line was that it looked as though the estate would be forced to hire a lawyer to handle the appeal.

On another subject, Barb reported that the office had received eleven phone calls that morning from the Crump clan, all demanding to see Ms. Kofer. Ms. Kofer said she planned to schedule a meeting later that afternoon. Not surprisingly, both Mattie and Annette had busy schedules with no time for the Crumps. Samantha rolled her eyes and said fine, but these folks are not going away.

Francine died at 4:30 that afternoon. She never regained consciousness, nor did she get around to revising the will Samantha prepared.

Early Tuesday afternoon, Jeff eased through the rear door and was standing at Samantha's desk before she realized it. Each smiled and said hello, but there was no movement toward anything more affectionate. Her door was open, and, as always, the place was filled with incredibly nosy women. He sat down and said, "So, when would you like to go hiking again?"

She put a finger to her lips and softly said, "Whenever I can work it into my schedule." She had thought about sex more in the last twenty-four hours than at any time in the last two years, since she broke up with Henry.

"I'll have to check with my secretary," she said. She still found it hard to believe that someone might be listening to conversations in her office, but she was taking no chances. And given his paranoia, he was saying almost nothing. He managed, "Okay."

"Would you like some coffee?"

"No."

"Then we'd better go."

They walked down the hall to the front conference room, where Mattie was waiting. At precisely 2:00 p.m., Agents Banahan, Frohmeyer, and Zimmer arrived in a rush and with such grim determination it seemed as if they might shoot first and ask questions later. Frohmeyer had led the troops during the raid on Donovan's office. Zimmer had been one of his gofers. Banahan had stopped by earlier. After quick introductions were made, they squared off, with Jeff sitting between Mattie and Samantha on one side and the government on the other. Annette held one end of the table and turned on a recorder.

Mattie again asked if Jeff was the subject of an investigation by the FBI, the U.S. Attorney, any other federal law enforcement agency, or anyone working for the Department of Justice. Frohmeyer assured her he was not.

Frohmeyer took charge and spent a few minutes digging through Jeff's background. Samantha took notes. After their rather intimate weekend, in which he had shared so much, she learned nothing new. Frohmeyer probed his relationship with his deceased brother. How long had he worked for him? What did he do? How much was he paid? As coached by Mattie and Annette, Jeff gave succinct answers and never offered anything extra.

Lying to an FBI agent is a crime in itself, regardless of where or how the interrogation takes place. Whatever you do, Mattie had said repeatedly, do not lie.

Like his brother, Jeff had seemed perfectly willing to lie if it would help the cause. He assumed the bad guys—the coal companies and now the government—would cut corners and cheat and do whatever to win. If they played dirty, why couldn't he? Because, Mattie had repeated, you can be sent to prison. The coal companies and their lawyers cannot.

Working from scripted notes, Frohmeyer finally got around to the important matters. He explained that the computers seized by the FBI one week ago on December 1 had been tampered with. The hard drives had been replaced. Did Jeff know anything about that?

Mattie snapped, "Don't answer that." She explained to Frohmeyer that she had spoken with the U.S. Attorney, and that it was clear that Donovan died without knowing that he was the subject of a new investigation. He had not been informed; there was nothing in writing. Therefore, with respect to his office files and records, any actions taken by his employees after his death were not done to impede an investigation.

Off the record, Jeff's version was that he removed the hard drives from the office and home computers and burned them. Samantha suspected, though, that they still existed. Not that it mattered. Jeff had assured her that there was nothing important, relative to Krull Mining, to be found in any of Donovan's computers.

And I know where the records are, Samantha thought to herself, almost in disbelief.

The fact that Mattie had gone to the U.S. Attorney irritated Frohmeyer. She didn't care. They haggled for a while over the questioning, and it became obvious who was in control, at least in this meeting. If Mattie told Jeff not to answer, Frohmeyer got nothing. He told the story of a bunch of records that disappeared from the headquarters of Krull Mining near Harlan, Kentucky, and asked Jeff if he knew anything about it. Jeff shrugged and shook his head no before Mattie could say, "Don't answer that."

"Do you plead the Fifth Amendment?" Frohmeyer asked in frustration.

"He's not under oath," Mattie shot back, as if Frohmeyer was stupid.

Samantha had to confess, at least to herself, that she was thoroughly enjoying the conflict. The FBI with all its power on one side. Jeff, their client, who was certainly guilty of something, on the other side, heavily protected by legal talent and winning, for the moment.

"I guess we're wasting our time," Frohmeyer said, throwing up his hands. "Thanks for the hospitality. I'm sure we'll be back."

"Don't mention it," Mattie said. "And no contact with my client unless I'm notified, got it?"

"We'll see," Frohmeyer said like a jerk as he kicked back his chair and stood. Banahan and Zimmer marched out with him.

An hour later, Samantha, Mattie, and Jeff were sitting in the back row in the main courtroom, waiting on the judge who would oversee the probate of Donovan's estate. Court was not in session and a handful of lawyers milled about the bench, swapping jokes with the clerks.

Jeff said quietly, "I talked to our experts this morning. So far, they've found no evidence of anyone tampering with Donovan's Cessna. The crash was caused by sudden engine failure, and the engine quit because the flow of fuel was cut off. The tank was full—we always filled up in Charleston because it's cheaper there. The miracle is that the plane did not burst into flames and burn a hole in the ground."

"How did the fuel get cut off?" Mattie asked.

"That's the big question. If you believe it was sabotage, then there's one real strong theory. There's a fuel line that runs from the fuel pump to the carburetor, where it's attached by what's called a B nut. If the B nut is deliberately loosened, the engine will start up just fine and operate smoothly until the vibration causes the B nut to slowly unscrew itself. The fuel line will come loose and engine failure is imminent. The engine will sputter and quickly shut down completely. Happens very fast with no warning, no alarm, and it's impossible to restart it. If a pilot is staring at his fuel gauge, which is something we glance at only periodically, then he might notice a sudden drop in fuel pressure at about the same time the engine begins to die. They make a big deal out of the fact that Donovan did not make a distress call. That's nonsense. Think about it. You're flying along at night and suddenly your engine quits. You have a few seconds to react, but it's total panic. You try to restart the engine, but that doesn't work. You're thinking about ten things at once, but the last thing you're thinking about is calling for help. How the hell is anyone going to help?"

"How easy is it to tamper with the B nut?" Samantha asked.

"It's not difficult if you know what you're doing. The trick is to do it without getting caught. You would have to wait until dark, sneak onto the tie-down area of the ramp, remove the cowling that covers the engine, use a flashlight and a wrench, and do your business. One expert said it can be done in about twenty minutes. On the night in question, there were seventeen other small aircraft tied down in the same area, but there was almost no traffic that night. The ramp was very quiet. We've checked the surveillance videos from the general aviation terminal and found nothing. We've talked to the ramp guys on duty that night, and they saw nothing. We've checked the maintenance records with the mechanic in Roanoke, and of course everything was working fine when he signed off on the last inspection."

"How badly was the engine damaged?" asked Mattie.

"It's a mess. Evidently, the Cessna clipped some trees. It looks like Donovan was trying to land on a county highway—he might have seen the headlights of a car, but who knows—and when he hit the trees the plane pitched forward and landed nose first. The engine was smashed and it's impossible to determine the position of the B nut. It's fairly easy to conclude that the fuel was cut off, but beyond that there aren't many clues."

The judge entered the courtroom and assumed the bench. He scanned the audience and said something to a clerk.

"What's next?" Samantha whispered.

"We'll keep digging," Jeff said, but with little confidence.

The judge looked toward the rear of the courtroom and said, "Ms. Wyatt."

Mattie introduced Jeff to His Honor, who politely passed along his condolences and said nice things about Donovan. Jeff thanked him as Mattie began producing orders for the judge to sign. The judge took his time reading the will and commented on various provisions. He and Mattie discussed the strategy of the estate hiring a lawyer to pursue the Tate appeal. Jeff was quizzed about Donovan's financial status, his assets and debts.

After an hour, all orders were signed and the estate was officially opened. Mattie stayed on to handle another matter, but Jeff was dismissed. As he walked back to the office with Samantha, he said, "I'm disappearing for a few weeks, so use the prepaid phone."

"Anyplace in particular?"

"No."

"No surprise there. I'm leaving myself, for the holidays, Washington and then New York. I guess I won't be seeing you for a while."

"So, is this Merry Christmas and Happy New Year?"

"I suppose so. Merry Christmas and Happy New Year."

He stopped and quickly pecked her on the cheek. "Same to you." He turned onto a side street and hurried away, as if someone might be trailing him.

The funeral for Francine Crump was held at 11:00 a.m. Wednesday, in a Holiness church deep in the hollows. Samantha never considered attending the service. Annette strongly advised against it, since it was likely they would pull out the snakes and start dancing. Samantha took this seriously. Annette later admitted she was exaggerating. There were no known snake-handling congregations still practicing in Virginia, she explained. "All the members are dead."

But a nest of angry rattlers could not have been worse than the mob of Crumps that showed up later in the day for a showdown with "Missus Kofer." They descended upon the clinic with a show of force unlike any Mattie had ever seen: the five siblings, some of their current spouses, a few of their large children, and a few assorted blood relatives.

Their beloved mother was dead, and it was time to split the money.

Mattie took charge and told most of them to leave. Only the five siblings would be allowed to take part in the meeting; the rest could go sit in their trucks. She and Annette herded them into a conference room, and when they were seated Samantha walked in and joined them. Collectively, they were a mess. They had just buried their mother. They were terrified they might lose the family land and whatever money that meant, and they were bitter at the lawyers for facilitating this. They were also getting pestered by relatives who'd heard rumors of coal money. They were away from home and missing work. And, as Samantha suspected, they had been fighting amongst themselves.

She began by explaining that no lawyer at the clinic had prepared another will for their mother; indeed, no one had heard a word from Francine since the last family meeting at that very table some nine days earlier. If Francine told them otherwise, then it simply wasn't true. Nor did Samantha know of any other lawyer in town who might have prepared a new will. Mattie explained that it was customary, though by no means obligatory, for one lawyer to call another when a different will is prepared. At any rate, as far as they knew, the will signed by Francine two months earlier was her last will and testament.

They listened and fumed, barely able to control their loathing for the lawyers. As Samantha wound down, she expected a torrent of abuse, probably from all five. Instead, there was a long pause. Jonah, the oldest at sixty-one, finally said, "Momma destroyed the will."

Samantha had no response. Annette frowned as her mind raced back to the old Virginia statutes regarding lost and destroyed wills. Mattie was impressed at the cleverness of their scheme and could barely suppress a grin.

Jonah went on, "I'm sure you have a copy of the will, but, as I understand things, when she destroyed the original the copy became useless. That right?"

Mattie nodded along, acknowledging the obvious fact that Jonah had paid for some quick legal advice. And why would he pay a lawyer for advice and not for a new will? Because Francine wouldn't agree to a new will. "How do you know she destroyed it?" she asked.

Euna Faye said, "She told me last week."

Irma said, "Told me too. Said she burned it in the fireplace."

DeLoss added, "And we've looked everywhere and can't find it."

It was all very well rehearsed, and as long as the five stuck together, the story would hold up. On cue, Lonnie asked, "And so if there's no will, then we get the land in five equal shares, right?"

"I suppose," Mattie said. "I'm not sure what position the Mountain Trust will take."

Jonah growled, "You tell the Mountain Trust to get lost, you hear? Hell, they never knew about our property until y'all brought 'em in. This is our family land, always has been."

His four siblings agreed wholeheartedly.

In a flash, Samantha switched teams. If Francine had in fact destroyed the will, or if these five were lying and there was no way to prove otherwise, then give them the damned eighty acres and say good-bye. The last thing she wanted was a will contest between the Crumps and the Mountain Trust, with her as the star witness taking flak from both sides. She never wanted to see these people again.

Nor did Annette and Mattie. They switched too, with Mattie saying, "Look, folks, we as lawyers will not try and probate the will. That's not our job. I doubt seriously if the Mountain Trust wants to get bogged down in a protracted will contest. The legal fees will cost more than the land is worth. If there's no will, then there's no will. Y'all need to find a lawyer who'll open the estate and get an administrator appointed."

"Do y'all do that?" Jonah asked.

All three lawyers recoiled in horror at the notion of representing these people. Annette managed to speak first, "Oh, no, we can't because we prepared the will."

"But it's pretty routine stuff," Mattie added quickly. "Almost any lawyer along Main Street can do it."

Euna Faye actually smiled and said, "Well, thanks."

Lonnie asked, "And we split it five ways, right?"

Mattie said, "That's the law, but you need to check with your lawyer." Lonnie was shifty-eyed to begin with, and he was already looking around the room. They would be fighting before they left Brady. And there were relatives waiting outside, ready to pounce on all that coal money.

They left in peace, and when the front door closed behind the last one, the three lawyers felt like celebrating. They locked the door, kicked off their shoes, and piled into the conference room for a late afternoon sip of wine and a lot of laughs. Annette attempted to describe the scene of the first one home, rummaging through the house in a desperate search for that damned will. Then the second, then the third. Their mother was on the slab at the funeral home and they were knocking over furniture and dumping out drawers in a frantic search. If they found it, they certainly burned it.

Not one of the three lawyers believed Francine actually destroyed her will.

And they were right. The original arrived in the mail the following day, with a note from Francine asking Samantha to please protect it.

The Crumps would be back after all.

30

For the third year in a row, Karen Kofer spent Christmas in New York City with her daughter. She had a close friend from college whose third husband was an aging industrialist, now sidelined by dementia and tucked away in a plush retirement home in Great Neck. Their rambling apartment on Fifth Avenue overlooked Central Park and was practically deserted. Karen was given her own suite for the week and treated like a queen. Samantha was offered one too, but chose instead to stay with Blythe in their apartment in SoHo. The lease expired on December 31, and she needed to pack her things and make arrangements to store furniture. Blythe, still hanging on at the world's fourth-largest law firm, was moving in with two friends in Chelsea.

After three months in Brady, Samantha felt liberated in the city. She shopped with her mother in midtown, battling the crowds but enjoying the frenetic energy. She had late afternoon drinks with friends in all the right, trendy bars, and, while enjoying the scene, found herself bored with the conversation. Careers, real estate, and the Great Recession. Karen sprang for two tickets to a Broadway musical, a rage that was nothing more than a made-for-tourists rip-off. They left at intermission and got a table at Orso. Samantha had brunch with an old Georgetown pal at Balthazar, where the friend almost squealed as she pointed out a famous TV actor Samantha had never seen nor heard of. She took long, solitary walks through lower Manhattan. Christmas dinner was a feast at the Fifth Avenue apartment with a bunch of strangers, though after a lot of wine the conversation loosened up and an ordeal became a riot that went on for hours. Samantha slept in a spare bedroom, one bigger than her apartment, and woke up with a mild hangover. A uniformed maid brought her orange juice, coffee, and ibuprofen. She had lunch with Henry, who had been pestering her, and realized they had nothing in common. He was assuming she would be back in the city in the near future and was eager to rekindle something. She tried to explain that she wasn't sure when she would return. There was no job waiting for her, and now no apartment. Her future was uncertain, as was his. He'd given up on acting and was considering an entry into the exciting world of hedge fund management. An odd choice these days, she thought. Aren't those guys bleeding cash and dodging indictments? His undergraduate degree from Cornell was in Arabic. He was headed to nowhere and she would not waste another minute with him.

Two days after Christmas, she was sitting in a coffee bar in SoHo when a phone buzzed. At first she didn't recognize the noise deep in her purse, then realized it was the prepaid phone Jeff had given her. She found it just in time and said hello. "Happy New Year," he said. "Where are you?"

"Same to you. I'm in the city. Where are you?"

"In the city. I'd like to see you. Got time for some coffee?"

For a moment, she thought he was joking. She couldn't imagine Jeff Gray walking the streets of Manhattan, but then, why not? The city attracted all types from everywhere. "Sure, in fact I'm having coffee right now. Alone."

"What's the address?"

While she waited, she became amused at her thought process. Her initial reaction was one of surprise, which was immediately followed by one of pure lust. How could she get him into her apartment and avoid Blythe? Not that Blythe would really care, but she didn't want a lot of questions. Where was he staying? A nice hotel; that would work. Was he alone? Or sharing a room with a friend?

Settle down girl, she told herself. He walked in twenty minutes later and they kissed on the lips. As they waited on double espressos, she asked him the obvious. "What are you doing here?"

"I've been here before," he said. "I'm moving around these days, and I wanted to see you."

"A call would've been nice." Faded jeans, black T-shirt, wool sports coat, chukka boots, three days' growth, hair just slightly untamed. He was definitely not one of the Wall Street clones, but in SoHo no one would suspect him of being from backwater Appalachia. And who would care? In reality, he looked more like an unemployed actor than Henry.

"I wanted to surprise you."

"Okay. I'm surprised. How did you get here?"

"A private jet. It's a long story."

"I'm so tired of long stories. Where are you staying?"

"The Hilton, midtown. Alone. Where are you staying?"

"My apartment, for a few more days anyway. Then the lease is up."

The barista said their coffee was ready and Jeff grabbed the two cups. He poured in a pack of sugar and stirred slowly. She passed on the sugar. They huddled closer together as the coffee bar became crowded. She said, "So, can we get back to this private jet matter. Care to elaborate?"

"I'm here for two reasons. First, I want to see you and maybe spend a little time together. Perhaps we could hike, you know, around the city and then find a fireplace somewhere. If not, maybe just a nice warm bed. That's what I'd like, but I understand if you're too busy. I'm not crashing your private time, okay?"

"You can forget the fireplace."

"Got it. I'm available from this moment on."

"I'm sure we'll find time. And what about the other reason?"

"Well, the jet is owned by a trial lawyer named Jarrett London, from Louisville. You may have heard of him by now."

"And how would I know a lawyer from Louisville?"

"Anyway, he and Donovan were very close, in fact Jarrett was at the funeral. Tall guy, about sixty, with long gray hair and a salt-and-pepper beard. Donovan considered him to be his mentor, almost his hero. His law firm is one of the other three who sued Krull Mining in the Hammer Valley case. They got raided the same day the FBI raided our office. Needless to say, a guy like London doesn't appreciate such Gestapo tactics, and he's spitting fire. Big ego, typical of the breed."

She was nodding. "My father."

"Yes, of course. In fact, London says he met your father years ago at some trial lawyer shindig. Anyway, London has a new girlfriend, a real dingbat, and she wanted to see the city. I hitched a ride."

"How convenient."

"He also wants to meet you, say hello, and talk about the documents."

"What documents? Come on, Jeff, I'm already in too deep. Where is this going?"

"You gotta help me here, Samantha. My brother is gone and I need someone to talk to, someone who knows the law and can give me advice."

Her spine stiffened and she pulled back. She glared at him and wanted to lash out. Instead, she glanced around, swallowed hard, and said, "You are deliberately sucking me into a conspiracy that can land me in serious trouble. The FBI is all over this, yet you want me to get involved. You're as reckless as your brother and you don't care what happens to me. Look, who says I'm even going back to Brady, Virginia? I feel incredibly safe right now. This is my home; it's where I belong."

His lanky frame seemed to shrink by inches as his chin dropped. He looked lost and helpless. "I do care about you, Samantha, and I care what happens to you. I just need help right now."

"Jeff, we had a wonderful time a couple of weeks ago at Gray Mountain. I've thought about it a lot, but what I don't understand is why you took me to that cave, or whatever the hell it's called, and showed me the documents. At that—"

"No one will ever know."

"At that point I became an accessory of some sort. I realize the documents are valuable and damaging and all that, but it doesn't change the fact that they're stolen."

"Someone has to know where they are, Samantha, in case something happens to me."

"Let Vic handle it."

"I told you. Vic is gone, checked out. His girlfriend is pregnant and he's a changed man. He's not risking anything. He will not answer the phone."

"He's smart."

The espresso was getting cold. Jeff noticed his and took a sip. Samantha ignored him and studied the crowd. Finally, Jeff said, "Can we get out of here?"

They found a bench in Washington Square Park. All the benches were empty because the wind was howling and the temperature was just below freezing. "How much does this London guy know about me?" she asked.

"He knows you have the Ryzer case, at least the black lung part. He knows you discovered the fraud and cover-up by the lawyers for Lonerock Coal. He's really impressed by that. He knows that I trust you and that Donovan trusted you. He knows that Donovan told you about the documents."

"Does he know I've seen them?"

"No. I told you, Samantha, no one will ever know that. I was wrong to take you there."

"Thank you."

"Let's at least meet with the guy and see what he says. Please. There's no harm in that, right?"

"I don't know."

"Yes, you do know. There is nothing even remotely out-of-bounds in meeting with Jarrett London. It will be extremely confidential, plus he's an interesting guy."

"When does he want to meet?"

"I'll call him. I'm freezing. Do you live around here?"

"Not far, but the apartment is a mess. We're packing up."

"I don't care."

————

Two hours later, Samantha walked into the lobby of the Peninsula hotel on Fifty-Fifth Street in midtown. She took the stairs to her left, climbed one floor, and saw Jeff sitting at the bar, as expected. Without a word, he handed her a scrap of paper with the message "Room 1926." He watched her turn around and leave, then stood by the stairs to see if anyone else noticed. She took the elevator to the nineteenth floor and pressed the buzzer to the room. A tall man with far too much gray hair opened the door within seconds and said, "Hello, Ms. Kofer, it's an honor. I'm Jarrett London."

Number 1926 was a huge suite with an entire den at one end. There was no sign of the girlfriend. Minutes after Samantha arrived, Jeff buzzed the door. They sat in the den and went through the required pleasantries. London mentioned something to drink, but everyone declined. He brought up her work in the Ryzer case and gushed on about how brilliant it was. He and Donovan had discussed it at length. London and his partners were still debating whether their firm should jump in the lawsuit with Donovan when he went ahead and filed the damned thing. "Much too premature," London said. "But then, that was Donovan."

He, London, was still considering the litigation. It's not every day you catch a major law firm like Casper Slate committing fraud red-handed, you know? The case could have enormous jury appeal, and so on. He went on and on about the beauty of the case, as if Samantha had never realized this. She'd heard it before, from Donovan and from her father. Now, on to Krull Mining. With Donovan out of the picture, London was now lead counsel for the plaintiffs. The lawsuit had been filed on October 29. Krull had been granted additional time to respond and file an answer. In early January, London and his team were expecting Krull to file a serious motion to dismiss, and the war would commence at full throttle. Soon, very soon, they would need the documents.

"How much do you know about them?" Samantha asked.

London exhaled loudly, as if the question was so loaded he had no idea where to begin, then he stood and walked to the minibar. "Beer, anyone?" Jeff and Samantha declined, again. He opened a Heineken and walked to a window. He took a long swig and said, "About a year ago, we had our first meeting, in Charleston, offices of Gordie Mace, one of our gang. Donovan had summoned all of us there to pitch the Hammer Valley lawsuit. He said he had possession of some documents, and the possession had not come about through the usual methods. We didn't ask; he didn't offer. Said there were over twenty thousand pages of highly incriminating stuff. Krull Mining knew about the contamination, knew it was leaking into the groundwater up and down the valley, knew people were still drinking the water, knew people were suffering and dying, knew it should clean up the site, but also knew it was less expensive to just screw the people and keep the money. He did not have the documents with him, but he had extensive notes, notes he destroyed after the meeting. He described about twenty of the documents, the most damaging ones, and, frankly, we were blown away. Stunned. Outraged. We signed on immediately and geared up for the lawsuit. Donovan was careful not to refer to the documents as stolen, and he kept them away from us. If he had given us the documents at any point during the past year, all of us, in all likelihood, would have been arrested earlier this month by the FBI."

"So how do you take possession of the documents now and avoid being arrested?" she asked.

"That's the great question. We're having indirect talks with one of the trial judge's law clerks, real back-channel stuff that's highly sensitive and highly unusual. We think we'll be able to take the documents, immediately tender them to the court, and have them locked away by the judge. We will then ask him to lean on the U.S. Attorney to back off the criminal investigation until the documents are reviewed. Let's face it, the person who stole the documents is dead. We've consulted with our criminal defense attorneys, and they agree that our exposure will be minimal. We are willing to take the risks. The danger is what might happen to the documents before they reach the court. Krull Mining will do anything to destroy them, and right now they have the FBI on their side. It's dangerous out there."

Samantha gave Jeff a look that could kill.

London sat near Samantha and looked deep into her eyes. "We could use some help in Washington."

"Uh, I'm sorry."

"The Attorney General has three people in his inner circle. One is Leonna Kent. I'm sure you know her."

Reeling, Samantha said, "I've, uh, met her years back."

"She and your mother started at Justice at the same time, thirty years ago. Your mother is highly regarded and has seniority. She also has some pull."

"But not in areas like this."

"Oh, yes, Samantha. A word or two from Karen Kofer to Leonna Kent, and from Leonna Kent to the Attorney General, and from the AG to the U.S. Attorney in Kentucky, and we could see the FBI back off. That would leave us with only the Krull thugs to worry about."

"Is that what this meeting is about? My mother?"

"Professionally, Samantha, not personally, you understand. Have you discussed this with your mother?"

"No, of course not. In fact, I haven't even thought about discussing it with her. This is out of her league, okay?"

"I don't think so. We have serious contacts in D.C. and they believe Karen Kofer could help us."

Samantha was bewildered and at a loss. She looked at Jeff and asked, "Is this why you came to New York? To get my mother involved?"

He quickly replied, "No, this is the first I've heard of it. I didn't even know where your mother worked." He was as sincere as a little boy being falsely accused, and she believed him.

"I didn't discuss it with him, Samantha," London said. "This is coming from our insiders in D.C."

"Your lobbyists."

"Yes, of course. Don't we all have lobbyists? Love 'em or hate 'em, but they know the landscape. I'm afraid you're taking this too personally. We're not asking you to ask your mother to get directly involved in a federal investigation, but at the same time we understand how things work. People are people, friends are friends, a quiet word here and there and things can happen. Just think about it, okay?"

Samantha took a deep breath and said, "I'll consider thinking about it."

"Thank you." He stood and stretched his legs again. She glared at Jeff, who was studying his boots. Rather awkwardly, London said, "Now, Jeff, can we discuss the delivery of the documents?"

Samantha jumped to her feet and said, "I'll see you guys later."

Jeff grabbed her arm, gently, and said, "Please, Samantha, don't go. I need your input here."

She shook free and said, "I'm not a part of your little conspiracy. You boys chat all you want to. You don't need me. It's been a pleasure." She yanked open the door and disappeared.

Jeff caught her in the lobby and they left the hotel together. He apologized, and she assured him she was not upset. She didn't know Jarrett London, certainly didn't trust him as a stranger, and wasn't about to discuss sensitive issues in his presence. They drifted up Fifth Avenue, lost in the crowd, and managed to move the conversation away from anything related to coal. She pointed out the building where her mother was currently living in luxury. She was expected at yet another dinner party there later in the evening, but she had already canceled. She had promised the night to Jeff.

Suspecting that he might not appreciate a three-hour marathon in a four-star restaurant, she avoided the fancy places and got a table at Mas in the West Village. On a frigid night it was the perfect choice—warm and cozy with the ambience of a real French farmhouse. The menu changed daily and was not extensive. Jeff read through it once and confessed he didn't recognize any of the dishes. A waiter suggested the four-course fixed-price offering for $68, and Samantha agreed. Jeff was appalled at the price, but soon impressed with the food. Shrimp crusted with spaghetti squash, pork and apple sausage, wild striped bass with leek fondue, and a chocolate torte. They drank a bottle of Syrah from the Rhône Valley. When the cheese cart rolled by Jeff almost chased it. Samantha called the waiter over and explained that they would like to add a cheese course, with more wine.

As they waited for the cart, Jeff leaned closer and said, "Will you think about something?"

"I'm not promising anything. I'm not sure I trust you."

"Thanks. Look, this may sound crazy, and I've really struggled with the idea of even mentioning this to you. So, I'm still struggling, but here it is."

For one horrible split second, Samantha thought he was going to propose marriage. They weren't even a couple! And she had no plans to get serious. So far they had put sex before any hint of love. Surely, this somewhat rustic mountain boy wasn't smitten enough to stumble into a proposal.

He wasn't, but his idea was almost as unsettling. He said, "I own the office building, or I will at some point after probate. I'm also the executor of Donovan's estate, so I'm in charge of his business. Me, Mattie, and the judge, I guess. You've seen the list of his cases; he left a lot of work behind. Mattie will take a few cases, but not many. Her desk is busy enough and it's not her type of work. What we need is for someone to take over the firm. The estate has the money to hire a lawyer to finish Donovan's business. Frankly, there's no one else in the county that we would even consider."

She was holding her breath, fearing a clumsy proposal, hearing a bizarre suggestion, and when he paused she finally exhaled and said, "Oh boy."

"You would work closely with Mattie and Annette, and I'll always be around."

It wasn't a complete shock. At least twice Mattie had vaguely broached the idea of hiring a lawyer to wrap up Donovan's cases. On both occasions, the words sort of hung in the air, but Samantha felt as though they were tossed at her.

She said, "I can think of at least ten reasons why that won't work."

"I can think of eleven why it will work," he shot back with a grin. The cheese cart stopped at the table, its pungent aromas and odors engulfing them. Samantha selected three. Jeff preferred sharp cheddar from the dairy case, but quickly caught on and said he'd take the same ones as Samantha. When the cart rolled away, he said, "You go first. Give me your best reason, and I'll match it."

"I'm not qualified."

"You're smart as hell and you're learning fast. With Mattie's help, you can handle anything. Next."

"I might be gone in a few months."

"But you can leave when you want to. There's no contract requiring you to return here in twelve months. You said yourself that the legal market is saturated and depressed and there are no jobs. Next."

"I'm not a litigator. Donovan's firm was all about litigation."

"You're twenty-nine years old and you can learn anything. Mattie told me you're very quick on your feet and already better than most local yokels in the courtroom."

"Did she really say that?"

"Would I lie?"

"Oh yes."

"I'm not lying. Next reason."

"I've never handled an appeal, much less an appeal with a big verdict."

"The lamest one yet. Appeals are all research and paperwork. Piece of cake. Next."

"I'm a city girl, Jeff. Look around you. This is my life. I can't survive in Brady."

"Okay, good point. But who says you have to stay there forever? Give it a go for two or three years, help us get his cases closed and the fees collected. There's some money out there that I don't want to lose. Next."

"Some of his cases could drag on for years. I can't make that commitment."

"Then commit to the Tate appeal. That's eighteen months max. It'll fly by and we'll figure out what to do next. Along the way, you can pick and choose other cases that look promising. I'll help. I'm a pretty good ambulance chaser. Next."

"I don't want to deal with Donovan's widow."

"You won't have to, I promise. Mattie and I will take care of Judy. Next."

She smeared some Camembert on a crostini and took a bite. Chewing, she said, "I don't want people following me. I don't like guns."

"You can practice law without a gun. Look at Mattie. They're afraid of her. And, like I said, I'll be close and I'll protect you. Next."

She swallowed and took a sip of port. "Okay, here's one you can't handle, and there's no way to say it without being blunt. You and Donovan played by different rules. You stole documents in the Krull Mining case, and I'm sure you've cut corners in other cases. I get the feeling that some of the files in that office are, shall we say, contaminated. I want no part of them. The FBI has raided the place once. I'm not going to be there when they raid it again."

"It's not going to happen, I swear. There's nothing, other than Krull, to worry about. And I will not jeopardize you or the office. I promise."

"I don't completely trust you."

"Thanks. I'll earn your trust."

Another bite of cheese, another sip of port. He was eating too, and waiting. He counted with his fingers and said, "That's only nine reasons, all of which I have just brilliantly shot down."

She said, "Okay, number ten, I'm not sure I would get much work done with you around."

"Good point. You want me to keep my hands off."

"I didn't say that. Look at me, Jeff. I'm not in the market for romance, okay? Period. We can fool around all we want, but it's just for fun. The moment things turn serious, then we'll have problems."

He smiled and chuckled and said, "So, let me get this straight.

You want to engage in all manner of sexual behavior but without the slightest twinge of commitment. Gee. That's a tough one. It's a deal. You win. Look, Samantha, I'm a thirty-two-year-old bachelor and I love being single. You need to understand that Donovan and I were scarred when we were very young. Our parents were miserable and couldn't stand the sight of each other. It was a war and we were the casualties. To us 'marriage' was a dirty word. There's a reason Donovan and Judy split."

"Annette said he was quite the tomcat."

"She should know."

"I suspected them. For a long time?"

"Who keeps records? And he didn't tell me everything. Donovan was very private, as you know. Did he put the move on you?"

"No."

"And if he had?"

"It would have been difficult to say no, I'll admit."

"Very few women said no to Donovan, including Annette."

"Does Mattie know?"

He took a sip of port and glanced around the dining room. "I doubt it. She doesn't miss much in Brady, but I'm guessing Donovan and Annette were very discreet. If Mattie found out, there would have been complications. She adores Judy and considers Haley a grandchild."

The waiter stopped by and she asked for the check. Jeff offered to pay for dinner, but she insisted on treating. "You can buy dinner in Brady," she said. "I'll pay in New York."

"Not a bad deal."

The cheese was gone and the port was disappearing. For a long time they sat and listened to the conversations around them, some in different languages. Jeff smiled and said, "Brady is far away, isn't it?"

"Indeed it is. Another world, and it's not mine. I gave you ten reasons, Jeff, and I'm sure I can think of ten more. I won't be there long, so please try and understand."

"I understand, Samantha, and I don't blame you."

31

Jeff began the New Year with a bang by getting himself arrested at the airport in Charleston, West Virginia. Around 10:00 p.m. on the first Sunday of the year, a guard strolling through the general aviation area noticed a man attempting to hide in the shadows of a Beech Bonanza, near several other small aircraft. The guard pulled a gun and ordered the man, Jeff, to step away from the airplane. The police were called. They put handcuffs on him and took him to jail. He called Samantha at six the following morning, but just for an update. He was not expecting her to come to the rescue because he had lawyer friends in Charleston. She asked the obvious: "What were you doing snooping around the airport on a Sunday night?"

"Investigating," he said. Someone was yelling in the background.

She shook her head in frustration at his recklessness. "Okay, what can I do?"

"Nothing. It's just trespassing. I'll be out in a few hours. I'll call."

Samantha hurried to the office and made the coffee before 7:00 a.m. She had little time to worry about Jeff and his latest adventure. She reviewed her notes, organized a file, poured a cup of coffee for the road, and at 7:30 took off for Colton, a one-hour drive in which she rehearsed her arguments with the judge and the lawyer for Top Market Solutions.

She walked into the Hopper County courthouse, alone. Gone were the days when either Mattie or Annette led interference. She was on her own now, at least for the Booker case. Pamela met her in the hallway and thanked her again. They entered the courtroom and sat at the same table where Donovan Gray had sat with Lisa Tate less than three months earlier, the same spot where they had held hands as the jury returned a just verdict. It was not lost on Samantha that in all likelihood she would be involved in the appeal of that verdict. But not today. Today they were not fighting over anything close to $3 million. Five thousand was more like it, but, judging from Samantha's nerves, it could have been millions.

The judge called them to order and asked Samantha to proceed. She breathed deeply, looked around, saw that there were no spectators, reminded herself that it was a simple case over a paltry sum, and plowed ahead. She made some brief opening remarks, and called Pamela to the witness stand. Pamela described the old credit card judgment, identified the divorce decree, described what it was like to have her paycheck garnished and her job terminated, and did a beautiful job of talking about living with her two children in her car. Samantha produced certified copies of the credit card judgment, the divorce decree, the garnishment order, and payroll records from the lamp factory. After an hour on the stand, Pamela returned to counsel table.

Top Market Solutions had a weak defense and an even weaker lawyer. His name was Kipling, a low-end litigator from a two-man firm in Abingdon, and it was obvious Kipling had little enthusiasm for the facts or for his client. He rambled on about how Top Market had been deceived by the credit card company and had acted in good faith. His client had no idea the judgment it was trying to enforce had expired.

The judge had no patience with Kipling and his ramblings. He said, "Your motion to dismiss is overruled, Mr. Kipling. Now, let's go off the record." The court reporter relaxed and reached for a coffee cup. The judge said, "I want this matter settled, and now.

Mr. Kipling, it's obvious your client has made a mistake and caused a lot of discomfort to Ms. Booker. We can have a full-blown trial in a month or so, right here, in front of me, no jury, but that would be a waste of time because I've already decided the case. I assure you it will cost your client less now if it agrees to settle."

"Well, uh, sure, Your Honor," Kipling stuttered, on his heels. It was highly unusual for a trial judge to be so blunt about a future ruling.

"Here's what I think is fair," the judge said. In other words, here's what my ruling will be. "Your client unlawfully garnished Ms. Booker's paychecks, eleven of them, for a total of $1,300. She was kicked out of her trailer because of this. Your client was directly responsible for her getting fired, though I understand she was able to regain her job. Nevertheless, she went through desperate times and ended up homeless and living in her car with her two children. All because of your client. Ms. Booker is entitled to damages for this. She has demanded $5,000 in her lawsuit, but that seems a bit low. If I decided the case today, I would award the $1,300 in lost wages, plus another $10,000 for damages. If I decide the case next month, I assure you this will seem like a bargain. What do you say, Mr. Kipling?"

Kipling was huddled up with his client, a representative to Top Market, a red-faced little stump of a man in a cheap, tight suit. He was furious and sweating, but he could also grasp what was happening. It was obvious the lawyer and the client did not trust one another. Finally, Kipling said, "Could we have five minutes, Your Honor?"

"Sure, but only five."

They stomped out of the courtroom.

Pamela leaned over and nervously whispered, "I can't believe this."

Samantha nodded smugly as if it were just another day in court. She pretended to be captivated by a document, frowning and underlining some terribly important words, while wanting to yell, "I can't believe it either. This is my first trial!"

Of course, it really wasn't a trial, but more of a hearing. But it was her first lawsuit, and to win in such a slam-dunk fashion was thrilling.

The main door opened and they stomped back to their table. Kipling looked at the judge and said, "Your Honor, well, uh, well it looks like my client made some mistakes and is truly sorry for all the trouble it caused. What you suggested is a fair settlement. We'll take it."

Samantha floated back to Brady. She thought of Donovan and Jeff after the Tate verdict, floating back to town with a $3 million verdict in their pocket. They could not have been more excited and overwhelmed than Samantha at that moment. She and her colleagues had rescued the Bookers from homelessness, even starvation, and returned them to a normal life. They had pursued justice with determination, and found it. The bad guys had been thoroughly routed.

As a lawyer, she had never felt so worthy. As a person, she had never felt so needed.

Monday's brown-bag lunch was spent celebrating Samantha's crushing victory in her first lawsuit. Annette advised her to savor the moment because victories were rare in their business. Mattie cautioned her about celebrating too soon; the check had not yet been received. Once they rehashed the Booker case, the conversation drifted to other matters. Mattie reported that Jeff was out of jail in Charleston. Did he post a bond or did he escape? Samantha asked. A prominent lawyer there, one of Donovan's pals, secured his release. No, he did not elaborate on his alleged crime.

Annette received an off-the-record call that morning from a clerk in the courthouse, alerting her to the possibility that an unnamed lawyer for the Crump family planned to file a petition to probate the prior will of Francine Crump, one she had signed five years earlier, and presumably the one she had shown Samantha. The family was claiming the prior will was valid because Francine had destroyed the later will, the free one prepared by the clinic. It was a looming mess that no one around the table wanted to jump into. Let the Crumps have their land and sell it to a coal company; they didn't care. However, as Mattie explained, as lawyers they were officers of the court, and thereby duty-bound to prevent, if possible, a fraud. They had the original free will, mailed to them by some mysterious person after Francine was felled by a stroke. She had not destroyed it; indeed, she was hiding it from her children and wanted the clinic to protect it, and to probate it. Should they produce the will now, and start a war that would rage for several years? Or should they wait and see what the Crumps alleged? There was a good chance the family would continue with its lying about Francine's destruction of the will. If these lies were told under oath, and then exposed, there could be serious implications for the family. In all likelihood, they were walking into a trap, one that the clinic could avoid by producing the will now.

It was a legal quagmire, a classic law school exam question, designed to drive students insane. They decided to wait another week, though all three lawyers, along with Claudelle and Barb, knew the will should be produced and the family alerted.

A heavy snowfall was expected to begin late in the afternoon, and they discussed the office contingencies. Mattie, Annette, and Samantha usually walked to work anyway, so the clinic would be open. Claudelle was eight months pregnant and would not be expected to show up. Barb lived deep in the countryside on a road that was seldom plowed.

By 3:00 p.m. the snow was already falling. Samantha was watching it from her desk, daydreaming and avoiding her files, when the prepaid phone buzzed in her purse. Jeff said he was still in the Charleston area. "How was jail?" she asked.

"Be careful what you say," he said.

"Oh right, I forgot." She stood and walked to the front porch.

He said he entered the ramp at the general aviation section of the airport by an unlocked gate in a chain-link fence. The small terminal was open but only a clerk was there, a young girl sitting at a desk flipping through tabloid magazines. From the shadows he watched the area for half an hour and saw no movements. In the distance, at the main terminal, there were a few flights, but nothing involving small aircraft. There were thirteen airplanes tied down on the ramp, including four Skyhawks. Two were unlocked, and he crawled inside one and sat in the darkness for ten minutes.

In other words, there was virtually no security. He could have tampered with any of the airplanes on the ramp. Then he saw a guard and decided to get arrested. It was only trespassing, a misdemeanor. He'd had more serious charges, he reminded her. The guard was nice and Jeff turned on the charm. He said he was a pilot and had always dreamed of owning a Beech Bonanza; he just wanted to see one up close. No harm intended. The guard believed him and was sympathetic, but he had a job to do.

Jail was no big deal. The lawyer would take care of things.

But while he was chatting up the guard, he asked about other guards who had worked there, other guys on the ramp who may not be around now. He got one name, a man who quit before Christmas, and he was tracking him down now.

She closed her eyes and told him to be careful. She also knew he would spend the rest of his life trying to find the men who killed his brother.

The thrill of litigation was tempered somewhat two days later when Samantha accompanied Mattie to a black lung hearing before an administrative law judge (ALJ) in the federal courthouse in Charleston. The miner, Wally Landry, was fifty-eight years old and had not worked in seven years. He was hooked to oxygen and confined to a wheelchair. Fourteen years earlier, he had filed a claim for black lung benefits based on a doctor's report that he was suffering from complicated black lung disease. The district director of the Department of Labor awarded him benefits. His employer, Braley Resources, appealed to the ALJ, who suggested to Mr. Landry that he find an attorney. Mattie eventually agreed to represent him. They prevailed before the ALJ, and Braley appealed to the Benefits Review Board (BRB) in Washington. The case bounced back and forth between the ALJ and the BRB for five years before the BRB issued a final ruling in Landry's favor.

The company appealed the ruling to the federal Court of Appeals where it sat for two years before being remanded back to the ALJ. The ALJ requested additional medical evidence and the experts went to war, again. Landry had started smoking at the age of fifteen, quit twenty years later, and as a smoker got hammered with the usual barrage of medical opinions stating that his lung problems were caused by tar and nicotine and not coal dust.

"Anything but coal dust," Mattie said over and over. "That's always their strategy."

Mattie had worked on the case for thirteen years, had 550 hours invested, and if she ultimately prevailed would have to fight to get approved at $200 an hour. The fee would be paid by Braley Resources and its insurance company, whose lawyers charged far more than $200 an hour. On those rare occasions when the clinic collected a fee in a black lung case, the money went into a special account that helped cover the expenses of future black lung cases. As of now, that fund had about $20,000 in it.

The hearing took place in a small courtroom. Mattie said it was at least the third time they had all gathered there to rehash the contrasting medical opinions. She and Samantha sat at one table. Not far away, a fashionable gang of sharply dressed lawyers from Casper Slate busily unpacked their thick briefcases and went about their work. Behind Samantha was Wally Landry, shriveled and breathing through a tube in his nose, his wife at his side. When Wally first filed his claim fourteen years earlier, he'd been entitled to $641 a month. The legal fees paid by Braley at that time amounted to at least $600 an hour, according to Mattie's off-the-cuff calculations, but don't try and make sense of it, she said. The legal fees paid by coal companies and their insurers far exceed the benefits they're fighting to avoid, but that's beside the point. The hurdles and delays discourage other miners from filing claims, and they certainly scare off the lawyers. In the long run, the companies win, as always.

A slick-rick in a black suit sauntered over to their table and said,

"Well, hello, Mattie. Nice to see you again." Mattie reluctantly got to her feet, offered a limp hand, and said, "Good morning, Trent. Always a pleasure."

Trent was about fifty with graying hair and confident looks. His smile was drippy and fake, and when he said, "So sorry about your nephew. Donovan was a fine lawyer," Mattie quickly withdrew her hand and snapped, "Let's not talk about him."

"Sorry, of course not. And who is this?" he asked, looking at Samantha. She was on her feet and said, "Samantha Kofer, an intern with the clinic."

"Ah, yes, the brilliant investigator who dug through the Ryzer records. I'm Trent Fuller." He extended a hand but Samantha ignored it.

"I'm a lawyer, not an investigator," she said. "And I represent Mr. Ryzer in his claim for black lung benefits."

"Yes, so I've heard." The smile vanished as his eyes narrowed and flashed with hatred. He actually pointed a finger at her as he spoke. "We deeply resent the allegations made against our law firm by your client in his ill-fated lawsuit. Don't make that mistake again, I'm warning you." His voice increased in volume as he lectured her. The other three suits from Castrate froze and glared at her.

Samantha was stunned, but there was nowhere to hide. "But you know the allegations are true," she said.

He took a step closer, jabbed his finger in her face, and said, "We'll sue you and your client for libel, do you understand?"

Mattie reached forward and gently shoved his hand away. "That's enough, Trent, go back to your box."

He relaxed and offered the same drippy smile. He kept glaring, though, and with a lower voice said to Samantha, "Your client caused us great embarrassment, Ms. Kofer. Even though that lawsuit has been dismissed, it still stings. His black lung claim will get the full treatment in our firm."

"Don't they all?" Mattie snapped. "Hell, this one's been on the docket for fourteen years and you're still fighting it tooth and nail."

"That's what we do, Mattie. That's what we do," he said proudly, backing away and returning to his fan club.

"Take a breath," Mattie said as they sat down.

"I'm not believing this," Samantha said, stunned. "I got threatened in open court."

"Oh, you haven't seen anything yet. They'll threaten you in court, out of court, in the hallways, on the phone, by e-mail, fax, or in court filings. Doesn't matter. They're bullies and brutes, just like their clients, and for the most part they get away with it."

"Who is he?"

"One of their more talented assassins. A senior partner, one of six in their black lung division. About a hundred associates, dozens of paralegals, and all the support staff they need. Can you imagine Wally Landry sitting here without a lawyer?"

"No." That visual seemed so far-fetched that it had to be illegal.

"Well, it happens all the time."

For a split second Samantha longed for the strength and security of Scully & Pershing, a firm four times as big as Casper Slate and far wealthier. No one bullied the litigators at her old firm; indeed, they were often regarded as the bullies. In a dogfight, they could always send in another pack of wolves to protect their clients.

Trent Fuller would never consider such an altercation with lawyers from another big firm. He swaggered over because he saw two women at the table, two ill-paid legal aid lawyers representing, pro bono, a dying miner, and he felt unrestrained in throwing his weight around. The audacity was astonishing: his firm was guilty of fraud and conspiracy, and had been caught red-handed by Samantha and exposed when Donovan filed the Ryzer lawsuit. Now that the lawsuit was gone, Fuller and his firm were not at all concerned with their own wrongdoing. Of course not—they were worried only about their tarnished image.

Nor would Fuller have ventured over and caused trouble had Donovan been there. Indeed, none of the four pretty boys at the other table would risk getting punched because of a stray word or idle threat.

They were women, viewed by the boys as easily intimidated and physically vulnerable. They were fighting a losing cause and not getting paid for it; therefore, they were obviously inferior.

Samantha stewed as Mattie shuffled papers. The judge took his place and called things to order. Samantha glanced across the courtroom and again caught Fuller staring at her. He smiled as if to say, "This is my turf, and you don't belong here."

32

The e-mail read:

Dear Samantha: I enjoyed our brief meeting in New York and look forward to another conversation with you. Yesterday, Jan 6, Krull Mining
filed a motion to dismiss our Hammer Valley lawsuit in federal court
in Charleston. This was expected, as was its length and forcefulness.
Obviously Krull Mining is terrified of the lawsuit and wants to get rid of
it. In 35 years, I've never seen a motion as strident in tone. And it will
be difficult to counter, absent proof yet to be developed. Can we meet
at some point in the near future? Also, no sign of relief from D.C. Your
friend, Jarrett London

On the one hand, she was hoping Jarrett London was a fading
memory. On the other, she had been thinking about him quite
a lot since her encounter with Trent Fuller. A trial lawyer with a
reputation and courtroom presence would not have been subjected
to such a demeaning ambush. Other than her father and Donovan,
London was the only trial lawyer she'd met, and none of those
three would have tolerated Fuller's antics. Indeed, Fuller, had they
been there, would have stayed on his side of the courtroom and
said nothing.

But she was not eager to meet him. He wanted complicity, and she had no plans to get further involved. The semi-vague "proof yet to be developed" meant he was desperate and wanted the documents.

She wrote back:

Hello Jarrett: Nice to hear from you. I'm sure I can be available for a meeting; just let me know when. Washington has been briefed. SK

Washington had not been briefed, not completely. On the train to Washington after the Christmas holiday, Samantha had told Karen part of the story, and in doing so emphasized the "abusive" tactics being used by the FBI in harassing the plaintiffs on behalf of Krull Mining. She said nothing about the hidden documents, nor did she touch on the other dramas currently unfolding in her little part of coal country.

Karen seemed interested, to a point, but commented that the FBI was known to overreach and get itself in trouble. From her lofty position at Justice, the agents way down there on the streets were in another world. Karen had no interest in what they were doing, whether in Appalachia or New York or Chicago. Her world these days was consumed with high-level strategies involving policies to be implemented relative to the reckless behavior of certain big banks and certain sub-prime mortgage lenders, and so on and on . . .

The second significant e-mail of the morning came from a Dr. Draper, a pulmonary specialist in Beckley who'd been selected by the Department of Labor to examine Buddy Ryzer. His note was to the point:

Attorney Kofer: Attached is my report. Mr. Ryzer is suffering from PMF—progressive massive fibrosis, also known as complicated coal workers' pneumoconiosis. His condition is advanced. I understand he is still working; frankly, I think he should not be, though there is nothing in my report to indicate this. I am available by e-mail for questions. LKD

She was poring over the report when the third one landed. It was from Andy Grubman, but not from his usual Scully & Pershing e-mail address.

Dear Samantha: Happy New Year. I trust this finds you doing well as you hustle about trying to save the world. I miss your smiling face and hope to see you soon. I'll be brief and get right to the point. I have decided to leave Scully & Pershing as of the end of February. I am not being forced out, or furloughed, or anything like that. We're parting on good terms. The truth is I can't stand working in tax law. I find it incredibly boring, and I miss my old beat. I have a friend who worked in commercial real estate at another firm for many years, and he's getting squeezed. We have decided to open our own shop—Spane & Grubman—with offices in the financial district. We have lined up two major clients— one a Korean bank and the other a fund out of Kuwait—and both are poised to pounce on distressed buildings along the East Coast. As you know, there is no shortage of over-leveraged units that have been swept underwater by the Recession. Also, these clients think it's the perfect time to start planning construction to begin in a couple of years when the Recession is over. They have plenty of cash and are ready to move.

Anyway, Nick Spane and I envision a firm of about twenty associates working under the two of us. Compensation will be close to that of Big Law, and we have no plans to kill ourselves or our associates. We want a nice little boutique firm where the lawyers work hard but also manage to have some fun. I promise the associates will never work more than 80 hours a week. We think 50 is a nice target. The term "quality of life" is an industry joke, but we're serious about it. I'm tired and I'm only 41.

I'm offering you a position. Izabelle is in. Ben has found something else—I'm afraid he's wandered off the reservation. What about it? No pressure, but I need an answer by the end of the month. Needless to say, there are a lot of lawyers out on the street these days.

Your favorite boss, Andy

She read it again, closed her door, and read it for a third time. Andy was basically a nice person from Indiana who'd spent too much time in New York. He sent a thoughtful letter that conveyed a generous and tempting offer, but he simply couldn't help himself by reminding her that there were plenty of lawyers begging for work. She turned off her computer and her office light, and sneaked out the back door without being heard. She got into her Ford and was a mile out of town before she asked herself where she might be headed. It didn't matter.

January 31 was twenty-four days away.

As she drove she thought about her clients. Buddy Ryzer came first. She had not committed to pushing his case until it was finished, but she had promised Mattie she would file the claim and do the initial heavy lifting. And that was almost a nuisance action compared with the mammoth lawsuit someone should refile against Lonerock Coal and Casper Slate. There was the brewing mess over the last will of Francine Crump, which, to be honest, was a beautiful reason to immediately call Andy and take the job. There were the Merryweathers, a nice, simple couple who'd sunk their savings into a small home that was now being threatened by a sleazy sub-prime lender suing for the entire balance. Samantha was seeking an injunction to stop the foreclosure. There were two divorces, still uncontested but unlikely to remain so. Of course, there was the Hammer Valley litigation that wouldn't leave her alone. Frankly, it was another reason to leave. She was helping Mattie with three bankruptcies and two employment discrimination cases. She was still waiting on a check for Pamela Booker, so that file had not been closed. She was helping Annette with two other divorces and Phoebe Fanning's mess—both Mom and Dad were headed to prison and no one wanted the kids.

To summarize things, Attorney Kofer, you have too many people leaning on you right now to pack up and run. The decision to return to New York was not supposed to be due now, only three months into a twelve-month furlough. You were supposed to have more time than this, time to open a few files, help a few folks, keep mildly occupied with one eye on the calendar as the months clicked by, the recession went away, and jobs sprang up all over Manhattan. That was the plan, wasn't it? Perhaps not a return to the drudgery of Big Law, but surely to a respectable job in something like a . . . boutique firm?

A small shop, a few happy lawyers, fifty hours a week, an impressive salary with all the usual goodies? In 2007, her last full year at Scully, she had billed three thousand hours. The math was easy—sixty billable hours a week for fifty weeks, though she had not been able to enjoy her two weeks of paid vacation. To bill sixty hours a week, she had to clock in at least seventy-five, often more. For those lucky enough to enjoy life without staring at a clock, seventy-five hours a week usually meant, for Samantha anyway, arriving at the office at 8:00 a.m. and leaving twelve hours later, Monday through Saturday, with a few spillover hours on the Sabbath. And that was normal. Toss in the pressure of a major deadline, one of Andy's clients in crisis, and a ninety-hour week was not unusual.

And now he was promising only fifty?

She was in Kentucky, approaching the small town of Whitesburg, an hour from Brady. The roads were clear but lined with piles of dirty snow. She saw a coffee shop and parked near it. The waitress informed her that there were hot biscuits fresh from the oven. How could one say no? At a table in the front window, she buttered the biscuit and waited for it to cool. She sipped coffee and watched the languid traffic along Main Street. She sent a text to Mattie, said she had to run some errands.

She ate a biscuit with strawberry jam and scribbled notes on a pad. She would not say no to Andy's offer, and she wouldn't say yes. She needed time, a few days anyway, to collect her thoughts, analyze them, gather all the information possible, and wait for some phantom voice to tell her what to do. She composed a response she would send later in the afternoon from her desk. The first draft read:

Dear Andy: Happy New Year to you. I must admit I'm shocked by your e-mail and the offer of such a promising position. Frankly, nothing has happened in the past three months to prepare me for such a quick return to the city. I thought I had at least a year to contemplate life and my future; now, though, you've suddenly turned things upside down. I need some time to think this through.

I haven't managed to save the world yet but I'm making progress. My clients are poor people who have no voice. They don't expect me to work miracles and all efforts are greatly appreciated. I go to court occasionally—imagine that, Andy, I've actually seen the inside of a courtroom—and it's far different from television. Though, as you know, I didn't have time for television. Last Monday I won my first trial. $10,000 for my client, and it felt like a million. With some experience, I might learn to enjoy trial work.

Now, about your offer. A few specifics. Who are the other associates and where are they coming from? No assholes, Andy, okay, I'm not working with a bunch of cutthroat gunners. What's the male/female breakdown? No all-boys club. Who is Nick Spane and what's his story? I'm sure he's a great lawyer but is he a nice person? Solid marriage or serial bed-hopper? If he touches me I'll sue for harassment and he needs to know that. Send me his bio, please. Where are the offices? I'm not subjecting myself to miserable working conditions. All I ever wanted was a small office—my office!—with a nice window, a little sunlight, and my own wall to hang whatever I choose. This fifty-hour-a-week guarantee—will you put that in writing? I'm currently on that schedule and it is delightful. Who will be the clients, other than the Koreans and Kuwaitis? I'm sure they'll be large corporations and such, or big guys with big egos; whatever, the point is I will not be yelled at by a client. (My clients here call me Miss Sam and bring me cookies.) We can talk about this. Lastly, what's the future? There's not one here so I won't be staying. I'm a New Yorker, Andy, more so now than three months ago, but I would like to know the structure of the new firm and where you and Spane see it ten years from now. Fair enough?

Thanks, Andy, for thinking of me. You were always fair; not always a sweetheart but then I'm not sure that's in your DNA.

Let's keep talking. Samantha

The temperature was somewhere under twenty degrees, and the snow was frozen and topped with a glaze that reflected moonlight. After a warm dinner with Annette and the kids, Samantha retired to her garage apartment, where the small furnace labored to break the chill. If she were paying a stiff rent in Manhattan she would have been giving someone an earful, but not in Brady. Not where there was no rent at all and her landlord was probably low on cash. So she bundled up and read in bed for two hours as the time slowly passed. She read a chapter, then put the book down and thought about New York, and Andy, and his brand-new firm. There were so many thoughts running through her mind.

There was no doubt she would say yes, and this excited her. The job was perfect; she would return to her home, to the city she loved, and to a job that was prestigious and promising. She could avoid the horrors of Big Law while pursuing a meaningful career. The bind was in the quitting. She could not simply walk away in a month or so and dump everything on Mattie. No, there had to be a more graceful and equitable exit. She was thinking of a short deferment—an acceptance now with an arrival on the job in six months or so. That would be fair, or as fair as possible. She could sell it to both Mattie and Andy, couldn't she?

A phone was buzzing under a pile of clothing. She finally found it and said, "Yes." It was Jeff's spy phone, and he responded with "Are you cold?"

She smiled and asked, "Where are you?"

"I'm about forty feet away, hiding in the dark, leaning against the back of the garage, my feet stuck in eight inches of frozen snow. Can you hear my teeth chattering?"

"I think so. What are you doing here?"

"That should be obvious. Look, Annette just turned off the lights over there, so the coast is clear. I think you should make some coffee, decaf if you have it, and open the damned door. Trust me, no one will see me. The neighbors have been asleep for two hours. Once again, all of Brady is dead."

She opened the door, and without as much as a squeak Jeff appeared from the dark stairs and pecked her on the lips. He took off his boots and parked them next to hers. "Staying, are we?" she asked as she poured water into the coffee machine.

He rubbed his hands together and said, "I think it's warmer outside. Have you complained to the landlord?"

"Haven't thought about it. No rent means no complaints. Nice to see you out of jail."

"You're not going to believe what I've dug up."

"And that's why you're here, to tell me all about it."

"Among other things."

On the night Donovan died, his Cessna was parked at the Charleston airport for about seven hours, from 3:20 to 10:31 p.m., according to air traffic control records and data from the general aviation terminal. After he landed, he rented a car and took off to meet with his legal team. While he was gone, four small planes arrived at the ramp; two bought fuel, dropped off a passenger, and left, and the other two tied down for the night. One of these was a Beech Baron, the other a King Air 210, a popular twin-engine turboprop that seats six passengers. The King Air arrived at 7:35 p.m. with two pilots and one passenger. All three got off the airplane, entered the terminal, did their paperwork, and left with a guy in a van.

Samantha listened without a word and poured the decaf.

According to Brad, an employee who worked the ramp that night, there were actually two passengers on the King Air, one of whom stayed behind. That's right—he spent the night on the airplane. As the two pilots were going through their postflight routines, Brad caught a glimpse of the passenger on the ground speaking to a passenger still on the plane. From a distance, he watched, and he waited, and sure enough the pilots closed the King Air's only door. When their aircraft was secure for the night, they walked into the terminal, with the passenger, as if all was well.

Bizarre, but Brad had actually seen this once before, a couple of years earlier when a pilot landed late at night, had neither a hotel reservation nor a rental car, and decided to just sleep a few hours in the cockpit and take off at dawn. The difference was that that pilot had made his intentions known and the ramp guys knew what he was doing. With the King Air, though, only Brad knew what was happening. He kept an eye on the airplane until 10:00 p.m., when he punched out and went home. Two days later he was fired for missing work. He had never liked his job and hated his boss. His brother got him a job in Florida and he left town. No one had ever interviewed him about the events of that night. Until now, of course.

"How'd you find him?" she asked.

"The guard who arrested me Sunday night gave me his name. Turns out Mack, the guard, is a pretty great guy. We had beers late Monday night, me buying of course, and Mack gave me the dirt on Brad. Brad's back in Charleston now. I found him last night, and, in another bar, we had some drinks. I'm detoxing tonight so don't offer me anything."

"There's not a drop in the house."

"Good."

"So, your theory is?"

"My theory is that this mysterious passenger waited until the right moment, opened the door of the King Air, walked about thirty yards in the darkness, straight to Donovan's Cessna, and in about twenty minutes loosened the B nut. Then he backtracked, climbed into the King Air, and was probably watching when Donovan showed up around 10:15 for his departure. After that, he kicked off his shoes and slept until sunrise."

"Sounds impossible to prove."

"Maybe, but I'm getting there."

"Who owns the King Air?"

"A charter service out of York, Pennsylvania, a company that does a lot of business with coal companies. The King Air is the workhorse in the coalfields because it's durable, has a nice payload, and works off short runways. This company has four available for charter. There are plenty of records so we'll soon know everything about the flight. Brad says he'll give an affidavit, though I'm a little worried about him."

"This is incredible, Jeff."

"It's huge. The investigators will grill the owners of the plane, the pilots, the passenger or passengers, and whoever chartered it for the trip. We're getting closer, Samantha. It's an unbelievable break."

"Nice work, Sherlock."

"Sometimes you just gotta get yourself arrested. You have an extra quilt somewhere around here?"

"They're all layered up on the bed. That's where I was, reading."

"Was that a pickup line?"

"We're already picked up, Jeff. The question at the moment is sex, and I hate to tell you it's not going to happen. Not the best time of the month."

"Oh, sorry."

"You could've called."

"I guess. Then why don't we just cuddle and share body heat and sleep together, I mean, you know, actually sleep?"

"I suppose that will work."

33

She had no idea what time he left. When she awoke, a few streaks of morning light penetrated the blinds and windows. It was almost 6:00 a.m. His side of the bed was not warm, as if he'd been gone for hours. Whatever. He lived in the shadows and left few trails, and that was fine with her. He carried burdens and baggage she would never understand, so why bother? She thought about him for a few moments, as she peeked from under the quilts and watched damp clouds follow her breathing. It was cold out there, and she had to admit she longed for his warmth.

She also longed for a hot shower, but that would not be happening. She counted to ten, threw off the covers, and raced to the coffeepot. It took forever to brew, and when she finally had a cup she crawled back under the covers and thought about New York. Her plans were to polish up her response to Andy and e-mail it first thing. Was it too pushy, too demanding? She was, after all, unemployed and he was offering a wonderful job. Did she have the right to nag about her associates and clients, about Mr. Nick Spane, and the dimensions of her new office? Would her deferment scheme please Andy, or irritate him? She wasn't sure, but Andy had a thick skin. If she didn't assert herself in the beginning she would certainly get run over later.

She skipped the cold shower and did a bird bath with lukewarm water in the sink. With no court appointments on the calendar, she dressed quickly in jeans and boots, flannel shirt and sweater. When she was properly bundled, she looped her satchel over one shoulder, her purse over the other, and left for work on foot. The air was crisp and still, the sun brilliant as it rose. It was a beautiful winter day, with snow still untouched in thick drifts against the houses. Not a bad way to get to work, she thought, as she walked through Brady.

On the negative side: In New York she would be packed into a subway train, then jostling through heavy foot traffic. Or perhaps sitting in the back of a dirty cab, waiting in traffic.

She spoke to Mr. Gantry as he fetched his newspaper off the sidewalk. He was pushing ninety, lived alone since his wife died last year, and in warmer weather had the prettiest lawn on the street. All snow on his property had been meticulously scraped and shoveled.

As usual these days, she arrived first at the office and, as the intern, went straight to the coffeepot. As it brewed, she tidied up the kitchen, emptied all the wastebaskets throughout the place, and straightened magazines in the reception area. No one had ever told her to do these things.

On the positive side: In New York, Spane & Grubman would pay someone else to do such chores.

On the neutral side: Samantha really didn't mind doing them, not here anyway. She wouldn't dare do them at a real firm, but at the Mountain Legal Aid Clinic everyone pitched in.

She sat in the conference room and watched the early traffic on Main Street. Now that she was planning to leave, she was astonished at how fond of the place she had become in three short months. She decided she would postpone the discussion with Mattie and wait until she knew more about Andy's offer. The thought of telling her she was leaving so soon was unsettling.

Mattie's mornings were still slower, but she seemed to be finding her old self. Donovan's absence was a jagged wound that would never heal, but she couldn't stop living. She had too many clients who needed her, too many entries in her calendar. She rolled in just after nine and asked Samantha to step into her office. With the door closed, she explained that she'd lost sleep the night before worrying about those wretched Crump people and poor old dead Francine. The only ethical thing to do was to poll the local bar and see if anyone had been hired by the family. If so, they would zip over a copy of the will and start the war. Mattie handed over a list and said, "Not including us, there are fourteen lawyers in Brady, all alphabetized with phone numbers. I've already talked to three, including Jackie Sporz, the lawyer who did the will five years ago. None has heard from the family. You pick five and let's get it done this morning. I'm tired of worrying about it."

Samantha had met all but two. She went to her office, grabbed the phone, and called Hump. He said no, he'd never heard of the Crumps. Lucky for him. The second call was to Hayes Sinclair, a lawyer who never came out of his office and was rumored to suffer from agoraphobia. No, he had never heard of the Crumps. The third call was to Lee Chatham, a lawyer who never stayed in his office but was always hanging around the courthouse, posturing as if he had important business there and trafficking in gossip, most of which he created. Bingo. Mr. Chatham said yes, he had met with several of the Crumps and had a contract to represent the family.

Evidently, they were pressing ahead with their fiction that their mother destroyed the free will prepared by those crooks over at legal aid, and therefore things would revert back to the prior will, which split everything equally. Mr. Chatham's plans were to open the estate in the near future and proceed with the prior will. However, they were bickering over who would serve as executor. Jonah, the oldest, had been appointed by Francine five years ago, but he was having heart problems (brought on by the stress of this situation), and probably couldn't serve. When Mr. Chatham mentioned replacing Jonah with a substitute executor, a fight started amongst the other four. He was currently trying to arbitrate matters.

Samantha dropped the bomb about the mysterious package they had received the day after the funeral. She made sure Mr. Chatham understood that neither she nor anyone at the clinic had any desire to get involved in a will contest, but it was important for him to know that his clients were lying. By the time she hung up, he was mumbling incoherently to himself. She faxed a copy of the last will to his office, and left to tell Mattie.

"That'll really piss 'em off, won't it?" she said when she heard the news. "One threat, and I'm going to the sheriff."

"Should we get some handguns?" Samantha asked.

"Not yet." She tossed some papers across the desk. "Take a look." It was thick, whatever it was, and Samantha sat down. "What is it?" she asked as she flipped a page.

"Strayhorn, notice of appeal in the Tate case. I talked to the trial judge late last week about the alleged settlement. Needless to say, he was not sympathetic, so we're screwed. Now we have to slog our way through the appeals process and hope the Supreme Court doesn't reverse."

"Why am I holding this?"

"I thought you might be interested. And, Samantha, we need you to handle the appeal."

"I think I saw this coming. I've never touched an appeal, Mattie."

"You've never touched most things around here. There's always a first time. Look, I'll supervise, and you'll learn quickly that it's just a lot of paperwork and research. Strayhorn goes first and files their thick brief in ninety days. They will allege all manner of grievous errors at trial. We respond, point counterpoint. In six months almost all of the work is done and you'll be waiting on oral argument."

But in six months I'll be gone, Samantha wanted to say.

"It'll be great experience," Mattie pressed on. "And for the rest of your life you can say you handled an appeal to the Supreme Court of the Commonwealth of Virginia. How can you top that?" She was aiming at levity but it was clear Mattie was anxious.

"How many hours?" Samantha asked. She was calculating quickly and already thinking that she could do virtually all of the research over the next six months, before she left.

"Donovan swore it was a clean trial, nothing major to quibble over on appeal. I'd guess five hundred hours, from now through oral argument, which is about fifteen months away. I know you'll be gone by then, so one of us will handle that part. The heavy lifting takes place now. Annette and I simply do not have the time."

Samantha smiled and said, "You're the boss."

"And you're a dear. Thanks Samantha."

Andy fired back:

Dear Miss Sam: Thanks so much for your lovely epistle. You've gotten so soft in only three months. Must be all those cookies. If I read you right, you want some assurances that you'll be (1) adored by your bosses, (2) worshipped by your colleagues, (3) appreciated by your clients, (4) virtually guaranteed a partnership which will lead to a long, full, happy life, and (5) given enough office space to make you happy, in spite of the obscene prices per square foot now being demanded by Manhattan landlords (our clients), recession or not.

I'll see what I can do. Attached is a bio of Nick Spane. Oddly enough, he's had just one divorce and has been married to the same great gal for about fifteen years now. As you'll see, he has no felony convictions for rape, child abuse, etc., nor has he been indicted for dealing in child porn. Too, he has never been sued for sexual harassment, or anything else for that matter. (His divorce was no-fault.) He's actually a great guy, I swear. A Southern guy—Tulane, Vanderbilt Law—with impeccable manners. Odd for these parts.

Later, Andy

The spy phone buzzed at 2:30 as Samantha was rereading Strayhorn's notice of appeal and reviewing the rules for appellate procedure. "Are you outside my office standing in the snow?" she asked, walking to the kitchen, which she assumed was bug-free.

"No, I'm in Pikeville meeting with some investigators. I enjoyed last night, slept warm and sound. You?"

"I slept well. What time did you leave this morning?"

"Just after four. I'm not sleeping much these days, you know. Somebody's back there, always watching. Kinda hard to sleep."

"Okay. What's on your mind?"

"Saturday, hiking around Gray Mountain, in the snow. Grilling a steak on the cabin porch. Drinking some red wine. Reading by the fire. That sort of thing. Are you up to it?"

"Let me think about it."

"What's there to think about? I'll bet that if you'll glance over at your calendar you'll see that there's nothing written down for this Saturday. Go ahead."

"I'm busy right now. I'll have to call you back."

Though it had not been mentioned by anyone at the clinic, Samantha was learning that the cold weather and short days of January slowed business considerably. The phone rang less and Barb spent more time away from her desk, always "running errands." Claudelle was eight months pregnant and on bed rest. The courts, never in a hurry, clunked along at even slower paces. Mattie and Annette were as busy as ever with existing cases, but new ones were not dropping in. It was as if conflict and misery took a break as the wintertime blues settled in. At least for some.

As Samantha was puttering around the office after dark on Friday, she heard the front door open. Mattie was still in with her door closed; everyone else was gone for the weekend. Samantha walked to the reception area and said hello to Buddy and Mavis Ryzer. They had no appointment; they had not called. Instead, they had driven an hour and a half from West Virginia to Brady late on a Friday afternoon to seek solace and guidance from their attorney. She hugged them both and knew immediately that their world had come to an end. She showed them to the conference room and offered a soft drink; they declined. She closed the door, asked what was going on, and both started crying.

Buddy had been fired by Lonerock Coal that morning. The

foreman said he was physically unfit to work; thus the immediate termination. No exit package, no farewell bonus, no cheap watch for a job well done and certainly no golden parachute, just a hard kick in the ass with a promise that the last paycheck was in the mail. He'd barely made it home when he collapsed on the sofa and tried to collect himself.

"I got nothing," he said between breaths as Mavis wiped tears and rattled away. "I got nothing."

"Just like that, he's outta work," Mavis said. "No paycheck, no black lung benefits, and no prospect of finding any kind of work. All he's ever done is work in the coalfields. What's he supposed to do now? You gotta help us, Samantha. You gotta do something. This ain't right."

"She knows it ain't right," Buddy said. Each word was labored as his chest rose and fell with each noisy breath. "But there's nothing you can do. They busted our union twenty years ago, so we got no protection from the company. Nothing."

Samantha listened with great sympathy. It was odd to see such a tough guy like Buddy wiping his cheeks with the back of a hand. His eyes were red and puffy. Normally, he would have been embarrassed at such emotion, but now there was nothing to hide. Eventually, she said, "We've filed our claim and we have a strong report from the doctor. That's all we can do right now. Unfortunately, in the states around here an employee can be terminated at will for any cause, or for no cause."

She thought the obvious but wasn't about to mention it: Buddy was in no shape to work. As much as she despised Lonerock Coal, she understood why the company would not want an employee in his condition operating heavy equipment.

There was a long silence, broken only by Mattie, who pecked on the door and stepped inside. She greeted the Ryzers, realized an unpleasant meeting was under way, and started a quick exit. "I'll see you for dinner, Sam?"

"I'll be there. Around seven?"

The door closed and they returned to the silence. Mavis finally said, "It took my cousin eleven years to get his black lung benefits. He's on oxygen now. My uncle, nine. I hear the average is something like five years. That about right?"

"For contested claims, yes, five to seven is the average."

"I'll be dead in five years," Buddy said, and they thought about this. No one argued with him.

"But you said all claims are contested, right?" Mavis asked.

"I'm afraid so."

Buddy just shook his head, slightly but without stopping. Mavis went silent and stared at the table. He coughed a few times and seemed on the verge of a gagging fit, but managed to swallow hard and fight it. His deep desperate breaths sounded like muffled roars from within. He cleared his throat again and said, "You know, I should've got my benefits ten years ago, and if I had I could've got out of the mines and found work somewhere else. I was only thirty back then, the kids were little, and I could've done something else, away from the dust, you know. Something that didn't make the disease any worse. But the company fought me and it won, and so I had no choice but to keep working in the mines, and keep breathing the dust. I could tell it was getting worse. You just know it. It creeps up on you but you know that walking up the four steps to the front porch is harder now than it was a year ago. Walking to the end of the driveway takes a bit longer. Not much, but things get slower." A pause for deep breaths. Mavis reached over and patted his hand. "I remember those guys in court, in front of the administrative law judge. Three or four of them, all in dark suits and shiny black shoes, all strutting around so important. They would look over at us like we was white trash, you know, just an ignorant coal miner with his ignorant wife, just another deadbeat trying to game the system for a monthly check. I can see them right now, arrogant little shits, so smart and smug and cocky because they knew how to win and we didn't. I know it's not very Christian-like to hate, but I really, really despised those guys. It's even worse now because we know the truth, and the truth is that those crooks knew I had black lung. They knew, yet they covered it up. They lied to the court. They brought in another set of lying doctors who said, under oath, that I didn't have black lung. Everybody lied. And they won. They kicked me outta court, put me back in the mines, for ten years now."

He stopped and rubbed his eyes with his fingers.

"They cheated, they won, and they'll do it again because they write the rules. I guess there's no way to stop them. They got the money, the power, the doctors, and I guess the judges. Some system."

"There's no way to stop them, Samantha?" Mavis pleaded.

"A lawsuit, I guess. The one Donovan filed, and there's still a chance that another firm might refile it. We haven't given up."

"But you're not taking the case, right?"

"Mavis, I've explained this before. I'm from New York, okay? I'm an intern, here for only a few months, then gone. I cannot initiate a lawsuit that will take five years of pretty intense litigation in federal court. We've covered this, right?"

Neither responded.

Minutes passed as the offices grew even quieter; the only sound was Buddy's painful breathing. He cleared his throat again and said, "Look, Samantha, you're the only lawyer we've ever had, the only one who's ever been willing to help us. If we'd had a lawyer ten years ago maybe things would be different. But anyway, we can't go back there. We drove over here today to say one thing, and that's to thank you for taking my case."

"And being so kind to us," Mavis said, jumping in. "We thank the Lord every day for you and your willingness to help us."

"It means more than you'll ever know."

"Just having a real lawyer out there fighting for us means so much."

Both were crying again.

34

Her first glimpse of Gray Mountain had been by air. Her second had been by boat and four-wheeler, a much more intimate visit two and a half weeks before last Christmas. Her third was by pickup truck, a more traditional means in those parts. Jeff picked her up in Knox, where she left her car in the same library parking lot. One look at the truck and she said, "You get a new one?" It was a massive vehicle, a Dodge something or other, and definitely not the one she'd seen before.

"No. It belongs to a friend," he said, vague as always. In the back were two red kayaks, a cooler, and several backpacks. "Let's go." They left town in a hurry. He seemed tense and his eyes kept darting from one mirror to the other.

"Are those canoes back there?" she asked.

"No, they're kayaks."

"Okay. What does one do with a kayak?"

"You've never been in a kayak?"

"Again, I'm from the city."

"Okay, with a kayak one goes kayaking."

"Or one sits by the fire with a book and a glass of wine. I'm not getting wet, you hear?"

"Relax, Sam."

"I still prefer Samantha, especially from the guy I'm currently sleeping with. Sam is okay when it's my father, never my mother, and now Mattie can get away with it. Sammie will get a person slapped. It's confusing, okay, but for now why don't you just stick with Samantha?"

"It's your name. I'm getting sex with no strings so I'll call you whatever you want."

"Get right to the point don't you?"

He laughed and turned up the stereo—Faith Hill. They left the main highway and bounced along a narrow county road. As they began a steep ascent, he suddenly turned onto a gravel road, one that ran along a ridge with forbidding canyons below. She tried not to look, but flashed back to her first adventure with Donovan, when they climbed to the top of Dublin Mountain and looked down at the Enid Mine site. Vic had startled them, and then they were spotted by security. It seemed so long ago, and now Donovan was dead.

Jeff turned again, and again. "I'm sure you know where you're going," she said, but only to register concern. "I grew up here," he said without looking. A dirt trail still half-covered with snow stopped at a dead end. Through the trees she could see the cabin.

As they were unloading the truck, she asked, "What about the kayaks? I'm not hauling these things."

"We'll have to check the creek. I'm afraid the water might be too low." They lifted the small cooler and backpacks from the truck and carried them to the cabin, fifty yards away. The snow was four inches deep and covered with the tracks of animals. There appeared to be no boot prints or signs of human visitors. Samantha was pleased that she noticed such things. A real mountain girl now.

He unlocked the cabin, entered slowly as if he might disturb something, and looked around. They placed the cooler in the small kitchen and the backpacks on a sofa. "Are those cameras still out there?" she asked.

"Yes, and we just triggered them."

"Any trespassers lately?"

"Not that I know of."

"When's the last time you were here?"

"It's been a long time. Too much traffic raises suspicions. Let's check the creek."

They walked over some rocks at the edge of the stream. Jeff said it was too low for the kayaks. Instead, they followed it deep into the hillsides, far away from the cabin and any land owned by his family. Though she wasn't sure, she thought they were going west, away from Gray Mountain. With the ground covered in snow, it was impossible to find trails, not that they were needed. Jeff, like his brother, moved through the terrain as if he walked it daily. They began a climb that grew steeper, and at one point stopped for water and a granola bar. He explained that they were on Chock Ridge, a long steep hill that was thick with coal and owned by people who would never sell. The Cosgrove family, from Knox. Donovan and Jeff had grown up with the Cosgrove kids. Good folks and so on. They climbed another five hundred feet and crested the ridge. In the distance, Jeff pointed out Gray Mountain. Even covered with a white blanket it looked bare, desolate, violated.

It was also far away, and after an hour trudging through the snow her feet were beginning to freeze. She decided to wait a few more minutes before complaining. As they began a descent, shots rang out, loud thunderous cracks of gunfire that echoed through the hills. She wanted to hit the ground but Jeff was unfazed. "Just deer hunters," he said, barely breaking stride. He had a backpack but no rifle. She was certain, though, that there was a weapon somewhere in there with the granola bars.

Finally, when she was convinced they were hopelessly lost in the woods, she asked, "Are we headed back to the cabin?"

He glanced at his watch and said, "Sure, it's getting late. Are you cold?"

"My feet are frozen."

"Has anyone ever told you that you have beautiful toes?"

"Happens every day."

"No, seriously?"

"Am I blushing? No, Jeff, I can honestly say that I do not remember anyone ever saying that."

"It's true."

"Thanks, I guess."

"Let's go thaw them."

The route back took almost twice as long as the venture out, and the valley was dark when they found the cabin. Jeff quickly built a fire, and the chill was replaced by a smoky warmth that Samantha could soon feel in her bones. He lit three gas lanterns, and as he hauled in enough firewood for the night, she unpacked the cooler and inspected dinner. Two steaks, two potatoes, and two ears of corn. There were three bottles of merlot, carefully selected by Jeff because of their screw-off caps. They drank the first cup as they warmed by the fire and talked about politics. Obama would take the oath in a few days, and Jeff was contemplating a road trip to D.C. for the festivities. Her father, long before his fall, had been active in the Democratic politics of the plaintiffs' bar, and now seemed to be regaining his enthusiasm for the fight. He had invited her to come share the moment. She liked the idea of watching history, but wasn't sure of her schedule.

She had told no one about the offer from Andy, and she would not bring it up now. Doing so would only complicate things. Halfway through the second cup he asked, "How are the toes?"

"They're tingling," she said. They were still tucked away in thick woolen socks, socks she planned to keep on regardless of what happened. He went to light the charcoal on the porch, and before long they were preparing dinner. They ate by candlelight on a primitive table built for two. After dinner, they attempted to read novels by the light of the fire, but quickly abandoned that idea for more pressing and important matters.

She awoke in the midst of the quilts and blankets, naked except for her socks, and it took a few seconds to realize Jeff was not somewhere in the pile. Coals smoldered in the fireplace as the last of the logs burned out. She found a flashlight and called his name, but he wasn't in the cabin. She checked her watch: 4:40 a.m. Pitch-black outside. She walked to the porch, shined the light over it, softly called his name, then quickly returned to her warm spot by the fire. She refused to panic. He wouldn't leave her alone if she were in danger. Or would he? She put on jeans and a shirt and tried to sleep, but she was too wired. She was also frightened, and as the minutes ticked by she tried to stifle her anger. Alone in a dark cabin deep in the woods—this was not supposed to happen. Every sound from the outside could be a threat. Five o'clock crept by. She almost dozed off but caught herself. She had brought a small back-pack with a toothbrush and a change of clothes. He had hauled in three large ones of the serious-backpacker variety. She had noticed them immediately in the back of the truck in Knox, and she had glanced at them occasionally. He used one for the hike; the other two appeared to be stuffed with something. They had been tossed on the sofa at first, then placed by the door. Now they were gone.

She took off her jeans and shirt and flung them on the sofa, as if nothing had happened. When she was still and warm again, she took deep breaths and assessed the situation. What was obvious became more so. For those watching Jeff's every move, today's visit to Gray Mountain was nothing more than a romantic getaway. The kayaks were a nice touch, bright and red and stacked in the back of the truck for all to see, but never close to actually getting wet. Kayaking, hiking, grilling on the porch, snuggling by the fire— just a pleasant little tryst with the new girl in town. In the early hours of the morning, when the valley was at its stillest, he awoke and eased away with the skill of a cat burglar. At that moment, he was deep in the bowels of Gray Mountain stuffing the backpacks with invaluable papers filched from Krull Mining.

He was using her for cover.

The door opened and her heart froze. She couldn't see it in the pitch blackness, and the sofa was blocking it too. She was lying on a thick mat layered with quilts and blankets, trying to breathe normally and praying that the person over there was Jeff. He stood perfectly still for what seemed like an hour, then moved slightly. When he placed his jeans on the sofa the belt buckle rattled slightly.

When he was undressed, he gently eased back under the covers, careful not to touch her or wake her.

She really hoped that naked man inches away was Jeff Gray. Feigning sleep, she rolled over and flung an arm across his chest. He pretended to be startled and mumbled something. She mumbled back, satisfied that she, in fact, knew the guy. With a hand that was a bit too cold for the occasion, he fondled her rear end. She mumbled no, and turned away. He moved closer, then pretended to fall asleep. Before she drifted off, she decided to play along with the game for the time being. Give it some time and thought, and keep an eye on those backpacks.

The cat burglar was moving again, now slowly getting to his feet and reaching for the stack of wood. He tossed two logs on the fire, stoked it, and whispered, "Are you awake?"

"I think so," she said.

"This place is freezing." He was on his knees, lifting covers and reburying himself next to her. "Let's sleep some more," he said, groping, going for the body heat. She grunted something in reply, as if she'd been in a coma. The fire was popping and crackling, the chill was suddenly gone, and Samantha managed to finally drift away.

35

The forecast for Monday was a high of fifty-five degrees and lots of sunshine. The last of the snow was melting quickly as Samantha walked to work. January 12, but it almost felt like spring. She unlocked the office and went about her early morning routine. The first e-mail was from Izabelle:

Hey Sam: Andy says he's made contact and you're almost on board. He made me promise not to discuss the job and the specifics; afraid we'll compare notes and try to squeeze him for a better package I guess. Can't say that I've really missed him that much. You? I certainly haven't missed the firm and the city and not sure I'm going back. I told Andy I'd take the job but having second thoughts. I certainly can't drop everything and be there in a month. You? Nor have I missed the thrill of reading and revising contracts ten hours a day. I need the money and all, but I'm surviving okay and I really enjoy the work. As I've told you, we advocate for kids who have been prosecuted as adults and are stuck in adult prisons. Don't get me started. The work is fascinating as well as depressing, but each day I feel like I'm making a small difference. We walked a kid out of prison last week. His parents were waiting by the gate, and everyone was in tears, including me. FYI—one of the other new associates at Spane & Grubman is that turd Sylvio from tax. Remember him? The worst halitosis in the entire firm. Knock you down from the other side of the conference table. And he insists on talking nose to nose. Spits too. Gross! FYI—according to unnamed sources, one of the blue ribbon clients at Spane & Grubman will be Chuck Randover, that great indictment-dodger who thinks just because he's paying you $900 an hour he has the right to rub your ass. You know him too well.

But you didn't hear this from me. FYI—Serious second thoughts. You? Izzie

Samantha chuckled as she read the e-mail, and wasted no time firing one right back:

Iz, I don't know what Andy is smoking, or telling, but I haven't said yes. And if he's playing this fast and loose with the facts it sort of makes me question everything else he says. No, I cannot pack up and leave here in a month, not with a clear conscience. I'm thinking of asking for a start date a few months down the road, say around September 1.

Randover was the only client who ever made me cry. He ridiculed me once in a meeting. I held things together until I could get to the restroom. And that chump Andy sat right there and watched it happen, no thought of protecting his people. No way. He wasn't about to cross a client. I was wrong, but it was such a simple and harmless mistake.

Any idea what the package will be?

Izabelle replied:

I swore I wouldn't divulge it. But it's impressive. Later.

The first surprise of the day came in the mail. Top Market Solutions sent a check for $11,300, made payable to Pamela Booker, with the required releases attached. Samantha made a copy of the check and planned to frame it. Her first lawsuit and her first victory. She proudly showed it to Mattie, who suggested that she drive it over to the lamp factory and surprise her client. An hour later, she entered the town of Brushy and found the near-vacant industrial park on the edge of town. She said hello to Mr. Simmons and again thanked him for rehiring Pamela.

On break, Pamela signed the release and cried over the check. She had never seen so much money and seemed thoroughly overwhelmed. They were sitting in Samantha's car, in the parking lot, among a sad collection of ancient pickup trucks and dirty little imports. "I'm not sure what to do with this," she said.

As a multitalented legal aid lawyer, Samantha had a bit of financial advice. "Well, first, don't tell anyone. Period. Open your mouth and you'll have all sorts of new friends. How much is your credit card debt?"

"Couple thousand."

"Pay it off, then cut up your cards. No debt for at least a year. Use cash and write checks, but no credit cards."

"Are you serious?"

"You need a car, so I'd put two thousand down on one and finance the rest over two years. Pay off your other bills, and put five thousand in a savings account, then forget about it."

"How much of this do you get?"

"Zero. We don't take fees, except in rare cases. It's all yours, Pamela, and you deserve every dime of it. Now hurry and stick it in the bank before those crooks bounce it."

With her lips twitching and tears dripping off her cheeks, she reached over and hugged her lawyer. "Thank you, Samantha. Thank you, thank you."

Driving away, she looked in her rearview mirror. Pamela was standing, watching, waving. Samantha wasn't crying, but she had a tightness in her throat.

The second surprise of the day came during the Monday brown-bag lunch. Just as Barb was telling a story about a man who'd fainted in church yesterday, Mattie's cell phone vibrated on the table beside her salad. Caller unknown. She said hello, and a strangely familiar, but unidentified, voice said, "The FBI will be there in thirty minutes with a search warrant. Back up your files immediately."

Her jaw dropped as the color drained from her face. "Who is this?" she asked. The caller was gone.

She calmly repeated the message, and everyone took a deep, fearful breath. Judging from the tactics used when the FBI raided Donovan's office, it was safe to assume they would walk out with just about everything they could carry. The first frantic order of business would be to find some flash drives and start downloading the important data from their desktops.

"We're assuming this is also related to Krull Mining," Annette said, looking suspiciously at Samantha.

Mattie was rubbing her temples, trying to stay calm. "There's nothing else. The Feds must think we have something because I'm the attorney for Donovan's estate. Bizarre, absurd, outrageous, I can't think of enough adjectives. I, we, have nothing they haven't already seen. There's nothing new."

To Samantha, though, the raid was far more ominous. She and Jeff had left Gray Mountain Sunday morning, and she was assuming the backpacks were loaded with documents. Barely twenty-four hours later, the FBI was charging in, snooping on behalf of Krull Mining. It was a fishing expedition, but also an act of effective intimidation. She mentioned nothing, but hurried to her office and began transferring data.

The women whispered as they scurried about. Annette had the bright idea of volunteering Barb to leave with their laptops. They would explain that she was driving over to Wise to have them serviced by a technician. Barb gathered them and was more than happy to leave town. Mattie called Hump, who was one of the better criminal lawyers in town, retained him on the spot, and asked him to saunter over once the raid started. Hump said he wouldn't miss it for anything. When the flash drives were loaded, Samantha placed them in a large envelope, along with her spy phone, and walked down to the courthouse. On the third floor, the county maintained a long-neglected law library that hadn't been cleaned in years. She hid the envelope in a pile of dusty *ABA Journals* from the 1970s and hurried back to the office.

Agents Frohmeyer and Banahan wore dark suits and led the fearless team as it barged into the heavily fortified offices of the Mountain Legal Aid Clinic. Three other agents—all in navy parkas with "FBI" stenciled from shoulder to shoulder in yellow letters as large and as bright as possible—followed their leaders. Mattie met them in the front hallway with "Oh no, not you again."

Frohmeyer said, "Afraid so. Here's the search warrant."

She took it and said, "I don't have time to read it. Just tell me what it covers."

"Any and all records relating to the legal files from the law offices of Donovan Gray and pertaining to correspondence, litigation, etc., relative to what is commonly known as the Hammer Valley case."

"You got it all last time, Frohmeyer. He's been dead seven weeks. You think he's still producing paperwork."

"I'm just following orders."

"Right, right. Look, Mr. Frohmeyer, his files are still over there, across the street. The file I have here is his probate file. We're not involved in the litigation. Understand? It's not complicated."

"I have my orders."

Hump made a noisy entrance, barking, "I represent the clinic. What the hell is this all about?" Annette and Samantha were watching from their open doors.

Mattie said, "Hump, this is Agent Frohmeyer, the leader of this little posse. He thinks he has the right to take all of our files and computers."

Annette suddenly barked, "Like hell you do. I don't have a single piece of paper in my office that's even remotely related to Donovan Gray or any of his cases. What I do have is an office full of sensitive and confidential files and cases involving such things as divorce, child molestation, domestic abuse, paternity, addiction and rehab, mental incompetency, and a long sad list of human misery. And you, sir, are not entitled to see any of it. If you try to touch any of it, I'll resist with all the physical might I can muster. Arrest me if you will, but I promise you first thing tomorrow morning I'll file a federal lawsuit with your name, Mr. Frohmeyer, and the names of the rest of you goons, front and center, as defendants. After that, I'll hound you to hell and back."

It took a lot to stun a tough guy like Frohmeyer, but for a second his shoulders slumped, slightly. The other four listened wide-eyed and uncertain. Samantha almost laughed out loud. Mattie was actually grinning.

"Very well put, Ms. Brevard," Hump said. "That sums up our position nicely, and I'll be happy to call the U.S. Attorney right now and clarify things."

Mattie said, "There are over two hundred active files and a thousand more in storage. None of which have anything to do with Donovan Gray and his business. Do you really want to haul them back to your office and dig through them?"

Annette snarled, "Surely, you have better things to do."

Hump raised both hands and called for quiet. Frohmeyer stiffened his back and glared at Samantha. "We'll start with your office. If we find what we're looking for, we'll take it and leave."

"And what might that be?"

"Read the search warrant."

Hump asked, "How many files do you have, Ms. Kofer?"

"Around fifteen, I think."

Hump said, "Okay, let's do this. Let's place her files on the conference room table and you boys have a look. Go through her office and inspect whatever you want, but before you remove anything let's have a chat. Okay?"

"We're taking her computers, desktop and laptop," Frohmeyer said.

The sudden interest in Samantha's files was puzzling to Mattie and Annette. Samantha shrugged as if she had no idea. "My laptop is not here," she said.

"Where is it?" Frohmeyer snapped.

"The technician has it. Some type of bug, I think."

"When did you take it in?"

Hump threw up another hand. "She doesn't have to answer

that. The search warrant doesn't give you the right to interrogate potential witnesses."

Frohmeyer took a deep breath, fumed for a second, then gave them a sappy grin. He followed Samantha to her office and watched closely as she removed her files from the army surplus cabinet. "Nice place you got here," he said like a real smart-ass. "Won't take long to search this office." Samantha ignored him. She carried her files to the conference room where Banahan and another agent began flipping through them. She returned to her office and watched Frohmeyer slowly poke through her two file cabinets and the drawers to her rickety desk. He touched every piece of paper but took nothing. She hated him for invading her private space.

One agent followed Mattie into her office; another followed Annette. Drawer by drawer, they looked at all the files but removed nothing. Hump walked from door to door, watching and waiting for an altercation.

"Are all the laptops gone?" Frohmeyer asked Hump when he finished digging through Samantha's office.

Annette heard the question and said, "Yes, we sent them all together."

"How convenient. Guess we'll be back with another search warrant."

"All fun and games."

They picked through hundreds of retired files. Three of them climbed into the attic and pulled out records Mattie hadn't seen in decades. The excitement gave way to monotony. Hump sat in the hallway and shot the bull with Frohmeyer while the ladies tried to return calls. After two hours, the raid lost steam and the agents left, taking with them nothing but Samantha's desktop computer.

As she watched it leave, she felt like the helpless victim in a backward country where the police ran rampant and rights were nonexistent. It was simply wrong. She was being bullied by the cops because of her association with Jeff. Now her property was being confiscated, and her clients' confidentiality was compromised. She had never felt so helpless.

The last thing she needed was a good grilling at the hands of

Mattie and Annette. They had to be highly suspicious of her at this point. How much did she know about the Krull matter? What had Jeff told her? Had she seen any of the documents? She managed to sneak out the back door and retrieve the flash drives and spy phone from the law library. She went for another long drive. Jeff was not answering the phone and this irritated her. Right now she needed him.

Mattie was waiting when she returned to the office at dark. The laptops were back, safe and untouched.

"Let's go sit on the porch and have a glass of wine," Mattie said. "We need to talk."

"Is Chester cooking?"

"Well, we never skip dinner."

They had a nice stroll to Mattie's house and decided along the way it was too chilly for porch sitting. Chester was busy elsewhere, so they were alone. They sat in the den and had a sip or two before Mattie said, "Now, tell me everything."

"Okay."

36

At about the same time, Buddy Ryzer parked his pickup truck at a scenic overlook, and walked two hundred yards along a trail to a picnic area. He sat on a table, put a gun in his mouth, and pulled the trigger. Two campers found his body late Monday night and called 911. Mavis, who'd been on the phone for hours, got the knock on the door. Panicked neighbors rushed over; the house was chaos.

Samantha was sleeping soundly when her cell phone began vibrating. She did not hear it. Absent an arrest, why would anyone feel the need to call his or her lawyer at midnight on a Monday?

She checked it at 5:30, soon after she awoke in the fog of reliving the FBI raid. There were three missed calls from Mavis Ryzer, the last one at 12:40. A message in a trembling voice delivered the news. Samantha suddenly forgot about the FBI.

She was really growing weary of all this death. Donovan's still haunted her. Francine Crump's was not untimely, but its aftermath was causing problems. Two days before, on Gray Mountain, Samantha had again seen the white cross marking the spot where Rose took her life. She had never met the Tate boys, but felt an attachment to their tragedy. She often thought of Mattie's father and the way black lung killed him. Life could be harsh in the coalfields, and at that moment she missed the rough streets of the big city.

Now her favorite client was dead, and she was facing another funeral. She put on jeans and a parka and went for a walk. As the sky began to lighten, she shivered in the cold and once again asked herself what, exactly, was she doing in Brady, Virginia. Why was she crying over a coal miner she had met only three months earlier? Why not just leave?

As always, there were no simple answers.

She saw a kitchen light on at Mattie's and pecked on the window. Chester, in his bathrobe, was making coffee. He let her in and went to fetch Mattie, who was supposedly awake. She took the news hard, and for a long time the two lawyers sat at the kitchen table and tried to make sense out of a senseless tragedy.

Somewhere in the pile of the Ryzers' records, Samantha had seen a payment on a life insurance policy of $50,000.

"Isn't there some type of exclusion for suicide?" she asked, cradling her cup with both hands.

"Typically, yes, but it's only for the first year or so. If not, then a person could load up on insurance and jump off a bridge. If Buddy's policy is older, then the exclusion has probably expired."

"So, it looks like he killed himself for the money."

"Who knows? A person who commits suicide is not thinking rationally, but I suspect we'll find out that life insurance was a factor. He had no job, no benefits, and their small savings account was gone. That, plus three kids at home and a wife with no job. He was facing years of even more bad health, and the end would not be pretty. Every coal miner knows a victim of the disease."

"Things start to add up."

"They do. Would you like some breakfast, maybe a piece of toast?"

"No thanks. I feel like I just left here. I guess I did." As Mattie topped off their coffees, Samantha said, "I have a hypothetical for you. A tough one. If Buddy had a lawyer ten years ago, what would have happened to his case?"

Mattie stirred in some sugar and frowned as she considered this. "You never know, but if you assume the lawyer was on the ball and found the medical records you discovered, and that he or she brought Casper Slate's fraud and cover-up to the court's attention, somewhere along the way, then you have to believe he would have been awarded benefits. Just speculating here, but I have a hunch Casper Slate would have acted quickly in order to keep their crimes away from the court. They would have conceded the claim, folded their tent so to speak, and Buddy would have received his checks."

"And he wouldn't have been breathing more coal dust for the past ten years."

"Probably not. The benefits aren't great, but they could have survived."

They sat in perfect silence for a while, neither wanting to speak or move. Chester appeared in the doorway with an empty cup, saw them frozen in deep thought, and disappeared without a sound. Finally, Mattie pushed back and stood. She reached for the wheat bread and put two slices in the toaster. From the fridge she withdrew butter and jam.

After a couple of bites, Samantha said, "I really don't want to go to the office today. It feels violated, you know? My computer got snatched yesterday, all my files were rifled through. Both Jeff and Donovan thought the place was bugged. I need a break."

"Take a personal day, or two. You know we don't care."

"Thanks. I'm leaving town and I'll see you tomorrow."

She left Brady and drove an hour before allowing herself one glance into the rearview mirror. No one, nothing. Jeff called twice but she refused to answer. At Roanoke, she headed east, away from the Shenandoah Valley and the interstate traffic. With hours to kill, she worked the phone, arranging details, leaning on people as she meandered through central Virginia. In Charlottesville, she had lunch with a friend from the Georgetown days. At ten minutes before 6:00 p.m., she took her position at a corner table at the bar in the Hay-Adams hotel, one block from the White House. Neutral turf was required.

Marshall Kofer arrived first, promptly at six, looking as dapper as ever. He had readily agreed to the meeting; Karen had been a bit more reluctant. In the end, though, her daughter needed help. What her daughter really needed was for her parents to listen and provide some guidance.

Karen was only five minutes late. She hugged Samantha, pecked her ex properly on the cheek, and sat down. A waiter took their drink orders. The table was away from the bar so there was privacy, for the moment anyway. Samantha would be in charge of the talking—it was her show all the way—and she would not allow any awkward pauses as her parents sat down together for the first time in at least eleven years. She had told them on the phone that this was not a social event, and it was certainly not a misguided effort to patch up old issues. More important matters were at hand.

The drinks arrived and everyone reached for a glass. Samantha thanked them for their time, apologized for the short notice, then plunged into her narrative. She began with the Hammer Valley litigation, and Krull Mining, and Donovan Gray and his lawsuit. Marshall had known the facts for some time, and Karen had heard most of it just after Christmas. But neither knew about the stolen documents, and Samantha spared no details. She had actually seen them, and was assuming they were still buried deep in Gray Mountain. Or at least most of them. Krull Mining was after them, and now the FBI had been enlisted to do its dirty work. She admitted she was seeing Jeff but assured them it was nothing serious. Frankly, she owed them no explanations. Both feigned disinterest in her new relationship.

The waiter was back. They ordered another round and something to snack on. Samantha described her meeting in New York with Jarrett London, and his efforts to pressure her and Jeff into delivering the documents as soon as possible. She admitted she felt like she was getting sucked into activity that, if not illegal, was clearly questionable. She had now been the target of an FBI raid, which, though misguided, had certainly been dramatic and frightening. As far as she knew, the U.S. Attorney in West Virginia was spearheading the investigation and evidently was convinced that Krull Mining was the victim of a theft and conspiracy. It should be the other way around, she argued. Krull Mining was the guilty party and should be brought to justice.

Marshall agreed wholeheartedly. He asked a few questions, all of them aimed at the U.S. Attorney and the Attorney General. Karen was cautious in her comments and questions. What Marshall was thinking, but could never say, was that Karen had most likely used her considerable influence to bust him and send him to prison a decade earlier. With clout like that, why couldn't she help her daughter now?

A cheese platter arrived but they ignored it. Both parents agreed that she should not touch the documents. Let Jeff run the risks if he so chose, but she should leave them alone. Jarrett London and his band of litigators had the brains and money to handle the dirty work, and if the documents were as valuable as they believed, they would figure out a way to nail Krull Mining.

Can you get the FBI to back off? Samantha asked her mother. Karen said she would give it her immediate attention, but cautioned that she had little influence with those guys.

The hell you don't, Marshall almost mumbled. He had sat in prison for three years and schemed of ways to retaliate against his ex-wife and her colleagues. But, with time, he accepted the reality that his problems had been caused by his own greed.

Have you thought about simply leaving? her mother asked. Pack up and get out? Call it an adventure and hustle back to the city? You gave it your best shot and now you've got the FBI breathing down your neck. What are you doing there?

Marshall seemed sympathetic to this line of questioning. He'd served time with some white-collar guys who, technically, had broken no laws. If the Feds want to get you, they'll figure out a way. Conspiracy was one of their favorites.

The more Samantha talked, the more she wanted to talk. She could not remember the last time she'd had the undivided attention of both parents. In fact, she was not sure it had ever happened. Perhaps as a toddler, but then who could remember? And, listening to her worries and troubles, both parents seemed to forget their own issues and rally to support her. The baggage was left behind, for the moment anyway.

Why did she feel compelled to stay "down there"? She answered by telling the story of Buddy Ryzer and his claim for black lung benefits. Her throat tightened when she told them of his suicide, about twenty-four hours ago. She would go to a funeral soon, at a pretty church out in the country, and watch from a distance as poor Mavis and the three kids melted down in emotional anguish. If they'd had a lawyer, things would have been different. Now that they had one, she couldn't pack up and run when the pressure was on. And there were other clients, other folks with little voices who needed her to at least hang around a few months and pursue some measure of justice.

She told them about the job offer from Andy Grubman. Marshall, predictably, disliked the idea and referred to it as "just a spiffed-up version of the same old corporate law." Just pushing paper around a desk with one eye on the clock. He warned that the firm would grow and grow and before long it would look and feel just like Scully & Pershing. Karen thought it was far more appealing than staying in Brady, Virginia. Samantha confessed she had mixed feelings about the offer, but, in reality, she expected to say yes at some point.

They had dinner in the hotel restaurant, salads, fish, and wine, even dessert and coffee. Samantha talked so much she was exhausted, but she allowed her fears to be heard by both parents, and the relief was enormous. No clear decisions had been made. Nothing had really been resolved. Their advice was largely predictable, but the act of talking about it all was therapeutic.

She had a room upstairs. Marshall had a car with a driver, and he offered Karen a ride home. When they said good-bye in the hotel lobby, Samantha had tears in her eyes as she watched her parents leave together.

37

Following instructions, she parked on Church Street in downtown Lynchburg, Virginia, and walked two blocks to Main. Midday traffic was heavy in the old section of town. The James River could be seen in the distance. She was certain someone was watching and she hoped it was Jeff. The reservation at the RA Bistro was in her name, again, pursuant to instructions. She asked the hostess for a booth in the rear, and that's where she sat at exactly noon, Wednesday, January 14. She ordered a soft drink and began fiddling with her cell phone. She also kept an eye on the door as the lunch crowd slowly drifted in. Ten minutes later, Jeff appeared from nowhere and sat across from her. They exchanged hellos. She asked, "Was I followed?"

"That's always the assumption, right? How was Washington?"

"I had a delightful dinner with my parents, for the first time in modern history. In fact, I cannot remember the last time the three of us ate a meal together. Pretty sad, don't you think?"

"At least you have both parents. Did you tell your mother about the FBI raid?"

"I did, and I asked her to make a call or two. She will, but she's not too sure what will happen."

"How's Marshall?"

"Swell, thanks, he sends his regards. I have a couple of questions for you. Did you call the office on Monday and warn us about the FBI raid?"

Jeff smiled and looked away, and it was one of those moments when she wanted to scream at him. She knew he would not answer the question. "Okay," she said. "Have you heard the news about Buddy Ryzer?"

He frowned and said, "Yes. Just awful. Another casualty in the coal wars. Too bad we can't find a lawyer willing to take on Lonerock Coal and the boys at Casper Slate."

"Was that a shot at me?"

"No, it was not."

A friendly waiter stopped by, went through the daily specials, and disappeared.

"Third question," Samantha said.

"Why am I getting grilled? I had in mind a pleasant little lunch a long way from the boredom of Brady. You seem pretty edgy."

"How many of the documents have you removed from Gray Mountain? We were there last weekend. I woke up at 4:40 a.m. Sunday and you were gone. I freaked out for a minute. You sneaked back in around five, got all cuddly as if nothing had happened. I saw the backpacks, all three of them. You kept moving them around, and they were noticeably heavier when we left. Level with me, Jeff. I know too much."

He took a deep breath, glanced around, cracked a few knuckles, and said, "About a third, and I need to get the rest of them."

"Where are you taking them?"

"Do you really want to know?"

"Yes."

"Let's say they're well hidden. Jarrett London needs the documents, all of them, as soon as possible. He'll tender them to the court and at that point they'll be safe. I need your assistance in getting them away from Gray Mountain."

"I know, Jeff, I know. I'm not stupid. You need me for cover, a chick who'll put out by the fire during long romantic weekends on the property. A girl, any girl will do, so that the bad guys will figure we're just kayaking and grilling on the porch, a couple of lovebirds screwing away the long winter nights while you sneak through the woods with the files."

He smiled and said, "Pretty close, but not just any girl will do, you know? You were carefully chosen."

"I'm so honored."

"If you'll help me, we can get them out this weekend and be done with it."

"I'm not touching the documents, Jeff."

"You don't have to. Just be the girl. They know who you are. They're watching you too. They picked up your trail three months ago when you came to town and started hanging around with Donovan."

The salads arrived and Jeff asked for a beer. After several bites, he said, "Please, Samantha, I need your help."

"I'm not sure I follow you. Why can't you just sneak onto the property tonight, or tomorrow night, all by yourself, get the documents, load them up, and take them to Jarrett London's office in Louisville? Why would that be so complicated?"

Another roll of the eyes, another glance at nearby eavesdroppers, another bite of salad. "Here's why. It's too risky. They're always watching, okay?"

"Right now, they're watching you?"

He rubbed his chin and pondered the question. "They probably know I'm somewhere in Lynchburg, Virginia. Maybe not exactly where, but they keep track. Remember, Samantha, they have all the money in the world and they make their own rules. They figure I'm the link to the documents. They can't find them anywhere else, so if it costs a fortune to track me, no big deal." The beer arrived and he took a sip. "If I go to Gray Mountain on the weekends with you, they're not suspicious, and why should they be? Two thirty-year-olds in a cabin deep in the woods, just having a little romance, as you say. I'm sure they're close by, but it makes sense that we're there. On the other hand, if I were to go there alone, their radar goes way up. They might provoke an encounter, something ugly so they could see what I'm doing. You never know.

It's a chess match, Samantha, they're trying to predict what I'll do, and I'm trying to stay one step ahead of them. I have the advantage of knowing my next move. They have the advantage of unlimited muscle. If either side makes a mistake, someone will get hurt." He took another sip and glanced at a couple reading menus ten feet away. "And, I gotta tell you. I'm tired. I'm really tired, exhausted, running on fumes, you know? I need to get rid of the documents before I do something stupid because of fatigue."

"What are you driving right now?"

"A Volkswagen Beetle, from Casey's Rent-A-Wreck in Roanoke. Forty bucks cash per day, plus gas and mileage. Really cute."

She shook her head in disbelief. "Do they know I'm here?"

"I don't know what they know, but I am assuming they're tracking you. And they'll continue to monitor both of us until the documents are turned over. I don't know this for a fact, but I would bet all the money I have."

"I find this hard to believe."

"Don't be naive, Samantha. There's too much at stake."

When she walked into her office at 5:20 that afternoon, her computer was sitting on her desk, precisely where it had been before the FBI took it on Monday. The keyboard and printer were in place; all wires running where they were supposed to run. As she stared at it Mattie walked to her door and said, "Surprise, surprise, huh?"

"When did this find its way back?"

"About an hour ago. One of the agents brought it over. Guess they realized there was nothing on it."

That, or Karen Kofer had far more friends than she would admit to. Samantha wanted to call her mother, but in her current state of paranoia she decided to wait.

"The Ryzer funeral is Friday afternoon," Mattie said. "You want to ride with me?"

"Sure. Thanks, Mattie."

38

Hello Sam: 1/16/09

I'm a bit confused, not sure why you think you have the right to veto the hiring of your future colleagues at Spane & Grubman. Likewise, I'm baffled by your concerns about possible clients the firm might attract. It seems as though the smartest course for us right now is to simply bring you in as the senior partner and get out of your way. You want a corner office? A car and driver?

No, we cannot wait for you until September 1. We open our doors in six weeks and things are already a bit chaotic. Word is out and we're getting flooded. Eight associates have signed on and there are around ten offers pending, including yours. The phone rings non-stop with young lawyers desperate for work—though few, of course, are as talented as you.

The offer: $150k a year and all the usual goodies. Three weeks paid vacation which I'll insist you take. The structure of the firm will be a work in progress, but I assure you it will hold more promise than any of the Big Law outfits.

We can wait until May 1 for your grand arrival, but I still need an answer by the end of this month. Love, Andy

Mattie predicted a full house, and she was right. During the drive to Madison, she tried to explain why rural funerals, especially those of dedicated churchgoers, draw such big crowds. In no particular order of importance, her reasons were (1) funerals are important religious services, as the living say good-bye to the departed, who by then are already in heaven reaping rewards; (2) there is an old and unshakable tradition that proper and well-raised people pay their respects to the family; (3) country folks are usually bored and looking for something to do; (4) everyone wants a crowd at his or her funeral, so you'd better play the game while you can; (5) there is always plenty of food. And so on. Mattie explained that a shocking death like Buddy's was guaranteed to draw a crowd. People want to play a role in the tragedy. They also want the gossip. She also attempted to explain the conflicting theologies behind suicide. Many Christians consider it an unpardonable sin. Others believe no sin is unpardonable. It would be interesting to see how the preacher handled the issue. When they buried her sister Rose, Jeff's mother, her suicide was never mentioned. And why should it have been? There was enough anguish without it. Everybody knew she'd killed herself.

They arrived at the Cedar Grove Missionary Baptist Church half an hour early and barely got in the door. An usher made room for them on the third pew from the rear. Within minutes all seats were taken and people began lining the walls. Through a window, Samantha could see the latecomers being directed to the fellowship hall, the same place she'd met with Buddy and Mavis after Donovan's death. When the organ started, the crowd grew still and expectant. At ten after four, the choir filed in behind the pulpit, and the preacher took his position. There was a commotion at the door. He raised his hands and said, "All rise."

The pallbearers rolled the casket down the aisle, slowly, so everyone could have a look. Thankfully, it was closed. Mattie said it would be, on account of the wound and all. Behind it, Mavis was supported by her son, the oldest, and they moved along in an anguished shuffle. They were followed by the two girls, Hope, age fourteen, and Keely, age thirteen. Through the mysteries of adolescence, Hope, who was only ten months older, was at least a foot taller than Keely. Both were sobbing as they suffered through this painful ritual.

Mattie had tried to explain that much of what they were about to see was designed to maximize the drama and grief. It would be Buddy's last hurrah, and they would milk it for all the emotion possible.

The rest of the family ambled by in loose formation—brothers, sisters, cousins, aunts, and uncles. The first two rows on both sides of the aisle were reserved for family, and by the time they took their seats the organ was blaring at full volume, the choir was humming loudly, and folks were breaking down all over the church.

The service was a one-hour marathon, and when it was over no tears were left un-shed. All emotions were expended. The mourners had given their all. Samantha was dry-eyed but drained nonetheless. She could not recall the last time she wanted so badly to run from a building. She walked, however, with the rest of the crowd to the cemetery behind the church where Buddy was laid to rest amidst lengthy prayers and a tear-jerking rendition of "How Great Thou Art." The solo baritone was a cappella, and profoundly moving. Samantha was stunned by it and finally had to wipe a tear.

In keeping with tradition, the family remained in their chairs next to the grave as everyone proceeded by for a comforting word or two. The line wrapped around the burial tent and moved slowly. Mattie said it was best if they did not sneak away. So they inched forward, in single file with hundreds of complete strangers, waiting to squeeze the hands of Mavis and the kids, who had been sobbing now for hours.

"What am I supposed to say?" Samantha whispered to Mattie as they approached the grave.

"Just say, 'God bless you,' or something like that, and keep moving." Samantha said this to the kids first, but when Mavis looked up and saw her she wailed anew and lunged for her in bear-hug fashion.

"This is our lawyer, kids, Miss Samantha, the one I told you about," Mavis said with far too much volume. But the kids were too numb to care. They wanted to leave more than Samantha. Mavis said, "Please stay and have some supper. We'll catch up later."

"Sure," Samantha said because there was nothing else to say. As she was released from the hug and scooted away from the tent, Mavis let loose with another shriek.

Supper was a "Baptist potluck," as Mattie called it, in the fellowship hall. Long tables were covered with casseroles and desserts, and the crowd seemed to grow even bigger as two buffet lines started. Samantha had no appetite and couldn't believe she was still there. She watched the horde attack the food and observed, to herself, that most could afford to skip a meal or two. Mattie brought her iced tea in a plastic cup, and they schemed ways to make a respectful departure. But Mavis had seen them, and they had promised to stay.

The family remained by the grave site until the casket was lowered. It was dark and supper was well under way when Mavis and her children entered the fellowship hall. They were given a preferred table in a corner and plates of food were taken to them. When Mavis saw Samantha and Mattie, she waved them over and insisted they sit with the family.

A piano played softly in the background and supper dragged on. As people began leaving, they stopped by for one last word with Mavis, who hadn't touched her food. She still cried off and on, but there were some smiles now, even a laugh when someone recalled a funny story about Buddy.

Samantha was tinkering with a wedge of some variety of red cake, trying to nibble just enough to be polite while trying to avoid it altogether, when Keely, the thirteen-year-old, eased into the chair next to her. She had short auburn hair and plenty of freckles, and her little eyes were red and swollen from the ordeal. She managed a smile, a gap-toothed grin more fitting for a ten-year-old. "My daddy liked you a lot," she said.

Samantha hesitated for a second and said, "He was a very nice man."

"Will you hold my hand?" she asked, reaching. Samantha took it and smiled at her. Everyone else at the table was either talking or eating. Keely said, "My daddy said you were the only lawyer brave enough to fight the coal companies."

Almost tongue-tied, Samantha managed to reply, "Well, that was very nice of him to say, but there are other good lawyers."

"Yes ma'am, but my daddy liked you the most. He said he hoped you didn't go back to New York. He said if he'd found you ten years ago, we wouldn't be in such a mess."

"Again, that was very nice of him."

"You're gonna stay and help us, aren't you, Miss Sam?" She was squeezing even harder, as if she could physically keep Samantha close by for protection.

"I'll stay as long as I can."

"You gotta help us, Miss Sam. You're the only lawyer who'll help us, at least that's what my daddy said."

39

A heavy, midweek rain drained into the rivers and streams of Curry County, and Yellow Creek was high enough for kayaking. It was warm for mid-January, and Samantha and Jeff spent most of Saturday afternoon racing up and down the creek in dueling kayaks, dodging boulders, floating on the still waters, and avoiding any mishaps. They built a fire on a sandbar and cooked hot dogs for a late lunch. Around 4:00 p.m., Jeff thought they should head for the cabin, which was about half a mile away upstream. By the time they arrived they were exhausted. Wasting no time, Jeff grabbed three backpacks and a rifle. He said, "Give me thirty minutes," and disappeared toward Gray Mountain.

Samantha put a log on the fire and decided to wait on the porch. She took a quilt outside, settled under it, and tried to read a novel. She watched two deer ease into the shallow water of the creek and take a drink. They left and vanished into the woods.

If everything went as planned, she and Jeff would leave after sunset. In the Jeep—Donovan's Jeep Cherokee—they would have in their possession all of the remaining Krull Mining documents. Jeff estimated their weight at about a hundred pounds. They would take them to a location he had yet to disclose. The less he told her, the less complicit she would be. Right? She wasn't so sure. He had promised she would not touch the documents, and hopefully not even see them. If somehow they got caught, now or later, he would take all the blame. She was reluctant to help, but she was also eager to close this complicated chapter of her life and move on.

Two rifle shots suddenly rang out, and she jumped out of her skin. Then two more! They were coming from just over the ridge, from Gray Mountain. She stood on the porch and looked in that direction. One more shot, for a total of five, and then nothing but silence. She could hear her heart pounding, but other than that there was complete silence. Five minutes passed, then ten. Fifteen. She was holding her cell phone but there was no service.

Minutes later Jeff emerged from the woods, not on the trail, but from the dense forest. He was walking as fast as possible as he lugged the three backpacks. She ran to meet him and took one of them. "Are you okay?"

"I'm fine," he said, then was silent as they tossed the backpacks onto the porch. He sat on the front steps, breathing heavily, almost heaving. She handed him a bottle of water and asked, "What happened?"

He slurped the water and poured some over his face. "As I was coming out of the cave, I saw two goons, both with rifles. They had followed me, then I guess they got turned around. I made a noise. They turned and fired, both missed. I hit one in the leg and scared the other one."

"You shot someone!"

"Damned right I shot someone. When they have guns it's best to hit them before they hit you. I think he's okay, not that I care. He screamed and his buddy was dragging him away last I saw." He gulped the water as his breathing settled down. "They'll be back. I'll bet they've called for help and more thugs are on the way."

"What are we going to do?"

"We're getting out of here. They were too close to the cave and they might have seen me go in. I can get it all in one more load."

"It's getting dark, Jeff. You can't go back there."

He didn't hear anything but mumbled, "We gotta work fast." He jumped to his feet, grabbed two of the backpacks and pointed to the third. "Get that one." Inside, they unzipped them, carefully removed stacks of paper and placed the loot on the kitchen table.

Two empty picnic coolers had been sitting suspiciously in a corner since Samantha's first visit. He pulled them over and opened them. From the inside pocket of his vest he produced a black pistol and laid it on the table. He grabbed her shoulders and said, "Listen to me, Samantha, as soon as I leave, place the documents into these coolers. There's a roll of cargo tape inside, make sure they're sealed tightly. I'll be back in about an hour."

"There's a gun on the table," she said, wide-eyed.

He picked it up and said, "Have you ever fired one?"

"Of course not. And I'm not doing it now."

"You'll do it if you have to. Look, it's a 9-millimeter Glock automatic. The safety is off so it's ready to go. Lock the door behind me and sit right here on the sofa. If anyone shows up and tries to get in, you have no choice but to pull this little trigger. You can do it."

"I want to go home."

"Buck up, Samantha, okay? You can do this. We're almost finished, and then we're outta here."

He did inspire confidence. Whether it was foolishness, bravery, the love of adventure, or a rush of adrenaline, he was assertive and sure of himself and made her believe she could hold the fort. If he was daring enough to return to Gray Mountain at dusk, the least she could do was sit by the fire and hold the gun.

The least she could do? Why was she even there?

He pecked her on the cheek and said, "I'm off. Does your phone have any coverage?"

"No. None."

He grabbed the empty backpacks and his rifle and left the cabin. She stood on the porch, watched him disappear into the woods, and shook her head at his guts. Donovan knew he would die young. What about Jeff? Once you accept death, is it easier to charge into the darkness? She would never know.

Inside, she gingerly picked up the Glock and placed it on the counter. She stared at the documents, and for a split second was tempted to at least scan a couple. Why not, after all their controversy? But her curiosity passed quickly and she stuffed them into the coolers. They barely fit, and as she was fumbling with the tape she heard two shots in the distance.

She forgot about the Glock and ran to the porch. After a few seconds, there was a third shot, then a shriek of an indistinguishable nature. Under the circumstances, she was reasonably sure it was the sound of a man getting hit by gunfire, not that she had any experience with such situations. As the seconds passed she became convinced it was Jeff who'd been hit. Ambushed by the backup thugs, or goons, or whatever.

She began walking along the creek, headed for the trail where she had seen him disappear. She stopped for a second and thought about the gun, then kept walking. The documents were not worth dying for, not when her life was on the line. If the bad guys grabbed her, she was betting that they would not kill her. Unarmed, anyway. If she burst into the woods blasting away, she wouldn't last three seconds. And how valuable was she in a gunfight? No, Samantha, guns are not your thing. Leave the Glock in the cabin. Leave it there with all those wretched documents and let the thugs have them all. Live another day and before long you'll be back in New York where you belong.

She was at the edge of the woods, staring into blackness. She froze and listened; nothing. She called out softly, "Jeff. Jeff. Are you okay?" Jeff did not answer. One foot slowly followed the other. Fifty feet in, she called out again. A hundred feet into the woods and she could not see the opening behind her.

Trying to find Jeff or anyone else, or anything in particular, at that moment in those woods was a ridiculous idea. She was not following orders. She was to stay inside the locked cabin and guard things. She turned around and hurried out of the woods. Something snapped loudly behind her and she gasped. She glanced back, saw nothing, but walked even faster. Out of the woods, the sky lightened a little and she could see the silhouette of the cabin a hundred yards away. She scampered along the creek until she hit the porch at full speed. She sat on the front steps, catching her breath, watching the trail, praying for a miracle.

She walked inside, locked the door, lit a lantern, and almost fainted.

The coolers were gone, as was the Glock.

There was a noise on the porch, heavy footsteps, bags being dropped, a man's cough. He tried to open the door, rattled it, yelled, "Samantha, it's me. Open up!"

She was wrapped in an old quilt, cowering in a corner, armed only with the poker from the fireplace, and ready to use it if necessary in a fight to the finish. He found a key and burst inside. "What the hell!" he demanded. She laid down her weapon and began crying. He rushed to her and said, "What happened?"

She told him. He kept his cool and said only, "Let's get outta here. Now!" He poured water on the fire, turned off the lantern, and locked the door. "Take that one," he said, pointing to a backpack. He threw one onto his back, slung the other over his shoulder, and had his rifle in a ready position. He was sweating and agitated and barked, "Follow me!"

As if she might choose another course of action.

They headed for the Jeep, which, along with everything else, was lost in the night. The last time Samantha checked her phone the time was 7:05. The trail was straight and within minutes they were in the opening. Jeff hit the key and the Jeep's lights came on. He yanked open the hatch, and as they tossed in the backpacks Samantha saw the two coolers. She barely managed to say, "What?"

"Get in. I'll explain." As they were driving away, he turned off the lights and drove slowly along the gravel road. He said, "It's a basic tactical maneuver. The good guys are on-site doing a mission. They know the bad guys are watching, trailing them. What the bad guys don't know is that the good guys have a backup team that's watching and trailing the bad guys, sort of a security ring."

She mumbled, "More stuff they didn't teach us in law school."

A yellow light flashed twice in front of them and Jeff stopped the Jeep. "Here's our backup team." Vic Canzarro yanked open a rear door and jumped inside. No greetings, no hellos, nothing but "Nice move, Sam, why did you leave the cabin?"

"Knock it off," Jeff barked over his shoulder. "Have you seen anything?"

"No. Let's go!"

Jeff turned on the lights and they were moving again, much faster now, and were soon on a paved county road. The fear was fading, replaced by a bit of relief. Each mile took them farther away, they thought. Five minutes passed without a word. Vic was texting away, his rifle still in his lap.

Finally, Jeff calmly asked her, "Why did you leave the cabin?"

"Because I heard gunshots, and I thought I heard someone scream. I thought you were hurt, so I panicked and went to the trail."

"What the hell were the gunshots?" Vic thundered from the backseat.

Jeff began laughing and was quite amused with himself. He said, "Well, I was racing through the woods, pitch-black, you know, and I ran into a black bear. A big one. They're hibernating this time of the year so they're practically brain-dead. This guy wasn't moving too quick, but he was irritated anyway. Figures it's his neck of the woods, you know, so he takes offense at getting run over by a trespasser. We had words, he wouldn't move, I had no choice but to shoot him."

"You shot the bear?"

"Yes, Samantha, I also shot a human, though I suspect he's okay."

"Aren't you worried about the police?"

Vic laughed loudly as he cracked a window and lit a cigarette.

"No smoking in here," Jeff said.

"Sure, sure."

Jeff glanced at Samantha and said, "No, dear, I'm not worried about the police or sheriff or anyone else, not for shooting an armed thug who was stalking me on my own property. This is Appalachia. No cop will investigate, and no prosecutor will prosecute because no jury will ever convict."

"What will happen to the guy?"

"I guess he'll have a sore leg. He's lucky. The bullet could have hit him between the eyes."

"Spoken like a true sniper."

Vic said, "He'll show up in an emergency room with a tall tale. Did you get everything?"

"Every piece of paper. Every scrap so skillfully confiscated by my dear brother."

"Donovan would be proud of us," Vic said.

In the town of Big Stone Gap, they turned in to a Taco Bell and waited in the drive-thru. Jeff ordered a sack of food with drinks, and as he was paying Vic opened the door and got out. He said, "We're headed to Bristol." Jeff nodded as if that was expected. He watched closely as Vic opened the door to his pickup, a truck Samantha recognized from her excursion into Hammer Valley with Donovan.

She said, "Okay, what are we doing now?"

"He'll follow us to Bristol and watch our tail. He also has the documents we hauled out last Saturday, the first batch."

"I thought you said Vic has a pregnant girlfriend and wanted no part of this."

"It's true. She is pregnant, but they got married a week ago. You want a taco?"

"I want a martini."

"I doubt if you can find a good one around here."

"What, may I ask, is in Bristol?"

"An airport. Beyond that, if I tell you then I'll have to kill you."

"You're on a rampage, go ahead."

The aroma hit them, and they were suddenly starving.

There were only five airplanes parked on the general aviation ramp at the Tri-Cities Regional Airport near Bristol, Tennessee.

The four small ones—two Cessnas and two Pipers—were dwarfed by the fifth, a sleek, glistening private jet with all lights on and the stairs down and waiting. Samantha, Jeff, and Vic admired the aircraft from a distance as they waited for instructions. After a few minutes, three large young men dressed in black met them outside the terminal. The documents—in two coolers, three backpacks, and two cardboard boxes—were handed over and immediately wheeled out to the jet.

One of the three men said to Jeff, "Mr. London would like to see you." Vic shrugged and said, "Oh why not? Let's check out his little toy."

"I've actually flown on it," Jeff said. "It's a step up from the Skyhawk."

"Well aren't you the big shot," Vic snarled.

They were led through the empty terminal, onto the ramp, and to the jet. Jarrett London was waiting at the top of the stairs with a huge smile and a drink in hand. He waved them up and welcomed them to his "second home."

Samantha had a friend at Georgetown whose family owned a jet, so this was not her first glimpse at one. The massive chairs were covered in deep, rich leathers. Everything was trimmed in gold plate. They sat around a table while a flight attendant took their drink orders. Just take me to Paris, Samantha wanted to say. And come get me in a month.

It was clear that Vic and London knew each other well. As Jeff gave the details of their escape from Gray Mountain, the drinks were served. "Would you like dinner?" London asked in Samantha's direction.

"Oh no, Jeff treated me to Taco Bell. I'm stuffed."

Her martini was perfect. Jeff and Vic had Dickel on the rocks. London explained that the documents would be flown right then to Cincinnati, where they would be copied on Sunday. On Monday, the originals would be flown to Charleston and handed over to a U.S. marshal. The judge had agreed to lock them up until he could review them. Krull Mining had not been informed of this agreement and had no idea what was about to happen. The FBI had backed off completely, for the moment anyway.

"Do we have friends in Washington to thank for this, Samantha?" London asked.

She smiled and said, "Perhaps. I'm not sure."

He took a sip, rattled his cubes, and said, "What are your plans now?"

"Why do you ask?"

"Well, it would be nice to have another lawyer on the ground in the Krull case. You're obviously familiar with it. Donovan trusted you, and his firm is still in the hunt for some serious money. There's a fifty-fifty chance Krull will surrender when they learn we have the documents. A settlement is not unlikely, albeit a confidential one. If they play hardball, then we crank it up and push for a trial. Frankly, that's what we want—a spectacle, a grand exposé, a two-month-long production in which all of the bad stuff gets hashed out in open court. Then, a spectacular verdict."

Shades of Donovan. Shades of Marshall Kofer.

He was on a roll: "There's plenty of work for all of us, including you, Samantha. You could join my firm in Louisville. You could hang out your shingle in Brady. You could take Donovan's office. A lot of options. My point is, we need you."

"Thanks, Mr. London," she said properly, then knocked back another gulp. She was on the spot and didn't like it.

Vic sensed this and changed the subject by quizzing him about the jet. A Gulfstream V, the latest marvel. Virtually unlimited range and so on, cruises at forty thousand, far above the airlines. Very quiet way up there. As the conversation lost steam, London glanced at his watch and asked, "Could I drop you guys off somewhere?"

Ah, the perks of a private jet. Drop-offs here, pickups there. Anything's possible.

They declined and said they had places to go. He thanked them profusely for delivering the documents and walked them back to the terminal.

40

Mattie arrived earlier on Monday, and they huddled in her office with the door closed. Samantha reported that the documents had been delivered, somewhat safely, and that if all went as planned they would be handed over to an officer of the court later in the day. She left out the more colorful aspects of the adventure—the shoot-out that left someone with a bum leg, the dead bear, the miraculous presence of Vic Canzarro, and the quick cocktail on Jarrett London's handsome jet. Some things were better left unsaid.

At any rate, the documents were now in safer hands, where they could be fought over by other lawyers. Somebody else would make sense of them. Samantha speculated that the FBI was now on the sidelines. There was even a hint that the investigation might turn 180 degrees and begin probing into the actions of Krull Mining. Nothing definite as of yet, just a word or two out of Washington.

After the death of Buddy Ryzer and the drama of the documents, life might possibly return to normal within the confines of the Mountain Legal Aid Clinic. The two lawyers certainly hoped so. Samantha was due in court at ten o'clock, in a case that had nothing to do with coal, documents, or federal authorities, and she was looking forward to an uneventful day. Jeff, though, was lurking around the courthouse, as if he knew her schedule. "Can we talk?" he said as they walked up the stairs to the main court-room.

"I was hoping I wouldn't see you for a while," she said.

"Sorry, no chance. How long will you be in court?"

"An hour."

"I'll meet you in Donovan's office. It's important."

Dawn, the secretary and receptionist, was gone, terminated. The firm was out of business, its offices shuttered and gathering dust. Jeff unlocked the front door, opened it for Samantha, then closed it and relocked it. They walked up the stairs to the sec-ond floor, to the war room where the walls were still lined with enlarged photos and courtroom exhibits from the Tate trial. Files and books and papers were scattered about, lingering evidence of the FBI raid. It seemed odd to her that no one had bothered to clean up the mess, to tidy up the room. Half the lights were out. The long table was covered in dust. Donovan had been dead for almost two months, and as Samantha looked around the room at his work, at the remains of his big cases, she was hit with a wave of sadness and nostalgia. She had known him so briefly, but for a second she longed to see his cocky smile.

They sat in folding chairs and drank coffee from paper cups. Jeff swept a hand over the room and said, "What am I supposed to do with this building? My brother left it to me in his will and no one wants it. We can't find a lawyer to take over his practice, and so far no one wants to buy it."

"It's early," she said. "It's a beautiful building and someone will buy it."

"Sure. Half the beautiful buildings on Main Street are empty. This town is dying."

"Is this the important matter you wanted to discuss?"

"No. I'm leaving for a few months, Samantha. I have a friend who runs a hunting lodge in Montana, and I'm going for a long visit. I need to get away. I'm tired of being followed, tired of worrying about who's back there, tired of thinking about my brother. I need a break."

"That's a great idea. What about your sniper work? I see where the reward is now a million bucks, cash. Things are heating up, huh?"

He took a long sip of the coffee and ignored her last comment. "I'll pop in from time to time to take care of Donovan's estate, whenever Mattie needs me. But long term, I think I'll relocate out west somewhere. There's just too much history around here, too many bad memories."

She nodded, understood, but did not respond. Was he attempting a bit of drama here with some lame lover's farewell? If so, she had nothing for him. She liked the boy all right, but at that moment she was relieved to hear he was headed for Montana. A full minute passed without a word, then another.

Finally, he said, "I think I know who killed Donovan." A pause as she was expected to ask "Who?" But she bit her tongue and let it pass. He went on: "It'll take some time, five maybe ten years, but I'll hide in the bushes, lay my traps, so to speak. They like airplane crashes, so I'll give them another."

"I don't want to hear this, Jeff. Do you really want to spend the rest of your life in prison?"

"I'm not going to."

"Famous last words. Look, I need to get to the office."

"I know. I'm sorry."

There was nothing at the office but the Monday brown-bag lunch, a rowdy gossip fest that she hated to miss. There seemed to be a code among the five women who participated in the lunch: If you skip it, you'll probably be discussed at length.

He said, "Okay, I know you're busy. I'll be back in a couple of months. Will you be here?"

"I don't know, Jeff, but don't think about me."

"But I will think about you, I can't help it."

"Here's the deal, Jeff. I'm not going to worry about whether you're coming back, and you don't worry about whether I'm here or in New York. Got it?"

"Okay, okay. Can I at least kiss you good-bye?"

"Yes, but watch your hands."

Samantha returned to her desk and was greeted with the latest from New York. Andy wrote:

Dear Samantha:

Old Spane & Grubman is growing by leaps and bounds. It now has 17 of the best and brightest associates signed on for what promises to be an exciting endeavor. We need two or three more. We need you! I've worked with a handful of these brilliant people—Nick Spane has worked with some others—so it's fair to say I don't know them all. But I know you, and I know I can trust you. I want you on my team and covering my back. A lot of sharks up here, as you know.

Here's the total package: (1) beginning salary of $160,000 (up slightly and the highest offer so far so please keep this quiet—wouldn't want to start trouble from the get-go); (2) an annual bonus to be determined by performance and overall firm productivity (no, the two partners do not plan to keep all the profits); (3) full health insurance—medical, dental, optical (everything but Botox and tummy tucks); (4) a savings and retirement plan which includes matching contributions to a rather generous 401K; (5) overtime pay beyond 50 hours a week (yes, dear, you read that right; S&G is probably the first law firm in history to offer overtime; we're serious about the 50 hour workweek); (6) three weeks of paid vacation; (7) your own private office with your own designated secretary (and probably your own paralegal too but can't make that promise right now); (8) advancement; we do not want our associates cutting throats to make partner, so we're considering a plan whereby one can stake out an equity position at 7 to 10 years with the firm.

Top that, will you? And you can start July 1 and not May 1.

I'm waiting, dear. I need an answer in a week or so. Please.

Andy

She read it twice, printed it, and admitted to herself that she was getting tired of Andy and his e-mails. She found her brown bag and went to lunch.

It was 6:00 p.m. before Mattie's last client left. Samantha had been puttering around her desk, stalling, waiting for the right moment. She poked her head into Mattie's office and said, "Got time for a drink?" Mattie smiled and said of course.

Monday's drinks were of the diet-soda variety. They poured themselves stiff ones and met in the conference room. Samantha slid Andy's latest e-mail across the table. Mattie read it slowly, smiled, laid it down, and said, "Wow. That's quite an offer. Nice to be wanted. I guess you'll be leaving sooner than expected." The smile was gone.

"I'm not ready to go back, Mattie. As generous as it sounds, the work is tedious, just hour after hour of reading and proofing and preparing documents. Try as they might, they can't jazz it up and make it even remotely exciting. I'm just not ready for that, and I don't think I ever will be. I'd like to stay awhile."

Mattie smiled again, a smug little grin that conveyed a lot of satisfaction. "I'm sure you have something in mind."

"Well, not long ago I was an unpaid intern. Now I'm dodging job offers, none of which I find that appealing. I'm not going back to New York, not now anyway. I'm not working for Jarrett London. He's too much like my father. I'm wary of trial lawyers who bounce around the country on their own jets. I don't want Donovan's office, too much baggage there. Jeff will own the building and be on the payroll, and knowing him as intimately as I do I can see a lot of trouble. He would assume the role of the boss and there would be tension from day one. He's dangerous and reckless and I'm shoving him away, not getting closer. We're having a romp every now and then but nothing serious. Besides, he says he's leaving town."

"So you're staying here?"

"If that's possible."

"For how long?"

"There are three things I want to do. The most important client is the Ryzer family. I feel like I'm needed there, and I can't just up and leave them in a few months. They're vulnerable right now, and for some reason they think I can help. I'll do the best I can. I like the idea of handling the Tate appeal, from start to finish. Lisa Tate needs us. The poor woman is living on food stamps and still grieving. I want to win the appeal and get her the money she deserves. And by the way, I think 40 percent is too much for Donovan's estate. He may have earned that money, but he's gone now. Lisa lost her boys; Donovan did not. With that set of facts, a lot of lawyers could have won the case. I guess we can discuss it later."

"I've had the same thought."

"During my second year of law school, we had to do a mock appellate case; write the briefs and argue before a three-judge panel, really just three law professors, but they were notorious for grilling the students. Oral argument was a big deal—coats and ties, dresses and pumps, you know?"

Mattie was nodding and smiling. "We did the same thing."

"I guess all law students suffered through it. I was so nervous I couldn't sleep the night before. My co-counsel gave me a Xanax two hours before the argument, but it didn't help. I was so stiff I could barely utter the first word, then something strange happened. One of the judges hit me with a cheap shot, and I got mad. I began arguing with him. I unloaded case after case to support our position and really blasted the guy. I forgot about being scared—I was too focused on showing this judge how right I was. My ten minutes flew by, and when I sat down everybody just stared at me. My co-counsel leaned over and whispered one word: 'Brilliant.'

"Anyway, it was my finest moment in law school, one I'll never forget. Which is to say, I'd love to take the Tate case all the way to the Supreme Court of Virginia, present the oral argument, make fools out of the lawyers for Strayhorn Coal, and win the case for Lisa Tate."

"Go girl. It's all yours."

"So that's eighteen months, right?"

"Something like that. You said there were three things you want to do."

"The third is simply to finish the cases I have, take some new ones as they come along, and try to help our clients. And in doing so, I'd like to spend more time in the courtroom."

"You have a flair for it, Samantha. It's pretty obvious."

"Thank you, Mattie. That's very kind. I don't like being shoved around by the Trent Fullers of the world. I want respect, and the only way to get it is to earn it. When I walk into a courtroom, I want all the boys to sit up straight and notice, and not just my ass."

"My, my, haven't we come a long way?"

"Yes, we have. Now, about this internship. If I'm spending the next two years here, I need some sort of a salary. Not much, but something I can live on."

"I've been thinking about that. We can't quite match your guy up in New York, but we can do okay for rural Virginia. Annette and I both make forty a year, so that's the ceiling. The clinic can pay you twenty. Since you'll be handling the Tate appeal, I can get the court to authorize another twenty out of Donovan's estate. How's that?"

"Forty might cause a little resentment from you know who."

"Annette?"

"Yes. Let's go with thirty-nine."

"We can do thirty-nine. Deal." Mattie thrust her hand across the table and Samantha shook it. She picked up Andy's e-mail and said, "Now I need to get rid of this jerk."

AUTHOR'S NOTE

Thankfully, there are dozens of nonprofits working diligently in the coalfields to protect the environment, change policy, and fight for the rights of miners and their families. One is the Appalachian Citizens' Law Center in Whitesburg, Kentucky. Mary Cromer and Wes Addington are wonderful lawyers there, and they provided guidance as I wandered through their region for the first time. Appalachian Voices is a feisty, grassroots environmental group out of Boone, North Carolina. Matt Wasson is its Director of Programs and was a great resource as I searched for facts.

Thanks also to Rick Middleton, Hayward Evans, Wes Blank, and Mike Nicholson.